Flying Colours

C. S. FORESTER

Introduction by Bernard Cornwell

PENGUIN BOOKS

PENGUIN BOOKS

Published by the Penguin Group
Penguin Books Ltd, 80 Strand, London WC2R 0RL, England
Penguin Group (USA) Inc., 375 Hudson Street, New York, New York 10014, USA
Penguin Group (Canada), 90 Eglinton Avenue East, Suite 700, Toronto, Ontario, Canada M4P 2Y3
(a division of Pearson Penguin Canada Inc.)
Penguin Ireland, 25 St Stephen's Green, Dublin 2, Ireland (a division of Penguin Books Ltd)
Penguin Group (Australia), 250 Camberwell Road, Camberwell, Victoria 3124, Australia
(a division of Pearson Australia Group Pty Ltd)
Penguin Books India Pvt Ltd, 11 Community Centre, Panchsheel Park,
New Delhi – 110 017, India
Penguin Group (NZ), 67 Apollo Drive, Rosedale, Auckland 0632, New Zealand
(a division of Pearson New Zealand Ltd)
Penguin Books (South Africa) (Pty) Ltd, 24 Sturdee Avenue, Rosebank, Johannesburg 2196, South Africa

Penguin Books Ltd, Registered Offices: 80 Strand, London WC2R 0RL, England

www.penguin.com

First published by Michael Joseph 1938
Published in Penguin Books 1956
Reissued in this edition 2011

1

Copyright © by C. S. Forester, 1938
Introduction copyright © Bernard Cornwell, 2006
All rights reserved

The moral right of the author has been asserted

Typeset in 11/13pt Monotype Dante
Set by Palimpsest Book Production Limited, Falkirk, Stirlingshire
Printed in England by Clays Ltd, St Ives plc

ISBN: 978-0-241-95549-9

www.greenpenguin.co.uk

Introduction

Flying Colours was the third Hornblower story to be written, but the seventh in chronological order, and it was written hard on the heels of *Ship of the Line*. That book ends in disaster. Hornblower has been taken prisoner by the French, after losing his ship in a battle against overwhelming forces. *Flying Colours* was published in 1938, the same year as *Ship of the Line*, so at least the growing number of Hornblower fans did not have long to wait to discover the fate of their hero.

They discover that Hornblower is now a prisoner in Rosas, a Spanish fort in French hands. His companions are Lieutenant Bush, who was grievously wounded at the end of *Ship of the Line*, and Coxswain Brown. The three men face a grim future. Forester, in his wide reading, had been struck by Napoleon's vengefulness, 'perhaps traceable to his Corsican childhood?' Suppose Napoleon wanted to make an example of Hornblower? A captured British naval captain would make a fine trophy for the vengeful Emperor so why not rig a trial and condemn him to death? So the story begins and you must discover the rest, right up to the splendid final scenes with the *Witch of Endor*.

The speed with which the first three Hornblower books were written shows that Forester knew he had struck a vein of purest gold. He was already a successful author, but the Hornblower tales were to make him famous. Cecil Scott Forester was born in Egypt to British parents in 1899. His real name was Cecil Lewis Troughton Smith and he was raised in Britain where, as a child, he was an avid reader, usually the first step in the making of a writer. In 1917, before his eighteenth birthday, he volunteered for the British army, fully expecting to fight on the Western Front, but he was rejected as medically unfit. He was a skinny, short-sighted six-footer who enjoyed sports, but the army's physical examination revealed a dangerously weak heart. So instead of serving as a soldier, Forester entered Guy's Hospital as a medical student – an experience as unhappy as it was unsuccessful – but Forester's ambitions were already fixed on writing. His first efforts failed, but in 1924, with *Payment Deferred*, he enjoyed his first success. During the Second World War he moved to the United States at the request of the British government, who wanted him to produce articles and stories that would encourage American support for the British war effort. It was sophisticated propaganda, and Forester was good at it. He also liked living in the States and most of the Hornblower books were written in California where, with his second wife, he remained until his death in 1966. By then he had become one of the world's most popular authors with almost sixty novels to his name and, even if he had never dreamed up Hornblower, he would be famous as the author of *The African Queen*, *The Gun*, *Brown on Resolution* or *Hunting the Bismarck*.

Flying Colours is an escape story, a tale of illicit passion, and a superb study of the three main characters. The relationship between Hornblower and the sturdy

Coxswain Brown is done especially well. Brown, aged twenty-eight, had served in the navy since he was eleven. 'He could knot and splice, hand, reef and steer, cast the lead or pull an oar, all of them far better than his captain. He could go aloft on a black night in a howling storm without thinking twice about it, but the sight of a knife and fork made his hands tremble.' When Brown is forced to eat off china in front of the officers, Hornblower immediately senses his embarrassment and makes it easy, but he also invites Brown to help himself to wine. This is not generosity, but 'a good moment for ascertaining if Brown could be trusted with liquor.' Brown could. Later Hornblower feels pangs of jealousy because of the pleasure Bush and Brown take in building a simple rowing boat. Hornblower could contribute nothing except 'unskilled labour' and it galls him. But then Hornblower is a complicated man, while Bush and Brown are simpler souls. Hornblower is complicated enough to envy 'Bush his complete inability to speak any other tongue than English'; an extraordinarily acute observation.

The writing of *Flying Colours* was interrupted by that most aggravating of duties, the need to read the proofs of the previous book. Forester was checking the proofs of *Ship of the Line* when his elder son, then a small boy, asked him to hurry with them. 'I want to read it,' he said, 'I liked the first book so much.' It was, Forester said, a reward for the trials of writing. He always claimed that writing was a difficult task, but reckoned *Flying Colours* was especially exhausting. He was filled with 'horrible doubts'; he was 'faced with disaster'. Yet he admitted that there were 'one or two mornings when I actually observed, with considerable astonishment – perhaps even dismay – that I was going eagerly to my worktable, that I was looking forward to a morning with Hornblower'. Dismay? It is a typical Forester touch in case we should believe he might actually have enjoyed himself too much, but those happy mornings show in this most intimate of Hornblower adventures and, if it does not give too much away, this story with the happiest of endings. And it was a good thing that *Flying Colours* ended so satisfactorily, for the world was about to be engulfed with horror and it was not until the Second World War was over that Hornblower, Bush, Brown and Lady Barbara would return.

I

Captain Hornblower was walking up and down along the sector of the ramparts of Rosas, delimited by two sentries with loaded muskets, which the commandant had granted him for exercise. Overhead shone the bright autumn sun of the Mediterranean, hanging in a blue Mediterranean sky and shining on the Mediterranean blue of Rosas Bay – the blue water fringed with white where the little waves broke against the shore of golden sand and grey-green cliff. Black against the sun above his head there flapped the tricolour flag of France, proclaiming to the world that Rosas was in the hands of the French, that Captain Hornblower was a prisoner. Not half a mile from where he walked lay the dismasted wreck of his ship the *Sutherland*, beached to prevent her from sinking, and in line beyond her there swung at their anchors the four ships of the line which had fought her. Hornblower, narrowing his eyes and with a twinge of regret for his lost telescope could see even at that distance that they were not ready for sea again, nor were likely to be. Even the two-decker which had emerged from the fight with all her masts intact still had her pumps at work every two hours to keep her afloat, and the other three had not yet succeeded in setting up masts to replace the ones lost in the battle. The French were a lubberly lot of no-seamen, as might be expected after seventeen years of defeat at sea and six of continuous blockade.

They had been all honey to him, in their French fashion praising him for his 'glorious defence' after his 'bold initiative' in dashing in with his ship to interpose between their four and their refuge at Rosas. They had expressed the liveliest pleasure at discovering that he had miraculously emerged unhurt from a battle which had left two-thirds of his men killed and wounded. But they had plundered in the fashion which had made the armed forces of the Empire hated throughout Europe. They had searched the pockets even of the wounded who had cumbered the *Sutherland*'s decks in moaning heaps. Their admiral, on his first encounter with Hornblower, had expressed surprise that the latter was not wearing the sword which the admiral had sent back to him in recognition of his gallantry, and on Hornblower's denial that he had ever seen the weapon again after giving it up had instituted a search which discovered the sword cast aside somewhere in his flagship, the glorious inscription still engraved upon the blade, but with the gold stripped from hilt and guard and scabbard. And the admiral had merely laughed at that and had not dreamed of instituting a search for the thief; the Patriotic Fund's gift still hung at Hornblower's side, the tang of the blade protruding nakedly from the scabbard without the gold and ivory and seed pearls which had adorned it.

The French soldiers and sailors which had swarmed over the captured ship had torn away even the brasswork in the same fashion; they had gorged upon the unappetizing provisions in a way which proved how miserable were the rations provided for the men who fought for the Empire – but it was only a few who had swilled themselves into insensibility from the rum casks.

In face of similar temptation (to which no British officer would have exposed his men) British seamen would have drunk until nine-tenths of them were incapable or fighting mad. The French officers had made the usual appeal to their prisoners to join the French ranks, making the usual tempting offers of good treatment and regular pay to anyone who cared to enlist either in the army or the navy. Hornblower was proud that no single man had succumbed to the temptation.

As a consequence the few sound men now languished in strict confinement in one of the empty storerooms of the fortress, deprived of the tobacco and rum and fresh air which for most of them represented the difference between heaven and hell. The wounded – the hundred and forty-five wounded – were rotting in a dank casemate where gangrene and fever would soon make an end of them. To the logical French mind the poverty-stricken Army of Catalonia, which could do little even for its own wounded, would be mad to expend any of its resources on attention to wounded who would be intolerable nuisances should they survive.

A little moan escaped Hornblower's lips as he paced the ramparts. He had a room of his own, a servant to wait on him, fresh air and sunshine, while the poor devils he had commanded were suffering all the miseries of confinement – even the three or four other unwounded officers were lodged in the town gaol. True, he suspected that he was being reserved for another fate. During those glorious days when, in command of the *Sutherland*, he had won for himself, unknowing, the nickname of 'the Terror of the Mediterranean', he had managed to storm the battery at Llanza by bringing his ship up close to it flying the tricolour flag. That had been a legitimate *ruse de guerre* for which historical precedents without number could be quoted, but the French government had apparently deemed it a violation of the laws of war. The next convoy to France or Barcelona would bear him with it as a prisoner to be tried by a military commission. Bonaparte was quite capable of shooting him, both from personal rancour and as a proof of the most convincing sort to Europe of British duplicity and wickedness, and during the last day or two Hornblower thought he had read as much in the eyes of his gaolers.

Just enough time had elapsed for the news of the *Sutherland*'s capture to have reached Paris and for Bonaparte's subsequent orders to have been transmitted to Rosas. The *Moniteur Universel* would have blazed out in a paean of triumph, declaring to the Continent that this loss of a ship of the line was clear proof that England was tottering to her fall like ancient Carthage; in a month or two's time presumably there would be another announcement to the effect that a traitorous servant of perfidious Albion had met his just deserts against a wall in Vincennes or Montjuich.

Hornblower cleared his throat nervously as he walked; he expected to feel afraid and was surprised that he did not. The thought of an abrupt and inevitable end of that sort did not alarm him as much as did his shapeless imaginings when he was going into action on his quarterdeck. In fact he could almost view it with relief, as putting an end to his worries about his wife Maria whom he had left pregnant, and to his jealous torments of longing for Lady Barbara who had married his admiral; in the eyes of England he would be regarded

4

as a martyr whose widow deserved a pension. It would be an honourable end, then, which a man ought to welcome – especially a man like Hornblower whose persistent and unfounded disbelief in his own capacity left him continually frightened of professional disgrace and ruin.

And it would be an end of captivity, too. Hornblower had been a prisoner once before, for two heartbreaking years in Ferrol, but with the passing of time he had forgotten the misery of it until his new experience. In those days, too, he had never known the freedom of his own quarterdeck, and had never tasted the unbounded liberty – the widest freedom on earth – of being a captain of a ship. It was torture now to be a prisoner, even with the liberty to look upon the sky and the sea. A caged lion must fret behind his bars in the same way as Hornblower fretted against his confinement. He felt suddenly sick and ill through restraint. He clenched his fists and only by an effort prevented himself from raising them above his head in a gesture of despair.

Then he took hold of himself again, with an inward sneer at his childish weakness. To distract himself he looked out again to the blue sea which he loved, the row of black cormorants silhouetted against the grey cliff, the gulls wheeling against the blue sky. Five miles out he could see the topsails of His Majesty's frigate *Cassandra* keeping sleepless watch over the four French ships huddled for shelter under the guns of Rosas, and beyond them he could see the royals of the *Pluto* and the *Caligula* – Admiral Leighton, the unworthy husband of his beloved Lady Barbara, was flying his flag in the *Pluto*, but he refused to let that thought worry him – where they awaited an accession of strength from the Mediterranean fleet before coming in to destroy the ships which had captured him. He could rely upon the British to avenge his defeat. Martin, the vice admiral with the Toulon blockading squadron, would see to it that Leighton did not make a hash of this attack, powerful as might be the guns of Rosas.

He looked along the ramparts at the massive twenty-four-pounders mounted there. The bastions at the angles carried forty-two-pounders – colossal pieces. He leaned over the parapet and looked down; it was a sheer drop from there of twenty-five feet to the bottom of the ditch, and along the bottom of the ditch itself ran a line of stout palisades, which no besieging army could damage until they had sapped right up to the lip of the ditch. No hurried, extemporized attack could carry the citadel of Rosas. A score of sentries paced the ramparts, even as did he; in the opposite face he could see the massive gates with the portcullis down, where a hundred men of the grand guard were always ready to beat back any surprise attack which might elude the vigilance of the twenty sentinels.

Down there, in the body of the place, a company of infantry was being put through its drill – the shrill words of command were clearly audible to him up here. It was Italian which was being spoken; Bonaparte had attempted his conquest of Catalonia mainly with the foreign auxiliaries of his Empire, Italians, Neapolitans, Germans, Swiss, Poles. The uniforms of the infantry down there were as ragged as the lines they were forming; the men were in tatters, and even the tatters were not homogeneous – the men wore white or blue or grey or brown according to the resources of the depots which had originally sent them out. They were half

6

starved, poor devils, as well. Of the five or six thousand men based on Rosas the ones he could see were all that could be spared for military duty; the others were all out scouring the countryside for food – Bonaparte never dreamed of trying to feed the men whom he compelled to serve him, just as he only paid them, as an after-thought, a year or two in arrears. It was amazing that his ramshackle Empire had endured so long – that was the clearest proof of the incompetence of the various kingdoms who had pitted their strength against it. Over on the other side of the Peninsula the French Empire was at this very minute putting out all its strength against a man of real ability and an army which knew what disci-pline was. On the issue of that struggle depended the fate of Europe. Hornblower was convinced that the redcoats with Wellington to lead them would be successful; he would have been just as certain even if Wellington were not his beloved Lady Barbara's brother.

Then he shrugged his shoulders. Not even Wellington would destroy the French Empire quickly enough to save him from trial and execution. Moreover, the time allowed him for his day's exercise was over now. The next items in his monotonous programme would be to visit the sick in the casemate, and then the prisoners in the storeroom – by the courtesy of the commandant he was allowed ten minutes for each, before being shut up again in his room, drearily to attempt to re-read the half-dozen books which were all that the garrison of Rosas possessed, or to pace up and down, three steps each way, or to lie huddled on his bed wondering about Maria and the child that was to be born in the New Year, and torturing himself with thoughts of Lady Barbara.

2

Hornblower awoke that night with a start, wondering what it was that had awakened him. A moment later he knew, when the sound was repeated. It was the dull thud of a gun fired on the ramparts above his head. He leaped from his bed with his heart pounding, and before his feet touched the floor the whole fortress was in a turmoil. Overhead there were guns firing. Somewhere else, outside the body of the fortress, there were hundreds of guns firing; through the barred windows of his room came a faint flickering as the flashes were reflected down from the sky. Immediately outside his door drums were beating and bugles were pealing as the garrison was called to arms – the courtyard was full of the sounds of nailed boots clashing on the cobbles.

That tremendous pulsation of artillery which he could hear could mean only one thing. The fleet must have come gliding into the bay in the darkness, and now he could hear the rolling of its broadsides as it battered the anchored ships. There was a great naval battle in progress within half a mile of him, and he could see nothing of it. It was utterly maddening. He tried to light his candle, but his trembling fingers could do nothing with his flint and steel. He dashed the tinder-box to the floor, and, fumbling in the darkness, he dragged on his coat and trousers and shoes and then beat upon the door madly with his fists. The sentry outside was Italian, he knew, and he spoke no Italian – only fluent Spanish and bad French.

'Officier! Officier!' he shouted, and then he heard the sentry call for the sergeant of the guard, and the measured step of the sergeant as he came up. The clatter of the garrison's falling in under arms had already died away.

'What do you want?' asked the sergeant's voice – at least so Hornblower fancied, for he could not understand what was said.

'Officier! Officier!' roared Hornblower, beating still on the heavy door. The artillery was still rolling terrifically outside. Hornblower went on pounding on the door even until he heard the key in the lock. The door swung open and he blinked at the light of a torch which shone into his eyes. A young subaltern in a neat white uniform stood there between the sergeant and the sentry.

'Qu'est-ce-que monsieur désire?' he asked – he at least understood French, even if he spoke it badly. Hornblower fumbled to express himself in an unfamiliar tongue.

'I want to see!' he stammered. 'I want to see the battle! Let me go on to the walls.'

The young officer shook his head reluctantly; like the other officers of the garrison, he felt a kindly feeling towards the English captain who – so rumour said – was so shortly to be conducted to Paris and shot.

'It is forbidden,' he said.

'I will not escape,' said Hornblower; desperate excitement was loosening his tongue now. 'Word of honour – I swear it! Come with me, but let me see! I want to see!'

The officer hesitated.

'I cannot leave my post here,' he said.

'Then let me go alone. I swear I will stay on the walls. I will not try to escape.'

'Word of honour?' asked the subaltern.

'Word of honour. Thank you, sir.'

The subaltern stood aside, and Hornblower dashed out of his room, down the short corridor to the court-yard, and up the ramp which led to the seaward bastion. As he reached it, the forty-two-pounder mounted there went off with a deafening roar, and the long tongue of orange flame nearly blinded him. In the darkness the bitter powder smoke engulfed him. Nobody in the groups bending over the guns noticed him, and he ran down the steep staircase to the curtain wall, where, away from the guns, he could see without being blinded.

Rosas Bay was all a-sparkle with gun flashes. Then, five times in regular succession, came the brilliant red glow of a broadside, and each glow lit up a stately ship gliding in rigid line ahead past the anchored French ships. The *Pluto* was there; Hornblower saw her three decks, her ensign at the peak, her admiral's flag at the mizzen, her topsails set and her other canvas furled. Leighton would be there, walking his quarterdeck – thinking of Barbara, perhaps. And that next astern was the *Caligula*. Bolton would be stumping about her deck revelling in the crash of her broadsides. She was firing rapidly and well – Bolton was a good captain, although a badly educated man. The words 'Oderint dum metuant' – the Caesar Caligula's maxim – picked out in letters of gold across the *Caligula*'s stern had meant nothing to Bolton until Hornblower translated and explained them to him. At this very moment, perhaps, those letters were being defaced and battered by the French shot.

But the French squadron was firing back badly and irregularly. There was no sudden glow of broadsides where they lay anchored, but only an irregular and intermittent sparkle as the guns were loosed off anyhow. In a night action like this, and after a sudden surprise, Hornblower would not have trusted even an English seaman with independent fire. He doubted if as many as one-tenth of the French guns were being properly served and pointed. As for the heavy guns pealing away beside him from the fortress, he was quite certain they were doing no good to the French cause and possibly some harm. Firing at half a mile in the darkness, even from a steady platform and with large calibre guns, they were as likely to hit friend as foe. It had well repaid Admiral Martin to send in Leighton and his ships in the moonless hours of the night, risking all the navigational perils of the bay.

Hornblower choked with emotion and excitement as his imagination called up the details of what would be going on in the English ships – the leadsman chanting the soundings with disciplined steadiness, the heave of the ship to the deafening crash of the broadside, the battle lanterns glowing dimly in the smoke of the lower decks, the squeal and rattle of the gun trucks as the guns were run up again, the steady orders of the officers in charge of sections of guns, the quiet voice of the captain addressing the helmsmen. He leaned far over the parapet in the darkness, peering down into the bay.

A whiff of wood smoke came to his nostrils, sharply

distinct from the acrid powder smoke which was drifting by from the guns. They had lit the furnaces for heating shot, but the commandant would be a fool if he allowed his guns to fire red-hot shot in these conditions. French ships were as inflammable as English ones, and just as likely to be hit in a close battle like this. Then his grip tightened on the stonework of the parapet, and he stared and stared again with aching eyes towards what had attracted his notice. It was the tiniest, most subdued little red glow in the distance. The English had brought in fire ships in the wake of their fighting squadron. A squadron at anchor like this was the best possible target for a fire ship, and Martin had planned his attack well in sending in his ships of the line first to clear away guard boats and beat down the French fire and occupy the attention of the crews. The red glow suddenly increased, grew brighter and brighter still, revealing the hull and masts and rigging of a small brig; still brighter it grew as the few daring spirits who remained on board flung open hatches and gunports to increase the draught. The tongues of flame which soared up were visible even to Hornblower on the ramparts, and they revealed to him, too, the form of the *Turenne* alongside her – the one French ship which had emerged from the previous battle with all her masts. Whoever the young officer in command of the fire ship might be, he was a man with a cool head and determined will, thus to select the most profitable target of all.

Hornblower saw points of fire begin to ascend the rigging of the *Turenne* until she was outlined in red like some setpiece in a firework display. Sudden jets of flame showed where powder charges on her deck were taking fire; and then the whole setpiece suddenly swung round and began to drift before the gentle wind as the burnt cables gave way. A mast fell in an upwards torrent of sparks, strangely reflected in the black water all round. At once the sparkle of gunfire in the other French ships began to die away as the crews were called from their guns to deal with the drifting menace, and a slow movement of the shadowy forms lit by the flames revealed that their cables had been cut by officers terrified of death by fire.

Then suddenly Hornblower's attention was distracted to a point closer in to shore, where the abandoned wreck of the *Sutherland* lay beached. There, too, a red glow could be seen, growing and spreading momentarily. Some daring party from the British squadron had boarded her and set her on fire, too, determined not to leave even so poor a trophy in the hands of the French. Farther out in the bay three red dots of light were soaring upwards slowly, and Hornblower gulped in sudden nervousness lest an English ship should have caught fire as well, but he realized next moment that it was only a signal – three vertical red lanterns – which was apparently the prearranged recall, for with their appearance the firing abruptly ceased. The blazing wrecks lit up now the whole of this corner of the bay with a lurid red in whose light could be distinctly seen the other French ships, drifting without masts or anchors towards the shore. Next came a blinding flash and a stunning explosion as the magazine of the *Turenne* took fire. For several seconds after the twenty tons of gunpowder had exploded Hornblower's eyes could not see nor his mind think; the blast of it had shaken him, like a child in the hands of an angry nurse, even where he stood.

He became aware that daylight was creeping into the bay, revealing the ramparts of Rosas in hard outlines, and dulling the flames from the wreck of the *Sutherland*. Far out in the bay, already beyond gunshot of the fortress, the five British ships of the line were standing out to sea in their rigid line-ahead. There was something strange about the appearance of the *Pluto*; it was only at his second glance that Hornblower realized that she had lost her main topmast – clear proof that one French shot at least had done damage. The other ships revealed no sign of having received any injury during one of the best managed affairs in the long history of the British Navy. Hornblower tore his gaze from his vanishing friends to study the field of battle. Of the *Turenne* and the fire ship there was no sign at all; of the *Sutherland* there only remained a few blackened timbers emerging from the water, with a wisp of smoke suspended above them. Two ships of the line were on the rocks to the westward of the fortress, and French seamanship would never make them seaworthy again. Only the three-decker was left, battered and mastless, swinging to the anchor which had checked her on the very edge of the surf. The next easterly gale would see her, too, flung ashore and useless. The British Mediterranean fleet would in the future have to dissipate none of its energies in a blockade of Rosas.

Here came General Vidal, the governor of the fortress, making his rounds with his staff at his heels, and just in time to save Hornblower from falling into a passion of despair at watching the English squadron disappear over the horizon.

'What are you doing here?' demanded the General, checking at the sight of him. Under the sternness of his expression could be read the kindly pity which Hornblower had noticed in the faces of all his enemies when they began to suspect that a firing party awaited him.

'The officer of the grand guard allowed me to come up here,' explained Hornblower in his halting French. 'I gave him my parole of honour not to try to escape. I will withdraw it again now, if you please.'

'He had no business to accept it, in any case,' snapped the General, but with that fateful kindliness still apparent. 'You wanted to see the battle, I suppose?'

'Yes, General.'

'A fine piece of work your companions have done.' The General shook his head sadly. 'It will not make the government in Paris feel any better disposed towards you, I fear, Captain.'

Hornblower shrugged his shoulders; he had already caught the infection of that gesture during his few days' sojourn among Frenchmen. He noted, with a lack of personal interest which seemed odd to him even then, that this was the first time that the Governor had hinted openly at danger threatening him from Paris.

'I have done nothing to make me afraid,' he said.

'No, no, of course not,' said the Governor hastily and out of countenance, like a parent denying to a child that a prospective dose of medicine would be unpleasant.

He looked round for some way of changing the subject, and fortunate chance brought one. From far below in the bowels of the fortress came a muffled sound of cheering – English cheers, not Italian screeches.

'That must be those men of yours, Captain,' said the General, smiling again. 'I fancy the new prisoner must have told them by now the story of last night's affair.'

'The new prisoner?' demanded Hornblower.

'Yes, indeed. A man who fell overboard from the admiral's ship – the *Pluto*, is it not? – and had to swim ashore. Ah, I suspected you would be interested, Captain. Yes, off you go and talk to him. Here, Dupont, take charge of the captain and escort him to the prison.'

Hornblower could hardly spare the time in which to thank his captor, so eager was he to interview the new arrival and hear what he had to say. Two weeks as a prisoner had already had their effect in giving him a thirst for news. He ran down the ramp, Dupont puffing beside him, across the cobbled court, in through the door which a sentry opened for him at a gesture from his escort, down the dark stairway to the iron-studded door where stood two sentries on duty. With a great clattering of keys the doors were opened for him and he walked into the room.

It was a wide low room – a disused storeroom, in fact – lit and ventilated only by a few heavily barred apertures opening into the fortress ditch. It stank of closely confined humanity and it was at present filled with a babel of sound as what was left of the crew of the *Sutherland* plied questions at someone hidden in the middle of the crowd. At Hornblower's entrance the crowd fell apart and the new prisoner came forward; he was naked save for his duck trousers and a long pigtail hung down his back.

'Who are you?' demanded Hornblower.

'Phillips, sir. Maintopman in the *Pluto*.'

His honest blue eyes met Hornblower's gaze without a sign of flinching. Hornblower could guess that he was neither a deserter nor a spy – he had borne both possibilities in mind.

'How did you come here?'

'We was settin' sail, sir, to beat out o' the bay. We'd just seen the old *Sutherland* take fire, an' Cap'n Elliott he says to us, he says, sir, "Now's the time, my lads. Top'sls and to'gar'ns." So up we went aloft, sir, an' I'd just taken the earring o' the main to'gar'n when down came the mast, sir, an' I was pitched off into the water. So was a lot o' my mates, sir, but just then the Frenchy which was burnin' blew up, an' I think the wreckage killed a lot of 'em, sir, 'cos I found I was alone, an' *Pluto* was gone away, an' so I swum for the shore, an' there was a lot of Frenchies what I think had swum from the burning Frenchy an' they took me to some sojers an' the sojers brought me here, sir. There was a orficer what arst me questions – it'd 'a made you laugh, sir, to hear him trying to speak English – but I wasn't sayin' nothin', sir. An' when they see that they puts me in here along with the others, sir. I was just telling 'em about the fight, sir. There was the old *Pluto*, an' *Caligula*, sir, an' –'

'Yes, I saw it,' said Hornblower, shortly. 'I saw that *Pluto* had lost her main topmast. Was she knocked about much?'

'Lor' bless you, sir, no, sir. We hadn't had half a dozen shot come aboard, an' they didn't do no damage, barrin' the one that wounded the Admiral.'

'The Admiral!' Hornblower reeled a little as he stood, as though he had been struck. 'Admiral Leighton, d'you mean?'

'Admiral Leighton, sir.'

'Was – was he badly hurt?'

'I dunno, sir. I didn't see it meself, o' course, sir, seein' as how I was on the main deck at the time. Sailmaker's mate, he told me, sir, that the Admiral had been hit by a splinter. Cooper's mate told *him*, sir, what helped to carry him below.'

Hornblower could say no more for the present. He could only stare at the kindly stupid face of the sailor before him. Yet even in that moment he could take note of the fact that the sailor was not in the least moved by the wounding of his Admiral. Nelson's death had put the whole fleet into mourning, and he knew of half a dozen other flag officers whose death or whose wounding would have brought tears into the eyes of the men serving under him. If it had been one of those, the man would have told of the accident to him before mentioning his own misadventures. Hornblower had known before that Leighton was not beloved by his officers, and here was a clear proof that he was not beloved by his men either. But perhaps Barbara had loved him. She had at least married him. Hornblower forced himself to speak, to bear himself naturally.

'That will do,' he said, curtly, and then looked round to catch his coxswain's eye. 'Anything to report, Brown?'

'No, sir. All well, sir.'

Hornblower rapped on the door behind him to be let out of prison, to be conducted by his guard back to his room again, where he could walk up and down, three steps each way, his brain seething like a pot on a fire. He only knew enough to unsettle him, to make him anxious. Leighton had been wounded, but that did not mean that he would die. A splinter wound – that might mean much or little. Yet he had been carried below. No admiral would have allowed that, if he had been able to resist – not in the heat of a fight, at any rate. His face might be lacerated or his belly torn open – Hornblower, shuddering, shook his mind free from the memories of all the horrible wounds he had seen received on board ship during twenty years' service. But, coldbloodedly, it was an even chance that Leighton would die – Hornblower had signed too many casualty lists to be unaware of the chances of a wounded man's recovery.

If Leighton were to die, Barbara would be free again. But what had that to do with him, a married man – a married man whose wife was pregnant? She would be no nearer to him, not while Maria lived. And yet it assuaged his jealousy to think of her as a widow. But then perhaps she would marry again, and he would have to go once more through all the torment he had endured when he had first heard of her marriage to Leighton. In that case he would rather Leighton lived – a cripple, perhaps mutilated or impotent; the implications of that train of thought drove him into a paroxysm of too-rapid thinking from which he only emerged after a desperate struggle for sanity.

In the cold reaction which followed he sneered at himself for a fool. He was the prisoner of a man whose empire extended from the Baltic to Gibraltar. He told himself he would be an old man, that his child and Maria's would be grown up before he regained his liberty. And then with a sudden shock he remembered that he might soon be dead – shot for violation of the laws of war. Strange how he could forget that possibility.

Sneering, he told himself that he had a coward's mind which could leave the imminence of death out of its calculations because the possibility was too monstrous to bear contemplation.

There was something else he had not reckoned upon lately, too. If Bonaparte did not have him shot, if he regained his freedom, even then he still had to run the gauntlet of a court martial for the loss of the *Sutherland*. A court martial might decree for him death or disgrace or ruin; the British public would not hear lightly of a British ship of the line surrendering, however great the odds against her. He would have liked to ask Phillips, the seaman from the *Pluto*, about what had been said in the fleet regarding the *Sutherland*'s action, whether the general verdict had been one of approval or not. But of course it would be impossible to ask; no captain could ask a seaman what the fleet thought of him, even if there was a chance of hearing the truth – which, too, was doubtful. He was compassed about with uncertainties – the uncertainties of his imprisonment, of the possibility of his trial by the French, of his future court martial, of Leighton's wound. There was even an uncertainty regarding Maria; she was pregnant – would the child be a girl or a boy, would he ever see it, would anyone raise a finger to help her, would she be able to educate the child properly without his supervision?

Once more the misery of imprisonment was borne in upon him. He grew sick with longing for his liberty, for his freedom, for Barbara and for Maria.

3

Hornblower was walking next day upon the ramparts again; the sentries with their loaded muskets stood one each end of the sector allotted to him, and the subaltern allotted to guard him sat discreetly against the parapet so as not to break in upon the thoughts which preoc-cupied him. But he was too tired to think much now – all day and nearly all night yesterday he had paced his room, three paces up and three paces back, with his mind in a turmoil. Exhaustion was saving him now, he could think no more.

He welcomed as a distraction a bustle at the main gate, the turning out of the guard, the opening of the gate, and the jingling entrance of a coach drawn by six fine horses. He stood and watched the proceedings with all the interest of a captive. There was an escort of fifty mounted men in the cocked hats and blue-and-red uniforms of Bonaparte's gendarmerie, coachmen and servants on the box, an officer dismounting hurriedly to open the door. Clearly the new arrival must be a man of importance. Hornblower experienced a faint feeling of disappointment when there climbed out of the coach not a Marshal with plumes and feathers, but just another officer of gendarmerie. A youngish man with a bullet black head, which he revealed as he held his cocked hat in his hand while stooping to descend; the star of the Legion of Honour on his breast; high black boots with spurs. Hornblower wondered idly why a colonel of gendarmerie who was obviously not crippled should arrive in a coach instead of on horseback. He watched him go clinking across the courtyard to the Governor's headquarters.

Hornblower's walk was nearly finished when one of the young French aides-de-camp of the Governor approached him on the ramparts and saluted.

'His Excellency sends you his compliments, sir, and he would be glad if you could spare him a few minutes of your time as soon as it is convenient to you.'

Addressed to a prisoner, as Hornblower told himself bitterly, these words might as well have been 'Come at once.'

'I will come now, with the greatest of pleasure,' said Hornblower, maintaining the solemn farce.

Down in the Governor's office the colonel of gendarmerie was standing conversing alone with His Excellency; the Governor's expression was sad.

'I have the honour of presenting to you, Captain,' he said, turning, 'Colonel Jean-Baptiste Caillard, Grand Eagle of the Legion of Honour, and one of His Imperial Majesty's personal aides-de-camp. Colonel, this is Captain Horatio Hornblower, of His Britannic Majesty's Navy.'

The Governor was clearly worried and upset. His hands were fluttering and he stammered a little as he spoke, and he made a pitiful muddle of his attempt on the aspirates of Hornblower's name. Hornblower bowed, but as the colonel remained unbending he stiffened to attention. He could recognize that type of man at once – the servant of a tyrant, and in close personal association with him, modelling his conduct not on the tyrant's, but on what he fancied should be the correct behaviour of a tyrant, far out-Heroding Herod in arbitrariness and cruelty. It might be merely a pose – the man might be a kind husband and the loving father of a family – but it was a pose which might have unpleasant results for anyone in his power. His victims would suffer in his attempt to prove, to himself as well as to others, that he could be more stern, more unrelenting – and therefore naturally more able – than the man who employed him.

Caillard ran a cold eye over Hornblower's appearance.

'What is he doing with that sword at his side?' he asked of the Governor.

'The Admiral returned it to him on the day of the battle,' explained the Governor hastily. 'He said –'

'It doesn't matter what he said,' interrupted Caillard. 'No criminal as guilty as he can be allowed a weapon. And a sword is the emblem of a gentleman of honour, which he most decidedly is not. Take off that sword, sir.'

Hornblower stood appalled, hardly believing he had understood. Caillard's face wore a fixed mirthless smile which showed white teeth, below the black moustache which lay like a gash across his olive face.

'Take off that sword,' repeated Caillard, and then, as Hornblower made no movement, 'If Your Excellency will permit me to call in one of my gendarmes, I will have the sword removed.'

At the threat Hornblower unbuckled his belt and allowed the weapon to fall to the ground; the clatter rang loud in the silence. The sword of honour which the Patriotic Fund had awarded him ten years ago for his heading of the boarding party which took the *Castilla* lay on the floor, jerked half out of its scabbard. The hiltless tang and the battered places on the sheath where the gold had been torn off bore mute witness to the lust for gold of the Empire's servants.

'Good!' said Caillard. 'Now will Your Excellency have the goodness to warn this man of his approaching departure?'

'Colonel Caillard,' said the Governor, 'has come to take you and your first lieutenant, Mistaire – Mistaire Bush, to Paris.'

'Bush?' blazed out Hornblower, moved as not even the loss of his sword could move him. 'Bush? That is impossible. Lieutenant Bush is seriously wounded. It might easily be fatal to take him on a long journey at present.'

'The journey will be fatal to him in any case,' said Caillard, still with the mirthless smile and the gleam of white teeth.

The Governor wrung his hands.

'You cannot say that, Colonel. These gentlemen have still to be tried. The Military Commission has yet to give its verdict.'

'These gentlemen, as you call them, Your Excellency, stand condemned out of their own mouths.'

Hornblower remembered that he had made no attempt to deny, while the Admiral was questioning him and preparing his report, that he had been in command of the *Sutherland* the day she wore French colours and her landing party stormed the battery at

Llanza. He had known the ruse to be legitimate enough, but he had not reckoned on a French emperor determined upon convincing European opinion of the perfidy of England and cunning enough to know that a couple of resounding executions might well be considered evidence of guilt.

'The colonel,' said the Governor to Hornblower, 'has brought his coach. You may rely upon it that Mistaire Bush will have every possible comfort. Please tell me which of your men you would like to accompany you as your servant. And if there is anything which I can provide which will make the journey more comfortable, I will do so with the greatest pleasure.'

Hornblower debated internally the question of the servant. Polwheal, who had served him for years, was among the wounded in the casemate. Nor, he fancied, would he have selected him in any case; Polwheal was not the man for an emergency – and it was just possible that there might be an emergency. Latude had escaped from the Bastille. Was not there a faint chance that he might escape from Vincennes? Hornblower thought of Brown's bulging muscles and cheerful devotion.

'I would like to take my coxswain, Brown, if you please,' he said.

'Certainly. I will send for him and have your present servant pack your things with him. And with regard to your needs for the journey?'

'I need nothing,' said Hornblower. At the same time as he spoke he cursed himself for his pride. If he were ever to save himself and Bush from the firing party in the ditch at Vincennes he would need gold.

'Oh, I cannot allow you to say that,' protested the

Governor. 'There may be some few comforts you would like to buy when you are in France. Besides, you cannot deprive me of the pleasure of being of assistance to a brave man. Please do me the favour of accepting my purse. I beg you to, sir.'

Hornblower fought down his pride and took the proffered wallet. It was of surprising weight and gave out a musical chink as he took it.

'I must thank you for your kindness,' he said. 'And for all your courtesy while I have been your prisoner.'

'It has been a pleasure to me, as I said,' replied the Governor. 'I want to wish you the – the very best of luck on your arrival in Paris.'

'Enough of this,' said Caillard. 'My orders from His Majesty call for the utmost expedition. Is the wounded man in the courtyard?'

The Governor led the way out, and the gendarmes closed up round Hornblower as they walked towards the coach. Bush was lying there on a stretcher, strangely pale and strangely wasted out there in the bright light. He was feebly trying to shield his eyes from the sun; Hornblower ran and knelt beside him.

'They're going to take us to Paris, Bush,' he said.

'What, you and me, sir?'

'Yes.'

'It's a place I've often wanted to see.'

The Italian surgeon who had amputated Bush's foot was plucking at Hornblower's sleeve and fluttering some sheets of paper. These were instructions, he explained in faulty Italian French, for the further treatment of the stump. Any surgeon in France would understand them. As soon as the ligatures came away the wound would heal at once. He had put a parcel of dressings into the coach for use on the journey. Hornblower tried to thank him, but was interrupted when the surgeon turned away to supervise the lifting of Bush, stretcher and all, into the coach. It was an immensely long vehicle, and the stretcher just fitted in across one door, its ends on the two seats.

Brown was there now, with Hornblower's valise in his hand. The coachman showed him how to put it into the boot. Then a gendarme opened the other door and stood waiting for Hornblower to enter. Hornblower looked up at the ramparts towering above him; no more than half an hour ago he had been walking there, worn out with doubt. At least one doubt was settled now. In a fortnight's time perhaps they would all be settled, after he had faced the firing party at Vincennes. A spurt of fear welled up within him at the thought, destroying the first momentary feeling almost of pleasure. He did not want to be taken to Paris to be shot; he wanted to resist. Then he realized that resistance would be both vain and undignified, and he forced himself to climb into the coach, hoping that no one had noticed his slight hesitation.

A gesture from the sergeant of gendarmerie brought Brown to the door as well, and he came climbing in to sit apologetically with his officers. Caillard was mounting a big black horse, a spirited, restless creature which champed at its bit and passaged feverishly about. When he had settled himself in the saddle the word was given, and the horses were led round the courtyard, the coach jolting and heaving over the cobbles, out through the gate and down to the road which wound under the

27

guns of the fortress. The mounted gendarmerie closed up round the coach, a whip cracked, and they were off at a slow trot, to the jingling of the harness and the clattering of the hoofs and the creaking of the leather-work.

Hornblower would have liked to have looked out of the windows at the houses of Rosas village going by – after three weeks' captivity the change of scene allured him – but first he had to attend to his wounded lieutenant.

'How is it going, Bush?' he asked, bending over him.

'Very well, thank you, sir,' said Bush.

There was sunlight streaming in through the coach windows now, and here a succession of tall trees by the roadside threw flickering shadows over Bush's face. Fever and loss of blood had made Bush's face less craggy and gnarled, drawing the flesh tight over the bones so that he looked unnaturally younger, and he was pale instead of being the mahogany brown to which Hornblower was accustomed. Hornblower thought he saw a twinge of pain cross Bush's expression as the coach lurched on the abominable road.

'Is there anything I can do?' he asked, trying hard to keep the helplessness out of his voice.

'Nothing, thank you, sir,' whispered Bush.

'Try and sleep,' said Hornblower.

Bush's hand which lay outside the blanket twitched and stirred and moved towards him; he took it and he felt a gentle pressure. For a few brief seconds Bush's hand stroked his feebly, caressing it as though it was a woman's. There was a glimmer of a smile on Bush's drawn face with its closed eyes. During all the years they had served together it was the first sign of affection either had shown for the other. Bush's head turned on the pillow, and he lay quite still, while Hornblower sat not daring to move for fear of disturbing him.

The coach had slowed to a walk – it must be breasting the long climb which carried the road across the roots of the peninsula of Cape Creux. Yet even at that speed the coach lurched and rolled horribly; the surface of the road must be utterly uncared for. The sharp ringing of the hoofs of the escorts' horses told that they were travelling over rock, and the irregularity of the sound was a dear indication of the way the horses were picking their way among the holes. Framed in the windows Hornblower could see the gendarmes in their blue uniforms and cocked hats jerking and swaying about with the rolling of the coach. The presence of fifty gendarmes as an escort was not a real indication of the political importance of himself and Bush, but only a proof that even here, only twenty miles from France, the road was unsafe for small parties – a little band of Spanish guerilleros was to be found on every inaccessible hilltop.

But there was always a chance that Claros or Rovira with their Catalan miqueletes a thousand strong might come swooping down on the road from their Pyrenean fastnesses. Hornblower felt hope surging up within him at the thought that at any moment, in that case, he might find himself a free man again. His pulse beat faster and he crossed and uncrossed his knees restlessly – with the utmost caution so as not to disturb Bush. He did not want to be taken to Paris to face a mockery of a trial. He did not want to die. He was beginning to fret himself into a fever, when common sense came to his rescue and he compelled himself to sink into a stolid indifference.

Brown was sitting opposite him, primly upright with his arms folded. Hornblower almost grinned, sympathetically, at sight of him. Brown was actually self-conscious. He had never in his life before, presumably, had to be at such close quarters with a couple of officers. Certainly he must be feeling awkward at having to sit in the presence of two such lofty individuals as a captain and a first lieutenant. For that matter, it was at least a thousand to one that Brown had never been inside a coach before, had never sat on leather upholstery with a carpet under his feet. Nor had he had any experience in gentlemen's service, his duties as captain's coxswain being mainly disciplinary and executive. There was something comic about seeing Brown, with the proverbial adaptability of the British seaman, aping what he thought should be the manners of the gentleman's gentleman, and sitting there as if butter would not melt in his mouth.

The coach lurched again, quickening its pace and the horses broke from a walk into a trot. They must be at the top of the long hill now, with a long descent before them, which would bring them back to the seashore somewhere near Llanza, where he had stormed the battery under protection of the tricolour flag. It was an exploit he had been proud of – still was, for that matter. He had never dreamed for one moment that it would lead him to Paris and a firing party. Through the window on Bush's side he could see the rounded brown slopes of the Pyrenees soaring upwards; on the other side, as the coach swung sickeningly round a bend, he caught a glimpse of the sea far below, sparkling in the rays of the afternoon sun. He craned his neck to look at it, the sea which had played him so many scurvy tricks and which he loved. He thought, with a little catch in his throat, that this would be the last day on which he would ever see it. Tonight they would cross the frontier; tomorrow they would plunge into France, and in ten days, a fortnight, he would be rotting in his grave at Vincennes. It would be hard to leave this life, even with all its doubts and uncertainties, to lose the sea with its whims and its treacheries, Maria and the child, Lady Barbara –

Those were white cottages drifting past the windows, and on the side towards the sea, perched on the grassy cliff, was the battery of Llanza. He could see a sentry dressed in blue and white; stooping and looking upwards he could see the French flag at the top of the flagstaff – Bush, here, had hauled it down not so many weeks ago. He heard the coachman's whip crack and the horses quickened their pace; it was still eight miles or so to the frontier and Caillard must be anxious to cross before dark. The mountains, bristling here with pines, were hemming the road in close between them and the sea. Why did not Claros or Rovira come to save him? At every turn of the road there was an ideal site for an ambush. Soon they would be in France and it would be too late. He had to struggle again to remain passive. The prospect of crossing into France seemed to make his fate far more certain and imminent.

It was growing dark fast – they could not be far now from the frontier. Hornblower tried to visualize the charts he had often handled, so as to remember the name of the French frontier town, but his mind was not sufficiently under control to allow it. The coach was coming to a standstill; he heard footsteps outside, heard Caillard's metallic voice saying, 'In the name of the Emperor,' and an unknown voice say, 'Passez, passez, monsieur.' The coach lurched and accelerated again; they were in France now. Now the horses' hoofs were ringing on cobblestones. There were houses, one or two lights to be seen. Outside the houses there were men in all kinds of uniforms, and a few women picking their way among them, dressed in pretty costumes with caps on their heads. He could hear laughter and joking. Then abruptly the coach swerved to the right and drew up in the courtyard of an inn. Lights were appearing in plenty in the fading twilight. Someone opened the door of the coach and drew down the steps for him to descend.

4

Hornblower looked round the room to which the innkeeper and the sergeant of gendarmerie had jointly conducted them. He was glad to see a fire burning there, for he was stiff and chilled with his long inactivity in the coach. There was a truckle bed against one wall, a table with a white cloth already spread. A gendarme appeared at the door, stepping slowly and heavily – he was the first of the two who were carrying the stretcher. He looked round to see where to lay it down, turned too abruptly, and jarred it against the jamb of the wall.

'Careful with that stretcher!' snapped Hornblower, and then, remembering he had to speak French, 'Attention! Mettez le brancard là. Doucement!'

Brown came and knelt over the stretcher.

'What is the name of this place?' asked Hornblower of the innkeeper.

'Cerbére. Hôtel Iéna, monsieur,' answered the innkeeper, fingering his leather apron.

'Monsieur is allowed no speech with anyone whatever,' interposed the sergeant. 'He will be served, but he must address no speech to the inn servants. If he has any wishes, he will speak to the sentry outside his door. There will be another sentry outside his window.'

A gesture of his hand called attention to the cocked hat and the musket barrel of a gendarme, darkly visible through the glass.

'You are too amiable, monsieur,' said Hornblower.

'I have my orders. Supper will be served in half an hour.'

'I would be obliged if Colonel Caillard would give orders for a surgeon to attend Lieutenant Bush's wounds at once.'

'I will ask him, sir,' said the sergeant, escorting the innkeeper from the room.

Bush, when Hornblower bent over him, seemed somehow a little better than in the morning. There was a little colour in his cheeks and more strength in his movements.

'Is there anything I can do, Bush?' asked Hornblower.

'Yes –'

Bush explained the needs of sick-room nursing. Hornblower looked up at Brown, a little helplessly.

'I am afraid it'll call for two of you, sir, because I'm a heavy man,' said Bush apologetically. It was the apology in his tone which brought Hornblower to the point of action.

'Of course,' he said with all the cheerfulness he could bring into his voice. 'Come on, Brown. Lift him from the other side.'

After the business was finished, with no more than a single half-stifled groan from Bush, Brown displayed more of the astonishing versatility of the British seaman.

'I'll wash you, sir, shall I? An' you haven't had your shave today, have you, sir?'

Hornblower sat and watched in helpless admiration the deft movements of the burly sailor as he washed and shaved his first lieutenant. The towels were so well

34

arranged that no single drop of water fell on the bedding.

'Thank 'ee, Brown, thank 'ee,' said Bush, sinking back on his pillow.

The door opened to admit a little bearded man in a semi-military uniform carrying a leather case.

'Good evening, gentlemen,' he said, sounding all his consonants in the manner which Hornblower was yet to discover was characteristic of the Midi. 'I am the surgeon, if you please. And this is the wounded officer? And these are the hospital notes of my confrére at Rosas? Excellent. Yes, exactly. And how are you feeling, sir?'

Hornblower had to translate, limpingly, the surgeon's question to Bush, and the latter's replies. Bush put out his tongue, and submitted to having his pulse felt, and his temperature gauged by a hand thrust into his shirt.

'So,' said the surgeon. 'And now let us see the stump. Will you hold the candle for me here, if you please, sir?'

He turned back the blankets from the foot of the stretcher, revealing the little basket which guarded the stump, laid the basket on the floor and began to remove the dressings.

'Would you tell him, sir,' asked Bush, 'that my foot which isn't there tickles most abominably, and I don't know how to scratch it?'

The translation taxed Hornblower's French to the utmost, but the surgeon listened sympathetically.

'That is not at all unusual,' he said. 'And the itchings will come to a natural end in course of time. Ah, now here is the stump. A beautiful stump. A lovely stump.'

Hornblower, compelling himself to look, was vaguely reminded of the knuckle end of a roast leg of mutton; the irregular folds of flesh were caught in by half-healed scars, but out of the scars hung two ends of black thread.

'When Monsieur le Lieutenant begins to walk again,' explained the surgeon, 'he will be glad of an ample pad of flesh at the end of the stump. The end of the bone will not chafe –'

'Yes, exactly,' said Hornblower, fighting down his squeamishness.

'A very beautiful piece of work,' said the surgeon. 'As long as it heals properly and gangrene does not set in. At this stage the surgeon has to depend on his nose for his diagnosis.'

Suiting the action to the word the surgeon sniffed at the dressings and at the raw stump.

'Smell, monsieur,' he said, holding the dressings to Hornblower's face. Hornblower was conscious of the faintest whiff of corruption.

'Beautiful, is it not?' said the surgeon. 'A fine healthy wound and yet every evidence that the ligatures will soon free themselves.'

Hornblower realized that the two threads hanging out of the scars were attached to the ends of the two main arteries. When corruption inside was complete the threads could be drawn out and the wounds allowed to heal; it was a race between the rotting of the arteries and the onset of gangrene.

'I will see if the ligatures are free now. Warn your friend that I shall hurt him a little.'

Hornblower looked towards Bush to convey the message, and was shocked to see that Bush's face was distorted with apprehension.

'I know,' said Bush. 'I know what he's going to do – sir.'

Only as an afterthought did he say that 'sir'; which was the clearest proof of his mental preoccupation. He grasped the bedclothes in his two fists, his jaw set and his eyes shut.

'I'm ready,' he said through his clenched teeth.

The surgeon drew firmly on one of the threads and Bush writhed a little. He drew on the other.

'A-ah,' gasped Bush, with sweat on his face.

'Nearly free,' commented the surgeon. 'I could tell by the feeling of the threads. Your friend will soon be well. Now let us replace the dressings. So. And so.' His dexterous plump fingers rebandaged the stump, replaced the wicker basket, and drew down the bed coverings.

'Thank you, gentlemen,' said the surgeon, rising to his feet and brushing his hands one against the other. 'I will return in the morning.'

'Hadn't you better sit down, sir,' came Brown's voice to Hornblower's ears as though from a million miles away, after the surgeon had withdrawn. The room was veiled in grey mist which gradually cleared away as he sat, to reveal Bush lying back on his pillow and trying to smile, and Brown's homely honest face wearing an expression of acute concern.

'Rare bad you looked for a minute, sir. You must be hungry, I expect, sir, not having eaten nothing since breakfast, like.'

It was tactful of Brown to attribute this faintness to hunger, to which all flesh might be subject without shame, and not merely to weakness in face of wounds and suffering.

'That sounds like supper coming now,' croaked Bush from the stretcher, as though one of a conspiracy to ignore their captain's feebleness.

The sergeant of gendarmerie came clanking in, two women behind him bearing trays. The women set the table deftly and quickly, their eyes downcast, and withdrew without looking up, although one of them smiled at the corner of her mouth in response to a meaning cough from Brown which drew a gesture of irritation from the sergeant. The latter cast one searching glance round the room before shutting and locking the door with a clashing of keys.

'Soup,' said Hornblower, peering into the tureen which steamed deliciously. 'And I fancy this is stewed veal.'

The discovery confirmed him in his notion that Frenchmen lived exclusively on soup and stewed veal – he put no faith in the more vulgar notions regarding frogs and snails.

'You will have some of this broth, I suppose, Bush?' he continued. He was talking desperately hard now to conceal the feeling of depression and unhappiness which was overwhelming him. 'And a glass of this wine? It has no label – let's hope for the best.'

'Some of their rotgut claret, I suppose,' grunted Bush. Eighteen years of war with France had given most Englishmen men the notion that the only wines fit for men to drink were port and sherry and Madeira, and that Frenchmen only drank thin claret which gave the unaccustomed drinker the bellyache.

'We'll see,' said Hornblower as cheerfully as he could. 'Let's get you propped up first.'

With his hand behind Bush's shoulders he heaved him up a little; as he looked round helplessly, Brown came to his rescue with pillows taken from the bed, and between them they settled Bush with his head raised and his arms free and a napkin under his chin. Hornblower brought him a plate of soup and a piece of bread.

'M'm,' said Bush, tasting. 'Might be worse. Please, sir, don't let yours get cold.'

Brown brought a chair for his captain to sit at the table, and stood in an attitude of attention beside it; there was another place laid, but his action proclaimed as loudly as words how far it was from his mind to sit with his captain. Hornblower ate, at first with a distaste and then with increasing appetite.

'Some more of that soup, Brown,' said Bush. 'And my glass of wine, if you please.'

The stewed veal was extraordinarily good, even to a man who was accustomed to meat he could set his teeth in.

'Dash my wig,' said Bush from the bed. 'Do you think I could have some of that stewed veal, sir? This travelling has given me an appetite.'

Hornblower had to think about that. A man in a fever should be kept on a low diet, but Bush could not be said to be in a fever now, and he had lost a great deal of blood which he had to make up. The yearning look on Bush's face decided him.

'A little will do you no harm,' he said. 'Take this plate to Mr Bush, Brown.'

Good food and good wine – the fare in the *Sutherland* had been repulsive, and at Rosas scanty – tended to loosen their tongues and make them more cheerful. Yet it was hard to unbend beyond a certain unstated limit. The awful majesty surrounding a captain of a ship of the line lingered even after the ship had been destroyed; more than that, the memory of the very strict reserve which Hornblower had maintained during his command acted as a constraint. And to Brown a first lieutenant was in a position nearly as astronomically lofty as a captain; it was awesome to be in the same room as the two of them, even with the help of making-believe to be their old servant. Hornblower had finished his cheese by now, and the moment which Brown had been dreading had arrived.

'Here, Brown,' he said rising, 'sit down and eat your supper while it's still hot.'

Brown, now at the age of twenty-eight, had served His Majesty in His Majesty's ships from the age of eleven, and during that time he had never made use at table of other instruments than his sheath knife and his fingers; he had never eaten off china, nor had he drunk from a wineglass. He experienced a nightmare sensation as if his officers were watching him with four eyes as large as footballs the while he nervously picked up a spoon and addressed himself to this unaccustomed task. Hornblower realized his embarrassment in a clairvoyant flash. Brown had thews and sinews which Hornblower had often envied; he had a stolid courage in action which Hornblower could never hope to rival. He could knot and splice, hand, reef and steer, cast the lead or pull an oar, all of them far better than his captain. He could go aloft on a black night in a howling storm without thinking twice about it, but the sight of a knife and fork made his hands tremble. Hornblower thought about how Gibbon would have pointed the moral epigrammatically in two vivid antithetical sentences.

Humiliation and nervousness never did any good to a man – Hornblower knew that if anyone ever did. He took a chair unobtrusively over beside Bush's stretcher and sat down with his back almost turned to the table, and plunged desperately into conversation with his first lieutenant while the crockery clattered behind him.

'Would you like to be moved into the bed?' he asked, saying the first thing which came into his head.

'No thank you, sir,' said Bush. 'Two weeks now I've slept in the stretcher. I'm comfortable enough, sir, and it'd be painful to move me, even if – if –'

Words failed Bush to describe his utter determination not to sleep in the only bed and leave his captain without one.

'What are we going to Paris for, sir?' asked Bush.

'God knows,' said Hornblower. 'But I have a notion that Boney himself wants to ask us questions.'

That was the answer he had decided upon hours before in readiness for this inevitable question; it would not help Bush's convalescence to know the fate awaiting him.

'Much good will our answers do him,' said Bush, grimly. 'Perhaps we'll drink a dish of tea in the Tuileries with Maria Louisa.'

'Maybe,' answered Hornblower. 'And maybe he wants lessons in navigation from you. I've heard he's weak at mathematics.'

That brought a smile. Bush notoriously was no good

with figures and suffered agonies when confronted with a simple problem in spherical trigonometry. Hornblower's acute ears heard Brown's chair scrape a little; presumably his meal had progressed satisfactorily.

'Help yourself to the wine, Brown,' he said, without turning round.

'Aye aye, sir,' said Brown cheerfully.

There was a whole bottle of wine left as well as some in the other. This would be a good moment for ascertaining if Brown could be trusted with liquor. Hornblower kept his back turned to him and struggled on with his conversation with Bush. Five minutes later Brown's chair scraped again more definitely, and Hornblower looked round.

'Had enough, Brown?'

'Aye aye, sir. A right good supper.'

The soup tureen and the dish of stew were both empty; the bread had disappeared all save the heel of the loaf; there was only a morsel of cheese left. But one bottle of wine was still two-thirds full – Brown had contented himself with a half bottle at most, and the fact that he had drunk that much and no more was the clearest proof that he was safe as regards alcohol.

'Pull the bellrope, then.'

The distant jangling brought in time the rattling of keys to the door, and in came the sergeant and the two maids; the latter set about clearing the tables under the former's eye.

'I must get something for you to sleep on, Brown,' said Hornblower.

'I can sleep on the floor, sir.'

'No, you can't.'

Hornblower had decided opinions about that; there had been occasions as a young officer when he had slept on the bare planks of a ship's deck, and he knew their unbending discomfort.

'I want a bed for my servant,' he said to the sergeant.

'He can sleep on the floor.'

'I will not allow anything of the kind. You must find a mattress for him.'

Hornblower was surprised to find how quickly he was acquiring the ability to talk French; the quickness of his mind enabled him to make the best use of his limited vocabulary and his retentive memory had stored up all sorts of words, once heard, and was ready to produce them from the subconscious part of his mind as soon as the stimulus of necessity was applied.

The sergeant had shrugged his shoulders and rudely turned his back.

'I shall report your insolence to Colonel Caillard tomorrow morning,' said Hornblower hotly. 'Find a mattress immediately.'

It was not so much the threat that carried the day as long-ingrained habits of discipline. Even a sergeant of French gendarmerie was accustomed to yielding deference to gold lace and epaulettes and an authoritative manner. Possibly the obvious indignation of the maids at the suggestion that so fine a man should be left to sleep on the floor may have weighed with him too. He called to the sentry at the door and told him to bring a mattress from the stables where the escort were billeted. It was only a palliasse of straw when it came, but it was something infinitely more comfortable than bare and draughty boards, all the same. Brown looked his gratitude to Hornblower as the mattress was spread out in the corner of the room.

'Time to turn in,' said Hornblower, ignoring it, as the door was locked behind the sergeant. 'Let's make you comfortable, first, Bush.'

It was some obscure self-conscious motive which made Hornblower select from his valise the embroidered nightshirt over which Maria's busy fingers had laboured lovingly – the nightshirt which he had brought with him from England for use should it happen that he should dine and sleep at a Governor's or on board the flagship. All the years he had been a captain he had never shared a room with anyone save Maria, and it was a novel experience for him to prepare for bed in sight of Bush and Brown, and he was ridiculously self-conscious about it, regardless of the fact that Bush, white and exhausted, was already lying back on his pillow with drooping eyelids, while Brown modestly stripped off his trousers with downcast eyes, wrapped himself in the cloak which Hornblower insisted on his using, and curled himself up on his palliasse without a glance at his superior.

Hornblower got into bed.

'Ready?' he asked, and blew out the candle; the fire had died down to embers which gave only the faintest red glow in the room. It was the beginning of one of those wakeful nights which Hornblower had grown by now able to recognize in advance. The moment he blew out the candle and settled his head on the pillow he knew he would not be able to sleep until just before dawn. In his ship he would have gone up on deck or walked his stern gallery; here he could only lie grimly immobile. Sometimes a subdued crackling told how Brown was turning over on his straw mattress; once or twice Bush moaned a little in his feverish sleep.

Today was Wednesday. Only sixteen days ago and Hornblower had been captain of a seventy-four, and absolute master of the happiness of five hundred seamen. His least word directed the operations of a gigantic engine of war; the blows it had dealt had caused an imperial throne to totter. He thought regretfully of night-time aboard his ship, the creaking of the timbers and the singing of the rigging, the impassive quarter-master at the wheel in the faint light of the binnacle and the officer of the watch pacing the quarterdeck.

Now he was a nobody; where once he had minutely regulated five hundred men's lives he was reduced to chaffering for a single mattress for the only seaman left to him; police sergeants could insult him with impunity; he had to come and to go at the bidding of someone he despised. Worse than that – Hornblower felt the hot blood running under his skin as the full realization broke upon him again – he was being taken to Paris as a criminal. Very soon indeed, in some cold dawn, he would be led out into the ditch at Vincennes to face a firing party. Then he would be dead. Hornblower's vivid imagination pictured the impact of the musket bullets upon his breast, and he wondered how long the pain would last before oblivion came upon him. It was not the oblivion that he feared, he told himself – indeed in his present misery he almost looked forward to it. Perhaps it was the finality of death, the irrevocableness of it.

No, that was only a minor factor. Mostly it was instinctive fear of a sudden and drastic change to something completely unknown. He remembered the night he had spent as a child in the inn at Andover, when he was going to join his ship next day and enter upon the unknown life of the Navy. That was the nearest comparison – he had been frightened then, he remembered, so frightened he had been unable to sleep; and yet 'frightened' was too strong a word to describe the state of mind of someone who was quite prepared to face the future and could not be readily blamed for this sudden acceleration of heartbeat and prickling of sweat!

A moaning sigh from Bush, loud in the stillness of the room, distracted him from his analysis of his fear. They were going to shoot Bush, too. Presumably they would lash him to a stake to have a fair shot at him – curious how, while it was easy to order a party to shoot an upright figure, however helpless, every instinct revolted against shooting a helpless man prostrate on a stretcher. It would be a monstrous crime to shoot Bush, who, even supposing his captain were guilty, could have done nothing except obey orders. But Bonaparte would do it. The necessity of rallying Europe round him in his struggle against England was growing ever more pressing. The blockade was strangling the Empire of the French as Antaeus had been strangled by Hercules. Bonaparte's unwilling allies – all Europe, that was to say, save Portugal and Sicily – were growing restive and thinking about defection; the French people themselves, Hornblower shrewdly guessed, were by now none too enamoured of this King Stork whom they had imposed on themselves. It would not be sufficient for Bonaparte merely to say that the British fleet was the criminal instrument of a perfidious tyranny; he had said that for a dozen years. The mere announcement that British naval officers had violated the laws of war would carry small enough weight, too. But to try a couple of officers and shoot them would be a convincing gesture, and the perverted statement of facts issued from Paris might help to sustain French public opinion – European public opinion as well – for another year or two in its opposition to England.

But it was bad luck that the victims should be Bush and he. Bonaparte had had a dozen British naval captains in his hands during the last few years, and he could have trumped up charges against half of them. Presumably it was destiny which had selected Hornblower and Bush to suffer. Hornblower told himself that for twenty years he had been aware of a premonition of sudden death. It was certain and inevitable now. He hoped he would meet it bravely, go down with colours flying; but he mistrusted his own weak body. He feared that his cheeks would be pale and his teeth would chatter, or worse still, that his heart would weaken so that he would faint before the firing party had done their work. That would be a fine opportunity for a mordant couple of lines in the *Moniteur Universel* – fine reading for Lady Barbara and Maria.

If he had been alone in the room he would have groaned aloud in his misery and turned over restlessly. But as it was he lay grimly rigid and silent. If his subordinates were awake they would never be allowed to guess that he was awake, too. To divert his mind from his approaching execution he cast round in search of something else to think about, and new subjects presented themselves in swarms. Whether Admiral

Leighton were alive or dead, and whether, if the latter were the case, Lady Barbara Leighton would think more often or less often about Hornblower, her lover; how Maria's pregnancy was progressing; what was the state of British public opinion regarding the loss of the *Sutherland*, and, more especially, what Lady Barbara thought about his surrendering – there were endless things to think and worry about; there was endless flotsam bobbing about in the racing torrent of his mind. And the horses stampeded in the stable, and every two hours he heard the sentries being changed outside window and door.

5

Dawn was not fully come, the room was only faintly illuminated by the grey light, when a clash of keys and a stamping of booted feet outside the door heralded the entrance of the sergeant of gendarmerie.

'The coach will leave in an hour's time,' he announced. 'The surgeon will be here in half an hour. You gentlemen will please be ready.'

Bush was obviously feverish; Hornblower could see that at his first glance as he bent over him, still in his embroidered silk nightshirt. But Bush stoutly affirmed that he was not ill.

'I'm well enough, thank you, sir,' he said; but his face was flushed and yet apprehensive, and his hands gripped his bedclothes. Hornblower suspected that the mere vibration of the floor as he and Brown walked about the room was causing pain to the unhealed stump of his leg.

'I'm ready to do anything you want done,' said Hornblower.

'No, thank you, sir. Let's wait till the doctor comes, if you don't mind, sir.'

Hornblower washed and shaved in the cold water in the wash-stand jug; during the time which had elapsed since he had left the *Sutherland* he had never been allowed hot. But he yearned for the cold shower bath he had been accustomed to take under the jet of the

49

wash-deck pump; his skin seemed to creep when he stopped to consider it, and it was a ghoulish business to make shift with washing glove and soap, wetting a few inches at a time. Brown dressed himself unobtrusively in his own corner of the room, scurrying out like a mouse to wash when his captain had finished.

The doctor arrived with his leather satchel.

'And how is he this morning?' he asked, briskly; Hornblower saw a shade of concern pass over his face as he observed Bush's evident fever.

He knelt down and exposed the stump, Hornblower beside him. The limb jerked nervously as it was grasped with firm fingers; the doctor took Hornblower's hand and laid it on the skin above the wound.

'A little warm,' said the doctor. It was hot to Hornblower's touch. 'That may be a good sign. We shall know now.'

He took hold of one of the ligatures and pulled at it. The thing came gliding out of the wound like a snake.

'Good!' said the doctor. 'Excellent!'

He peered closely at the debris entangled in the knot, and then bent to examine the trickle of pus which had followed the ligature out of the wound.

'Excellent,' repeated the doctor.

Hornblower went back in his mind through the numerous reports which surgeons had made to him regarding wounded men, and the verbal comments with which they had amplified them. The words 'laudable pus' came up in his mind; it was important to distinguish between the drainage from a wound struggling to heal itself and the stinking ooze of a poisoned limb. This was clearly laudable pus, judging by the doctor's comments.

'Now for the other one,' said the doctor. He pulled at the remaining ligature, but all he got was a cry of pain from Bush – which seemed to go clean through Hornblower's heart – and a convulsive writhing of Bush's tortured body.

'Not quite ready,' said the doctor. 'I should judge that it will only be a matter of hours, though. Is your friend proposing to continue his journey today?'

'He is under orders to continue it,' said Hornblower in his limping French. 'You would consider such a course unwise?'

'Most unwise,' said the doctor. 'It will cause him a great deal of pain and may imperil the healing of the wound.'

He felt Bush's pulse and rested his hand on his fore-head.

'Most unwise,' he repeated.

The door opened behind him to reveal the gendarmerie sergeant.

'The carriage is ready.'

'It must wait until I have bandaged this wound. Get outside,' said the doctor testily.

'I will go and speak to the Colonel,' said Hornblower.

He brushed past the sergeant who tried too late to intercept him, into the main corridor of the inn, and out into the courtyard where stood the coach. The horses were being harnessed up, and a group of gendarmes were saddling their mounts on the farther side. Chance dictated that Colonel Caillard should be crossing the courtyard, too, in his blue and red uniform and his gleaming high boots, the star of the Legion of Honour dancing on his breast.

'Sir,' said Hornblower.

'What is it now?' demanded Caillard.

'Lieutenant Bush must not be moved. He is very badly wounded and a crisis approaches.'

The broken French came tumbling disjointedly from Hornblower's lips.

'I can do nothing in contravention of my orders,' said Caillard. His eyes were cold and his mouth hard.

'You were not ordered to kill him,' protested Hornblower.

'I was ordered to bring you and him to Paris with the utmost dispatch. We shall start in five minutes.'

'But, sir – cannot you wait even today?'

'Even as a pirate you must be aware of the impossibility of disobeying orders,' said Caillard.

'I protest against those orders in the name of humanity.'

That was a melodramatic speech, but it was a melodramatic moment, and in his ignorance of French Hornblower could not pick and choose his words. A sympathetic murmur in his ear attracted his notice, and, looking round, he saw the two aproned maids and a fat woman and the innkeeper all listening to the conversation with obvious disapproval of Caillard's point of view. They shut themselves away behind the kitchen door as Caillard turned a terrible eye upon them, but they had granted Hornblower a first momentary insight into the personal unpopularity which Imperial harshness was causing to develop in France.

'Sergeant,' said Caillard abruptly. 'Put the prisoners into the coach.'

There was no hope of resistance. The gendarmes

carried Bush's stretcher into the courtyard and perched it up on the seats, with Brown and Hornblower running round it to protect it from unnecessary jerks. The surgeon was scribbling notes hurriedly at the foot of the sheaf of notes regarding Bush's case which Hornblower had brought from Rosas. One of the maids came clattering across the courtyard with a steaming tray which she passed in to Hornblower through the open window. There was a platter of bread and three bowls of a black liquid which Hornblower was later to come to recognize as coffee – what blockaded France had come to call coffee. It was no pleasanter than the infusion of burnt crusts which Hornblower had sometimes drunk on shipboard during a long cruise without the opportunity of renewing cabin stores, but it was warm and stimulating at that time in the morning.

'We have no sugar, sir,' said the maid apologetically.

'It doesn't matter,' answered Hornblower, sipping thirstily.

'It is a pity the poor wounded officer has to travel,' she went on. 'These wars are terrible.'

She had a snub nose and a wide mouth and big black eyes – no one could call her attractive, but the sympathy in her voice was grateful to a man who was a prisoner. Brown was propping up Bush's shoulders and holding a bowl to his lips. He took two or three sips and turned his head away. The coach rocked as two men scrambled up on to the box.

'Stand away, there!' roared the sergeant.

The coach lurched and rolled and wheeled round out of the gates, the horses' hoofs clattering loud on the cobbles, and the last Hornblower saw of the maid was the slight look of consternation on her face as she realized that she had lost the breakfast tray for good.

The road was bad, judging by the way the coach lurched; Hornblower heard a sharp intake of breath from Bush at one jerk. He remembered what the swollen and inflamed stump of Bush's leg looked like; every jar must be causing him agony. He moved up the seat to the stretcher and caught Bush's hand.

'Don't you worry yourself, sir,' said Bush. 'I'm all right.'

Even while he spoke Hornblower felt him grip tighter as another jolt caught him unexpectedly.

'I'm sorry, Bush,' was all he could say; it was hard for the captain to speak at length to the lieutenant on such personal matters as his regret and unhappiness.

'We can't help it, sir,' said Bush, forcing his peaked features into a smile.

That was the main trouble, their complete helplessness. Hornblower realized that there was nothing he could say, nothing he could do. The leather-scented stuffiness of the coach was already oppressing him, and he realized with horror that they would have to endure this jolting prison of theirs for another twenty days, perhaps, before they should reach Paris. He was restless and fidgety at the thought of it, and perhaps his restlessness communicated itself by contact to Bush, who gently withdrew his hand and turned his head to one side, leaving his captain free to fidget within the narrow confines of the coach.

Still there were glimpses of the sea to be caught on one side, and of the Pyrenees on the other. Putting his head out of the window Hornblower ascertained that their escort was diminished today. Only two troopers rode ahead of the coach, and four clattered behind at the heels of Caillard's horse. Presumably their entry into France made any possibility of a rescue far less likely. Standing thus, his head awkwardly protruding through the window, was less irksome than sitting in the stuffiness of the carriage. There were the vineyards and the stubble field to be seen, and the swelling heights of the Pyrenees receding into the blue distance. There were people, too – nearly all women, Hornblower noted – who hardly looked up from their hoeing to watch the coach and its escort bowling along the road. Now they were passing a party of uniformed soldiers – recruits and convalescents, Hornblower guessed, on their way to their units in Catalonia – shambling along the road more like sheep than soldiers. The young officer at their head saluted the glitter of the star on Caillard's chest and eyed the coach curiously at the same time.

Strange prisoners had passed along that road before him; Alvarez, the heroic defender of Gerona, who died on a wheelbarrow – the only bed granted him – in a dungeon on his way to trial, and Toussaint l'Ouverture, the Negro hero of Haiti, kidnapped from his sunny island and sent to die, inevitably, of pneumonia in a rocky fortress in the Jura; Palafox of Zaragoza, young Mina from Navarre – all victims of the tyrant's Corsican rancour. He and Bush would only be two more items in a list already notable. D'Enghien who had been shot in Vincennes six years ago was of the blood-royal, and his death had caused a European sensation, but Bonaparte had murdered plenty more. Thinking of all those who had preceded him made Hornblower gaze more yearningly from the carriage window, and breathe more deeply of the free air.

Still in sight of sea and hills – Mount Canigou still dominating the background – they halted at a posting inn beside the road to change horses. Caillard and the escort took new mounts; four new horses were harnessed up to the coach, and in less than a quarter of an hour they were off again, breasting the steep slopes before them with renewed strength. They must be averaging six miles to the hour at least, thought Hornblower, his mind beginning to make calculations. How far Paris might be he could only guess – five or six hundred miles, he fancied. From seventy to ninety hours of travel would bring them to the capital, and they might travel eight, twelve, fifteen hours a day. It might be five days, it might be twelve, days, before they reached Paris – vague enough figures. He might be dead in a week's time, or he might still be alive in three weeks. Still alive! As Hornblower thought those words he realized how greatly he desired to live; it was one of those moments when the Hornblower whom he observed so dispassionately and with faint contempt suddenly blended with the Hornblower who was himself, the most important and vital person in the whole world. He envied the bent old shepherd in the distance with the plaid rug over his shoulders, hobbling over the hillside bent over his stick.

Here was a town coming – there were ramparts, a frowning citadel, a lofty cathedral. They passed through a gateway and the horses' hoofs rang loudly on cobble-stones as the coach threaded its way through narrow streets. Plenty of soldiers here, too; the streets were filled with variegated uniforms. This must be Perpignan, of course, the French base for the invasion of Catalonia. The coach stopped with a jerk in a wider street where an avenue of plane trees and a flagged quay bordered a little river, and, looking upward, Hornblower read the sign 'Hôtel de la Poste et du Perdrix. Route Nationale 9. Paris 849'. With a rush and bustle the horses were changed, Brown and Hornblower were grudgingly allowed to descend and stretch their stiff legs before returning to attend to Bush's wants – they were few enough in his present fever. Caillard and the gendarmes were snatching a hasty meal – the latter at tables outside the inn, the former visible through the windows of the front room. Someone brought the prisoners a tray with slices of cold meat, bread, wine, and cheese. It had hardly been handed into the coach when the escort climbed upon their horses again, the whip cracked and they were off. The coach heaved and dipped like a ship at sea as it mounted first one hump-backed bridge and then another, before the horses settled into a steady trot along the wide straight road bordered with poplars.

'They waste no time,' said Hornblower, grimly.

'No, sir, that they don't!' agreed Brown.

Bush would eat nothing, shaking his head feebly at the offer of bread and meat. All they could do for him was to moisten his lips with wine, for he was parched and thirsty; Hornblower made a mental note to remember to ask for water at the next posting house, and cursed himself for forgetting anything so obvious up to now. He and Brown shared the food, eating with their fingers and drinking turn and turn about from the bottle of wine, Brown apologetically wiping the bottle's mouth with the napkin after drinking. And as soon as the food was finished Hornblower was on his feet again craning through the carriage window, watching the countryside drifting by. A thin chill rain began, soaking his scanty hair as he stood there, wetting his face and even running in trickles down his neck, but still he stood there, staring out at freedom.

The sign of the inn where they stopped at nightfall read 'Hôtel de la Poste de Sigean. Route Nationale 9. Paris 805. Perpignan 44'. This place Sigean was no more than a sparse village, straggling for miles along the high road, and the inn was a tiny affair, smaller than the posting stables round the other three sides of the court-yard. The staircase to the upper rooms was too narrow and winding for the stretcher to be carried up them; it was only with difficulty that the bearers were able to turn with it into the salon which the innkeeper reluctantly yielded to them. Hornblower saw Bush wincing as the stretcher jarred against the sides of the door.

'We must have a surgeon at once for the lieutenant,' he said to the sergeant.

'I will inquire for one.'

The innkeeper here was a surly brute with a squint; he was ungracious about clearing his best sitting room of its spindly furniture, and bringing beds for Hornblower and Brown, and producing the various arti-cles they asked for to help make Bush comfortable. There were no wax candles nor lamps; only tallow dips which stank atrociously.

'How's the leg feeling?' asked Hornblower, bending over Bush.

'All right, sir,' said Bush, stubbornly, but he was so

58

obviously feverish and in such obvious pain that Hornblower was anxious about him.

When the sergeant escorted in the maid with the dinner he asked, sharply:

'Why has the surgeon not come?'

'There is no surgeon in this village.'

'No surgeon? The lieutenant is seriously ill. Is there no – no apothecary?'

Hornblower used the English word in default of French.

'The cow-doctor went across the hills this afternoon and will not be back tonight. There is no one to be found.'

The sergeant went out of the room, leaving Hornblower to explain the situation to Bush.

'All right,' said the latter, turning his head on the pillow with the feeble gesture which Hornblower dreaded. Hornblower nerved himself.

'I'd better dress that wound of yours myself,' he said. 'We might try cold vinegar on it, as they do in our service.'

'Something cold,' said Bush, eagerly.

Hornblower pealed at the bell, and when it was eventually answered he asked for vinegar and obtained it. Not one of the three had a thought for their dinner cooling on the side table.

'Now,' said Hornblower.

He had a saucer of vinegar beside him, in which lay the soaking lint, and the clean bandages which the surgeon at Rosas had supplied were at hand. He turned back the bedclothes and revealed the bandaged stump. The leg twitched nervously as he removed the bandages;

it was red and swollen and inflamed, hot to the touch for several inches above the point of amputation.

'It's pretty swollen here, too, sir,' whispered Bush. The glands in his groin were huge.

'Yes,' said Hornblower.

He peered at the scarred end, examined the dressings he had removed, with Brown holding the light. There had been a slight oozing from the point where the ligature had been withdrawn yesterday; much of the rest of the scar was healed and obviously healthy. There was only the other ligature which could be causing this trouble; Hornblower knew that if it were ready to come out it was dangerous to leave it in. Cautiously he took hold of the silken thread. The first gentle touch of it conveyed to his sensitive fingers a suggestion that it was free. It moved distinctly for a quarter of an inch, and judging by Bush's quiescence, it caused him no sudden spasm of pain. Hornblower set his teeth and pulled; the thread yielded very slowly, but it was obviously free, and no longer attached to the elastic artery. He pulled steadily against a yielding resistance. The ligature came slowly out of the wound, knot and all. Pus followed it in a steady trickle, only slightly tinged with blood. The thing was done.

The artery had not burst, and clearly the wound was in need of the free drainage open to it now with the withdrawal of the ligature.

'I think you're going to start getting well now,' he said, aloud, making himself speak cheerfully, 'How does it feel?'

'Better,' said Bush. 'I think it's better, sir.'

Hornblower applied the soaking lint to the scarred

surface. He found his hands trembling, but he steadied them with an effort as he bandaged the stump – not an easy job, this last, but one which he managed to complete in adequate fashion. He put back the wicker shield, tucked in the bedclothes, and rose to his feet. The trembling was worse than ever now, and he was shaken and sick, which surprised him.

'Supper, sir?' asked Brown. 'I'll give Mr Bush his.'

Hornblower's stomach resisted a protest at the suggestion of food. He would have liked to refuse, but that would have been too obvious a confession of weakness in front of a subordinate.

'When I've washed my hands,' he said loftily.

It was easier to eat than he had expected, when he sat down to force himself. He managed to choke down enough mouthfuls to make it appear as if he had eaten well, and with the passage of the minutes the memory of the revolting task on which he had been engaged became rapidly less clear. Bush displayed none of the appetite nor any of the cheerfulness which had been noticeable last night; that was the obvious result of his fever. But with free drainage to his wound it could be hoped that he would soon recover. Hornblower was tired now, as a result of his sleepless night the night before, and his emotions had been jarred into a muddle by what he had had to do; it was easier to sleep tonight, waking only at intervals to listen to Bush's breathing, and to sleep again reassured by the steadiness and tranquillity of the sound.

6

After that day the details of the journey became more blurred and indistinct – up to that day they had had all the unnatural sharpness of a landscape just before rain. Looking back at the journey, what was easiest to remember was Bush's convalescence – his steady progress back to health from the moment that the ligature was withdrawn from his wound. His strength began to come back fast, so that it would have been astonishing to anyone who did not know of his iron constitution and of the Spartan life he had always led. The transition was rapid between the time when his head had to be supported to allow him to drink and the time when he could sit himself up by his own unaided strength.

Hornblower could remember those details when he tried to, but all the rest was muddled and vague. There were memories of long hours spent at the carriage window, when it always seemed to be raining, and the rain wetted his face and hair. Those were hours spent in a sort of melancholy; Hornblower came to look back on them afterwards in the same way as someone recovered from insanity must look back on the blank days in the asylum. All the inns at which they stayed and the doctors who had attended to Bush were confused in his mind. He could remember the relentless regularity with which the kilometre figures displayed at the posting stations indicated the dwindling distance between them and Paris – Paris 525, Paris 383, Paris 287; somewhere at that point they changed from Route Nationale No. 9 to Route Nationale No. 7. Each day was bringing them nearer to Paris and death, and each day he sank farther into apathetic melancholy. Issoire, Clermont-Ferrand, Moulins; he read the names of the towns through which they passed without remembering them.

Autumn was gone now, left far behind down by the Pyrenees. Here winter had begun. Cold winds blew in melancholy fashion through the long avenues of leafless trees, and the fields were brown and desolate. At night he was sleeping heavily, tormented by dreams which he could not remember in the morning; his days he spent standing at the carriage window staring with sightless eyes over a dreary landscape where the chill rain fell. It seemed as if he had spent years consecutively in the leathery atmosphere of the coach, with the clatter of the horses' hoofs in his ears, and, visible in the tail of his eye, the burly figure of Caillard riding at the head of the escort close to the offside hind wheel.

During the bleakest afternoon they had yet experienced it did not seem as if Hornblower would be roused from his stupor even by the sudden unexpected stop which to a bored traveller might provide a welcome break in the monotony of travel. Dully, he watched Caillard ride up to ask the reason; dully, he gathered from the conversation that one of the coach horses had lost a shoe and gone dead lame. He watched with indifference the unharnessing of the unfortunate brute, and heard without interest the unhelpful answers of a passing travelling salesman with a pack-mule of whom

Caillard demanded the whereabouts of the nearest smith. Two gendarmes went off at a snail's pace down a side track, leading the crippled animal; with only three horses the coach started off again towards Paris.

Progress was slow, and the stage was a long one. Only rarely before had they travelled after dark, but here it seemed that night would overtake them long before they could reach the next town. Bush and Brown were talking quite excitedly about this remarkable mishap – Hornblower heard their cackle without noticing it, as a man long resident beside a waterfall no longer hears the noise of the fall. The darkness which was engulfing them was premature. Low black clouds covered the whole sky, and the note of the wind in the trees carried with it something of menace. Even Hornblower noted that, nor was it long before he noticed something else, that the rain beating upon his face was changing to sleet, and then from sleet to snow; he felt the big flakes upon his lips, and tasted them with his tongue. The gendarme who lit the lamps beside the driver's box revealed to them through the windows the front of his cloak caked thick with snow, shining faintly in the feeble light of the lamp. Soon the sound of the horses' feet was muffled and dull, the wheels could hardly be heard, and the pace of the coach diminished still further as it ploughed through the snow piling in the road. Hornblower could hear the coachman using his whip mercilessly upon his weary animals – they were heading straight into the piercing wind, and were inclined to take every opportunity to flinch away from it.

Hornblower turned back from the window to his subordinates inside the coach – the faint light which the glass front panel allowed to enter from the lamps was no more than enough to enable him just to make out their shadowy forms. Bush was lying huddled under all his blankets; Brown was clutching his cloak round him, and Hornblower for the first time noticed the bitter cold. He shut the coach window without a word, resigning himself to the leathery stuffiness of the interior. His dazed melancholy was leaving him without his being aware of it.

'God help sailors,' he said cheerfully, 'on a night like this.'

That drew a laugh from the others in the darkness – Hornblower just caught the note of pleased surprise in it which told him that they had noticed and regretted the black mood which had gripped him during the last few days, and were pleased with this first sign of his recovery. Resentfully he asked himself what they expected of him. They did not know, as he did, that death awaited him and Bush in Paris. What was the use of thinking and worrying, guarded as they were by Caillard and six gendarmes? With Bush a hopeless cripple, what chance was there of escape? They did not know that Hornblower had put aside all thought of escaping by himself. If by a miracle he had succeeded, what would they think of him in England when he arrived there with the news that he had left his lieu-tenant to die? They might sympathize with him, pity him, understand his motive – he hated the thought of any of that; better to face a firing party at Bush's side, never to see Lady Barbara again, never to see his child. And better to spend his last few days in apathy than in fretting. Yet the present circumstances, so different from the monotony of the rest of the journey, had stimulated him. He laughed and chatted with the others as he had not done since they had left Béziers.

The coach crawled on through the darkness with the wind shrieking overhead. Already the windows on one side were opaque with the snow which was plastered upon them – there was not warmth enough within the coach to melt it. More than once the coach halted, and Hornblower, putting his head out, saw that they were having to clear the horses' hoofs of the snow balled into ice under their shoes.

'If we're more than two miles from the next post house,' he announced, sitting back again, 'we won't reach it until next week.'

Now they must have topped a small rise, for the horses were moving quicker, almost trotting, with the coach swaying and lurching over the inequalities of the road. Suddenly from outside they heard an explosion of shouts and yells.

'Hé, hé, hé!'

The coach swung round without warning, lurching frightfully, and came to a halt leaning perilously over to one side. Hornblower sprang to the window and looked out. The coach was poised perilously on the bank of a river; Hornblower could see the black water sliding along almost under his nose. Two yards away a small rowing boat, moored to a post, swayed about under the influence of wind and stream. Otherwise there was nothing to be seen in the blackness. Some of the gendarmes had run to the coach horses' heads; the animals were plunging and rearing in their fright at the sudden apparition of the river before them.

Somehow in the darkness the coach must have got off the road and gone down some side track leading to the river here; the coachman had reined his horses round only a fraction of a second before disaster threatened. Caillard was sitting his horse blaring sarcasms at the others.

'A fine coachman you are, God knows. Why didn't you drive straight into the river and save me the trouble of reporting you to the sous-chef of the administration? Come along, you men. Do you want to stay here all night? Get the coach back on the road, you fools.'

The snow came driving down in the darkness, the hot lamps sizzling continuously as the flakes lighted on them. The coachman got his horses under control again, the gendarmes stood back, and the whip cracked. The horses plunged and slipped, pawing for a footing, and the coach trembled without stirring from the spot.

'Come along, now!' shouted Caillard. 'Sergeant, and you, Pellaton, take the horses. You other men get to the wheels! Now, altogether. Heave! Heave!'

The coach lurched a scant yard before halting again. Caillard cursed wildly.

'If the gentlemen in the coach would descend and help,' suggested one of the gendarmes, 'it would be better.'

'They can, unless they would rather spend the night in the snow,' said Caillard; he did not condescend to address Hornblower directly. For a moment Hornblower thought of telling him that he would see him damned first – there would be some satisfaction in that – but on the other hand he did not want to condemn

Bush to a night of discomfort merely for an intangible self-gratification.

'Come on, Brown,' he said, swallowing his resentment, and he opened the door and they jumped down into the snow.

Even with the coach thus lightened, and with five men straining at the spokes of the wheels, they could make no progress. The snow had piled up against the steep descent to the river, and the exhausted horses plunged uselessly in the deep mass.

'God, what a set of useless cripples!' raved Caillard. 'Coachman, how far is it to Nevers?'

'Six kilometres, sir.'

'You mean you think it's six kilometres. Ten minutes ago you thought you were on the right road and you were not. Sergeant, ride into Nevers for help. Find the mayor, and bring every able-bodied man in the name of the Emperor. You, Ramel, ride with the sergeant as far as the high road, and wait there until he returns. Otherwise they'll never find us. Go on, sergeant, what are you waiting for? And you others, tether your horses and put your cloaks on their backs. You can keep warm digging the snow away from that bank. Coachman, come off that box and help them.'

The night was incredibly dark. Two yards from the carriage lamps nothing was visible at all, and with the wind whistling by they could not hear, as they stood by the coach, the movements of the men in the snow. Hornblower stamped about beside the coach and flogged himself with his arms to get his circulation back. Yet this snow and this icy wind were strangely refreshing. He felt no desire at the moment for the cramped stuffiness of the coach. And as he swung his arms an idea came to him, which checked him suddenly in his movements, until, ridiculously afraid of his thoughts being guessed, he went on stamping and swinging more industriously than ever. The blood was running hot under his skin now, as it always did when he was making plans – when he had outmanoeuvred the *Natividad*, for instance, and when he had saved the *Pluto* in the storm off Cape Creux.

There had been no hope of escape without the means of transporting a helpless cripple; now, not twenty feet from him, there was the ideal means – the boat which rocked to its moorings at the river bank. On a night like this it was easy to lose one's way altogether – except in a boat on a river; in a boat one had only to keep shoving off from shore to allow the current to carry one away faster than any horse could travel in these conditions. Even so, the scheme was utterly harebrained. For how many days would they be able to preserve their liberty in the heart of France, two able-bodied men and one on a stretcher? They would freeze, starve – possibly even drown. But it was a chance, and nothing nearly as good would present itself (as far as Hornblower could judge from his past observations) between now and the time when the firing party at Vincennes would await them. Hornblower observed with mild interest that his fever was abating as he formed his resolve; and he was sufficiently amused at finding his jaw set in an expression of fierce resolution to allow his features to relax into a grim smile. There was always something laughable to him in being involved in heroics.

Brown came stamping round the coach and Hornblower addressed him, contriving with great effort to keep his voice low and yet matter of fact.

'We're going to escape down the river in that boat, Brown,' he said.

'Aye, aye, sir,' said Brown, with no more excitement in his voice than if Hornblower had been speaking of the cold. Hornblower saw his head in the darkness turn towards the nearly visible figure of Caillard, pacing restlessly in the snow beside the coach.

'That man must be silenced,' said Hornblower.

'Aye, aye, sir.' Brown meditated for a second before continuing. 'Better let me do that, sir.'

'Very good.'

'Now, sir?'

'Yes.'

Brown took two steps towards the unsuspecting figure.

'Here,' he said. 'Here, you.'

Caillard turned and faced him, and as he turned he received Brown's fist full on his jaw, in a punch which had all Brown's mighty fourteen stone behind it. He dropped in the snow, with Brown leaping upon him like a tiger, Hornblower behind him.

'Tie him up in his cloak,' whispered Hornblower. 'Hold on to his throat while I get it unbuttoned. Wait. Here's his scarf. Tie his head up in that first.'

The sash of the Legion of Honour was wound round and round the wretched man's head. Brown rolled the writhing figure over and with his knee in the small of his back tied his arms behind him with his neckcloth. Hornblower's handkerchief sufficed for his ankles –

Brown strained the knot tight. They doubled the man in two and bundled him into his cloak, tying it about him with his swordbelt. Bush, lying on his stretcher in the darkness of the coach, heard the door open and a heavy load drop upon the floor.

'Mr Bush,' said Hornblower – the formal 'Mr' came naturally again now the action had begun again – 'We are going to escape in the boat.'

'Good luck, sir,' said Bush.

'You're coming too. Brown, take that end of the stretcher. Lift. Starboard a bit. Steady.'

Bush felt himself lifted out of the coach, stretcher and all, and carried down through the snow.

'Get the boat close in,' snapped Hornblower. 'Cut the moorings. Now, Bush, let's get these blankets round you. Here's my cloak, take it as well. You'll obey orders, Mr Bush. Take the other side, Brown. Lift him into the stern-sheets. Lower away. Bow thwart, Brown. Take the oars. Right. Shove off. Give way.'

It was only six minutes from the time when Hornblower had first conceived the idea. Now they were free, adrift on the black river, and Caillard was gagged and tied into a bundle on the floor of the coach. For a fleeting moment Hornblower wondered whether Caillard would suffocate before being discovered, and he found himself quite indifferent in the matter. Bonaparte's personal aides-de-camp, especially if they were colonels of gendarmerie as well, must expect to run risks while doing the dirty work which their situation would bring them. Meanwhile he had other things to think about.

'Easy!' he hissed at Brown. 'Let the current take her.'

The night was absolutely black; seated on the stern

thwart he could not even see the surface of the water overside. For that matter, he did not know what river it was. But every river runs to the sea. The sea! Hornblower writhed in his seat in wild nostalgia at a vivid recollection of sea breezes in the nostrils and the feel of a heaving deck under his feet. Mediterranean or Atlantic, he did not know which, but if they had fantastic luck they might reach the sea in this boat by following the river far enough, and the sea was England's and would bear them home, to life instead of death, to freedom instead of imprisonment, to Lady Barbara, to Maria and his child.

The wind shrieked down on them, driving snow down his neck – thwarts and bottom boards were thick with snow. He felt the boat swing round under the thrust of the wind, which was in his face now instead of on his cheek.

'Turn her head to wind, Brown,' he ordered, 'and pull slowly into it.'

The surest way of allowing the current a free hand with them was to try to neutralize the effect of the wind – a gale like this would soon blow them on shore, or even possibly blow them upstream; in this blackness it was impossible to guess what was happening to them.

'Comfortable, Mr Bush?' he asked.

'Aye, aye, sir.'

Bush was faintly visible now, for the snow had driven up already against the grey blankets that swathed him and could just be seen from where Hornblower sat, a yard away.

'Would you like to lie down?'

'Thank you, sir, but I'd rather sit.'

Now that the excitement of the actual escape was over, Hornblower found himself shivering in the keen wind without his cloak. He was about to tell Brown that he would take one of the sculls when Bush spoke again.

'Pardon, sir, but d'you hear anything?'

Brown rested on his oars, and they sat listening.

'No,' said Hornblower. 'Yes, I do, by God!'

Underlying the noise of the wind there was a distant monotonous roaring.

'H'm,' said Hornblower, uneasily.

The roar was growing perceptibly louder; now it rose several notes in the scale, suddenly, and they could distinguish the sound of running water. Something appeared in the darkness beside the boat; it was a rock nearly covered, rendered visible in the darkness by the boiling white foam round it. It came and was gone in a flash, the clearest proof of the speed with which the boat was travelling.

'Jesus!' said Brown in the bows.

Now the boat was spinning round, lurching, jolting. All the water was white overside, and the bellowing of the rapid was deafening. They could do no more than sit and cling to their seat as the boat heaved and jerked. Hornblower shook himself free from his dazed helplessness, which seemed to have lasted half an hour and probably lasted no more than a couple of seconds.

'Give me a scull,' he snapped at Brown. 'You fend off port side. I'll take starboard.'

He groped in the darkness, found a scull, and took it from Brown's hand; the boat spun, hesitated, plunged again. All about them was the roar of the rapid. The starboard side of the boat caught on a rock; Hornblower felt icy water deluge his legs as it poured in over the side behind him. But already he was thrusting madly and blindly with his scull against the rock, he felt the boat slip and swing, he thrust so that the swing was accentuated, and next moment they were clear, wallowing sluggishly with the water up to the thwarts. Another rock slid hissing past, but the roar of the fall was already dwindling.

'Christ!' said Bush, in a mild tone contrasting oddly with the blasphemy. 'We're through!'

'D'you know if there's a bailer in the boat, Brown?' demanded Hornblower.

'Yessir, there was one at my feet when I came on board.'

'Find it and get this water out. Give me your other scull.'

Brown splashed about in the icy water in a manner piteous to hear as he groped for the floating wooden basin.

'Got it, sir,' he reported, and they heard the regular sound of the water being scooped overside as he began work.

In the absence of the distraction of the rapids they were conscious of the wind again now, and Hornblower turned the boat's bows into it and pulled slowly at the sculls. Past experience appeared to have demonstrated conclusively that this was the best way to allow the current a free hand to take the boat downstream and away from pursuit. Judging by the speed with which the noise of the rapid was left behind the current of this river was very fast indeed – that was only to be expected,

74

too, for all the rain of the past few days must have brought up every river brim full. Hornblower wondered vaguely again what river this was, here in the heart of France. The only one with whose name he was acquainted and which it might possibly be was the Rhône, but he felt a suspicion that the Rhône was fifty miles or so farther eastward. This river presumably had taken its origin in the gaunt Cevennes whose flanks they had turned in the last two days' journey. In that case it would run northward, and must presumably turn west-ward to find the sea – it must be the Loire or one of its tributaries. And the Loire fell into the Bay of Biscay below Nantes, which must be at least four hundred miles away. Hornblower's imagination dallied with the idea of a river four hundred miles long, and with the prospect of descending it from source to mouth in the depth of winter.

A ghostly sound as if from nowhere brought him back to earth again. As he tried to identify it it repeated itself more loudly and definitely, and the boat lurched and hesitated. They were gliding over a bit of rock which providence had submerged to a depth sufficient just to scrape their keel. Another rock, foam covered, came boiling past them dose overside. It passed them from stern to bow, telling him what he had no means of discovering in any other way in the blackness, that in this reach the river must be running westward, for the wind was in the east and he was pulling into it.

'More of those to come yet, sir,' said Bush – already they could hear the growing roar of water among rocks.

'Take a scull and watch the port side, Brown,' said Hornblower.

'Aye aye, sir. I've got the boat nearly dry,' volunteered Brown, feeling for the scull.

The boat was lurching again now, dancing a little in the madness of the river. Hornblower felt bow and stem lift successively as they dropped over what felt like a downward step in the water; he reeled as he stood, and the water remaining in the bottom of the boat surged and splashed against his ankles. The din of the rapid in the darkness round them was tremendous; white water was boiling about them on either side. The boat swung and pitched and rolled. Then something invisible struck the port side amidships with a splinter crash. Brown tried unavailingly to shove off, and Hornblower swung round and with his added strength forced the boat clear. They plunged and rolled again; Hornblower, feeling in the darkness, found the gunwale stove in, but apparently only the two upper stakes were damaged – chance might have driven that rock through below the water line as easily as it had done above it. Now the keel seemed to have caught; the boat heeled hideously, with Bush and Hornblower falling on their noses, but she freed herself and went on through the roaring water. The noise was dying down again and they were through another rapid.

'Shall I bail again, sir?' asked Brown.

'Yes. Give me your scull.'

'Light on the starboard bow, sir' interjected Bush.

Hornblower craned over his shoulder. Undoubtedly it was a light, with another close beside it, and another farther on, barely visible in the driving snow. That must be a village on the river bank, or a town – the town of Nevers, six kilometres, according to the coachman, from

76

where they had embarked. They had come four miles already.

'Silence now!' hissed Hornblower. 'Brown, stop bailing.'

With those lights to guide him in the darkness, stable, permanent things in this insane world of infinite indefiniteness, it was marvellous how he felt master of his fate once more. He knew again which was upstream and which was down – the wind was still blowing downstream. With a touch of the sculls he turned the boat downstream, wind and current sped her along fast and the lights were gliding by rapidly. The snow stung his face – it was hardly likely there would be anyone in the town to observe them on a night like this. Certainly the boat must have come down the river faster than the plodding horses of the gendarmes whom Caillard had sent ahead. A new roaring of water caught his ear, different in timbre from the sound of a rapid. He craned round again to see the bridge before them silhouetted in white against the blackness by reason of the snow driven against the arches. He tugged wildly, first at one scull and then at both, heading for the centre of an arch; he felt the bow dip and the stern heave as they approached – the water was banked up above the bridge and rushed down through the arches in a long sleek black slope. As they whirled under Hornblower bent to his sculls, to give the boat sufficient way to carry her through the eddies which his seaman's instinct warned him would await them below the piers. The crown of the arch brushed his head as he pulled – the floods had risen as high as that. The sound of rushing water echoed strangely under the stonework for a second, and then they were through, with Hornblower tugging madly at the sculls.

One more light on the shore, and then they were in utter blackness again, their sense of direction lost.

'Christ!' said Bush again, this time with utter solemnity, as Hornblower rested on his sculls. The wind shrieked down upon them, blinding them with snow. From the bows came a ghostly chuckle.

'God help sailors,' said Brown, 'on a night like this.'

'Carry on with the bailing, Brown, and save your jokes for afterwards,' snapped Hornblower. But he giggled, nevertheless, even despite of the faint shock he experienced at hearing the lower deck cracking jokes to a captain and a first lieutenant. His ridiculous habit of laughing insanely in the presence of danger or hardship was already ready to master him, and he giggled now, while he dragged at the oars and fought against the wind – he could tell by the way the blades dragged through the water that the boat was making plenty of leeway. He only stopped giggling when he realized with a shock that it was hardly more than two hours back that he had first uttered the prayer about God helping sailors on a night like this. It seemed like a fortnight ago at least that he had last breathed the leathery stuffiness of the inside of the coach.

The boat grated heavily over gravel, caught, freed itself, bumped again, and stuck fast. All Hornblower's shoving with the sculls would not get her afloat again.

'Nothing to do but shove her off,' said Hornblower, laying down his sculls.

He stepped over the side into the freezing water, slipping on the stones, with Brown beside him. Between them they ran her out easily, scrambled on board, and Hornblower made haste to seize the sculls and pull her into the wind. Yet a few seconds later they were aground again. It was the beginning of a nightmare period. In the darkness Hornblower could not guess whether their difficulties arose from the action of the wind in pushing them against the bank, or from the fact that the river was sweeping round in a great bend here, or whether they had strayed into a side channel with scanty water. However it was, they were continually having to climb out and shove the boat off. They slipped and plunged over the invisible stones; they fell waist deep into unseen pools, they cut themselves and bruised themselves in this mad game of blind man's buff with the treacherous river. It was bitterly cold now; the sides of the boat were glazed with ice. In the midst of his struggles with the boat Hornblower was consumed with anxiety for Bush, bundled up in cloak and blankets in the stern.

'How is it with you, Bush?' he asked.

'I'm doing well, sir,' said Bush.

'Warm enough?'

'Aye aye, sir. I've only one foot to get wet now, you know, sir.'

He was probably being deceitfully cheerful, thought Hornblower, standing ankle deep in rushing water and engaged in what seemed to be an endless haul of the boat through invisible shallows. Blankets or no blankets, he must be horribly cold and probably wet as well, and he was a convalescent who ought to have been kept in bed. Bush might die out here this very night. The boat came free with a run, and Hornblower staggered back waist deep in the chill water. He swung himself in over

79

the swaying gunwale while Brown, who apparently had been completely submerged, came spluttering in over the other side. Each of them grabbed a scull in their anxiety to have something to do while the wind cut them to the bone.

The current whirled them away. Their next contact with the shore was among trees – willows, Hornblower guessed in the darkness. The branches against which they scraped volleyed snow at them, scratched them and whipped them, held the boat fast until by feeling round in the darkness they found the obstruction and lifted it clear. By the time they were free of the willows Hornblower had almost decided that he would rather have rocks if he could choose and he giggled again, feebly, with his teeth chattering. Naturally, they were among rocks again quickly enough; at this point apparently there was a sort of minor rapid down which the river rolled among rocks and banks of stones.

Already Hornblower was beginning to form a mental picture of the river – long swift reaches alternating with narrow and rock-encumbered stretches, looped back and forth at the whim of the surrounding country. This boat they were in had probably been built close to the spot where they had found her, had been kept there as a ferry boat, probably by farming people, on the clear reach where they had started, and had probably never been more than half a mile from her moorings before. Hornblower, shoving off from a rock, decided that the odds were heavily against her ever seeing her moorings again.

Below the rapid they had a long clear run – Hornblower had no means of judging how long. Their eyes were quick now to pick out the snow-covered shore when it was a yard or more away, and they kept the boat clear. Every glimpse gave them a chance to guess at the course of the river compared with the direction of the wind, so that they could pull a few lusty strokes without danger of running aground as long as there was no obstructions in mid-channel. In fact, it had almost stopped snowing – Hornblower guessed that what little snow was being flung at them by the wind had been blown from branches or scooped from drifts. That did not make it any warmer; every part of the boat was coated with ice – the floorboards were slippery with it except where his heels rested while rowing.

Ten minutes of this would carry them a mile or more – more for certain. He could not guess at all how long they had been travelling, but he could be sure that with the countryside under thick snow they were well ahead of any possible pursuit, and the longer this wonderful rock-free reach endured the safer they would be. He tugged away fiercely, and Brown in the bows responded, stroke for stroke.

'Rapids ahead, sir,' said Bush at length.

Resting on his oar Hornblower could hear, far ahead, the familiar roar of water pouring over rocks; the present rate of progress had been too good to last, and soon they would be whirling down among rocks again, pitching and heaving.

'Stand by to fend off on the port side, Brown,' he ordered.

'Aye aye, sir.'

Hornblower sat on his thwart with his scull poised; the water was sleek and black overside. He felt the boat swing round. The current seemed to be carrying her over to one side, and he was content to let her go. Where the main mass of water made its way was likely to be the clearest channel down the rapid. The roar of the fall was very loud now.

'By God!' said Hornblower in sudden panic, standing up to peer ahead.

It was too late to save themselves – he had noticed the difference in the sound of the fall only when they were too close to escape. Here there was no rapid like those they had already descended, not even one much worse. Here there was a rough dam across the river – a natural transverse ledge, perhaps, which had caught and retained the rocks rolled down in the bed, or else something of human construction. Hornblower's quick brain turned these hypotheses over even as the boat leaped at the drop. Along its whole length water was brimming over the obstruction; at this particular point it surged over in a wide swirl, sleek at the top, and plunging into foaming chaos below. The boat heaved sickeningly over the summit and went down the slope like a bullet. The steep steady wave at the foot was as unyielding as a brick wall as they crashed into it.

Hornblower found himself strangling under the water, the fall still roaring in his ears, his brain still racing. In nightmare helplessness he was scraped over the rocky bottom. The pressure in his lungs began to hurt him. It was agony – agony. Now he was breathing again – one single gulp of air like fire in his throat as he went under again, and down to the rocks at the bottom until his breast was hurting worse than before. Then another quick breath – it was as painful to breathe as it was to strangle. Over and down, his ears roaring and his head swimming. The grinding of the rocks of the river bed over which he was scraped was louder than any clap of thunder he had ever heard. Another gulp of air – it was as if he had been anticipating it, but he had to force himself to make it, for he felt as if it would be easier not to, easier to allow this agony in his breast to consume him.

Down again, to the roar and torment below the surface. His brain, still working like lightning, guessed how it was with him. He was caught in the swirl below the dam, was being swept downstream on the surface, pushed into the undertow and carried up again along the bottom, to be spewed up and granted a second in which to breathe before being carried round again. He was ready this time to strike out feebly, no more than three strokes, sideways, at his next breathing space. When he was next sucked down the pain in his breast was inconceivably greater and blending with that agony was another just as bad of which he now became conscious – the pain of the cold in his limbs. It called for every scrap of his resolution to force himself to take another breath and to continue his puny effort sideways when the time came for it. Down again; he was ready to die, willing, anxious to die, now, so that this pain would stop. A bit of board had come into his hand, with nails protruding from one end. That must be a plank from the boat, shattered to fragments and whirling round and round with him, eternally. Then his resolution flickered up once more. He caught a gulp of air as he rose to the surface, striking out for the shore, waiting in apprehension to be dragged down. Marvellous; he had time for a second breath, and a third. Now he wanted to live, so heavenly were these painless breaths he was taking. But he was so tired, and so sleepy. He got to his feet, fell as the water swept his legs away again from under him, splashed and struggled in mad panic, scrambling through the shallows on his hands and knees. Rising, he took two more steps, before falling with his face in the snow and his feet still trailing in the rushing water.

He was roused by a human voice bellowing apparently in his ear. Lifting his head he saw a faint dark figure a yard or two away, bellowing with Brown's voice.

'Ahoy! Cap'n, Cap'n! Oh, Cap'n!'

'I'm here,' moaned Hornblower, and Brown came and knelt over him.

'Thank God, sir,' he said, and then, raising his voice, 'The cap'n's here, Mr Bush.'

'Good!' said a feeble voice five yards away.

At that Hornblower fought down his nauseating weakness and sat up. If Bush were still alive he must be looked after at once. He must be naked and wet, exposed in the snow to this cutting wind. Hornblower reeled to his feet, staggered, clutched Brown's arm, and stood with his brain whirling.

'There's a light up there, sir,' said Brown, hoarsely. 'I was just goin' to it if you hadn't answered my hail.'

'A light?'

Hornblower passed his hands over his eyes and peered up the bank. Undoubtedly it was a light shining faintly, perhaps a hundred yards away. To go there meant surrender – that was the first reaction of Hornblower's mind. But to stay here meant death. Even if by a miracle they could light a fire and survive the night here they would be caught next morning – and Bush would be dead for certain. There had been a faint chance of life when he planned the escape from the coach, and now it was gone.

'Well carry Mr Bush up,' he said.

'Aye aye, sir.'

They plunged through the snow to where Bush lay.

'There's a house just up the bank, Bush. We'll carry you there.'

Hornblower was puzzled by his ability to think and to speak while he felt so weak; the ability seemed unreal, fictitious.

'Aye aye, sir.'

They stooped and lifted him up between them, linking hands under his knees and behind his back. Bush put his arms round their necks; his flannel nightshirt dripped a further stream of water as they lifted him. Then they started trudging, knee deep in the snow, up the bank towards the distant light.

They stumbled over obstructions hidden in the snow. They slipped and staggered. Then they slid down a bank and fell, all together, and Bush gave a cry of pain.

'Hurt, sir?' asked Brown.

'Only jarred my stump. Captain, leave me here and send down help from the house.'

Hornblower could still think. Without Bush to burden them they might reach the house a little quicker, but he could imagine all the delays that would ensue after they had knocked at the door – the explanations which would have to be made in his halting French, the hesitation and the time wasting before he could get a carrying party started off to find Bush – who meanwhile would be lying wet and naked in the snow. A quarter of an hour of it would kill Bush, and he might be exposed for twice as long as that. And there was the chance that there would be no one in the house to help carry him.

'No,' said Hornblower cheerfully. 'It's only a little way. Lift, Brown.'

They reeled along through the snow towards the light. Bush was a heavy burden – Hornblower's head was swimming with fatigue and his arms felt as if they were being dragged out of their sockets. Yet somehow within the shell of his fatigue the inner kernel of his brain was still active and restless.

'How did you get out of the river?' he asked, his voice sounding flat and unnatural in his ears.

'Current took us to the bank at once, sir,' said Bush, faintly surprised. 'I'd only just kicked my blankets off when I touched a rock, and there was Brown beside me hauling me out.'

'Oh,' said Hornblower.

The whim of a river in flood was fantastic; the three of them had been within a yard of each other when they entered the water, and he had been dragged under while the other two had been carried to safety. They could not guess at his desperate struggle for life, and they would never know of it, for he would never be able to tell them about it. He felt for the moment a bitter sense of grievance against them, resulting from his weariness and his weakness. He was breathing heavily, and he felt as if he would give a fortune to lay down his burden and rest for a couple of minutes; but his pride forbade, and they went on through the snow, stumbling over the inequalities below the surface. The light was coming near at last.

They heard a faint inquiring bark from a dog.

'Give 'em a hail, Brown,' said Hornblower.

'Ahoy!' roared Brown. 'House ahoy!' Instantly two dogs burst into a clamorous barking.

'Ahoy!' yelled Brown again, and they staggered on. Another light flashed into view from another part of the house. They seemed to be in some kind of garden now; Hornblower could feel plants crushing under his feet in the snow, and the thorns of a rose tree tore at his trouser leg. The dogs were barking furiously. Suddenly a voice came from a dark upper window.

'Who is there?' it asked in French.

Hornblower prodded at his weary brain to find words to reply.

'Three men,' he said. 'Wounded.'

That was the best he could do.

'Come nearer,' said the voice, and they staggered forward, slipped down an unseen incline, and halted in the square of light cast by the big lighted window in the ground floor, Bush in his nightshirt resting in the arms of the bedraggled other two.

'Who are you?'

'Prisoners of war,' said Hornblower.

'Wait one moment, if you please,' said the voice politely.

They stood shuddering in the snow until a door opened near the lighted window, showing a bright rectangle of light and some human silhouettes.

'Come in, gentlemen,' said the polite voice.

7

The door opened into a stone flagged hall; a tall thin man in a blue coat with a glistening white cravat stood there to welcome them, and at his side was a young woman, her shoulders bare in the lamplight. There were three others, too – maidservants and a butler, Hornblower fancied vaguely, as he advanced into the hall under the burden of Bush's weight. On a side table the lamplight caught the ivory butts of a pair of pistols, evidently laid there by their host on his deciding that his nocturnal visitors were harmless. Hornblower and Brown halted again for a moment, ragged and dishevelled and daubed with snow, and water began to trickle at once to the floor from their soaking garments; and Bush was between them, one foot in a grey worsted sock slicking out under the hem of his flannel nightshirt. Hornblower's constitutional weakness almost overcame him again and he had to struggle hard to keep himself from giggling as he wondered how these people were explaining to themselves the arrival of a nightshirted cripple out of a snowy night.

At least his host had sufficient self-control to show no surprise.

'Come in, come in,' he said. He put his hand to a door beside him and then withdrew it. 'You will need a better fire than I can offer you in the drawing room. Felix, show the way to the kitchen – I trust you gentlemen will pardon my receiving you there? This way, sirs. Chairs, Felix, and send the maids away.'

It was a vast low-ceilinged room, stone-flagged like the hall. Its grateful warmth was like Paradise; in the hearth glowed the remains of a fire and all round them kitchen utensils winked and glittered. The woman without a word piled fresh billets of wood upon the fire and set to work with bellows to work up a blaze. Hornblower noticed the glimmer of her silk dress; her piled-up hair was golden, nearly auburn.

'Cannot Felix do that, Marie, my dear? Very well, then. As you will,' said their host. 'Please sit down, gentlemen. Wine, Felix.'

They lowered Bush into a chair before the fire. He sagged and wavered in his weakness, and they had to support him; their host clucked in sympathy.

'Hurry with those glasses, Felix, and then attend to the beds. A glass of wine, sir? And for you, sir? Permit me.'

The woman he had addressed as 'Marie' had risen from her knees, and withdrew silently; the fire was crackling bravely amid its battery of roasting spits and cauldrons. Hornblower was shivering uncontrollably, nevertheless, in his dripping clothes. The glass of wine he drank was of no help to him; the hand he rested on Bush's shoulder shook like a leaf.

'You will need dry clothes,' said their host. 'If you will permit me, I will –'

He was interrupted by the re-entrance of the butler and Marie, both of them with their arms full of clothes and blankets.

'Admirable!' said their host. 'Felix, you will attend these gentlemen. Come, my dear.'

The butler held a silken nightshirt to the blaze while Hornblower and Brown stripped Bush of his wet clothes and chafed him with a towel.

'I thought I should never be warm again,' said Bush, when his head came out through the collar of the nightshirt. 'And you, sir? You shouldn't have troubled about me. Won't you change your clothes now, sir? I'm all right.'

'We'll see you comfortable first,' said Hornblower. There was a fierce perverse pleasure in neglecting himself to attend to Bush. 'Let me look at that stump of yours.'

The blunt seamed end still appeared extraordinarily healthy. There was no obvious heat or inflammation when Hornblower took it in his hand, no sign of pus exuding from the scars. Felix found a cloth in which Hornblower bound it up, while Brown wrapped him about in a blanket.

'Lift him now, Brown. We'll put him into bed.'

Outside in the flagged hall they hesitated as to which way to turn, when Marie suddenly appeared from the left hand door.

'In here,' she said; her voice was a harsh contralto. 'I have had a bed made up on the ground floor for the wounded man. I thought it would be more convenient.'

One maid – a gaunt old woman, rather – had just taken a warming pan from between the sheets; the other was slipping a couple of hot bottles into the bed. Hornblower was impressed by Marie's practical forethought. He tried with poor success to phrase his thanks in French while they lowered Bush into bed, and covered him up.

'God, that's good, thank you, sir,' said Bush.

They left him with a candle burning at his bedside – Hornblower was in a perfect panic now to strip off his wet clothes before that roaring kitchen fire. He towelled himself with a warm towel and slipped into a warm woollen shirt; standing with his bare legs toasting before the blaze he drank a second glass of wine. Fatigue and cold fell away from him, and he felt exhilarated and lightheaded as a reaction. Felix crouched before him tendering him a pair of trousers, and he stepped into them and suffered Felix to tuck in his shirt tails and button him up – it was the first time since childhood that he had been helped into his trousers, but this evening it seemed perfectly natural. Felix crouched again to put on his socks and shoes, stood to buckle his stock and help him on with waistcoat and coat.

'Monsieur le Comte and Madame la Vicomtesse await monsieur in the drawing room,' said Felix – it was odd how, without a word of explanation, Felix had ascertained that Brown was of a lower social level. The very clothes he had allotted to Brown indicated that.

'Make yourself comfortable here, Brown,' said Hornblower.

'Aye aye, sir,' said Brown, standing at attention with his black hair in a rampant mass – only Hornblower had had an opportunity so far of using a comb.

Hornblower stepped in to look at Bush, who was already asleep, snoring faintly at the base of his throat. He seemed to have suffered no ill effects from his immersion and exposure – his iron frame must have grown accustomed to wet and cold during twenty-five years at sea. Hornblower blew out the candle and softly closed the door, motioning to the butler to precede him. At the drawing-room door Felix asked Hornblower his name, and when he announced him Hornblower was oddly relieved to hear him make a sad hash of the pronunciation – it made Felix human again.

His host and hostess were seated on either side of the fire at the far end of the room, and the Count rose to meet him.

'I regret,' he said, 'that I did not quite hear the name which my majordomo announced.'

'Captain Horatio Hornblower, of His Britannic Majesty's ship *Sutherland*,' said Hornblower.

'It is the greatest pleasure to meet you, Captain,' said the Count, sidestepping the difficulty of pronunciation with the agility to be expected of a representative of the old régime. 'I am Lucien Antoine de Ladon, Comte de Graçay.'

The men exchanged bows.

'May I present you to my daughter-in-law? Madame la Vicomtesse de Graçay.'

'Your servant, ma'am,' said Hornblower, bowing again, and then felt like a graceless lout because the English formula had risen to his lips by the instinct the action prompted. He hurriedly racked his brains for the French equivalent, and ended in a shamefaced mumble of 'Enchanté.'

The Vicomtesse had black eyes in the maddest contrast with her nearly auburn hair. She was stoutly – one might almost say stockily – built, and was somewhere near thirty years of age, dressed in black silk which left sturdy white shoulders exposed. As she curtseyed her eyes met his in complete friendliness.

'And what is the name of the wounded gentleman

whom we have the honour of entertaining?' she asked; even to Hornblower's unaccustomed ear her French had a different quality from the Count's.

'Bush,' said Hornblower, grasping the import of the question with an effort. 'First Lieutenant of my ship. I have left my servant, Brown, in the kitchen.'

'Felix will see that he is comfortable,' interposed the Count. 'What of yourself, Captain? Some food? A glass of wine?'

'Nothing, thank you,' said Hornblower. He felt in no need of food in this mad world, although he had not eaten since noon.

'Nothing, despite the fatigues of your journey?'

There could hardly be a more delicate allusion than that to Hornblower's recent arrival through the snow, drenched and battered.

'Nothing, thank you,' repeated Hornblower.

'Will you not sit down, Captain?' asked the Vicomtesse. They all three found themselves chairs.

'You will pardon us, I hope,' said the Count, 'if we continue to speak French. It is ten years since I last had occasion to speak English, and even then I was a poor scholar, while my daughter-in-law speaks none.'

'Bush,' said the Vicomtesse. 'Brown. I can say those names. But your name, Captain, is difficult. Orrenblor – I cannot say it.'

'Bush! Orrenblor!' exclaimed the Count, as though reminded of something. 'I suppose you are aware, Captain, of what the French newspapers have been saying about you recently?'

'No,' said Hornblower. 'I should like to know, very much.'

'Pardon me, then.'

The Count took up a candle and disappeared through a door; he returned quickly enough to save Hornblower from feeling too self-conscious in the silence that ensued.

'Here are recent copies of the *Moniteur*,' said the Count. 'I must apologize in advance, Captain, for the statements made in them.'

He passed the newspapers over to Hornblower, indicating various columns in them. The first one briefly announced that a dispatch by semaphore just received from Perpignan informed the Ministry of Marine that an English ship of the line had been captured at Rosas. The next was the amplification. It proclaimed in triumphant detail that the hundred-gun ship *Sutherland* which had been committing acts of piracy in the Mediterranean had met a well-deserved fate at the hands of the Toulon fleet directed by Admiral Cosmao. She had been caught unawares and overwhelmed, and had 'pusillanimously hauled down the colours of perfidious Albion under which she had committed so many dastardly crimes.' The French public was assured that her resistance had been of the poorest, it being advanced in corroboration that only one French ship had lost a topmast during the cannonade. The action took place under the eyes of thousands of the Spanish populace, and would be a salutory lesson to those few among them who, deluded by English lies or seduced by English gold, still cherished notions of resistance to their lawful sovereign King Joseph.

Another article announced that the infamous Captain Hornblower and his equally wicked lieutenant Bush had surrendered in the *Sutherland*, the latter being one of the few wounded in the encounter. All those peace-loving

94

French citizens who had suffered as a result of their piratical depredations could rest assured that a military court would inquire immediately into the crimes these two had committed. Too long had the modern Carthage sent forth her minions to execute her vile plans with impunity! Their guilt would soon be demonstrated to a world which would readily discriminate between the truth and the vile lies which the poisoned pens in Canning's pay so persistently poured forth.

Yet another article declared that as a result of Admiral Cosmao's great victory over the *Sutherland* at Rosas English naval action on the coasts of Spain had ceased, and the British army of Wellington, so imprudently exposed to the might of the French arms, was already suffering seriously from a shortage of supplies. Having lost one vile accomplice in the person of the detestable Hornblower, perfidious Albion was about to lose another on Wellington's inevitable surrender.

Hornblower read the smudgy columns in impotent fury. 'A hundred-gun ship', forsooth, when the *Sutherland* was only a seventy-four and almost the smallest of her rate in the list! 'Resistance of the poorest!' 'One topmast lost!' The *Sutherland* had beaten three bigger ships into wrecks and had disabled a fourth before surrendering. 'One of the few wounded!' Two-thirds of the *Sutherland*'s crew had given life or limb, and with his own eyes he had seen the blood running from the scuppers of the French flagship. 'English naval action had ceased!' There was not a hint that a fortnight after the capture of the *Sutherland* the whole French squadron had been destroyed in the night attack on Rosas Bay.

His professional honour had been impugned; the circumstantial lies had been well told, too – that subtle touch about only one topmast being lost had every appearance of verisimilitude. Europe might well believe that he was a poltroon as well as a pirate, and he had not the slightest chance of contradicting what had been said. Even in England such reports must receive a little credit – most of the *Moniteur*'s bulletins, especially the naval ones, were reproduced in the English press. Lady Barbara, Maria, his brother captains, must all be wondering at the present moment just how much credence should be given to the *Moniteur*'s statements. Accustomed as the world might be to Bonaparte's exaggerations people could hardly be expected to realize that in this case everything said – save for the bare statement of his surrender – had been completely untrue. His hands shook a little with the passion that consumed him, and he was conscious of the hot flush in his cheeks as he looked up and met the eyes of the others.

It was hard to grope for his few French words while he was so angry.

'He is a liar!' he spluttered at length. 'He dishonours me!'

'He dishonours everyone,' said the Count, quietly.

'But this – but this,' said Hornblower, and then gave up the struggle to express himself in French. He remembered that while he was in captivity in Rosas he had realized that Bonaparte would publish triumphant bulletins regarding the capture of the *Sutherland*, and it was only weakness to be enraged by them now that he was confronted by them.

'Will you forgive me,' asked the Count, 'if I change

the subject and ask you a few personal questions?'

'Certainly.'

'I presume you have escaped from an escort which was taking you to Paris?'

'Yes,' said Hornblower.

'Where did you escape?'

Hornblower tried to explain that it was at a point where a by-road ran down to the river's edge, six kilometres on the farther side of Nevers. Haltingly, he went on to describe the conditions of his escape, the silencing of Colonel Caillard, and the wild navigation of the river in the darkness.

'That must have been about six o'clock, I presume?' asked the Count.

'Yes.'

'It is only midnight now, and you have come twenty kilometres. There is not the slightest chance of your escort seeking you here for some time. That is what I wanted to know. You will be able to sleep in tranquillity tonight, Captain.'

Hornblower realized with a shock that he had long taken it for granted that he would sleep in tranquillity, at least as far as immediate recapture was concerned; the atmosphere of the house had been too friendly for him to feel otherwise. By way of reaction, he began to feel doubts.

'Are you going to – to tell the police we are here?' he asked; it was infernally difficult to phrase that sort of thing in a foreign language and avoid offence.

'On the contrary,' said the Count. 'I shall tell them, if they ask me, that you are not here. I hope you will consider yourself among friends in this house, Captain, and that you will make your stay here as long as is convenient to you.'

'Thank you, sir. Thank you very much,' stammered Hornblower.

'I may add,' went on the Count, 'that circumstances – it is too long a story to tell you – make it quite certain that the authorities will accept my statement that I know nothing of your whereabouts. To say nothing of the fact that I have the honour to be mayor of this commune and so represent the government, even though my *adjoint* does all the work of the position.'

Hornblower noticed his wry smile as he used the word 'honour', and tried to stammer a fitting reply, to which the Count listened politely. It was amazing, now Hornblower came to think about it, that chance should have led him to a house where he was welcomed and protected, where he might consider himself safe from pursuit, and sleep in peace. The thought of sleep made him realize that he was desperately tired, despite his excitement. The impassive face of the Count, and the friendly face of his daughter-in-law, gave no hint as to whether or not they too were tired; for a moment Hornblower wrestled with the problem which always presents itself the first evening of one's stay in a strange house – whether the guest should suggest going to bed or wait for a hint from his host. He made his resolve, and rose to his feet.

'You are tired,' said the Vicomtesse – the first words she had spoken for some time.

'Yes,' said Hornblower.

'I will show you your room, sir. Shall I ring for your servant? No?' said the Count.

Out in the hall, after Hornblower had bowed good night, the Count indicated the pistols still lying on the side table.

'Perhaps you would care to have those at your bedside?' he asked politely. 'You might feel safer?'

Hornblower was tempted, but finally he refused the offer. Two pistols would not suffice to save him from Bonaparte's police should they come for him.

'As you will,' said the Count, leading the way with a candle. 'I loaded them when I heard your approach because there was a chance that you were a party of réractaires – young men who evade the conscription by hiding in the woods and mountains. Their number has grown considerably since the latest decree anticipating the conscription. But I quickly realized that no gang meditating mischief would proclaim its proximity with shouts. Here is your room, sir. I hope you will find here everything you require. The clothes you are wearing appear to fit so tolerably that perhaps you will continue to wear them tomorrow? Then I shall say good night. I hope you will sleep well.'

The bed was deliciously warm as Hornblower slid into it and closed the curtains. His thoughts were pleasantly muddled; disturbing memories of the appalling swoop of the little boat down the long black slope of water at the fall, and of his agonized battle for life in the water, were overridden by mental pictures of the Count's long, mobile face and of Caillard bundled in his cloak and dumped down upon the carriage floor. He did not sleep well, but he could hardly be said to have slept badly.

8

Felix entered the next morning bearing a breakfast tray, and he opened the bed curtains while Hornblower lay dazed in his bed. Brown followed Felix, and while the latter arranged the tray on the bedside table he applied himself to the task of gathering together the clothes which Hornblower had flung down the night before, trying hard to assume the unobtrusive deference of a gentleman's servant. Hornblower sipped gratefully at the steaming coffee, and bit into the bread; Brown recollected another duty and hurried across to open the bedroom curtains.

'Gale's pretty nigh dropped, sir,' he said. 'I think what wind there's left is backing southerly, and we might have a thaw.'

Through the deep windows of the bedroom Hornblower could see from his bed a wide landscape of dazzling white, falling steeply away down to the river which was black by contrast, appearing like a black crayon mark on white paper. Trees stood out starkly through the snow where the gale had blown their branches bare; down beside the river the willows there – some of them stood in the flood, with white foam at their feet – were still domed with white. Hornblower fancied he could hear the rushing of water, and was certain that he could hear the regular droning of the fall, the tumbling water at whose foot was just visible over the shoulder of the bank. Far beyond the river could be seen the snow-covered roofs of a few small houses.

'I've been in to Mr Bush already, sir,' said Brown – Hornblower felt a twinge of remorse at being too interested in the landscape to have a thought to spare for his lieutenant – 'and he's all right an' sends you his best respects, sir. I'm goin' to help him shave after I've attended to you, sir.'

'Yes,' said Hornblower.

He felt deliciously languorous. He wanted to be idle and lazy. The present was a moment of transition between the miseries and dangers of yesterday and the unknown activities of today, and he wanted that moment to be prolonged on and on indefinitely; he wanted time to stand still, the pursuers who were seeking him on the other side of Nevers to be stilled into an enchanted rigidity while he lay here free from danger and responsibility. The very coffee he had drunk contributed to his ease by relieving his thirst without stimulating him to activity. He sank imperceptibly and delightfully into a vague daydream; it was hateful of Brown to recall him to wakefulness again by a respectful shuffling of his feet.

'Right,' said Hornblower resigning himself to the inevitable.

He kicked off the bedclothes and rose to his feet, the hard world of the matter-of-fact closing round him, and his daydreams vanishing like the cloud-colours of a tropical sunrise. As he shaved and washed in the absurdly small basin in the corner, he contemplated grimly the prospect of prolonged conversation in French with his hosts. He grudged the effort it would involve, and he envied Bush his complete inability to speak any other tongue than English. Having to exert himself today loomed as large to his self-willed mind as the fact that he was doomed to death if he were caught again. He listened absentmindedly to Bush's garrulity when he went in to visit him, and did nothing at all to satisfy his curiosity regarding the house in which they had found shelter, and the intentions of their hosts. Nor was his mood relieved by his pitying contempt for himself at thus working off his ill temper on his unoffending lieutenant. He deserted Bush as soon as he decently could and went off in search of his hosts in the drawing room.

The Vicomtesse alone was there, and she made him welcome with a smile.

'M. de Graçay is at work in his study,' she explained. 'You must be content with my entertaining you this morning.'

To say even the obvious in French was an effort for Hornblower, but he managed to make the suitable reply, which the lady received with a smile. But conversation did not proceed smoothly, with Hornblower having laboriously to build up his sentences beforehand and to avoid the easy descent into Spanish which was liable to entrap him whenever he began to think in a foreign tongue. Nevertheless, the opening sentences regarding the storm last night, the snow in the fields, and the flood, elicited for Hornblower one interesting fact – that the river whose roar they could hear was the Loire, four hundred miles or more from its mouth in the Bay of Biscay. A few miles upstream lay the town of Nevers; a little way downstream the large tributary, the Allier, joined the Loire, but there was hardly a house and no village on the river in that direction for twenty miles as far as Pouilly – from whose vineyards had come the wine they had drunk last night.

'The river is only as big as this in winter,' said the Vicomtesse. 'In summer it dwindles away to almost nothing. There are places where one can walk across it, from one bank to the other. Then it is blue, and its banks are golden, but now it is black and ugly.'

'Yes,' said Hornblower.

He felt a peculiar tingling sensation down his thighs and calves as the words recalled his experience of the night before, the swoop over the fall and the mad battle in the flood. He and Bush and Brown might easily all be sodden corpses now, rolling among the rocks at the bottom of the river until the process of corruption should bring them to the surface.

'I have not thanked you and M. de Graçay for your hospitality,' he said, picking his words with care. 'It is very kind of the Count.'

'Kind? He is the kindest man in the whole world. I can't tell you how good he is.'

There was no doubting the sincerity of the Count's daughter-in-law as she made this speech; her wide humorous mouth parted and her dark eyes glowed.

'Really?' said Hornblower – the word 'vraiment' slipped naturally from his lips now that some animation had come into the conversation.

'Yes, really. He is good all the way through. He is sweet and kind, by nature and not – not as a result of experience. He has never said a word to me, not once, not a word, about the disappointment I have caused him.'

'You, madame?'

'Yes. Oh, isn't it obvious? I am not a great lady –
Marcel should not have married me. My father is a
Normandy peasant, on his own land, but a peasant all
the same, while the Ladons, Counts of Graçay, go back
to – to Saint Louis, or before that. Marcel told me how
disappointed was the Count at our marriage, but I
should never have known of it otherwise – not by word
or by action. Marcel was the eldest son then, because
Antoine had been killed at Austerlitz. And Marcel is
dead, too – he was wounded at Aspern – and I have no
son, no child at all, and the Count has never reproached
me, never.'

Hornblower tried to make some kind of sympathetic
noise.

'And Louis-Marie is dead as well now. He died of fever
in Spain. He was the third son, and M. de Graçay is the
last of the Ladons. I think it broke his heart, but he has
never said a bitter word.'

'The three sons are all dead?' said Hornblower.

'Yes, as I told you. M. de Graçay was an émigré – he
lived in your town of London with his children for years
after the Revolution. And then the boys grew up and
they heard of the fame of the Emperor – he was First
Consul then – and they all wanted to share in the glory
of France. It was to please them that the Count took
advantage of the amnesty and returned here – this is all
that the Revolution has left of his estates. He never went
to Paris. What would he have in common with the
Emperor? But he allowed his sons to join the army, and
now they are all dead, Antoine and Marcel and Louis-
Marie. Marcel married me when his regiment was

billeted in our village, but the others never married. Louis-Marie was only eighteen when he died.'

'Terrible!' said Hornblower.

The banal words did not express his sense of the pathos of the story, but it was all he could think of. He understood now the Count's statement of the night before that the authorities would be willing to accept his bare word that he had seen nothing of any escaped prisoners. A great gentleman whose three sons had died in the Imperial service would never be suspected of harbouring fugitives.

'Understand me,' went on the Vicomtesse. 'It is not because he hates the Emperor that he makes you welcome here. It is because he is kind, because you needed help – I have never known him to deny help to anyone. Oh, it is hard to explain, but I think you understand.'

'I understand,' said Hornblower, gently.

His heart warmed to the Vicomtesse. She might be lonely and unhappy; she was obviously as hard as her peasant upbringing would make her, and yet her first thought was to impress upon this stranger the goodness and virtue of her father-in-law. With her nearly-red hair and black eyes she was a striking-looking woman, and her skin had a thick creaminess which enhanced her looks; only a slight irregularity of feature and the wideness of her mouth prevented her from being of dazzling beauty. No wonder the young subaltern in the Hussars – Hornblower took it for granted that the dead Vicomte de Graçay had been a subaltern of Hussars – had fallen in love with her during the dreary routine of training, and had insisted on marrying her despite his father's opposition. Hornblower thought he would not find it hard to fall in love with her himself if he were mad enough to allow such a thing to happen while his life was in the hands of the Count.

'And you?' asked the Vicomtesse. 'Have you a wife in England? Children?'

'I have a wife,' said Hornblower.

Even without the handicap of a foreign language it was difficult to describe Maria to a stranger; he said that she was short and dark, and he said no more. Her red hands and dumpy figure, her loyalty to him which cloyed when it did not irritate – he could not venture on a fuller description lest he should betray the fact that he did not love her, and he had never betrayed it yet.

'So that you have no children either?' asked the Vicomtesse again.

'Not now,' said Hornblower.

This was torment. He told of how little Horatio and little Maria had died of smallpox in a Southsea lodging, and then with a gulp he went on to say that there was another child due to be born in January next.

'Let us hope you will be home with your wife then,' said the Vicomtesse. 'Today you will be able to discuss plans of escape with my father-in-law.'

As if this new mention of his name had summoned him, the Count came into the room on the tail of this sentence.

'Forgive my interrupting you,' he said, even while he returned Hornblower's bow, 'but from my study window I have just seen a gendarme approaching this house from a group which was riding along the river bank. Would it be troubling you too much, Captain, to ask you to go into Monsieur Bush's room for a time? I shall send your servant in to you, too, and perhaps then you would be good enough to lock the door. I shall interview the gendarme myself, and you will only be detained for a few minutes, I hope.'

A gendarme! Hornblower was out of the room and was crossing over to Bush's door before this long speech was finished, while M. de Graçay escorted him thither, unruffled, polite, his words unhurried. Bush was sitting up in bed as Hornblower entered, but what he began to say was broken off by Hornblower's abrupt gesture demanding silence. A moment later Brown tapped at the door and was admitted, Hornblower carefully locking the door after him.

'What is it, sir?' whispered Bush, and Hornblower whispered an explanation, still standing with his hand on the handle, stooping to listen.

He heard a knocking on the outer door, and the rattling of chains as Felix went to open it. Feverishly he tried to hear the ensuing conversation, but he could not understand it. But the gendarme was speaking with respect, and Felix in the flat passionless tones of the perfect butler. He heard the tramp of booted feet and the ring of spurs as the gendarme was led into the hall, and then all the sounds died away with the closing of a door upon them. The minutes seemed like hours as he waited. Growing aware of his nervousness he forced himself to turn and smile at the others as they sat with their ears cocked, listening.

The wait was too long for them to preserve their tension; soon they relaxed, and grinned at each other, not with hollow mirth as Hornblower's had been at the start. At last a renewed burst of sound from the hall keyed them up again, and they stayed rigid listening to the penetrating voices. And then they heard the clash of the outside door shutting, and the voices ceased. Still it was a long time before anything more happened – five minutes – ten minutes, and then a tap on the door startled them as though it were a pistol shot.

'Can I come in, Captain?' said the Count's voice.

Hurriedly Hornblower unlocked the door to admit him, and even then he had to stand and wait in feverish patience, translating awkwardly while the Count apologized to Bush for intruding upon him, and made polite inquiries about his health and whether he slept well.

'Tell him I slept nicely, if you please, sir,' said Bush.

'I am delighted to hear it,' said the Count 'Now in the matter of this gendarme –'

Hornblower brought forward a chair for him. He would not allow it to be thought that his impatience overrode his good manners.

'Thank you, Captain, thank you. You are sure I will not be intruding if I stay? That is good of you. The gendarme came to tell me –'

The narrative was prolonged by the need for interpreting to Bush and Brown. The gendarme was one of those posted at Nevers; every available man in that town had been turned out shortly before midnight by a furious Colonel Caillard to search for the fugitives. In the darkness they had been able to do little, but with the coming of the dawn Cailliard had begun a systematic search of both banks of the river, seeking for traces of the prisoners and making inquiries at every house and cottage along the banks. The visit of the gendarme had been merely one of routine – he had come to ask if anything had been seen of three escaped Englishmen, and to give warning that they might be in the vicinity. He had been perfectly satisfied with the Count's assurance upon the point. In fact, the gendarme had no expectation of finding the Englishmen alive. The search had already revealed a blanket, one of those which had been used by the wounded Englishman, lying on the bank down by the Bec d'Allier, which seemed a sure indication that their boat had capsized, in which case, with the river in flood, there could be no doubt that they had been drowned. Their bodies would be discovered somewhere along the course of the river during the next few days. The gendarme appeared to be of the opinion that the boat must have upset somewhere in the first rapid they had encountered, before they had gone a mile, so madly was the river running.

'I hope you will agree with me, Captain, that this information is most satisfactory,' added the Count.

'Satisfactory!' said Hornblower. 'Could it be better?'

If the French should believe them to be dead there would be an end to the pursuit. He turned and explained the situation to the others in English, and they endeavoured with nods and smiles to indicate to the Count their gratification.

'Perhaps Bonaparte in Paris will not be satisfied with this bald story,' said the Count. 'In fact I am sure he will not, and will order a further search. But it will not trouble us.'

'Thank you, sir,' said Hornblower, and the Count made a deprecatory gesture.

'It only remains,' he said, 'to make up our minds

about what you gentlemen would find it best to do in the future. Would it be officious of me to suggest that it might be inadvisable for you to continue your journey while Lieutenant Bush is still unwell?'

'What does he say, sir?' asked Bush – the mention of his name had drawn all eyes on him. Hornblower explained.

'Tell his lordship, sir,' said Bush, 'that I can make myself a jury leg in two shakes, an' this time next week I'll be walking as well as he does.'

'Excellent!' said the Count, when this had been translated and expurgated for him. 'And yet I cannot see that the construction of a wooden leg is going to be of much assistance in our problem. You gentlemen might grow beards, or wear disguises. It was in my mind that by posing as German officers in the Imperial service you might, during your future journey, provide an excuse for your ignorance of French. But a missing foot cannot be disguised; for months to come the arrival of a stranger without a foot will recall to the minds of inquisitive police officers the wounded English officer who escaped and was believed to be drowned.'

'Yes,' said Hornblower. 'Unless we could avoid all contact with police officers.'

'That is quite impossible,' said the Count with decision. 'In this French Empire there are police officers everywhere. To travel you will need horses certainly, a carriage very probably. In a journey of a hundred leagues horses and a carriage will bring you for certain to the notice of the police. No man can travel ten miles along a road without having his passport examined.'

The Count pulled in perplexity at his chin; the deep

parentheses at the corners of his mobile mouth were more marked than ever.

'I wish,' said Hornblower, 'that our boat had not been destroyed last night. On the river, perhaps –'

The idea came up into his mind fully formed and as it did so his eyes met the Count's. He was conscious afresh of a strange sympathy between him and the Count. The same idea was forming in the Count's mind, simultaneously – it was not the first time that he had noticed a similar phenomenon.

'Of course!' said the Count, 'the river! How foolish of me not to think of it. As far as Orleans the river is unnavigable; because of the winter floods the banks are practically deserted save at the towns, and there are few of those, which you could pass at night if necessary, as you did at Nevers.'

'Unnavigable, sir?'

'There is no commercial traffic. There are fishermen's boats here and there, and there are a few others engaged in dredging sand from the river bed. That is all. From Orleans to Nantes Bonaparte has been making efforts to render the river available to barges, but I understand he has had small success. And above Briare the new lateral canal carries all the traffic, and the river is deserted.'

'But could we descend it, sir?' persisted Hornblower.

'Oh, yes,' said the Count, meditatively. 'You could do so in summer in a small rowing boat. There are many places where it would be difficult, but never dangerous.'

'In summer!' exclaimed Hornblower.

'Why, yes. You must wait until the lieutenant here is well, and then you must build your boat – I suppose

111

you sailors can build you own boat? You cannot hope to start for a long time. And then in January the river usually freezes, and in February come the floods, which last until March. Nothing could live on the river then – especially as it would be too cold and wet for you. It seems to be quite necessary that you should give me the pleasure of your company until April, Captain.'

This was something entirely unexpected, this prospect of waiting for four months the opportunity to start. Hornblower was taken by surprise; he had supposed that a few days, three or four weeks at most, would see them on their way towards England again. For ten years he had never been as long as four months consecutively in the same place – for that matter during those ten years he had hardly spent four months on shore altogether. His mind sought unavailingly for alternatives. To go by road undoubtedly would involve horses, carriages, contact with all sorts of people. He could not hope to bring Bush and Brown successfully through. And if they went by river they obviously would have to wait; in four months Bush could be expected to make a complete recovery, and with the coming of summer they would be able to dispense with the shelter of inns or houses, sleeping on the river bank, avoiding all intercourse with Frenchmen, drifting downstream until they reached the sea.

'If you have fishing rods with you,' supplemented the Count, 'anyone observing you as you go past the towns will look on you as a fishing party out for the day. For some reason which I cannot fully analyse a freshwater fisherman can never be suspected of evil intent – except possibly by the fish.'

Hornblower nodded. It was odd that at that very moment he too had been visualizing the boat drifting downstream, with rods out, watched by incurious eyes from the bank. It was the safest way of crossing France which he could imagine.

And yet – April? His child would be born. Lady Barbara might have forgotten that he ever existed.

'It seems monstrous,' he said, 'that you should be burdened with us all through the winter.'

'I assure you, Captain, your presence will give the greatest pleasure both to Madame la Vicomtesse and myself.'

He could only yield to circumstances.

9

Lieutenant Bush was watching Brown fastening the last strap of his new wooden leg, and Hornblower, from across the room, was watching the pair of them.

"Vast heaving,' said Bush. 'Belay.'

Bush sat on the edge of his bed and moved his leg tentatively.

'Good,' he said. 'Give me your shoulder. Now, heave and wake the dead.'

Hornblower saw Bush rise and stand; he watched his lieutenant's expression change to one of hurt wonderment as he clung to Brown's burly shoulders.

'God!' said Bush feebly, 'how she heaves!'

It was the giddiness only to be expected after weeks of lying and sitting. Evidently to Bush the floor was pitching and tossing, and, judging by the movement of his eyes, the walls were circling round him. Brown stood patiently supporting him as Bush confronted this unexpected phenomenon. Hornblower saw Bush set his jaw, his expression hardening as he battled with his weakness.

'Square away,' said Bush to Brown. 'Set a course for the captain.'

Brown began walking slowly towards Hornblower, Bush clinging to him, the leather-tipped end of the wooden leg falling with a thump on the floor at each effort to take a stride with it – Bush was swinging it too high, while his sound leg sagged at the knee in its weakness.

'God!' said Bush again. 'Easy! Easy!'

Hornblower rose in time to catch him and to lower him into the chair, where Bush sat and gasped. His big white face, already unnaturally pale through long confinement, was whiter than ever. Hornblower remembered with a pang the old Bush, burly and self-confident, with a face which might have been rough-hewn from a solid block of wood; the Bush who feared nothing and was prepared for anything. This Bush was frightened of his weakness. It had not occurred to him that he would have to learn to walk again – and that walking with a wooden leg was another matter still.

'Take a rest,' said Hornblower, 'before you start again.'

Desperately anxious as Bush had been to walk, weary as he was of helplessness, there were times during the next few days when Hornblower had to give him active encouragement while he was learning to walk. All the difficulties that arose had been unforeseen by him, and depressed him out of proportion to their importance. It was a matter of some days before he mastered his giddiness and weakness, and then as soon as he was able to use the wooden leg effectively they found all manner of things wrong with it. It was none too easy to find the most suitable length, and they discovered to their surprise that it was a matter of some importance to set the leather tip at exactly the right angle to the shaft – Brown and Hornblower between them, at a work-table in the stable yard, made and remade that wooden leg half a dozen times. Bush's bent knee, on which his weight rested when he walked, grew sore and inflamed; they had to pad the kneecap and remake the socket to fit, more than once, while Bush had to take his exercise in small amounts until the skin over his kneecap grew calloused and more accustomed to its new task. And when he fell – which was often – he caused himself frightful agony in his stump, which was hardly healed; with his knee bent at right angles the stump necessarily bore the brunt of practically any fall, and the pain was acute.

But teaching Bush to walk was one way of passing the long winter days, while orders from Paris turned out the conscripts from every depot round, and set them searching once more for the missing English prisoners. They came on a day of lashing rain, a dozen shivering boys and a sergeant, wet through, and made only the poorest pretence at searching the house and its stabling – Hornblower and Bush and Brown were safe enough behind the hay in an unobtrusive loft. The conscripts were given in the kitchen a better meal by the servants than they had enjoyed for some time, and marched off to prosecute their inquiries elsewhere – every house and village for miles round was at least visited.

After that the next occurrence out of the ordinary was the announcement in Bonaparte's newspapers that the English captain and lieutenant, Hornblower and Bush, had met a well-deserved fate by being drowned in the Loire during an attempt to escape from an escort which was conducting them to their trial; undoubtedly (said the bulletin) this had saved the miscreants from the firing party which awaited them for the purpose of exacting the penalty of their flagrant piracy in the Mediterranean.

Hornblower read the announcement with mixed feelings when the Count showed it to him; not every man has the privilege of reading his own obituary. His first reaction was that it would make their escape considerably easier, seeing that the police would no longer be on the watch for them. But that feeling of relief was swamped by a wave of other feelings. Maria in England would think herself a widow, at this very moment when their child was about to be born. What would it mean to her? Hornblower knew, only too acutely, that Maria loved him as dearly as a woman could love a man, although he only admitted it to himself at moments like this. He could not guess what she would do when she believed him dead. It would be the end of everything she had lived for. And yet she would have a pension, security, a child to cherish. She might set herself, unconsciously, to make a new life for herself. In a clairvoyant moment Hornblower visualized Maria in deep mourning, her mouth set in prim resignation, the coarse red skin of her cheeks wet with tears, and her red hands nervously clasping and unclasping. She had looked like that the summer day when little Horatio and little Maria had been buried in their common grave.

Hornblower shuddered away from the recollection. Maria would at least be in no need of money; the British press would see that the government did its duty there. He could guess at the sort of articles which would be appearing in reply to this announcement of Bonaparte's, the furious indignation that a British officer should be accused of piracy, the openly expressed suspicions that he had been murdered in cold blood and had not died while attempting to escape, the clamour for reprisals.

To this day a British newspaper seldom discussed Bonaparte without recalling the death of another British naval captain, Wright, who was said to have committed suicide in prison in Paris. Everyone in England believed that Bonaparte had had him murdered – they would believe the same in this case. It was almost amusing that nearly always the most effective attacks on the tyrant were based on actions on his part which were either trivial or innocent. The British genius for invective and propaganda had long discovered that it paid better to exploit trivialities rather than inveigh broadly against policies and principles; the newspapers would give more space to a condemnation of Bonaparte for causing the death of a single naval officer than to a discussion of the criminal nature of, say, the invasion of Spain, which had resulted in the wanton slaughter of some hundreds of thousands of innocent people.

And Lady Barbara would read that he was dead, too. She would be sorry – Hornblower was prepared to believe that – but how deep her sorrow would be he could not estimate at all. The thought called up all the flood of speculations and doubts which lately he had been trying to forget – whether she cared for him at all or not, whether or not her husband had survived his wound, and what he could do in the matter in any event.

'I am sorry that this announcement seems to cause you so much distress,' said the Count, and Hornblower realized that his expression had been anxiously studied during the whole reading. He had for once been caught off his guard, but he was on guard again at once. He made himself smile.

'It will make our journey through France a good deal easier,' he said.

'Yes. I thought the same as soon as I read it. I can congratulate you, Captain.'

'Thank you,' said Hornblower.

But there was a worried look in the Count's face; he had something more to say and was hesitating to say it.

'What are you thinking about, sir?' asked Hornblower.

'Only this – Your position is in one way more dangerous now. You have been pronounced dead by a government which does not admit mistakes – cannot afford to admit them. I am afraid in case I have done you a disservice in so selfishly accepting the pleasure of your company. If you are recaptured you *will* be dead; the government will see that you die without further attention being called to you.'

Hornblower shrugged his shoulders with a carelessness quite unassumed for once.

'They were going to shoot me if they caught me. This makes no difference.'

He dallied with the notion of a modern government dabbling in secret murder, for a moment was inclined to put it aside as quite impossible, as something one might believe of the Turks or perhaps even of the Sicilians, but not of Bonaparte, and then he realized with a shock that it was not at all impossible, that a man with unlimited power and much at stake, with underlings on whose silence he could rely, could not be expected to risk appearing ridiculous in the eye of his public when a mere murder would save him. It was a sobering thought, but he made himself smile again, bravely.

'You have all the courage characteristic of your

nation, Captain,' said the Count. 'But this news of your death will reach England. I fear that Madame Orrenblor will be distressed by it?'

'I am afraid she will.'

'I could find means of sending a message to England – my bankers can be trusted. But whether it would be advisable is another matter.'

If it were known in England that he was alive it would be known in France, and a stricter search would be instituted for him. It would be terribly dangerous. Maria would draw small profit from the knowledge that he was alive if that knowledge were to cause his death.

'I think it would not be advisable,' said Hornblower.

There was a strange duality in his mind; the Hornblower for whom he could plan so coolly, and whose chances of life he could estimate so closely, was a puppet of the imagination compared with the living, flesh and blood Hornblower whose face he had shaved that morning. He knew by experience now that only when a crisis came, when he was swimming for his life in a whirlpool, or walking a quarterdeck in the heat of action, that the two blended together – that was the moment when fear came.

'I hope, Captain,' said the Count, 'that this news has not disturbed you too much?'

'Not at all, sir,' said Hornblower.

'I am delighted to hear it. And perhaps you will be good enought to give Madame la Vicomtesse and myself the pleasure of your company again tonight at whist, you and Mr Bush?'

Whist was the regular way of passing the evening. The Count's delight in the game was another bond of sympathy between him and Hornblower. He was not a player of the mathematical variety, as was Hornblower. Rather did he rely upon a flair, an instinctive system of tactics. It was marvellous how often his blind leads found his partner's short suit and snatched tricks from the jaws of the inevitable, how often he could decide intuitively upon the winning play when confronted by a dilemma. There were rare evenings when this faculty would desert him, and when he would sit with a rueful smile losing rubber after rubber to the remorseless precision of his daughter-in-law and Hornblower. But usually his uncanny telepathic powers would carry him triumphantly through, to the exasperation of Hornblower if they had been opponents, and to his intense satisfaction if they had been partners – exasperation at the failure of his painstaking calculations, or satisfaction of their complete vindication.

The Vicomtesse was a good well-taught player of no brilliance whose interest in the game, Hornblower suspected, was entirely due to her devotion to her father-in-law. It was Bush to whom these evenings of whist were a genuine penance. He disliked card games of any sort – even the humble vingt-et-un – and in the supreme refinement of whist he was hopelessly at a loss. Hornblower had cured him of some of his worst habits – of asking, for instance, 'What are trumps?' halfway through every hand – had insisted on his counting the cards as they fell, on his learning the conventional leads and discards, and by so doing had made of him a player whose presence three good players could just tolerate rather than miss their evening's amusement; but the evenings to him were periods of agonized, hard-breathing concentration, of flustered mistakes and shamefaced apology – misery made no less acute by the fact that conversation was carried on in French in which he could never acquire any facility. Bush mentally classed together French, whist, and spherical trigonometry as subjects in which he was too old ever to make any further progress, and which he would be content, if he were allowed, to leave entirely to his admired captain.

For Hornblower's French was improving rapidly, thanks to the need for continual use of the language. His defective ear would never allow him to catch the trick of the accent – he would always speak with the tonelessness of the foreigner – but his vocabulary was widening and his grammar growing more certain and he was acquiring a fluency in the idiom which more than once earned him a pretty compliment from his host. Hornblower's pride was held in check by the astonishing fact that below stairs Brown was rapidly acquiring the same fluency. He was living largely with French people, too – with Felix and his wife the housekeeper, and their daughter Louise the maid, and, living over the stables across the yard, the family of Bertrand, who was Felix's brother and incidentally the coachman; Bertrand's wife was the cook, with two daughters to help her in the kitchen, while one of her young sons was footman under Felix and the other two worked in the stables under their father.

Hornblower had once ventured to hint to the Count that the presence of himself and the others might well be betrayed to the authorities by one of all these servants, but the Count merely shook his head with a serene confidence that could not be shaken.

'They will not betray me,' he said, and so intense was his conviction on the point that it carried conviction to Hornblower – and the better he came to know the Count the more obvious it became that no one who knew him well would ever betray him. And the Count added with a wry smile –

'You must remember, too, Captain, that here I *am* the authorities.'

Hornblower could allow his mind to subside into security and sloth again after that – a sense of security with a fantastic quality about it that savoured of a nightmare. It was unreal to be mewed for so long within four walls, deprived of the wide horizons and the endless variety of the sea. He could spend his mornings tramping up and down the stable yard, as though it were a quarterdeck and as though Bertrand and his sons chattering about their duties were a ship's crew engaged on their morning's deck-washing. The smell of the stables and the land winds which came in over the high walls were a poor substitute for the keen freshness of the sea. He spent hours in a turret window of the house, with a spyglass which the Count found for him, gazing round the countryside; the desolate vineyards in their winter solitude, the distant towers of Nevers – the ornate Cathedral tower and the graceful turrets of the Gonzaga palace; the rushing black river, its willows half submerged – the ice which came in January and the snow which three times covered the blank slopes that winter were welcome variations of the monotonous landscape; there were the distant hills and the nearby slopes; the trace of the valley of the Loire winding off into the unknown, and of the valley of the Allier coming down to meet it – to a landman's eye the prospect from the turret window would have been delightful, even perhaps in the lashing rain that fell so often, but to a seaman and a prisoner it was revolting. The indefinable charm of the sea was wanting, and so were the mystery and magic and freedom of the sea. Bush and Brown, noting the black bad temper in which Hornblower descended from the turret window after a sitting with his spyglass, wondered why he spent his time in that fashion. He wondered why himself, but weakly he could not stop himself from doing so. Specially marked was his bad temper when the Count and his daughter-in-law went out riding, returning flushed and healthy and happy after some brisk miles of the freedom for which he craved – he was stupidly jealous, he told himself, angrily, but he was jealous all the same.

He was even jealous of the pleasure Bush and Brown took in the building of the new boat. He was not a man of his hands, and once the design of the boat had been agreed upon – its fifteen feet of length and four feet of beam and its flat bottom – he could contribute nothing towards the work except unskilled labour. His subordinates were far more expert with tools than he was, with plane and saw and drill, and characteristically found immense pleasure in working with them. Bush's childish delight in finding his hands, softened by a long period of convalescence, forming their distinguishing callouses again, irritated him. He envied them the simple creative pleasure which they found in watching the boat grow under their hands in the empty loft which they had adopted as a workshop – more still he envied Brown the accuracy of eye he displayed, working with a spokeshave shaping the sculls without any of the apparatus of templates and models and stretched strings which Hornblower would have found necessary.

They were black days, all that winter of confinement. January came, and with it the date when his child would be born; he was half mad with the uncertainty of it all, with his worry about Maria and the child, with the thought that Barbara would think him dead and would forget him. Even the Count's sweetness of temper and unvarying courtesy irritated him as soon as it began to cloy. He felt he would give a year of his life to hear him make a tart rejoinder to one of Bush's clumsy speeches; the impulse to be rude to the Count, to fire up into a quarrel with him even though – or perhaps because – he owed him his life, was sometimes almost irresistible, and the effort of self-control tried his temper still further. He was surfeited with the Count's unwearying goodness, even with the odd way in which their thoughts ran so frequently together; it was queer, even uncanny, to see in the Count so often what seemed like reflections of himself in a mirror. It was madder still to remember that he had felt similar ties of sympathy, sometimes with the wickedest man he had ever known – with el Supremo in Central America.

El Supremo had died for his crime on a scaffold at Panama; Hornblower was worried by the thought that the Count was risking the guillotine at Paris for his friend's sake – it was mad to imagine any parallelism between the careers of el Supremo and the Count, but Hornblower was in a mad mood. He was thinking too much and he had too little to do, and his overactive brain was racketing itself to pieces. There was insanity in indulging in ridiculous mystic speculations about spiritual relationships between himself and the Count and el Supremo, and he knew it. Only self-control and patience were necessary, he told himself, to come safely through these last few weeks of waiting, but his patience seemed to be coming to an end, and he was so weary of exerting self-control.

It was the flesh that saved him when his spirit grew weak. One afternoon, descending from a long and maddening sitting with his telescope in the turret, he met the Vicomtesse in the upper gallery. She was at her boudoir door, about to enter, and she turned and smiled at him as he approached. His head was whirling; somehow his exasperation and feverishness drove him into holding out both his hands to her, risking a rebuff, risking everything, in his longing for some kind of comfort, something to ease this unbearable strain. She put her hands in his, smiling still, and at the touch self-possession broke down. It was madness to yield to the torrent of impulses let loose, but madness was somehow sweet. They were inside the room now, and the door was closed. There was sweet, healthy, satisfying flesh in his arms. There were no doubts nor uncertainties; no mystic speculations. Now blind instinct could take charge, all the bodily urges of months of celibacy. Her lips were ripe and rich and ready, the breasts which he crushed against him were hillocks of sweetness. In his nostrils was the faint intoxicating scent of womanhood.

Beyond the boudoir was the bedroom; they were there now and she was yielding to him. Just as another man might have given way to drink, might have stupefied his brain in beastly intoxication, so Hornblower numbed his own brain with lust and passion. He forgot every-thing, and he cared for nothing, in this mad lapse from self-control.

And she understood his motives, which was strange, and she did not resent them, which was stranger still. As his passion ebbed away, he could see her face again clearly, and her expression was tender and detached and almost maternal. She was aware of his unhappiness as she had been aware of his lust for that splendid body of hers. She had given him her body because of his crying need for it, as she might have given a cup of water to a man dying of thirst. Now she held his head to her breast, and stroked his hair, rocking a little as though he were a child, and murmuring little soothing words to him. A tear fell from her eye on to Horn-blower's temple. She had come to love this Englishman, but she knew only too well that it was not love which had brought him into her arms. She knew of the wife and child in England, she guessed at the existence of the other woman whom he loved. It was not the thought of them which brought the tears to her eyes; it was the knowledge that she was not any part of his real life, that this stay of his on the banks of the Loire was as unreal to him as a dream, something to be endured until he could escape again to the sea, into the mad world which to him was sanity, where every day he would encounter peril and discomfort. These kisses he was giving her meant nothing to him compared with the business of life, which was war – the same war which had killed her young husband, the wasteful, prodigal, beastly busi-ness which had peopled Europe with widows and disfigured it with wasted fields and burned villages. He was kissing her as a man might pat his dog's head during an exciting business deal.

Then Hornblower lifted his face to hers again, and read the tragedy in her eyes. The sight of her tears moved him inexpressibly. He stroked her cheek.

'Oh, my dear,' he said in English, and then began to try to find French words to express what he wanted to say. Tenderness was welling up within him. In a blinding moment of relevation he realized the love she bore him, and the motives which had brought her submissively into his arms. He kissed her mouth, he brushed away the splendid red hair from her pleading eyes. Tenderness reawoke passion; and under his caresses her last reserve broke down.

'I love you!' she sighed, her arms about him. She had not meant to admit it, either to him or to herself. She knew that if she gave herself to him with passion he would break her heart in the end, and that he did not love her, not even now, when tenderness had replaced the blind lust in his eyes. He would break her heart if she allowed herself to love him; for one more second she had that clairvoyance before she let herself sink into the self-deception which she knew in the future she would not believe to be self-deception. But the temptation to deceive herself into thinking he loved her was overwhelming. She gave herself to him passionately.

10

The affair thus consummated seemed, to Hornblower's mind at least, to clear the air like a thunderstorm. He had something more definite to think about now than mystic speculations; there was Marie's loving kindness to soothe him, and for counter-irritant there was the pricking of his conscience regarding his seduction of his host's daughter-in-law under his host's roof. His uneasiness lest the Count's telepathic powers should enable him to guess at the secret he shared with Marie, the fear lest someone should intercept a glance or correctly interpret a gesture, kept his mind healthily active.

And the love-affair while it ran its course brought with it a queer unexpected happiness. Marie was everything Hornblower could desire as a mistress. By marriage she was of a family noble enough to satisfy his liking for lords, and yet the knowledge that she was of peasant birth saved him from feeling any awe on that account. She could be tender and passionate, protective and yielding, practical and romantic; and she loved him so dearly, while at the same time she remained reconciled to his approaching departure and resolute to help it on in every way, that his heart softened towards her more and more with the passage of the days.

That departure suddenly became a much nearer and more likely possibility – by coincidence it seemed to come up over the horizon from the hoped-for into the expected only a day or two after Hornblower's meeting with Marie in the upper gallery. The boat was finished, and lay, painted and equipped, in the loft ready for them to use; Brown kept it filled with water from the well and proudly announced that it did not leak a drop. The plans for their journey to the sea were taking definite shape. Fat Jeanne the cook baked biscuit for them – Hornblower came triumphantly into his own then, as the only person in the house who knew how ship's biscuit should be baked, and Jeanne worked under his supervision.

Anxious debate between him and the Count had ended in his deciding against running the risk of buying food while on their way unless compelled; the fifty pounds of biscuit which Jeanne baked for them (there was a locker in the boat in which to store it) would provide the three of them with a pound of bread each day for seventeen days, and there was a sack of potatoes waiting for them, and another of dried peas; and there were long thin Arles sausages – as dry as sticks, and, to Hornblower's mind, not much more digestible, but with the merit of staying eatable for long periods – and some of the dry cod which Hornblower had come to know during his captivity at Ferrol, and a corner of bacon; taken all in all – as Hornblower pointed out to the Count who was inclined to demur – they were going to fare better on their voyage down the Loire than they had often fared in the ships of His Majesty King George. Hornblower, accustomed for so long to sea voyages, never ceased to marvel at the simplicity of planning a river trip thanks to the easy solution of the problem of water supply; overside they would have unlimited fresh water for drinking and washing and bathing – much better water, too, as he told the Count again, than the stinking green stuff, alive with animalculae, doled out at the rate of four pints a head a day, with which people in ships had to be content.

He could anticipate no trouble until they neared the sea; it was only with their entry into tidal waters that they would be in any danger. He knew how the French coast swarmed with garrisons and customs officers – as a lieutenant under Pellew he had once landed a spy in the salt marshes of Bourgneuf – and it would be under their noses that they would have to steal a fishing boat and make their way to sea. Thanks to the Continental system, and the fear of English descents, and precautions against espionage, tidal waters would be watched closely indeed. But he felt he could only trust to fortune – it was hard to make plans against contingencies which might take any shape whatever, and besides, those dangers were weeks away, and Hornblower's newly contented mind was actually too lazy to devote much thought to them. And as he grew fonder of Marie, too, it grew harder to make plans which would take him away from her. His attachment for her was growing even as strong as that.

It was left to the Count to make the most helpful suggestion of all.

'If you would permit me,' he said, one evening, 'I would like to tell you of an idea I have for simplifying your passage through Nantes.'

'It would give me pleasure to hear it, sir,' said Hornblower – the Count's long-winded politeness was infectious.

'Please do not think,' said the Count, 'that I wish to interfere in any way in the plans you are making, but it occurred to me that your stay on the coast might be made safer if you assumed the role of a high official of the customs service.'

'I think it would, sir,' said Hornblower, patiently, 'but I do not understand how I could do it.'

'You would have to announce yourself, if necessary, as a Dutchman,' said the Count. 'Now that Holland is annexed to France and King Louis Bonaparte has fled, it is to be presumed that his employés will join the Imperial service. I think it is extremely likely that, say, a colonel of Dutch douaniers should visit Nantes to learn how to perform his duties – especially as it was over the enforcement of customs regulations that Bonaparte and his brother fell out. Your very excellent French would be just what might be expected of a Dutch customs officer, even though – please pardon my frankness – you do not speak quite like a native Frenchman.'

'But – but –,' stammered Hornblower; it really seemed to him that the Count's customary good sense had deserted him '– it would be difficult, sir –'

'Difficult?' smiled the Count. 'It might be dangerous, but, if you will forgive my contradicting you so directly, it would hardly be difficult. In your English democracy you perhaps have had no opportunity of seeing how much weight an assured manner and a uniform carry with them in a country like this, which has already made the easy descent from an autocracy to a bureaucracy. A colonel of douaniers on the coast can go anywhere, command anything. He never has to account for himself – his uniform does that for him.'

'But I have no uniform, sir,' said Hornblower, and before the words were out of his mouth he guessed what the Count was going to say.

'We have half a dozen needlewomen in the house,' smiled the Count, 'from Marie here to little Christine the cook's daughter. It would be odd if between them they could not make uniforms for you and your assistants. I might add that Mr Bush's wound, which we all so much deplore, will be an actual advantage if you adopt the scheme. It is exactly consonant with Bonaparte's methods to provide for an officer wounded in his service by giving him a position in the customs. Mr Bush's presence with you would add a touch of – shall we say realism? – to the effect produced by your appearance.'

The Count gave a little bow to Bush, in apology for thus alluding to Bush's crippled condition, and Bush returned it awkwardly from his chair in bland ignorance of at least two thirds of what had been said.

The value of the suggestion was obvious to Hornblower at once, and for days afterwards the women in the house were at work cutting and stitching and fitting, until the evening came when the three of them paraded before the Count in their neat coats of blue piped with white and red, and their rakish képis – it was the making of these which had taxed Marie's ingenuity most, for the képi was still at that time an unusual headdress in the French government services. On Hornblower's collar glittered the eight-pointed stars of colonel's rank, and the top of his képi bore the gold-lace rosette; as the three of them rotated solemnly before the Count the latter nodded approvingly.

'Excellent,' he said, and then hesitated. 'There is only one addition which I can think of to add realism. Excuse me a moment.'

He went off to his study leaving the others looking at each other, but he was back directly with a little leather case in his hand which he proceeded to open. Resting on the silk was a glittering cross of white enamel, surmounted by a golden crown and with a gold medallion in the centre.

'We must pin this on you,' he said. 'No one reaches colonel's rank without the Legion of Honour.'

'Father!' said Marie – it was rare that she used the familiar mode of address with him – 'that was Louis-Marie's.'

'I know, my dear, I know. But it may make the difference between Captain Hornblower's success or – or failure.'

His hands trembled a little, nevertheless, as he pinned the scarlet ribbon to Hornblower's coat.

'Sir – sir, it is too good of you,' protested Hornblower.

The Count's long, mobile face, as he stood up, was sad, but in a moment he had twisted it into his usual wry smile.

'Bonaparte sent it to me,' he said, 'after – after my son's death in Spain. It was a posthumous award. To me of course it is nothing – the trinkets of the tyrant can never mean anything to a Knight of the Holy Ghost. But because of its sentimental value I should be grateful if you would endeavour to preserve it unharmed and return it to me when the war is over.'

'I cannot accept it, sir,' said Hornblower, bending to unpin it again, but the Count checked him.

'Please, Captain,' he said, 'wear it, as a favour to me. It would please me if you would.'

More than ever after his reluctant acceptance did Hornblower's conscience prick him at the thought that he had seduced this man's daughter-in-law while enjoying his hospitality, and later in the evening when he found himself alone with the Count in the drawing room the conversation deepened his sense of guilt.

'Now that your stay is drawing to an end, Captain,' said the Count, 'I know how much I shall miss your presence after you have gone. Your company has given me the very greatest pleasure.'

'I do not think it can compare with the gratitude I feel towards you, sir,' said Hornblower.

The Count waved aside the thanks which Hornblower was endeavouring awkwardly to phrase.

'A little while ago we mentioned the end of the war. Perhaps there will come an end some day, and although I am an old man perhaps I shall live to see it. Will you remember, me then, and this little house beside the Loire?'

'Of course, sir,' protested Hornblower. 'I could never forget.'

He looked round the familiar drawing room, at the silver candelabra, the old-fashioned Louis Seize furniture, the lean figure of the Count in his blue dress-coat.

'I could never forget you, sir,' repeated Hornblower.

'My three sons were all young when they died,' said the Count. 'They were only boys, and perhaps they would not have grown into men I could have been proud of. And already when they went off to serve Bonaparte they looked upon me as an old-fashioned reactionary for whose views they had only the smallest patience – that was only to be expected. If they had lived through the wars we might have become better friends later. But they did not, and I am the last Ladon. I am a lonely man, Captain, lonely under this present régime, and yet I fear that when Bonaparte falls and the reactionaries return to power I shall be as lonely still. But I have not been lonely this winter, Captain.'

Hornblower's heart went out to the lean old man with the lined face sitting opposite him in the uncomfortable armchair.

'But that is enough about myself, Captain,' went on the Count. 'I wanted to tell you of the news which has come through – it is all of it important. The salute which we heard fired yesterday was, as we thought, in honour of the birth of an heir to Bonaparte. There is now a King of Rome, as Bonaparte calls him, to sustain the Imperial throne. Whether it will be any support I am doubtful – there are many Bonapartists who will not, I fancy, be too pleased at the thought of the retention of power indefinitely in a Bonaparte dynasty. And the fall of Holland is undoubted – there was actual fighting between the troops of Louis Bonaparte and those of Napoleon Bonaparte over the question of customs enforcement. France now extends to the Baltic – Hamburg and Lubeck are French towns like Amsterdam and Leghorn and Trieste.'

Hornblower thought of the cartoons in the English newspapers which had so often compared Bonaparte with the frog who tried to blow himself up as big as an ox.

'I fancy it is symptomatic of weakness,' said the

Count. 'Perhaps you do not agree with me? You do? I am glad to have my suspicions confirmed. More than that; there is going to be war with Russia. Already troops are being transferred to the East, and the details of a new conscription were published at the same time as the proclamation of a King of Rome. There will be more refractories than ever hiding about the country now. Perhaps Bonaparte will find he has undertaken a task beyond his strength when he comes to grips with Russia.'

'Perhaps so,' said Hornblower. He had not a high opinion of Russian military virtues.

'But there is more important news still,' said the Count. 'There has at last been published a bulletin of the Army of Portugal. It was dated from Almeida.'

It took a second or two for Hornblower to grasp the significance of this comment, and it only dawned upon him gradually, along with the endless implications.

'It means,' said the Count, 'that your Wellington has beaten Bonaparte's Masséna. That the attempt to conquer Portugal has failed, and that the whole of the affairs of Spain are thrown into flux again. A running sore has been opened in the side of Bonaparte's empire, which may drain him of his strength – at what cost to poor France one can hardly imagine. But of course, Captain, you can form a more reliable opinion of the military situation than I can, and I have been presumptuous in commenting on it. Yet you have not the facilities which I have of gauging the moral effect of this news. Wellington has beaten Junot, and Victor, and Soult. Now he has beaten Masséna, the greatest of them all. There is only one man now against whom European opinion can measure him, and that is Bonaparte. It is not well for a tyrant to have rivals in prestige. Last year how many years of power would one have given Bonaparte if asked? Twenty? I think so. Now in 1811 we change our minds. Ten years, we think. In 1812 we may revise our estimate again, and say five. I myself do not believe the Empire as we know it will endure after 1814 – Empires collapse at a rate increasing in geometrical progression, and it will be your Wellington who will pull this one down.'

'I hope sincerely you are right, sir,' said Hornblower.

The Count was not to know how disturbing this mention of Wellington was to his audience; he could not guess that Hornblower was daily tormented by speculations as to whether Wellington's sister was widowed or not, whether Lady Barbara Leighton, née Wellesley, ever had a thought to devote to the naval captain who had been reported dead. Her brother's triumphs might well occupy her mind to the exclusion of everything else, and Hornblower feared that when at last he should reach England she would be far too great a lady to pay him any attention at all. The thought irked him.

He went to bed in a peculiarly sober mood, his mind busy with problems of the most varying nature – from speculations about the approaching fall of the French Empire to calculations regarding the voyage down the Loire which he was about to attempt. Lying awake, long after midnight, he heard his bedroom door quietly open and close; he lay rigid, instantly, conscious of a feeling of faint distaste at this reminder of the intrigue which he was conducting under a hospitable roof. Very gently, the curtains of his bed were drawn open, and in the darkness he could see, through half opened eyes, a shadowy ghost bending over him. A gentle hand found his cheek and stroked it; he could no longer sham sleep, and he pretended to wake with a start.

'It is Marie, 'Oratio,' said a voice, softly.

'Yes,' said Hornblower.

He did not know what he should say or do – for that matter he did not know what he wanted. Mostly he was conscious of Marie's imprudence in thus coming to his room, risking discovery and imperilling everything. He shut his eyes as though still sleepy, to gain time for consideration; the hand ceased to stroke his cheek. Hornblower waited for a second or two more, and was astonished to hear the slight click of the latch of the door again. He sat up with a jerk. Marie had gone, as silently as she had come. Hornblower continued to sit up, puzzling over the incident, but he could make nothing of it. Certainly he was not going to run any risks by going to seek Marie in her room and asking for explanations; he lay down again to think about it, and this time, with its usual capriciousness, sleep surprised him in the midst of his speculations, and he slept soundly until Brown brought him his breakfast coffee.

It took him half the morning to nerve himself for what he foresaw to be a very uncomfortable interview; it was only then that he tore himself away from a last inspection of the boat, in Bush's and Brown's company, and climbed the stairs to Marie's boudoir and tapped at the door. He entered when she called, and stood there in the room of so many memories – the golden chairs with their oval backs upholstered in pink and white, the windows looking out on the sunlit Loire, and Marie in the window-seat with her needlework.

'I wanted to say "good morning",' he said at length, as Marie did nothing to help him out.

'Good morning,' said Marie. She bent her head over her needlework – the sunshine through the windows lit her hair gloriously – and spoke with her face concealed. 'We only have to say "good morning" today, and tomorrow we shall say "goodbye".'

'Yes,' said Hornblower stupidly.

'If you loved me,' said Marie, 'it would be terrible for me to have you go, and to know that for years we should not meet again – perhaps for ever. But as you do not, then I am glad that you are going back to your wife and your child, and your ships, and your fighting. That is what you wanted, and I am pleased that you should have it all.'

'Thank you,' said Hornblower.

Still she did not look up.

'You are the sort of man,' she went on, 'whom women love very easily. I do not expect that I shall be the last. I don't think that you will ever love anybody, or know what it is to do so.'

Hornblower could have said nothing in English in reply to these two astonishing statements, and in French he was perfectly helpless. He could only stammer.

'Goodbye,' said Marie.

'Goodbye, madame,' said Hornblower, lamely.

His cheeks were burning as he came out into the upper hall, in a condition of mental distress in which humiliation only played a minor part. He was thoroughly conscious of having acted despicably, and of having been dismissed without dignity. But he was puzzled by the other remarks Marie had made. It had never occurred to him that women loved him easily. Maria – it was odd, that similarity of names, Maria and Marie – loved him, he knew; he had found it a little tiresome and disturbing. Barbara had offered herself to him, but he had never ventured to believe that she had loved him – and had she not married someone else? And Marie loved him; Hornblower remembered guiltily an incident of a few days ago, when Marie in his arms had whispered hotly, 'Tell me you love me,' and he had answered with facile kindness, 'I love you, dear.' 'Then I am happy,' answered Marie. Perhaps it was a good thing that Marie knew now that he was lying, and had made easy his retreat. Another woman with a word might have sent him and Bush to prison and death – there were women capable of it.

And this question of his never loving anyone; surely Marie was wrong about that. She did not know the miseries of longing he had been through on Barbara's account, how much he had desired her and how much he still desired her. He hesitated guiltily here, wondering whether his desire would survive gratification. That was such an uncomfortable thought that he swerved away from it in a kind of panic. If Marie had merely revengefully desired to disturb him she certainly had achieved her object; and if on the other hand she had wanted to win him back to her she was not far from success either. What with the torments of remorse and his sudden uneasiness about himself Hornblower would have returned to her if she had lifted a finger to him, but she did not.

At dinner that evening she appeared young and lighthearted, her eyes sparkling and her expression animated, and when the Count lifted his glass for the toast of 'a prosperous voyage home' she joined in with every appearance of enthusiasm. Hornblower was glum beneath his forced gaiety. Only now, with the prospect of an immediate move ahead of him, had he become aware that there were decided arguments in favour of the limbo of suspended animation in which he had spent the past months. Tomorrow he was going to leave all this certainty and safety and indifferent negativeness. There was physical danger ahead of him; that he could face calmly and with no more than a tightening of the throat, but besides that there was the resolution of all the doubts and uncertainties which had so troubled him.

Hornblower was suddenly aware that he did not so urgently desire his uncertainties to be resolved. At present he could still hope. If Leighton were to declare that Hornblower had fought at Rosas contrary to the spirit of his orders; if the court martial were to decide that the *Sutherland* had not been fought to the last gasp – and courts martial were chancy affairs; if – if – if. And there was Maria with her cloying sweetness awaiting him, and the misery of longing for Lady Barbara, all in contrast with the smoothness of life here with the Count's unruffled politeness and the stimulus of Marie's healthy animalism. Hornblower had to force a smile as he lifted his glass.

II

The big green Loire was shrinking to its summer level. Hornblower had seen its floods and its ice come and go, had seen the willows at its banks almost submerged, but now it was back safely in its wide bed, with a hint of golden-brown gravel exposed on either bank. The swift green water was clear now, instead of turbid, and under the blue sky the distant reaches were blue as well, in charming colour contrast with the springtime emerald of the valley and the gold of the banks.

The two sleek dun oxen, patient under the yoke, had dragged the travois-sledge down to the water's edge in the first early light of dawn, Brown and Hornblower walking beside to see that the precious boat balanced on it came to no harm, and Bush stumping breathlessly behind them. The boat slid gently into the water, and under Bush's supervision the stable hands loaded her with the bags of stores which they had carried down. The faint morning mist still lay in the valley, and wreathed over the surface of the water, awaiting the coming of the sun to drink it up. It was the best time for departure: the mist would shield them from inquisitive persons who might be unduly curious at the sight of the expedition starting off. Up at the house farewells had all been said – the Count as unruffled as ever, as though it were usual for him to rise at five in the morning, and Marie smiling and calm. In the stable yard and the kitchen there had been tears; all the women had lamented Brown's going, weeping unashamed and yet laughing through their tears as he laughed and joked in the voluble French which he had acquired, and as he smacked their broad posteriors. Hornblower wondered how many of them Brown had seduced that winter, and how many Anglo-French children would be born next autumn as a result.

'Remember your promise to return after the war,' the Count had said to Hornblower. 'Marie will be as delighted to see you as I shall be.'

His smile had conveyed no hint of a hidden meaning – but how much did he guess, or know? Hornblower gulped as he remembered.

'Shove off,' he rasped. 'Brown, take the sculls.'

The boat scraped over the gravel, and then floated free as the current took her, dancing away from the little group of stable hands and the stolid oxen, vague already in the mist. The rowlocks creaked and the boat swayed to Brown's pulls; Hornblower heard the noises, and felt Bush seated in the stern beside him, but for some seconds he saw nothing. There was a mist about him far denser than the reality.

The one mist cleared with the other, as the sun came breaking through, warm on Hornblower's back. High up the bank on the opposite side was the orchard at which Hornblower had often gazed from his window; it was marvellous now under its load of blossom. Looking back he saw the château shining in the sun. The turrets at the corners had been added, he knew, no more than fifty years ago by a Comte de Graçay with a rococo taste for the antique, but they looked genuine enough at a distance. It was like a fairy castle in the pearly light, a dream castle; and already the months he had spent there seemed like a dream too, a dream from which he regretted awakening.

'Mr Bush,' he said sharply. 'I'll trouble you to get out your rod and make an appearance of fishing. Take a slower stroke, Brown.'

They went drifting on down the noble river, blue in the distance and green overside, clear and transparent, so that they could actually see the bottom passing away below them. It was only a few minutes before they reached the confluence of the Allier, itself a fine river almost the size of the Loire, and the united stream was majestically wide, a hundred and fifty fathoms at least from bank to bank. They were a long musket shot from land, but their position was safer even than that implied, for from the water's edge on either side stretched an extensive no man's land of sand and willow which the periodic floods kept free from human habitations and which was only likely to be visited by fishermen and laundering housewives.

The mist had entirely vanished now, and the hot sun bore with all the promise of one of those splendid spring days of central France. Hornblower shifted in his seat to make himself more comfortable. The hierarchy of this, his new command, was top-heavy. A proportion of one seaman to one lieutenant and one captain was ludicrous. He would have to exercise a great deal of tact to keep them all three satisfied – to see that Brown was not made resentful by having all the work to do and yet that discipline was not endangered by a too democratic division of labour. In a fifteen-foot boat it would be difficult to keep up the aloof dignity proper to a captain.

'Brown,' he said. 'I've been very satisfied with you so far. Keep in my good books and I'll see you're properly rewarded when we get back to England. There'll be a warrant for you as master's mate if you want it.'

'Thank 'ee, sir. Thank 'ee very kindly. But I'm happy as I am, beggin' your pardon, sir.'

He meant he was happy in his rating as a coxswain, but the tone of his voice implied more than that. Hornblower looked at him as he sat with his face turned up to the sun, pulling slowly at the sculls. There was a blissful smile on his face – the man was marvellously happy. He had been well fed and well housed for months, with plenty of women's society, with light work and no hardship. Even now there was a long prospect ahead of him of food better than he had ever known before he entered France, of no harder work than a little gentle rowing, of no need ever to turn out on a blustering night to reef topsails. Twenty years of the lower deck in King George's Navy, Hornblower realized, must make any man form the habit of living only in the present. Tomorrow might bring a flogging, peril, sickness, death; certainly hardship and probably hunger, and all without the opportunity of lifting a finger to ward off any of these, for any lifting of a finger would make them all more certain. Twenty years of being at the mercy of the incalculable, and not merely in the major things of life but in the minor ones, must make a fatalist of any man who survived them. For a moment Hornblower felt a little twinge of envy of Brown, who would never know the misery of helplessness, or the indignity of indecision.

The river channel here was much divided by islands each bordered by a rim of golden gravel; it was

Hornblower's business to select what appeared to be the most navigable channel – no easy task. Shallows appeared mysteriously right in the centre of what had seemed to be the main stream; over these the clear green water ran faster and faster and shallower and shallower until the bottom of the boat was grating on the pebbles. Sometimes the bank would end there with astonishing abruptness, so that one moment they were in six inches of rushing water and the next in six feet of transparent green, but more than once now they found themselves stuck fast, and Brown and Hornblower, trousers rolled to the knee, had to get out and haul the boat a hundred yards over a barely covered bank before finding water deep enough. Hornblower thanked his stars that he had decided on having the boat built flat-bottomed – a keel would have been a hampering nuisance.

Then they came to a dam, like the one which had brought them disaster in the darkness during their first attempt to navigate the river. It was half natural, half artificial, roughly formed of lumps of rock piled across the river bed, and over it the river poured in fury at a few points.

'Pull over to the bank there, Brown,' snapped Hornblower as his coxswain looked to him for orders.

They ran the boat up on to the gravel just above the dam, and Hornblower stepped out and looked downstream. There was a hundred yards of turbulent water below the dam; they would have to carry everything down. It took three journeys on the part of Hornblower and Brown to carry all their stores to the point he chose for them to re-enter the river – Bush with his wooden leg could only just manage to stumble over the uneven surface unladen – and then they addressed themselves to the business of transporting the boat. It was not easy; there was a colossal difference between dragging the boat through shallows even an inch deep only and carrying her bodily. Hornblower contemplated the task glumly for some seconds before plunging at it. He stooped and got his hands underneath.

'Take the other side, Brown. Now – lift.'

Between them they could just raise it; they had hardly staggered a yard with it before all the strength was gone from Hornblower's wrists and fingers and the boat slipped to the ground again. He avoided Brown's eye and stooped again, exasperated.

'Lift!' he said.

It was impossible to carry the heavy boat that way. He had no sooner lifted it than he was compelled to drop it again.

'It's no go, sir,' said Brown gently. 'We'll have to get her upon our backs, sir. That's the only way.'

Hornblower heard the respectful murmur as if from a long distance.

'If you take the bows, beggin' your pardon, sir, I'll look after the stern. Here, sir, lift t'other way round. Hold it, sir, 'till I can get aft. Right, sir. Ready. Lift!'

They had the boat up on their backs now, stooping double under the heavy load. Hornblower, straining under the lighter bows, thought of Brown carrying the much heavier stern, and he set his teeth and vowed to himself that he would not rest until Brown asked to. Within five seconds he was regretting his vow. His breath was coming with difficulty and there were stabbing pains in his chest. It grew harder and harder to take the trouble

148

to attend to the proper placing of his feet as he stumbled over the uneven surface. Those months in the Château de Graçay had done their work in making him soft and out of condition; for the last few yards of the portage he was conscious of nothing save the overwhelming weight on his neck and shoulders and his difficulty of breathing. Then he heard Bush's bluff voice.

'Right, sir. Let me get hold, sir.'

With the small but welcome help that Bush could afford he was able to disengage himself and lower the boat to the ground; Brown was standing over the stern gasping, and sweeping the sweat off his forehead with his forearm. Hornblower saw him open his mouth to make a remark, presumably regarding the weight of the boat, and then shut it again when he remembered that now he was under discipline again and must only speak when spoken to. And discipline, Hornblower realized, required that he himself should display no sign of weakness before his subordinates – it was bad enough that he should have had to receive advice from Brown as to how to lift the boat.

'Take hold again, Brown, and we'll get her into the water,' he said, controlling his breathing with a vast effort.

They slid the boat in, and heaved the stores on board again. Hornblower's head was swimming with the strain; he thought longingly of his comfortable seat in the stern, and then put the thought from him.

'I'll take the sculls, Brown,' he said.

Brown opened and shut his mouth again, but he could not question explicit orders. The boat danced out over the water, with Hornblower at the sculls happy in the rather baseless conviction that he had demonstrated that a captain in the King's Navy was the equal even in physical strength of any mere coxswain, however Herculean his thews.

Once or twice that day shallows caught them out in midstream which they were unable to pass without lightening the boat to a maximum extent. When Hornblower and Brown, ankle-deep in rushing water, could drag the boat no farther, Bush had to get out too, his wooden leg sinking in the sand despite its broad leather sole, and limp downstream to the edge of the shallows and wait until the others dragged the lightened boat up to him – once he had to stand holding the bag of bread and the roll of bedding before they could tug the boat over the shallows, and on that occasion they had to unstrap his wooden leg, help him in, and then tug the leg free from the sand, so deeply had it sunk. There was another portage to be made that day, fortunately not nearly such a long one as the first; altogether there was quite enough interest in the day's journey to keep them from growing bored.

On that big lonely river it was almost like travelling through an uninhabited country. For the greater part of the day there was hardly a soul in sight. Once they saw a skiff moored to the bank which was obviously used as a ferry-boat, and once they passed a big wagon ferry – a flat-bottomed scow which was moored so as to swing itself across the river by the force of the current, pendulum-fashion on long mooring ropes. Once they passed a small boat engaged in the task of dredging sand for building purposes from the river bed; there were two weather-beaten men on board, hard at work with small hand dredgers on poles, which they scraped over the bottom and emptied into the boat. It was a nervous moment as they approached them, Bush and Brown with their ornamental fishing rods out, Hornblower forcing himself to do no more with the sculls than merely keep the boat in midstream. He had thought, as they drifted down, of giving orders to Bush and Brown regarding the instant silencing of the two men if they appeared suspicious, but he checked himself. He could rely on their acting promptly without warning, and his dignity demanded that he should betray none of the apprehension which he felt.

But the apprehension was quite baseless. There was no curiosity in the glances which the two sand dredgers threw at them, and there was cordiality in their smiles and in their polite 'Bonjour, messieurs.'

'Bonjour,' said Hornblower and Brown – Bush had the sense to keep shut the mouth which would instantly have betrayed them, and devoted his attention instead to his rod. Clearly boats with fishing parties on board were just common enough on the Loire to escape comment; and, besides, the intrinsic innocence of fishing as a pastime shielded them from suspicion, as Hornblower and the Count had agreed long before. And nobody could ever dream that a small boat in the heart of France was manned by escaped prisoners of war.

The commonest sight of all along the river was the women washing clothes, sometimes singly, sometimes in little groups whose gossiping chatter floated out to them distinctly over the water. The Englishmen could hear the 'clop clop clop' of the wooden beaters smacking the wet clothes on the boards, and could see the kneeling women sway down and up as they rinsed them in the current; most of the women looked up from their work and gave them a glance as they drifted by, but it was never more than a long glance, and often not as much. In time of war and upheaval there were so many possible explanations for the women not to know the occupants of the boat that their inability did not trouble them.

Of the roaring rapids such as had nearly destroyed them once before, they saw nothing; the junction of the Allier, and the cessation of the winter floods, accounted for that. The rock-strewn sand bars represented the sites of winter rapids and were far easier to navigate, or rather to circumvent. In fact, there were no difficulties at all. Even the weather was benign, a lovely clear day of sunshine, comfortably warm, lighting up the changing panorama of gold and blue and green. Brown basked in it all unashamedly, and the hardbitten Bush took his ease whenever the peacefulness of it caught him napping; in Bush's stern philosophy mankind – naval mankind at least – was born to sorrow and difficulty and danger, and any variation from such a state of affairs must be viewed with suspicion and not enjoyed too much lest it should have to be paid for at compound interest. It was too good to be true, this delightful drifting down the river, as morning wore into noon and noon into prolonged and dreamy afternoon, with a delicious lunch to eat of a cold pâté (a parting gift from fat Jeanne) and a bottle of wine.

The little towns, or rather villages, which they passed were all perched up high on the distant banks beyond the flood limits; Hornblower, who already knew by heart the brief itinerary and table of distances which the Count had made out for him, was aware that the first town with a bridge was at Briare, which they could not reach until late evening. He had intended to wait above the town until nightfall and then to run through in the darkness, but as the day wore on his resolve steadily hardened to push on without waiting. He could not analyse his motives. He was aware that it was a very remarkable thing for him to do, to run into danger, even the slightest, when urged neither by the call of duty nor the thirst for distinction. Here the only benefit would be the saving of an hour or two's time. The Nelsonian tradition to 'lose not an hour' was grained deeply into him, but it was hardly that which influenced him.

Partly it was his innate cross-grainedness. Everything had gone so supremely well. Their escape from their escort had been almost miraculous, the coincidence which had brought them to the Château de Graçay, where alone in all France they could have found safety, was more nearly miraculous still. Now this voyage down the river bore every promise of easy success. His instinctive reaction to all this unnatural prosperity was to put himself into the way of trouble – there had been so much trouble in his life that he felt uneasy without it.

But partly he was being driven by devils. He was morose and cantankerous. Marie was being left behind, and he was regretting that more with every yard that divided them. He was tormented by the thought of the shameful part he had played, and by memories of the hours they had spent together; sentimentally he was obsessed with longing for her. And ahead of him lay England where they thought him dead, where Maria would by now have reconciled herself to her loss and would be doubly and painfully happy with him in consequence, and where Barbara would have forgotten him, and where a court martial to inquire into his conduct awaited him. He thought grimly that it might be better for everyone if he *were* dead; he shrank a little from the prospect of returning to England as one might shrink from a cold plunge, or as he shrank from the imminent prospect of danger. That was the ruling motive. He had always forced himself to face danger, to advance bravely to meet it. He had always gulped down any pill which life had presented to him, knowing that any hesitation would give him a contempt for himself more bitter still. So now he would accept no excuse for delay.

Briare was in sight now, down at the end of the long wide reach of the river. Its church tower was silhouetted against the evening sky, and its long straggling bridge stood out black against the distant silver of the water. Hornblower at the sculls looked over his shoulder and saw all this; he was aware of his subordinate's eye turned inquiringly upon him.

'Take the sculls, Brown,' he growled.

They changed places silently, and Bush handed over the tiller to him with a puzzled look – he had been well aware of the design to run past bridges only at night. There were two vast black shapes creeping over the surface of the river down there, barges being warped out of the lateral canal on one side and into the canal of Briare on the other by way of a channel across the river dredged for the purpose. Hornblower stared forward as they approached under the impulse of Brown's steady strokes. A quick examination of the water surface told him which arch of the bridge to select, and he was able to discern the tow-ropes and warps of the barges – there were teams of horses both on the bridge and on the banks, silhouetted clearly against the sky as they tugged at the ropes to drag the bulky barges across the rushing current.

Men were looking at them now from the bridge, and there was just sufficient gap left between the barges to enable the boat to slip between without the necessity to stop and make explanations.

'Pull!' he said to Brown, and the boat went careering headlong down the river. They slid under the bridge with a rush, and neatly rounded the stern of one of the barges; the burly old man at the tiller, with a little grandchild beside him, looked down at them with a dull curiosity as they shot by. Hornblower waved his hand gaily to the child – excitement was a drug which he craved, which always sent his spirits high – and looked up with a grin at the other men on the bridge and on the banks. Then they were past, and Briare was left behind.

'Easy enough, sir,' commented Bush.

'Yes,' said Hornblower.

If they had been travelling by road they certainly would have been stopped for examination of their pass-ports; here on the unnavigable river such a proceeding occurred to no one. The sun was low now, shining right into his eyes as he looked forward, and it would be dark in less than an hour. Hornblower began to look out for a place where they could be comfortable for the night. He allowed one long island to slide past them before he saw the ideal spot – a tiny hummock of an island with three willow trees, the green of the central part surrounded by a broad belt of golden brown where the receding river had left the gravel exposed.

'We'll run the boat aground over there, Brown,' he announced. 'Easy. Pull starboard. Pull both. Easy.'

It was not a very good landing. Hornblower, despite his undoubted ability in handling big ships, had much to learn regarding the behaviour of flat-bottomed boats amid the shoals of a river. There was a black eddy, which swung them round; the boat had hardly touched bottom before the current had jerked her free again. Brown, tumbling over the bows, was nearly waist deep in water and had to grab the painter and brace himself against the current to check her. The tactful silence which ensued could almost be felt while Brown tugged the boat up to the gravel again – Hornblower, in the midst of his annoyance, was aware of Bush's restless movement and thought of how his first lieutenant would have admonished a midshipman guilty of such a careless piece of work. It made him grin to think of Bush bottling up his feelings, and the grin made him forget his annoyance.

He stepped out into the shallow water and helped Brown run the lightened boat farther up the bank, checking Bush when he made to step out too – Bush could never accustom himself to seeing his captain at work while he sat idle. The water was no more than ankle-deep by the time he allowed Bush to disembark; they dragged the boat up as far as she could go and Brown made fast the painter to a peg driven securely into the earth, as a precaution in case any unexpected rise in the water level should float the boat off. The sun had set now in the flaming west, and it was fast growing dark.

'Supper,' said Hornblower. 'What shall we have?'

A captain with strict ideas of discipline would merely have announced what they should eat, and would certainly not have called his subordinates into consultation, but Hornblower was too conscious of the top-heavy organization of his present ship's company to be able to maintain appearances to that extent. Yet Bush and Brown were still oppressed by a life-long experience of subordination and could not bring themselves to proffer advice to their captain; they merely fidgeted and stood silent, leaving it to Hornblower to decree that they should finish off the cold pâté with some boiled potatoes. Once the decision was made, Bush proceeded to amplify and interpret his captain's original order, just as a good first lieutenant should.

'I'll handle the fire here,' he said. 'There ought to be all the driftwood we need, Brown. Yes, an' I'll want some sheer-legs to hang the pan over the fire – cut me three off those trees, there.'

Bush felt it in his bones that Hornblower was meditating taking part in the preparation of supper, and could not bear the thought. He looked up at his captain half appealingly, half defiantly. A captain should not merely never be seen doing undignified work, but he should be kept in awful isolation, screened away in the mysterious recesses of his cabin. Hornblower left them to it, and wandered off round the tiny island, looking over at the distant banks and the far houses, fast disappearing in the growing twilight. It was a shock to discover that the pleasant green which carpeted most of the island was not the grass he had assumed it to be, but a bank of nettles, knee high already despite the earliness of the season. Judging by his language, Brown on the other side had just made the same discovery while seeking fuel with his feet bare.

Hornblower paced the gravel bank for a space, and on his return it was an idyllic scene which met his eyes.

Brown was tending the little fire which flickered under the pot swinging from its tripod, while Bush, his wooden leg sticking stiffly out in front of him, was peeling the last of the potatoes. Apparently Bush had decided that a first lieutenant could share menial work with the sole member of the crew without imperilling discipline. They all ate together, wordless but friendly, beside the dying fire; even the chill air of the evening did not cool the feeling of comradeship of which each was conscious in his own particular way.

'Shall I set a watch, sir?' asked Bush, as supper ended.

'No,' said Hornblower.

The minute additional security which would be conferred by one of them staying awake would not compare with the discomfort and inconvenience of everyone losing four hours' sleep each night.

Bush and Brown slept in cloak and blanket on the bare soil, probably, Hornblower anticipated, most uncomfortably. For himself there was a mattress of cut nettles cunningly packed under the boat cover which Brown had prepared for him on the most level part of the gravel spit, presumably at a grave cost in stings. He slept on it peacefully, the dew wetting his face and the gibbous moon shining down upon it from the starry sky. Vaguely he remembered, in a troubled fashion, the stories of the great leaders of men – Charles XII especially – who shared their men's coarse fare and slept like them on the bare ground. For a second or two he feared he should be doing likewise, and then his common sense overrode his modesty and told him that he did not need to have recourse to theatrical tricks to win the affections of Bush and Brown.

12

Those days on the Loire were pleasant, and every day was more pleasant than the one preceding. For Hornblower there was not merely the passive pleasure of a fortnight's picnic, but there was the far more active one of the comradeliness of it all. During his ten years as a captain his natural shyness had reinforced the restrictions surrounding his position, and had driven him more and more in upon himself until he had grown unconscious of his aching need for human companionship. In that small boat, living at close quarters with the others, and where one man's misfortune was everyone's, he came to know happiness. His keen insight made him appreciate more than ever the sterling good qualities of Bush, who was secretly fretting over the loss of his foot, and the inactivity to which that loss condemned him, and the doubtfulness of his future as a cripple.

'I'll see you posted as captain,' said Hornblower, on the only occasion on which Bush hinted at his troubles, 'if it's my last act on earth.'

He thought he might possibly contrive that, even if disgrace awaited him personally in England. Lady Barbara must still remember Bush and the old days in the *Lydia*, and must be aware of his good qualities as Hornblower was himself. An appeal to her, properly worded – even from a man broken by court martial – might have an effect, and might set turning the hidden wheels of Government patronage. Bush deserved post rank more than half the captains he knew on the list.

Then there was Brown with his unfailing cheerfulness. No one could judge better than Hornblower the awkwardness of Brown's position, living in such close proximity to two officers. But Brown always could find the right mixture of friendliness and deference; he could laugh gaily when he slipped on a rounded stone and sat down in the Loire, and he could smile sympathetically when the same thing happened to Hornblower. He busied himself over the jobs of work which had to be done, and never, not even after ten days' routine had established something like a custom, appeared to take it for granted that his officers would do their share. Hornblower could foresee a great future for Brown, if helped by a little judicious exertion of influence. He might easily end as a captain, too – Darby and Westcott had started on the lower deck in the same fashion. Even if the court martial broke him Hornblower could do something to help him. Elliott and Bolton at least would not desert him entirely, and would rate Brown as midshipman in their ships if he asked them to with special earnestness.

In making these plans for the future of his friends, Hornblower could bring himself to contemplate the end of the voyage and the inevitable court martial with something like equanimity; for the rest, during those golden days, he was able to avoid all thought of their approaching end. It was a placid journey through a placid limbo. He was leaving behind him in the past the shameful memory of his treatment of Marie, and the troubles to come were still in the future; for once in his life he was able to live in the lotus-eating present.

All the manifold little details of the journey helped towards this desirable end – they were so petty and yet temporarily so important. Selecting a course between the golden sandbanks of the river; stepping out over-side to haul the boat over when his judgement was incorrect; finding a lonely island on which to camp at night, and cooking supper when one was found; drifting past the gravel dredgers and the rare fishing parties; avoiding conspicuous behaviour while passing towns; there were always trifles to occupy the mind. There were the two nights when it rained, and they all slept huddled together under the shelter of a blanket stretched between willow trees – there had been a ridiculous pleasure about waking up to find Bush snoring beside him with a protective arm across him.

There was the pageantry of the Loire – Gien with its château-fortress high on its terraces, and Sully with its vast rounded bastions, and Château-Neuf-sur-Loire, and Jargeau. Then for miles along the river they were in sight of the gaunt square towers of the cathedral of Orleans – Orleans was one of the few towns with an extensive river front, past which they had to drift unobtrusively and with special care at its difficult bridges. Orleans was hardly out of sight before they reached Beaugency with its interminable bridges of countless arches and its strange square tower. The river was blue and gold and green. The rocks above Nevers were succeeded by the gravel banks of the middle reaches, and now the gravel gave way to sand, golden sand amid the shimmering blue of the river whose water was a clear green overside. All the contrasted greens delighted Hornblower's eyes, the green of the never-ending willows, of the vineyards and the cornfields and the meadows.

They passed Blois, its steeply-humped bridge crowned by the pyramid whose inscription proclaimed the bridge to be the first public work of the infant Louis XV, and Chaumont and Amboise, their lovely châteaux towering above the river, and Tours – an extensive water front to sidle past here, too – and Langeais. The wild desolation of the island-studded river was punctuated everywhere by towers and châteaux and cathedrals on the distant banks. Below Langeais the big placid Vienne entered the river on their left, and appeared to convey some of its own qualities to the united stream, which was now a little slower and more regular in its course, its shallows becoming less and less frequent. After Saumur and the innumerable islands of Les Ponts de Cé, the even bigger Maine came in on their right, and finally deprived the wild river of all the characteristics which had endeared it to them. Here it was far deeper and far slower, and for the first time they found the attempt to make the river available for commercial traffic successful here – they had passed numerous traces of wasted work on Bonaparte's part higher up.

But below the confluence of the Maine the groynes and dykes had withstood the winter floods and the continual erosion, had piled up long beaches of golden sand on either bank, and had left in the centre a deep channel navigable to barges – they passed several working their way up to Angers from Nantes. Mostly they were being towed by teams of mules, but one or two were taking advantage of a westerly wind to make the ascent under vast gaff-mainsails. Hornblower stared hungrily at them, for they were the first sails he had seen for months, but he put aside all thought of stealing one. A glance at their clumsy lines assured him that it would be more dangerous to put to sea, even for a short distance, in one of those than in the cockleshell boat they had already.

That westerly wind that brought the barges up brought something else with it, too. Brown, diligently tugging at the sculls as he forced the boat into it, suddenly wrinkled his nose.

'Begging your pardon, sir,' he said, 'I can smell the sea.'

They sniffed at the breeze, all three of them.

'By God, you're right, Brown,' said Bush.

Hornblower said nothing, but he had smelt the salt as well, and it had brought with it such a wave of mixed feelings as to leave him without words. And that night after they had camped – there were just as many desolate islands to choose from, despite the changes in the river – Hornblower noticed that the level of the water had risen perceptibly above where it had stood when they beached the boat. It was not flood water like the time when after a day of heavy rain their boat had nearly floated during the night; on this evening above Nantes there had been no rain, no sign of it, for three days. Hornblower watched the water creep up at a rate almost perceptible, watched it reach a maximum, dally there for a space, and then begin to sink. It was the tide. Down at Paimboeuf at the mouth there was a rise and fall of ten or twelve feet, at Nantes one of four or six; up here he was witnessing the last dying effort of the banked up sea to hold the river back in its course.

*

There was a strange emotion in the thought. They had reached tidewater at last, the habitat on which he had spent more than half his life; they had travelled from sea to sea, from the Mediterranean to what was at least technically the Atlantic; this same tide he was witnessing here washed also the shores of England, where were Barbara, and Maria, and his unknown child, and the Lords Commissioners of the Admiralty. But more than that. It meant that their pleasant picnic on the Loire was over. In tidal water they could not hope to move about with half the freedom they had known inland; strange faces and new arrivals would be scanned with suspicion, and probably the next forty-eight hours or so would determine whether he was to reach England to face a court martial or be recaptured to face a firing squad. Hornblower knew that moment the old sensation of excitement, which he called fear to himself – the quickened heart beat, the dampening palms, the tingling in the calves of his legs. He had to brace himself to master these symptoms before returning to the others to tell them of his observations.

'High water half an hour back, sir?' repeated Bush in reply.

'Yes.'

'M'm,' said Bush.

Brown said nothing, as accorded with his position in life, but his face bore momentarily the same expression of deep cogitation. They were both assimilating the fact, in the manner of seamen. Hornblower knew that from now on, with perhaps a glance at the sun but not necessarily with a glance at the river, they would be able to tell offhand the state of the tide, producing the information without a thought by the aid of a subconscious calculating ability developed during a lifetime at sea. He could do the same himself – the only difference between them was that he was interested in the phenomenon while they were indifferent to it or unaware of it.

13

For their entrance into Nantes Hornblower decided that they must wear their uniforms as officials of the customs service. It called for long and anxious thought to reach this decision, a desperately keen balancing of chances. If they arrived in civilian clothes they would almost certainly be questioned, and in that case it would be almost impossible to explain their lack of papers and passports, whereas in uniform they might easily not be questioned at all, and if they were a haughty demeanour might still save them. But to pose as a colonel of douaniers would call for histrionic ability on the part of Hornblower, and he mistrusted himself – not his ability, but his nerve. With remorseless self-analysis he told himself that he had played a part for years, posing as a man of rigid imperturbability when he was nothing of the kind, and he asked himself why he could not pose for a few minutes as a man of swaggering and over-bearing haughtiness, even under the additional handicap of having to speak French. In the end it was in despite of his doubts that he reached his decision, and put on the neat uniform and pinned the glittering Legion of Honour on his breast.

As always, it was the first moment of departure which tried him most – getting into the sternsheets of the boat and taking the tiller while Brown got out the sculls. The tension under which he laboured was such that he knew that, if he allowed it, the hand that rested on the tiller would tremble, and the voice which gave the orders to Brown would quaver. So he carried himself with the unbending rigidity which men were accustomed to see in him, and he spoke with the insensitive harshness he always used in action.

Under the impulse of Brown's sculls the river glided away behind them, and the city of Nantes came steadily nearer. Houses grew thicker and thicker on the banks, and then the river began to break up into several arms; to Hornblower the main channel between the islands was made obvious by the indications of traces of commercial activity along the banks – traces of the past, largely, for Nantes was a dying town, dying of the slow strangulation of the British blockade. The lounging idlers along the quays, the deserted warehouses, all indicated the dire effects of war upon French commerce.

They passed under a couple of bridges, with the tide running strongly, and left the huge mass of the ducal château to starboard; Hornblower forced himself to sit with careless ease in the boat, as though neither courting nor avoiding observation; the Legion of Honour clinked as it swung upon his breast. A side glance at Bush suddenly gave him enormous comfort and reassurance, for Bush was sitting with a masklike immobility of countenance which told Hornblower that he was nervous too. Bush could go into action and face an enemy's broadside with an honest indifference to danger, but this present situation was trying his nerves severely, sitting watched by a thousand French eyes, and having to rely upon mere inactivity to save himself from death or imprisonment. The sight was like a tonic to Hornblower.

His cares dropped from him, and he knew the joy and thrill of reckless bravery.

Beyond the next bridge the maritime port began. Here first were the fishing boats – Hornblower looked keenly at them, for he had in mind to steal one of them. His experience under Pellew in the blockading squadron years ago was serving him in good stead now, for he knew the ways of those fishing boats. They were accustomed to ply their trade among the islands of the Breton coast, catching the pilchards which the French persisted in calling 'sardines', and bringing their catch up the estuary to sell in the market at Nantes. He and Bush and Brown between them could handle one of those boats with ease, and they were seaworthy enough to take them safely out to the blockading squadron, or to England if necessary. He was practically certain that he would decide upon such a plan, so that as they rowed by he sharply ordered Brown to pull more slowly, and he turned all his attention upon them.

Below the fishing boats two American ships were lying against the quay, the Stars and Stripes fluttering jauntily in the gentle wind. His attention was caught by a dreary clanking of chains – the ships were being emptied of their cargoes by gangs of prisoners, each man staggering bent double under a bag of grain. That was interesting. Hornblower looked again. The chain gangs were under the charge of soldiers – Hornblower could see the shakos and the flash of the musket barrels – which gave him an insight into who the poor devils might be. They were military criminals, deserters, men caught sleeping at their posts, men who had disobeyed an order, all the unfortunates of the armies Bonaparte maintained in every corner of Europe. Their sentences condemned them to 'the galleys' and as the French Navy no longer used galleys in which they could be forced to tug at the oars, they were now employed in all the hard labour of the ports; twice as lieutenant in Pellew's *Indefatigable* Hornblower had seen picked up small parties of desperate men who had escaped from Nantes in much the same fashion as he himself proposed now to do.

And then against the quay below the American ships they saw something else, something which caused them to stiffen in their seats. The tricolour here was hoisted above a tattered blue ensign, flaunting a petty triumph.

'*Witch of Endor*, ten-gun cutter,' said Bush hoarsely. 'A French frigate caught her on a lee shore off Noirmoutier last year. By God, isn't it what you'd expect of the French? It's eleven months ago and they're still wearing French colours over British.'

She was a lovely little ship; even from where they were they could see the perfection of her lines – speed and seaworthiness were written all over her.

'The Frogs don't seem to have over-sparred her the way you'd expect 'em to,' commented Bush.

She was ready for sea, and their expert eyes could estimate the area of the furled mainsail and jib. The high graceful mast nodded to them, almost imperceptibly, as the cutter rocked minutely beside the quay. It was as if a prisoner were appealing to them for aid, and the flapping colours, tricolour over blue ensign, told a tragic story. In a sudden rush of impulse Hornblower put the helm over.

'Lay us alongside the quay,' he said to Brown.

A few strokes took them there; the tide had turned some time ago, and they headed against the flood. Brown caught a ring and made the painter fast, and first Hornblower, nimbly, and then Bush, with difficulty, mounted the stone steps to the top of the quay.

'Suivez-nous,' said Hornblower to Brown, remembering at the last moment to speak French.

Hornblower forced himself to hold up his head and walk with a swagger; the pistols in his side pockets bumped reassuringly against his hips, and his sword tapped against his thigh. Bush walked beside him, his wooden leg thumping with measured stride on the stone quay. A passing group of soldiers saluted the smart uniform, and Hornblower returned the salute nonchalantly, amazed at his new coolness. His heart was beating fast, but ecstatically he knew he was not afraid. It was worth running this risk to experience this feeling of mad bravery.

They stopped and looked at the *Witch of Endor* against the quay. Her decks were not of the dazzling whiteness upon which an English first lieutenant would have insisted, and there was a slovenliness about her standing rigging which was heartbreaking to contemplate. A couple of men were moving lackadaisically about the deck under the supervision of a third.

'Anchor watch,' muttered Bush. 'Two hands and a master's mate.'

He spoke without moving his lips, like a naughty boy in school, lest some onlooker should read his words and realize that he was not speaking French.

'Everyone else on shore, the lubbers,' went on Bush.

Hornblower stood on the quay, the tiny breeze

blowing round his ears, soldiers and sailors and civilians walking by, the bustle of the unloading of the American ships noisy in the distance. Bush's thoughts were following on the heels of his own. Bush was aware of the temptation Hornblower was feeling, to steal the *Witch of Endor* and to sail her to England – Bush would never have thought of it himself, but years of service under his captain made him receptive of ideas, however fantastic.

Fantastic was the right word. Those big cutters carried a crew of sixty men, and the gear and tackle were planned accordingly. Three men – one a cripple – could not even hope to be able to hoist the big main-sail, although it was just possible that the three of them might handle her under sail in the open sea in fair weather. It was that possibility which had given rise to the train of thought, but on the other hand there was all the tricky estuary of the Loire between them and the sea; and the French, Hornblower knew, had removed the buoys and navigation marks for fear of an English raid. Unpiloted they could never hope to find their way through thirty-five miles of shoals without going aground, and besides, there were batteries at Paimboeuf and Saint Nazaire to prohibit unauthorized entrance arid exit. The thing was impossible – it was sheer senti-mentality to think of it, he told himself, suddenly self-critical again for a moment.

He turned away and strolled up towards the American ships, and watched with interest the wretched chain gangs staggering along the gang planks with their loads of grain. The sight of their misery sickened him; so did the bullying sergeants who strutted about in charge of them. Here, if anywhere, he told himself, was to be found the nucleus of that rising against Bonaparte which everyone was expecting. All that was needed was a desperate leader – that would be something worth reporting to the Government when he reached home. Farther down the river yet another ship was coming up to the port, her topsails black against the setting sun, as, with the flood behind her, she held her course close hauled to the faint southerly breeze. She was flying the Stars and Stripes – American again. Hornblower experienced the same feeling of exasperated impotence which he had known in the old days of his service under Pellew. What was the use of blockading a coast, and enduring all the hardships and perils of that service, if neutral vessels could sail in and out with impunity? Their cargoes of wheat were officially noncontraband, but wheat was of as vital importance to Bonaparte as ever was hemp, or pitch, or any other item on the contraband list – the more wheat he could import, the more men he could draft into his armies. Hornblower found himself drifting into the eternal debate as to whether America, when eventually she became weary of the indignities of neutrality, would turn her arms against England or France – she had actually been at war with France for a short time already, and it was much to her interest to help pull down the imperial despotism, but it was doubtful whether she would be able to resist the temptation to twist the British lion's tail.

The new arrival, smartly enough handled, was edging in now to the quay. A backed topsail took the way off her, and the warps creaked round the bollards. Homnblower watched idly, Bush and Brown beside him.

As the ship was made fast, a gang plank was thrown to the quay, and a little stout man made ready to walk down it from the ship. He was in civilian clothes, and he had a rosy round face with a ridiculous little black moustache with upturned ends. From his manner of shaking hands with the captain, and from the very broken English which he was speaking, Hornblower guessed him to be the pilot.

The pilot! In that moment a surge of ideas boiled up in Hornblower's mind. It would be dark in less than an hour, with the moon in its first quarter – already he could see it, just visible in the sky high over the setting sun. A clear night, the tide about to ebb, a gentle breeze, southerly with a touch of east. A pilot available on the one hand, a crew on the other. Then he hesitated. The whole scheme was rash to the point of madness – beyond that point. It must be ill-digested, unsound. His mind raced madly through the scheme again, but even as it did so he was carried away by the wave of recklessness. There was an intoxication about throwing caution to the winds which he had forgotten since his boyhood. In the tense seconds which were all he had, while the pilot was descending the gang plank and approaching them along the quay, he had formed his resolution. He nudged his two companions, and then stepped forward and intercepted the fat little pilot as he walked briskly past them.

'Monsieur,' he said. 'I have some questions to ask you. Will you kindly accompany me to my ship for a moment?'

The pilot noted the uniform, the star of the Legion of Honour, the assured manner.

'Why, certainly,' he said. His conscience was clear; he was guilty of no more than venal infringements of the Continental system. He turned and trotted alongside Hornblower. 'You are a newcomer to this port, Colonel, I fancy?'

'I was transferred here yesterday from Amsterdam,' answered Hornblower shortly.

Brown was striding along at the pilot's other elbow; Bush was bringing up the rear, gallantly trying to keep pace with them, his wooden leg thumping the pavement. They came up to the *Witch of Endor*, and made their way up her gang plank to her deck; the officer there looked at them with a little surprise. But he knew the pilot, and he knew the customs uniform.

'I want to examine one of your charts, if you please,' said Hornblower. 'Will you show us the way to the cabin?'

The mate had not a suspicion in the world. He signed to his men to go on with their work and led the way down the brief companion to the after cabin. The mate entered, and politely Hornblower thrust the pilot in next, before him. It was a tiny cabin, but there was sufficient room to be safe when they were at the farther end. He stood by the door and brought out his two pistols.

'If you make a sound,' he said, and excitement rippled his lips into a snarl, 'I will kill you.'

They simply stood and stared at him, but at last the pilot opened his mouth to speak – speech was irrepressible with him.

'Silence!' snapped Hornblower.

He moved far enough into the room to allow Brown and Bush to enter after him.

'Tie 'em up,' he ordered.

Belts and handkerchiefs and scarves did the work efficiently enough; soon the two men were gagged and helpless, their hands tied behind them.

'Under the table with 'em,' said Hornblower. 'Now, be ready for the two hands when I bring 'em down.'

He ran up on deck.

'Here, you two,' he snapped. 'I've some question to ask you. Come down with me.'

They put down their work and followed him meekly, to the cabin where Hornblower's pistols frightened them into silence. Brown ran on deck for a generous supply of line with which to bind them and to make the lashings of the other two more secure yet. Then he and Bush – neither of them had spoken as yet since the adventure began – looked to him for further orders.

'Watch 'em,' said Hornblower. 'I'll be back in five minutes with a crew. There'll be one more man at least to make fast.'

He went up to the quay again, and along to where the gangs of galley slaves were assembling, weary after their day's work of unloading. The ten chained men under the sergeant whom he addressed looked at him with lacklustre eyes, only wondering faintly what fresh misery this spruce colonel was bringing them.

'Sergeant,' he said. 'Bring your party down to my ship. There is work for them there.'

'Yes, Colonel,' said the sergeant.

He rasped an order at the weary men, and they followed Hornblower down the quay. Their bare feet made no sound, but the chain which ran from waist to waist clashed rhythmically with their stride.

'Bring them down on to the deck,' said Hornblower. 'Now come down into the cabin for your orders.'

It was all so easy, thanks to that uniform and star. Hornblower had to try hard not to laugh at the sergeant's bewilderment as they disarmed him and tied him up. It took no more than a significant gesture with Hornblower's pistol to make the sergeant indicate in which pocket was the key of the prisoner's chain.

'I'll have these men laid out under the table, if you please, Mr Bush,' said Hornblower. 'All except the pilot. I want him on deck.'

The sergeant and the mate and the two hands were laid out, none too gently, and Hornblower went out on deck while the others dragged the pilot after him; it was nearly quite dark now, with only the moon shining. The galley slaves were squatting listlessly on the hatch-coaming. Hornblower addressed them quietly. Despite his difficulty with the language, his boiling excitement conveyed itself to them.

'I can set you men free,' he said. 'There will be an end of beatings and slavery if you will do what I order. I am an English officer, and I am going to sail this ship to England. Does anyone not want to come?'

There was a little sigh from the group; it was as if they could not believe they were hearing aright – probably they could not.

'In England,' went on Hornblower, 'you will be rewarded. There will be a new life awaiting you.'

Now at last they were beginning to understand that they had not been brought on board the cutter for further toil, that there really was a chance of freedom.

'Yes, sir,' said a voice.

'I am going to unfasten your chain,' said Hornblower. 'Remember this. There is to be no noise. Sit still until you are told what to do.'

He fumbled for the padlock in the dim light, unlocked it and snapped it open – it was pathetic, the automatic gesture with which the first man lifted his arms. He was accustomed to being locked and unlocked daily, like an animal. Hornblower set free each man in turn, and the chain clanked on the deck; he stood back with his hands on the butts of his pistols ready in case of trouble, but there was no sign of any. The men stood dazed – the transition from slavery to freedom had taken no more than three minutes.

Hornblower felt the movement of the cutter under his feet as the wind swung her; she was bumping gently against the fends-off hung between her and the quay. A glance over the side confirmed his conclusions – the tide had not yet begun to ebb. There were still some minutes to wait, and he turned to Brown, standing restless aft of the mainmast with the pilot sitting miserably at his feet.

'Brown,' he said quietly, 'run down to our boat and bring me my parcel of clothes. Run along now – what are you waiting for?'

Brown went unhappily. It seemed dreadful to him that his captain should waste precious minutes over recovering his clothes, and should even trouble to think of them. But Hornblower was not as mad as he might appear. They could not start until the tide turned, and Brown might as well be employed fetching clothes as standing fidgeting. For once in his life Hornblower had no intention of posing before his subordinates. His head was clear despite his excitement.

'Thank you,' he said, as Brown returned, panting with the canvas bag. 'Get me my uniform coat out.'

He stripped off his colonel's tunic and put on the coat which Brown held for him, experiencing a pleasant thrill as his fingers fastened the buttons with their crown and anchor. The coat was sadly crumpled, and the gold lace bent and broken, but still it was a uniform, even though the last time he had worn it was months ago when they had been capsized in the Loire. With this coat on his back he could no longer be accused of being a spy, and should their attempt result in failure and recapture it would shelter both himself and his subordinates. Failure and recapture were likely possibilities, as his logical brain told him, but secret murder now was not. The stealing of the cutter would attract sufficient public attention to make that impossible. Already he had bettered his position – he could not be shot as a spy nor be quietly strangled in prison. If he were recaptured now he could only be tried on the old charge of violation of the laws of war, and Hornblower felt that his recent exploits might win him sufficient public sympathy to make it impolitic for Bonaparte to press even that charge.

It was time for action now. He took a belaying pin from the rail, and walked up slowly to the seated pilot, weighing the instrument meditatively in his hand.

'Monsieur,' he said, 'I want you to pilot this ship out to sea.'

The pilot goggled up at him in the faint moonlight.

'I cannot,' he gabbled. 'My professional honour – my duty –'

Hornblower cut him short with a menacing gesture of the belaying pin.

'We are going to start now,' he said. 'You can give instructions or not, as you choose. But I tell you this, monsieur. The moment this ship touches ground, I will beat your head into a paste with this.'

Hornblower eyed the white face of the pilot – his moustache was lopsided and ridiculous now after his rough treatment. The man's eyes were on the belaying pin with which Hornblower was tapping the palm of his hand, and Hornblower felt a little thrill of triumph. The threat of a pistol bullet through the head would not have been sufficient for this imaginative southerner. But the man could picture so clearly the crash of the belaying pin upon his skull, and the savage blows which would beat him to death, that the argument Hornblower had selected was the most effective one.

'Yes, monsieur,' said the pilot, weakly.

'Right,' said Hornblower. 'Brown, lash him to the rail, there. Then we can start. Mr Bush, will you take the tiller, if you please?'

The necessary preparations were brief; the convicts were led to the halliards and the ropes put in their hands, ready to haul on the word of command. Hornblower and Brown had so often before had experience in pushing raw crews into their places, thanks to the all-embracing activities of the British press-gangs, and it was good to see that Brown's French, eked out by the force of his example, was sufficient for the occasion.

'Cut the warps, sir?' volunteered Brown.

'No. Cast them off,' snapped Hornblower.

Cut warps left hanging to the bollards would be a sure proof of a hurried and probably illegal departure; to cast them off meant possibly delaying inquiry and pursuit by a few more minutes, and every minute of delay might be precious in the uncertain future. The first of the ebb was tightening the ropes now, simplifying the business of getting away from the quay. To handle the tiny fore-and-aft rigged ship was an operation calling for little either of the judgement or of the brute strength which a big square rigger would demand, and the present circumstances – the wind off the quay and the ebbing tide – made the only precaution necessary that of casting off the stern warp before the bow, as Brown understood as clearly as Hornblower. It happened in the natural course of events, for Hornblower had to fumble in the dim light to disentangle the clove hitches with which some French sailor had made fast, and Brown had completed his share long before him. The push of the tide was swinging the cutter away from the quay. Hornblower, in the uncertain light, had to time his moment for setting sail, making allowance for the unreliability of his crew, the eddy along the quayside, the tide and the wind.

'Hoist away,' said Hornblower, and then, to the men, 'Tirez'.

Mainsail and jib rose, to the accompaniment of the creaking of the blocks. The sails flapped, bellied, flapped again. Then they filled, and Bush at the tiller – the cutter steered with a tiller, not a wheel – felt a steady pressure. The cutter was gathering way; she was changing from a dead thing to a live. She heeled the tiniest fraction to the breeze with a subdued creaking of her cordage, and simultaneously Hornblower heard a little musical chuckle from the bows as her forefoot bubbled through the water. He picked up the belaying pin again, and in three strides was at the pilot's side, balancing the instrument in his hand.

'To the right, monsieur,' gabbled the individual. 'Keep well to the right.'

'Port your helm, Mr Bush. We're taking the starboard channel,' said Hornblower, and then, translating the further hurried instructions of the pilot. 'Meet her! Keep her at that!'

The cutter glided on down the river in the faint moonlight. From the bank of the river she must make a pretty picture – no one would guess that she was not setting forth on some quite legitimate expedition.

The pilot was saying something else now; Hornblower bent his ear to listen. It had regard to the advisability of having a man at work with the lead taking soundings, and Hornblower would not consider it for a moment. There were only Brown and himself who could do that, and they both might be wanted at any moment in case it should be necessary for the cutter to go about – moreover, there would be bound to be a muddle about fathoms and metres.

'No,' said Hornblower. 'You will have to do your work without that. And my promise still holds good.'

He tapped his palm with the belaying pin, and laughed. That laugh surprised him, it was so blood-curdling in its implications. Anyone hearing it would be quite sure that Hornblower was determined upon club-bing the pilot to death if they went aground. Hornblower asked himself if he were acting and was puzzled to discover that he could not answer the question. He could not picture himself killing a helpless man – and yet he could not be sure. This fierce, relentless determination that consumed him was something new to him, just as it always was. He was aware of the fact that once he had set his hand to a scheme he never allowed any consideration to stop his carrying it through, but he always looked upon himself as fatalistic or resigned. It was always startling to detect in himself qualities which he admired in other men. But it was sufficient, and satisfactory, for the moment, to know that the pilot was quite sure that he would be killed in an unpleasant fashion if the cutter should touch ground.

Within half a mile it was necessary to cross to the other side – it was amusing to note how this vast estuary repeated on a grand scale the characteristics of the upper river, where the clear channel serpentined from shore to shore between the sandbanks. At the pilot's warning Hornblower got his motley crew together in case it might be necessary to go about, but the precaution was needless. Closehauled, and with the tide running fast behind her, the cutter glided across, Hornblower and Brown at the sheets, and Bush at the tiller demonstrating once more what an accomplished seaman he was. They steadied her with the wind again over her quarter, Hornblower anxiously testing the direction of the wind and looking up at the ghostly sails.

'Monsieur,' pleaded the pilot. 'Monsieur, these cords are tight.'

Hornblower laughed again, horribly.

'They will serve to keep you awake, then,' he said.

His instinct had dictated the reply; his reason confirmed it. It would be best to show no hint of weakness towards this man who had it in his power to wreck everything – the more firmly the pilot was convinced of his captor's utter pitilessness the less chance there was of his playing them false. Better that he should endure the pain of tight ligatures than that three men should risk imprisonment and death. And suddenly Hornblower remembered the four other men – the sergeant and the mate and the two hands – who lay gagged and bound in the cabin. They must be highly uncomfortable, and probably fairly near to suffocation. It could not be helped. No one could be spared for a moment from the deck to go below and attend them. There they must lie until there was no hope of rescue for them.

He found himself feeling sorry for them, and put the feeling aside. Naval history teemed with stories of recaptured prizes, in which the prisoners had succeeded in overpowering weak prize crews. He was going to run no risk of that. It was interesting to note how his mouth set itself hard at the thought without his own volition; and it was equally interesting to observe how his reluctance to go home and face the music reacted contrariwise upon his resolution to see this affair through. He did not want to fail, and the thought that he might be glad of failure because of the postponement of the settlement of his affairs only made him more set in his determination not to fail.

'I will loosen the cords,' he said to the pilot, 'when we are off Noirmoutier. Not before.'

14

They were off Noirmoutier at dawn, with the last dying puff of wind. The grey light found them becalmed and enwreathed in a light haze which drifted in patches over the calm surface of the sea, awaiting the rising of the sun to dissipate it. Hornblower looked round him as the details became more clear. The galley slaves were all asleep on the foredeck, huddled together for warmth like pigs in a sty, with Brown squatting on the hatch beside them, his chin on his hand. Bush still stood at the tiller, betraying no fatigue after his sleepless night; he held the tiller against his hip with his wooden leg braced against a ring bolt. Against the rail the pilot drooped in his bonds; his face which yesterday had been plump and pink was this morning drawn and grey with pain and fatigue.

With a little shudder of disgust Hornblower cut him loose.

'I keep my promise, you see,' he said, but the pilot only dropped to the deck, his face distorted with pain, and a minute later he was groaning with the agony of returning circulation.

The big mainsail boom came inboard with a clatter as the sail flapped.

'I can't hold the course, sir,' said Bush.

'Very well,' said Hornblower.

He might have expected this. The gentle night wind

which had wafted them down the estuary was just the sort to die away with the dawn, leaving them becalmed. But had it held for another half hour, had they made another couple of miles of progress, they would be far safer. There lay Noirmoutier to port, and the mainland astern; through the shredding mist he could make out the gaunt outlines of the semaphore station on the mainland – sixteen years ago he had been second in command of the landing party which Pellew had sent ashore to destroy it. The islands were all heavily garrisoned now, with big guns mounted, as a consequence of the incessant English raids. He scanned the distance which separated them from Noirmoutier, measuring it with his eye – they were out of big gun range, he fancied, but the tide might easily drift them in closer. He even suspected, from what he remembered of the set of the tides, that there was danger of their being drifted into the Bay of Bourgneuf.

'Brown,' he called, sharply. 'Wake those men up. Set them to work with the sweeps.'

On either side of every gun was a thole for a sweep, six on each side of the ship; Brown shoved his bleary-eyed crew into their positions and showed them how to get out the big oars, with the long rope joining the looms.

'One, two, three, pull!' shouted Brown.

The men put their weight on the oars; the blades bubbled ineffectively through the still water.

'One, two, three, pull! One, two, three, pull!'

Brown was all animation, gesticulating, running from man to man beating time with his whole body. Gradually the cutter gathered way, and as she began to move the oar blades began to bite upon the water with more effect.

'One, two, three, pull!'

It did not matter that Brown was counting time in English, for there was no mistaking his meaning, nor the meaning of the convulsive movements of his big body.

'Pull!'

The galley slaves sought for foothold on the deck as they tugged; Brown's enthusiasm was infectious, so that one or two of them even raised their voices in a cracked cheer as they leaned back. Now the cutter was perceptibly moving; Bush swung the tiller over, felt the rudder bite, and steadied her on her course again. She rose and fell over the tiny swell with a clattering of blocks.

Hornblower looked away from the straining men over the oily sea. If he had been lucky he might have found one of the ships of the blockading squadron close inshore – often they would come right in among the islands to beard Bonaparte. But today there was no sail in sight. He studied the grim outlines of the island for signs of life. Even as he looked the gallows-like arms of the semaphore station on the mainland sprang up to attention. They made no further movement, and Hornblower guessed that they were merely announcing the operators' readiness to receive a message from the station further inshore invisible to him – he could guess the purport of the message. Then the arms started signalling, moving jerkily against the blue sky, transmitting a brief reply to the interior. Another period of quiescence, and then Hornblower saw the signal arms swing round towards him – previously they had been nearly in profile. Automatically he turned towards Noirmoutier, and he saw the tiny speck of the flag at the masthead there dip in acknowledgement. Noirmoutier was ready to receive orders from the land. Round and round spun the arms of the semaphore; up and down went the flag in acknowledgement of each sentence.

Near the foot of the mast appeared a long jet of white smoke, rounding off instantly into a ball, and one after the other four fountains of water leaped from the glassy surface of the sea as a shot skipped over it, the dull report following after. The nearest fountain was a full half mile away, so that they were comfortably out of range.

'Make those men pull!' roared Hornblower to Brown.

He could guess what would be the next move. Under her sweeps the cutter was making less than a mile in the hour, and all day long they would be in danger, unless a breeze came, and his straining eye could see no hint of a breeze on the calm surface of the sea, nor in the vivid blue of the morning sky. At any moment boats crowded with men would be putting off towards them – boats whose oars would move them far faster than the cutter's sweeps. There would be fifty men in each, perhaps a gun mounted in the bows as well. Three men with the doubtful aid of a dozen galley slaves could not hope to oppose them.

'Yes I can, by God,' said Hornblower to himself.

As he sprang into action he could see the boats heading out from the tip of the island, tiny dots upon the surface of the sea. The garrison must have turned out and bundled into the boats immediately on receiving the order from the land.

'Pull!' shouted Brown.

The sweeps groaned on the tholes, and the cutter lurched under the impulse.

Hornblower had cleared away the aftermost six-pounder on the port side. There was shot in the locker under the rail, but no powder.

'Keep the men at work, Brown,' he said, 'and watch the pilot.'

'Aye aye, sir,' said Brown.

He stretched out a vast hand and took hold of the pilot's collar, while Hornblower dived into the cabin. One of the four prisoners there had writhed and wriggled his way to the foot of the little companion – Hornblower trod on him in his haste. With a curse he dragged him out of the way; as he expected there was a hatchway down into the lazarette. Hornblower jerked it open and plunged through; it was nearly dark, for the only light was what filtered through the cabin skylight and down the hatchway, and he stumbled and blundered upon the piled-up stores inside. He steadied himself; whatever the need for haste there was no profit in panic. He waited for his eyes to grow accustomed to the darkness, while overhead he could hear Brown still bellowing and the sweeps still groaning on the tholes. Then in the bulkhead before him he saw what he sought, a low doorway with a glass panel, which must indicate the magazine – the gunner would work in there by the light of a lantern shining through.

He heaved the piled-up stores out of his way, sweating in his haste and the heat, and wrenched open the door. Feeling about him in the tiny space, crouching nearly double, his hands fell upon four big hogsheads of gunpowder. He fancied he could feel the grittiness of gunpowder under his feet; any movement on his part might start a spark and blow the cutter to fragments – it was just like the French to be careless with explosives. He sighed with relief when his fingers encountered the paper – containers of ready charges. He had hoped to find them, but there had always been the chance that there were no cartridges available, and he had not been enamoured of the prospect of using a powder-ladle. He loaded himself with cartridges and backed out of the tiny magazine to the cabin, and sprang up on deck again, to the clear sunshine.

The boats were appreciably nearer, for they were no longer black specks but boats, creeping beetle-like over the surface towards them, three of them, already spaced out in their race to effect a recapture. Hornblower put down his cartridges upon the deck. His heart was pounding with his exertions and with excitement, and each successive effort that he made to steady himself seemed to grow less successful. It was one thing to think and plan and direct, to say 'Do this' or 'Go there', and it was quite another to have success dependent upon the cunning of his own fingers and the straightness of his own eye.

His sensations were rather similar to those he experienced when he had drunk a glass of wine too many – he knew clearly enough what he had to do, but his limbs were not quite as ready as usual to obey the orders of his brain. He fumbled more than once as he rigged the train-tackle of the gun.

That fumbling cured him; he rose from the task shaking his unsteadiness from him like Christian losing his burden of sin. He was cool now, set completely on the task in hand.

'Here, you,' he said to the pilot.

The pilot demurred for a moment, full of fine phrases regarding the impossibility of training a gun upon his fellow countrymen, but a sight of the alteration in Hornblower's expression reduced him to instant humble submission. Hornblower was unaware of the relentless ferocity of his glance, being only conscious of a momentary irritation at anyone crossing his will. But the pilot had thought that any further delay would lead to Hornblower's killing him, pitilessly – and the pilot may have been right. Between them they laid hold of the train-tackle and ran the gun back. Hornblower took out the tampion and went round to the breech; he twirled the elevating screw until his eye told him that the gun was at the maximum elevation at which it could be run out. He cocked the lock, and then, crouching over the gun so that the shadow of his body cut off the sunlight, jerked the lanyard. The spark was satisfactory.

He ripped open a cartridge, poured the powder into the muzzle of the gun, folded the paper into a wad, and rammed the charge home with the flexible rammer. A glance towards the boats showed that they were still probably out of range, so that he was not pressed for time. He devoted a few seconds to turning over the shot in the locker, selecting two or three of the roundest, and then strolled across the deck to the starboard side locker and made a selection from there. For long range work with a six-pounder he did not want shot that bounced about during its passage up the gun and was liable to fly off God-knew-where when it emerged. He rammed his eventual selection well down upon the wad – at this elevation there was no need for a second wad – and, ripping open a second cartridge, he primed the breach.

'Allons!' he snapped at the pilot, and then ran the gun up. Two men were the barest minimum crew for a six-pounder, but Hornblower's long slight body was capable of exerting extraordinary strength at the behest of his mind.

With a handspike he trained the gun round aft as far as possible. Even so, the gun did not point towards the leading boat, which lay far abaft the beam; the cutter would have to yaw to fire at her. Hornblower straightened himself up in the sunlight. Brown was chanting hoarsely at the galley slaves almost in his ear, and the aftermost sweep had been working right at his elbow, and he had not noticed either, so intent had he been on his task. For the cutter to yaw meant losing a certain amount of distance; he had to balance that certain loss against the chances of hitting a boat with a six-pounder ball at two thousand yards. It would not pay at present; it would be better to wait a little, for the range to shorten, but it was an interesting problem, even though it could have no exact solution in consequence of the presence of an unknown, which was the possibility of the coming of a wind.

Of that there was still no sign, long and anxiously though Hornblower stared over the glassy sea. As he looked round he caught the eye of Bush at the tiller directed anxiously at him – Bush was awaiting the order to yaw. Hornblower smiled at him and shook his head, resuming his study of the horizon, the distant islands, the unbroken expanse to seaward where lay freedom. A seagull was wheeling overhead, dazzling white against the blue, and crying plaintively. The cutter was nodding a little in the faint swell.

'Beggin' your pardon, sir,' said Brown in his ear. 'Beggin' your pardon, sir – Pull! – These men can't go on much longer, sir. Look at that one over there on the starboard side, sir – Pull!'

There could be no doubt of it; the men were swaying with fatigue as they reached forward with the long sweeps. Dangling from Brown's hand was a length of knotted cord; clearly he had already been using the most obvious argument to persuade them to work.

'Give 'em a bit of a rest, sir, and summat to eat an' drink, an' they'll go on all right, sir. Pull, you bastards! They haven't had no breakfast, sir, nor no supper yesterday.'

'Very good,' said Hornblower. 'You can rest 'em and get 'em fed. Mr Bush! Let her come slowly round.'

He bent over the gun, oblivious at once to the clatter of the released sweeps as the galley slaves ceased work, just as he was oblivious that he himself had not eaten or drunk or slept since yesterday. At the touch of the tiller and with her residual way the cutter turned slowly. The black mass of a boat appeared in the V of the dispart sight, and he waved his hand to Bush. The boat had disappeared again, and came back into his field of vision as Bush checked the turn with the tiller, but not quite in alignment with the gun. Hornblower eased the gun round with the handspike until the aim was true, drew himself up, and stepped out of the way of the recoil, lanyard in hand. Of necessity, he was far more doubtful of the range than of the direction, and it was vital to observe the fall of the shot. He took note of the motion of the cutter on the swell, waited for the climax of the roll, and jerked the lanyard. The gun roared out and recoiled past him; he sprang sideways to get clear of the smoke. The four seconds of the flight of the shot seemed to stretch out indefinitely, and then at last he saw the jet of water leap into brief existence, fully two hundred yards short and a hundred yards to the right. That was poor shooting.

He sponged out the gun and reloaded it, called the pilot to him with an abrupt gesture, and ran the gun out again. It was necessary, he realized, to get acquainted with the weapon if he wanted to do any fancy shooting with it, so that he made no alteration in elevation, endeavoured to lay the gun exactly as before, and jerked the lanyard at as nearly the same instant of the roll as possible. This time it appeared that the elevation was correct, for the shot pitched well up to the boat, but it was out to the right again, fifty yards off at least. It seemed likely that the gun, therefore, had a tendency to throw to the right. He trained the gun round a trifle to the left, and, still without altering the elevation, fired again. Too far to the left, and two hundred yards short again.

Hornblower told himself that a variation of two hundred yards in the fall of shot from a six-pounder at full elevation was only to be expected, and he knew it to be true, but that was cold comfort to him. The powder varied from charge to charge, the shot were never truly round, quite apart from the variations in atmospheric conditions and in the temperature of the gun. He set his teeth, aimed and fired again. Short, and a trifle to the left. It was maddening.

'Breakfast, sir,' said Brown at his elbow.

Hornblower turned abruptly, and there was Brown with a tray, bearing a basin of biscuit, a bottle of wine, a jug of water, a pewter mug; the sight made Hornblower realize that he was intensely hungry and thirsty.

'What about you?' asked Hornblower.

'We're all right, sir,' said Brown.

The galley slaves were squatting on the deck wolfing bread and drinking water; so was Bush, over by the tiller. Hornblower discovered that his tongue and the roof of his mouth were dry as leather – his hands shook as he mixed water with wine and gulped it down. Beside the cabin skylight lay the four men who had been left in bonds in the cabin. Their hands were free now, although their feet were still bound. The sergeant and one of the seamen were noticeably pale.

'I took the liberty of bringing 'em up, sir,' said Brown. 'Those two was pretty nigh dead, 'cause o' their gags, sir. But they'll be all right soon, I fancy, sir.'

It had been thoughtless cruelty to leave them bound, thought Hornblower. But going back in his mind through the events of the night he could not think of any time until now when any attention could have been spared for them. In war there was always plenty of cruelty.

'These beggars,' said Brown, indicating the galley slaves, 'wanted to throw the sojer overboard when they saw 'im, sir.'

He grinned widely, as though that were very amusing. The remark opened a long vista of thought, regarding the miseries of the life of a galley slave and the brutalities of their guards.

'Yes,' said Hornblower, gulping down a morsel of biscuit and drinking again. 'You had better set 'em all to work at the sweeps.'

'Aye aye, sir. I had the same idea, beggin' your pardon, sir. We can have two watches with all these men.'

'Arrange it as you like,' said Hornblower, turning back to the gun.

The nearest boat was appreciably nearer now; Hornblower judged it advisable to make a small reduction in the elevation, and this time the shot pitched close to the boat, almost among the oars on one side, apparently.

'Beautiful, sir!' said Bush beside the tiller.

Hornblower's skin was prickling with sweat and powder smoke. He took off his gold laced coat, suddenly conscious of the heavy weight of the pistols in the side pockets; he proffered them to Bush, but the latter shook his head and grinned, pointing to the bell-mouthed blunderbuss on the deck beside him. That would be a far more efficacious weapon if there was trouble with their motley crew. For an exasperated moment Hornblower wondered what to do with the pistols, and finally laid them handy in the scuppers before sponging out and reloading the gun. The next shot was a close one, too – apparently the small reduction of range had had a profound effect on the accuracy of the gun. Hornblower saw the shot pitch close to the bows of the boat; it would be a matter of pure chance at that range if he scored an actual hit, for no gun could be expected to be accurate to fifty yards.

'Sweeps are ready, sir,' said Brown.

'Very good. Mr Bush, kindly lay a course so that I can keep that boat under fire.'

Brown was a pillar of strength. He had had rigged only the three foremost sweeps on each side, setting six men to work on them. The others were herded together forward, ready to relieve the men at work when they were tired – six sweeps would only just give the big cutter steerage way, but continuous slow progress was preferable to an alternation of movement and passivity. What arguments he had used to persuade the four Frenchmen who were not galley slaves to work at the sweeps Hornblower judged it best not to inquire – it was sufficient that they were there, their feet hobbled, straining away at the sweeps while Brown gave them the time, his knotted rope's end dangling from his fist.

The cutter began to creep through the blue water again, the rigging rattling at each tug on the sweeps. To make the chase as long as possible she should have turned her stern to her pursuers, instead of keeping them on her quarter. But Hornblower had decided that the chance of scoring a hit with the gun was worth the loss in distance – a decision of whose boldness he was painfully aware and which he had to justify. He bent over the gun and aimed carefully, and this time the shot flew wide again. Watching the splash from the rail Hornblower felt a surge of exasperation. For a moment he was tempted to hand the gun over to Bush, for him to try his hand, but he put the temptation aside. In the face of stark reality, without allowing false modesty to enter into the debate, he could rely on himself to lay a gun better than Bush could.

'Tirez!' he snapped at the pilot, and between them they ran the gun up again.

The pursuing boats, creeping black over the blue sea, had shown no sign so far of being dismayed by the bombardment to which they were being subjected. Their oars kept steadily at work, and they maintained resolutely a course which would cut the *Witch of Endor*'s a mile or so further on. They were big boats, all three of them, carrying at least a hundred and fifty men between them – only one of them need range alongside to do the business. Hornblower fired again and then again, doggedly, fighting down the bitter disappointment at each successive miss. The range was little over a thousand yards now, he judged – what he would call in an official report 'long cannon shot'. He hated those black boats creeping onward, immune, threatening his life and liberty, just as he hated this cranky gun which would not shoot the same two rounds running. The sweat was making his shirt stick to him, and the powder-grains were irritating his skin.

At the next shot there was no splash; Hornblower could see no sign of its fall anywhere. Then he saw the leading boat swing half round, and her oars stop moving.

'You've hit her, sir,' called Bush.

Next moment the boat straightened on her course again, her oars hard at work. That was disappointing – it had hardly been likely that a ship's long boat could survive a direct hit from a six-pounder ball without injury to her fighting ability, but it was possible, all the same. Hornblower felt for the first time a sense of impending failure. If the hit he had scored with such difficulty was of no avail, what was the sense in continuing the struggle? Then, doggedly, he bent over the gun again, staring along the sights to allow for the small amount of right hand bias which the gun exhibited. Even as he looked he saw the leading boat cease rowing again. She wavered and then swung round, signalling wildly to the other boats. Hornblower trained the gun round upon her and fired again and missed, but he could see that she was perceptibly lower in the water. The other boats drew up alongside her, evidently to transfer her crew.

'Port a point, Mr Bush!' yelled Hornblower – already the group of boats was out of the field of fire of the gun, and yet was far too tempting a mark to ignore. The French pilot groaned as he helped to run the gun up, but Hornblower had no time for his patriotic protests. He sighted carefully, and fired. Again there was no sign of a splash – the ball had taken effect, but presumably upon the boat which had already been hit, for immediately afterwards the other two drew away from their waterlogged fellow to resume the pursuit.

Brown was changing over the men at the sweeps – Hornblower remembered now that he had heard him cheering hoarsely when he had scored his hit – and Hornblower found a second in which to admire his masterful handling of the men, prisoners of war and escaping slaves alike. There was time for admiration, but no time for envy. The pursuers were changing their tactics – one boat was heading straight at them, while the other, diverging a little, was still heading to intercept them. The reason was soon obvious, for from the bows of the former boat came a puff of smoke, and a cannon-ball raised a splash from the surface of the water on the cutter's quarter and skipped past the stern.

Hornblower shrugged his shoulders at that – a three-pounder boat gun, fired from a platform far more unsteady even than the *Witch of Endor*, could hardly do them any harm at that range, and every shot meant delay in the pursuit. He trained his gun round upon the intercepting boat, fired, and missed. He was already taking aim again before the sound of the second shot from the boat gun reached his ears, and he did not trouble to find out where the ball went. His own shot fell close to its target, for the range was shortening and he was growing more experienced with the gun and more imbued with the rhythm of the long Atlantic swell which rocked the *Witch of Endor*. Three times he dropped a shot so close to the boat that the men at the oars must have been wetted by the splashes – each shot deserved to be a hit, he knew, but the incalculable residuum of variables in powder and ball and gun made it a matter of chance just where the ball fell in a circle of fifty yards, radius, however well aimed. Ten guns properly controlled, and fired together in a broadside, would do the business, but there was no chance of firing ten guns together.

There was a crash from forward, a fountain of splinters from the base of a stanchion, and a shot scarred the deck diagonally close beside the fore hatchway.

'No you don't,' roared Brown, leaping forward with his rope's end. 'Keep pulling, you bastard!'

He jerked the scared galley slave who had dropped his sweep – the shot must have missed him by no more than a yard – back into position.

'Pull!' he shouted, standing, magnificent in his superb physique, right in the midst of them, the weary ones lying on the deck, the others sweating at the sweeps, the knotted rope swinging from his hand. He was like a lion tamer in a cage. Hornblower could see there was no need for him and his pistols, and he bent again, this time with a real twinge of envy, over his gun.

The boat which was firing at them had not closed in at all – if anything she had fallen a trifle back – but the other one was far nearer by now. Hornblower could see the individual men in her, the dark heads and the brown shoulders. Her oars were still for the moment, and there was some movement in her, as if they were rearranging the men at the oars. Now she was in motion again, and moving far faster, and heading straight at them. The officer in charge, having worked up as close as this, had double-banked his oars so as to cover the last, most dangerous zone with a rush, pouring out the carefully conserved energy of his men prodigally in his haste to come alongside.

Hornblower estimated the rapidly diminishing range, twirled the elevating screw, and fired. The shot hit the water ten yards from her bows and must have ricochetted clean over her. He sponged and loaded and rammed – a miss-fire now, he told himself, would be fatal, and he forced himself to go through the routine with all the exactness he had employed before. The sights of the gun were looking straight at the bows of the boat, it was point blank range. He jerked the lanyard and sprang instantly to reload without wasting time by seeing where the shot went. It must have passed close over the heads of the men at the oars, for when he looked along the sights again there she was, still heading straight at him. A tiny reduction in elevation, and he stepped aside and jerked the lanyard. He was dragging at the train tackles before he could look again. The bows of the boat had opened like a fan. In the air above her there was a black dot – a water breaker, presumably, sent flying like a football by the impact of the shot, which had hit clean and square upon her stem at water level. Her bows were lifted a little out of the water, the loose stakes spread wide, and then they came down again and the water surged in, and she was gunwale deep in a flash, her bottom smashed, presumably, as well as her bows, by the passage of the shot.

Brown was cheering again, and Bush was capering as well as he could with a wooden leg while steering, and the little French pilot at his side pulling in his breath with a sharp hissing noise. There were black dots on the surface of the blue water where men struggled for their lives – it must be bitter cold and they would die quickly, those who could not find support on the shattered hull, but nothing could be done to help them. Already they had more prisoners than they could conveniently handle, and any delay would bring the other boat alongside them.

'Keep the men at work!' said Hornblower, harshly, to Brown, and unnecessarily. Then he bent to reload the gun once more.

'What course, sir?' asked Bush, from the tiller. He wanted to know if he should steer so as to allow fire to be opened on the third boat, which had ceased firing now and was pulling hastily towards the wreck.

'Keep her as she is,' snapped Hornblower. He knew

perfectly well that the boat would not annoy them further; having seen two of her fellows sunk and being of necessity vastly overcrowded she would turn back sooner than maintain the contest. And so it proved. After the boat had picked up the survivors they saw her swing round and head towards Noirmoutier, followed by a derisive cheer from Brown.

Hornblower could look round him now. He walked aft to the taffrail beside Bush – it was curious how much more natural it felt to be there than at the gun – and scanned the horizon. During the fight the cutter had made very decided progress under her sweeps. The mainland was lost in the faint haze; Noirmoutier was already far behind. But there was still no sign of a breeze. They were still in danger – if darkness should find them where boats could reach them from the islands a night attack would tell a very different story. They needed every yard they could gain, and the men must go on slaving at the sweeps all through the day, all through the night too, if necessary.

He was conscious now that he ached in every joint after the frantic exertions of serving the gun the whole morning, and he had had a whole night without sleep – so had Bush, so had Brown. He felt that he stank of sweat and smoke, and his skin tingled with powder grains. He wanted rest, yet automatically he walked over to make the gun secure again, to put the unused cartridges out of harm's way, and to repocket the pistols which he noticed reproaching his carelessness from the scuppers.

15

At midnight, and not before, a tiny breeze came whispering over the misty surface of the water, at first merely swinging over the big mainsail and setting the rigging chattering, but then breathing more strongly until the sails could catch it and hold it, filling out in the darkness until Hornblower could give the word for the exhausted men at the sweeps to abandon their labour and the cutter could glide on with almost imperceptible motion, so slowly that there was hardly a bubble at her bows, yet even at that faster than the sweeps had moved her. Out of the east came that breath of wind, steady even though feeble; Hornblower could feel hardly any pull as he handled the mainsheet, and yet the cutter's big area of canvas was able to carry her graceful hull forward over the invisible surface as though in a dream.

It was like a dream indeed – weariness and lack of sleep combined to make it so for Hornblower, who moved about his tasks in a misty unreality which matched the misty darkness of the sea. The galley slaves and prisoners could lie and sleep – there was no fear of trouble from them at present, when they had spent ten hours out of the last twenty pulling at the sweeps with hands which by nightfall were running with blood, but there was no sleep for him nor for Bush and Brown. His voice sounded strange and distant in his own ears, like that of a stranger speaking from another room, as he issued his orders; the very hands with which he held the ropes seemed not to belong to him. It was as if there was a cleavage between the brain with which he was trying to think and the body which condescended to obey him.

Somewhere to the northwest lay the fleet which maintained its unsleeping watch over Brest; he had laid the cutter on a northwesterly course with the wind comfortably on her quarter, and if he could not find the Channel fleet he would round Ushant and sail the cutter to England. He knew all this – it made it more like a dream than ever that he could not believe it although he knew it. The memory of Marie de Graçay's upper boudoir, or of his battle for life in the flood-water of the Loire, was far more real to him than this solid little ship whose deck he trod and whose mainsheet he was handling. Setting a course for Bush to steer was like playing a make-believe game with a child. He told himself desperately that this was not a new phenomenon, that often enough before he had noticed that although he could dispense with one night's sleep without missing it greatly, on the second in succession his imagination began to play tricks with him, but it did not help to clear his mind.

He came back to Bush at the tiller, when the faint binnacle light made the lieutenant's face just visible in the darkness; Hornblower was even prepared to enter into conversation in exchange for a grasp at reality.

'Tired, Mr Bush?' he asked.

'No, sir. Of course not. But how is it with you, sir?'

Bush had served with his captain through too many fights to have an exaggerated idea of his strength.

'Well enough, thank you.'

'If this breeze holds, sir,' said Bush, realizing that this was one of the rare occasions when he was expected to make small talk with his captain, 'we'll be up to the fleet in the morning.'

'I hope so,' said Hornblower.

'By God, sir,' said Bush, 'what will they say of this in England?'

Bush's expression was rapt. He was dreaming of fame, of promotion, for his captain as much as for himself.

'In England?' said Hornblower vaguely.

He had been too busy to dream any dreams himself, to think about what the British public, sentimental as always, would think of an escaping British captain retaking almost single-handed a captured ship of war and returning in her in triumph. And he had seized the *Witch of Endor* in the first place merely because the opportunity had presented itself, and because it was the most damaging blow he could deal the enemy; since the seizure he had been at first too busy, and latterly too tired, to appreciate the dramatic quality of his action. His distrust of himself, and his perennial pessimism regarding his career, would not allow him to think of himself as dramatically successful. The unimaginative Bush could appreciate the potentialities better than he could.

'Yes, sir,' said Bush, eagerly – even with tiller and compass and wind claiming so much of his attention he could be loquacious at this point – 'It'll look fine in the *Gazette*, this recapture of the *Witch*. Even the *Morning Chronicle*, sir –'

The *Morning Chronicle* was a thorn in the side of the government, ever ready to decry a victory or make capital of a defeat. Hornblower remembered how during the bitter early days of his captivity at Rosas he had worried about what the *Morning Chronicle* would say regarding his surrender of the *Sutherland*.

He felt sick now, suddenly. His mind was active enough now. Most of its vagueness must have been due, he told himself, because he had been refusing in cowardly fashion to contemplate the future. Until this night everything had been uncertain – he might have been recaptured at any moment, but now, as sure as anything could be at sea, he would see England again. He would have to stand his trial for the loss of the *Sutherland*, and face a court martial, after eighteen years of service. The court might find him guilty of not having done his utmost in the presence of the enemy, and for that there was only one penalty, death – that Article of War did not end, as others did, with the mitigating words 'or such less penalty –'. Byng had been shot fifty years before under that Article of War.

Absolved on that account, the wisdom of his actions in command of the *Sutherland* might still be called into question. He might be found guilty of errors of judgement in hazarding his ship in a battle against quadruple odds, and be punished by anything from dismissal from the service, which would make him an outcast and a beggar, down to a simple reprimand which would merely wreck his career. A court martial was always a hazardous ordeal from which few emerged unscathed – Cochrane, Sydney Smith, half a dozen brilliant captains had suffered damage at the hands of a court martial, and the friendless Captain Hornblower might be the next.

And a court martial was only one of the ordeals that awaited him. The child must be three months old now; until this moment he had never been able to think clearly about the child – boy or girl, healthy or feeble. He was torn with anxiety for Maria – and yet, gulping at the pill of reality, he forced himself to admit that he did not want to go back to Maria. He did not want to. It had been in mad jealousy of the moment, when he heard of Lady Barbara's marriage to Admiral Leighton, that the child had been conceived. Maria in England, Marie in France – his conscience was in a turmoil about both of them, and underlying the turmoil was an unregenerate hunger for Lady Barbara which had remained quiescent during his preoccupation but which he knew would grow into an unrelenting ache, an internal cancer, the moment his other troubles ceased, if ever they did.

Bush was still babbling away happily beside him at the tiller. Hornblower heard the words, and attached no meaning to them.

'Ha – h'm,' he said. 'Quite so.'

He could find no satisfaction in the simple pleasures Bush had been in ecstasy about – the breath of the sea, the feeling of a ship's deck underfoot – not now, not with all these bitter thoughts thronging his mind. The harshness of his tone checked Bush in the full career of his artless and unwonted chatter, and the lieutenant pulled himself up abruptly. Hornblower thought it was absurd that Bush should still cherish any affection for him after the cutting cruelty with which he sometimes used him. Bush was like a dog, thought Hornblower bitterly – too cynical for the moment to credit Bush with any perspicacity at all – like a dog, coming fawning to the hand that beat him. Hornblower despised himself as he walked forward again to the mainsheet, to a long, long, period of a solitary black hell of his own.

There was just the faintest beginning of daylight, the barest pearly softening of the sombreness of night, a greyness instead of a blackness in the haze, when Brown came aft to Hornblower.

'Beggin' your pardon, sir, but I fancy I see the loom of something out there just now. On the port bow, sir – there, d'you see it, sir?'

Hornblower strained his eyes through the darkness. Perhaps there was a more solid nucleus to the black mist out there, a tiny something. It came and went as his eyes grew tired.

'What d'you make of it, Brown?'

'I thought it was a ship, sir, when I first saw it, but in this haze, sir –'

There was a faint chance she might be a French ship of war – it was about as likely as to find the king unguarded when leading from a suit of four to an ace. Much the most likely chance was that she was an English ship of war, and the next most likely that she was a merchantman. The safest course was to creep down upon her from the windward, because the cutter, lying nearer the wind than any square-rigged ship could do, could escape if necessary the way she came, trusting to the mist and darkness and surprise to avoid being disabled before she got out of range.

'Mr Bush, I fancy there's a sail to leeward. Put the cutter before the wind and run down to her, if you please. Be ready to go about if I give the word. Jib-sheet, Brown.'

Hornblower's head was clear again now, in the face of a possible emergency. He regretted the quickening of his pulse – uncertainly always had that effect. The cutter steadied upon her new course, creeping before the wind over the misty water, mainsail boom far out to port. Hornblower experienced a moment's doubt in case Bush was sailing her by the lee, but he would not allow himself to call a warning – he knew he could trust a sailor of Bush's ability not to risk a gibe in an emergency of this sort. He strained his eyes through the darkness; the mist was patchy, coming and going as he looked, but that was a ship without any doubt. She was under topsails alone – that made it almost certain that she was an English ship of war, one of the fleet which maintained unceasing watch over Brest. Another patch of mist obscured her again, and by the time they had run through it she was appreciably nearer, and dawn was at hand – her sails were faint grey in the growing light. Now they were close upon her.

Suddenly the stillness was rent by a hail, high-pitched, penetrating, its purity of quality almost unspoilt by the speaking trumpet – the voice which uttered it was trained in clarity in Atlantic gales.

'Cutter ahoy! What cutter's that?'

At the sound of the English speech Hornblower relaxed. There was no need now to go about, to claw to windward, to seek shelter in the mist. But on the other hand all the unpleasantness of the future which he had been visualizing was certain now. He swallowed hard, words failing him for the moment.

'What cutter's that?' repeated the hail, impatiently.

Unpleasant the future might be; he would fly his colours to the last, and if his career were ending, he would end it with a joke.

'His Britannic Majesty's armed cutter *Witch of Endor*, Captain Horatio Hornblower. What ship's that?'

'*Triumph*, Captain Sir Thomas Hardy – *what* did you say that cutter was?'

Hornblower grinned to himself. The officer of the watch in the strange sail had begun his reply automatically; it was only after he had stated the names of his ship and captain that it had suddenly dawned upon him that the cutter's statement was quite incredible. The *Witch of Endor* had been a prize to the French for nearly a year, and Captain Horatio Hornblower had been dead six months.

Hornblower repeated what he had said before; both Bush and Brown were chuckling audibly at a joke which appealed to them forcibly indeed.

'Come under my lee, and no tricks, or I'll sink you,' hailed the voice.

From the cutter they could hear the guns being run out in the *Triumph;* Hornblower could picture the bustle on board, hands being turned up, the captain being called – Sir Thomas Hardy must be Nelson's late flag captain at Trafalgar, two years Hornblower's senior in the captains' list. Hornblower had known him as a lieutenant, although since then their paths had hardly crossed. Bush eased the cutter under the stern of the two-decker, and brought her to the wind under her lee. Dawn was coming up fast now, and they could see the details of the ship, as she lay hove to, rolling in the swell, and a long shuddering sigh burst from Hornblower's breast. The sturdy beauty of the ship, the two yellow streaks along her sides, checkered with black gunports, the pendant at the main, the hands on the deck, the red coats of the marines, the boatswain's voice roaring at dilatory seamen – all the familiar sights and sounds of the Navy in which he had grown up moved him inexpressibly at this moment, the end of his long captivity and flight.

The *Triumph* had launched a boat, which came dancing rapidly over to them, and a young midshipman swung himself dexterously on board, dirk at his hip, arrogant suspicion on his face, four seamen at his back with pistols and cutlasses.

'What's all this?' demanded the midshipman. His glance swept the cutter's deck, observing the sleepy prisoners rubbing their eyes, the wooden-legged civilian at the tiller, the bare-headed man in a King's coat awaiting him.

'You call me "sir",' barked Hornblower, as he had done to midshipmen ever since he became a lieutenant.

The midshipman eyed the gold laced coat – undoubtedly it was trimmed in the fashion of the coat of a captain of more than three years' seniority, and the man who wore it carried himself as though he expected deference.

'Yes, sir,' said the midshipman, a little abashed.

'That is Lieutenant Bush at the tiller. You will remain here with these men under his orders, while I go to interview your captain.'

'Aye aye, sir,' said the midshipman, stiffening to attention.

The boat bore Hornblower to the *Triumph*'s side; the coxswain made the four-finger gesture which indicated the arrival of a captain, but marines and side-boys were not in attendance as Hornblower went up the side – the Navy could not risk wasting her cherished compliments on possible impostors. But Hardy was there on deck, his huge bulk towering over everyone round him; Hornblower saw the expression of his beefy face alter as he saw him.

'Good God, it's Hornblower all right,' said Hardy, striding forward, with his hand outstretched. 'Welcome back, sir. How do you come here, sir? How did you retake the *Witch*? How –'

What Hardy wanted to say was 'How have you risen from the grave?' but such a question seemed to savour of impoliteness. Hornblower shook hands, and trod gratefully the quarterdeck of a ship of the line once more. His heart was too full for speech, or his brain was too numb with fatigue, and he could make no reply to Hardy's questioning.

'Come below to my cabin,' said Hardy, kindly – phlegmatic though he was, he still could just appreciate the other's difficulty.

There was more ease in the cabin, sitting on the cushioned locker under the portrait of Nelson that hung on the bulkhead, and with the timbers groaning faintly all round, and the blue sea visible through the great stern window. Hornblower told a little of what happened to him – not much, and not in detail; only half a dozen brief sentences, for Hardy was not a man with much use for words. He listened with attention, pulling at his whiskers, and nodding at each point.

'There was a whole *Gazette*,' he remarked, 'about the attack in Rosas Bay. They brought Leighton's body back for burial in St Paul's.'

The cabin swam round Hornblower; Hardy's homely face and magnificent whiskers vanished in a mist.

'He was killed, then?' Hornblower asked.

'He died of his wounds at Gibraltar.'

So Barbara was a widow – had been one for six months now.

'Have you heard anything of my wife?' asked Hornblower. The question was a natural one to Hardy, little use though he himself had for women; and he could see no connexion between it and the preceding conversation.

'I remember reading that she was awarded a Civil List pension by the government when the news of – of your death arrived.'

'No other news? There was a child coming.'

'None that I know of. I have been four months in this ship.'

Hornblower's head sunk on his breast. The news of Leighton's death added to the confusion of his mind. He did not know whether to be pleased or sorry about it. Barbara would be as unattainable to him as ever, and perhaps there would be all the jealous misery to endure of her remarriage.

'Now,' said Hardy. 'Breakfast?'

'There's Bush and my coxswain in the cutter,' said Hornblower. 'I must see that all is well with them first.'

16

A midshipman came into the cabin as they ate breakfast.

'The fleet's in sight from the masthead, sir,' he reported to Hardy.

'Very good.' As the midshipman went out again Hardy turned back to Hornblower. 'I must report your arrival to His Lordship.'

'Is he still in command?' asked Hornblower, startled. It was a surprise to him that the government had left Admiral Lord Gambier in command of the Channel Fleet for three years, despite the disastrous waste of opportunity at the Basque Roads.

'He hauls down his flag next month,' said Hardy, gloomily. Most officers turned gloomy when discussing 'Dismal Jimmy'. 'They whitewashed him at the court martial, and had to leave him his full three years.'

A shade of embarrassment appeared in Hardy's expression; he had let slip the mention of a court martial to a man who soon would endure the same ordeal.

'I suppose they had to,' said Hornblower, his train of thought following that of his fellow captain as he wondered if there would be any whitewash employed at his trial.

Hardy broke the embarrassed silence which followed.

'Would you care to come on deck with me?' he asked.

Over the horizon to leeward was appearing a long line of ships, closehauled. They were in rigid, regular line, and as Hornblower watched they went about in succession in perfect order, as if they were chained together. The Channel Fleet was at drill – eighteen years of drill at sea had given them their unquestioned superiority over any other fleet in the world.

'*Victory*'s in the van,' said Hardy, handing his glass to Hornblower. 'Signal midshipman! "*Triumph* to flag. Have on board –".'

Hornblower looked through the glass while Hardy dictated his message. The three-decker with her admiral's flag at the main was leading the long line of ships, the broad stripes on her side glistening in the sunlight. She had been Jervis's flagship at St Vincent, Hood's in the Mediterranean, Nelson's at Trafalgar. Now she was Dismal Jimmy's – a tragedy if ever there was one. Signal-hoists were soaring up to her yardarms; Hardy was busy dictating replies.

'The Admiral is signalling for you to go on board, sir,' he said at last, turning back to Hornblower. 'I trust you will do me the honour of making use of my barge?'

The *Triumph*'s barge was painted primrose yellow picked out with black, and so were the oarblades; her crew wore primrose-coloured jumpers with black neckcloths. As Hornblower took his seat, his hand still tingling with Hardy's handclasp, he reminded himself gloomily that he had never been able to afford to dress his barge's crew in a fancy rig-out; he always felt sore on the point. Hardy must be a wealthy man with his Trafalgar prize money and his pension as Colonel of Marines. He contrasted their situations – Hardy, a baronet, moneyed, famous, and he himself poor, undistinguished, and awaiting trial.

They piped the side for him in the *Victory*, as Admiralty regulations laid down – the marine guard at the present, the side-boys in white gloves to hand him up, the pipes of the boatswain's mates all a-twittering; and there was a captain on the quarterdeck ready to shake hands with him – odd, that was to Hornblower, seeing that soon he would be on trial for his life.

'I'm Calendar, Captain of the Fleet,' he said. 'His Lordship is below, waiting for you.'

He led the way below, extraordinarily affable.

'I was first of the *Amazon*,' he volunteered, 'when you were in *Indefatigable*. Do you remember me?'

'Yes,' said Hornblower. He had not risked a snub by saying so first.

'I remember you plainly,' said Calendar. 'I remember hearing what Pellew had to say about you.'

Whatever Pellew said about him would be favourable – he had owed his promotion to Pellew's enthusiastic recommendation – and it was pleasant of Calendar to remind him of it at this crisis of his career.

Lord Gambier's cabin was not nearly as ornate as Captain Hardy's had been – the most conspicuous item of furniture therein was the big brass-bound Bible lying on the table. Gambier himself, heavy-jowled, gloomy, was sitting by the stern window dictating to a clerk who withdrew on the arrival of the two captains.

'You can make your report verbally, sir, for the present,' said the Admiral.

Hornblower drew a deep breath and made the plunge. He sketched out the strategic situation at the moment when he took the *Sutherland* into action against the French squadron off Rosas. Only a sentence or two had to be devoted to the battle itself – these men had fought in battles themselves and could fill in the gaps. He described the whole crippled mass of ships drifting helpless up Rosas Bay to where the guns of the fortress awaited them, and the gunboats creeping out under oars.

'One hundred and seventeen killed,' said Hornblower. 'One hundred and forty-five wounded, of whom forty-four died before I was removed from Rosas.'

'My God!' said Calendar. It was not the deaths in hospital which called forth the exclamation – that was a usual proportion – but the total casualty list. Far more than half the crew of the *Sutherland* had been put out of action before surrendering.

'Thompson in the *Leander* lost ninety-two out of three hundred, my lord,' he said. Thompson had surrendered the *Leander* to a French ship of the line off Crete after a defence which had excited the admiration of all England.

'I was aware of it,' answered Gambier. 'Please go on, Captain.'

Hornblower told of how he witnessed the destruction of the French squadron, of how Caillard arrived to take him to Paris, of his escape, first from his escort and then from drowning. He made only a slight mention of Count de Graçay and of his voyage down the Loire – that was not an admiral's business – but he descended to fuller details when he told of his recapture of the *Witch of Endor*. Details here were of importance, because in the course of the manifold activities of the British Navy it might easily happen that a knowledge of harbour arrangements at Nantes and of the navigational difficulties of the lower Loire might be useful.

'Good God Almighty, man,' said Calendar, 'how can you be so cold-blooded about it? Weren't you –'

'Captain Calendar,' interrupted Gambier, 'I have requested you before not to allude to the Deity in that blasphemous fashion. Any repetition will incur my serious displeasure. Kindly continue, Captain Hornblower.'

There was only the brush with the boats from Noirmoutier to be described now. Hornblower continued, formally, but this time Gambier himself interrupted him.

'You say you opened fire with a six-pounder,' he said. 'The prisoners were at the sweeps, and the ship had to be steered. Who laid the gun?'

'I did, my lord. The French pilot helped me.'

'M'm. And you frightened 'em off?'

Hornblower confessed that he had succeeded in sinking two out of the three boats sent against him. Calendar whistled his surprise and admiration, but the hard lines in Gambier's face only set harder still.

'Yes?' he said. 'And then?'

'We went on under sweeps until midnight, my lord, and then we picked up a breeze. We sighted *Triumph* at dawn.'

There was silence in the cabin, only broken by the noises on deck, until Gambier stirred in his chair.

'I trust, Captain,' he said, 'that you have given thanks to the Almighty for these miraculous preservations of yours. In all these adventures I can see the finger of God. I shall direct my chaplain at prayers this evening to make a special mention of your gratitude and thankfulness.'

'Yes, my lord.'

'Now you will make your report in writing. You can

have it ready by dinner time – I trust you will give me the pleasure of your company at dinner? I will then be able to enclose it in the packet I am about to despatch to Their Lordships.'

'Yes, my lord.'

Gambier was still thinking deeply.

'*Witch of Endor* can carry the despatches,' he said. Like every admiral the world over, his most irritating and continuous problem was how to collect and disseminate information without weakening his main body by detachments; it must have been an immense relief to him to have the cutter drop from the clouds as it were, to carry these despatches. He went on thinking.

'I will promote this lieutenant of yours, Bush, into her as Commander,' he announced.

Hornblower gave a little gasp. Promotion to Commander meant almost certain post rank within the year, and it was this power of promotion which constituted the most prized source of patronage an Admiral in command possessed. Bush deserved the step, but it was surprising that Gambier should give it to him – Admirals generally had some favourite lieutenant, or some nephew or some old friend's son awaiting the first vacancy. Hornblower could imagine Bush's delight at the news that he was at last on his way to becoming an admiral himself if he lived long enough.

But that was not all, by no means all. Promotion of a captain's first lieutenant was a high compliment to the captain himself. It set the seal of official approval on the captain's proceedings. This decision of Gambler's was a public – not merely a private – announcement that Hornblower had acted correctly.

'Thank you, my lord, thank you,' said Hornblower.

'She is your prize, of course,' went on Gambier. 'Government will have to buy her on her arrival.'

Hornblower had not thought of that. It meant at least a thousand pounds in his pocket.

'That coxswain of yours will be in clover,' chuckled Calendar. 'He'll take all the lower deck's share.'

That was true, too. Brown would have a quarter of the value of the *Witch of Endor* for himself. He could buy a cottage or land and set up in business on his own account if he wished to.

'*Witch of Endor* will wait until your report is ready,' announced Gambier. 'I will send my secretary in to you. Captain Calendar will provide you with a cabin and the necessities you lack. I hope you will continue to be my guest until I sail for Portsmouth next week. It would be best, I think.'

The last words were a delicate allusion to that aspect of the matter which had occupied most of Hornblower's thoughts on his arrival, and which had not as yet been touched upon – the fact that he must undergo court martial for the loss of the *Sutherland*, and was of necessity under arrest until that time. By old established custom he must be under the supervision of an officer of equal rank while under arrest; there could be no question of sending him home in the *Witch of Endor*.

'Yes, my lord,' said Hornblower.

Despite all Gambler's courtesy and indulgence towards him, despite Calendar's open admiration, he still felt a constriction of the throat and a dryness of the mouth at the thought of that court martial; they were symptoms which persisted even when he tried to settle down and compose his report with the aid of the compe-tent young clergyman who made his appearance in the cabin to which Calendar conducted him.

'Arma virumque cano,' quoted the Admiral's secre-tary after the first halting sentences – Hornblower's report naturally began with the battle of Rosas. 'You begin in medias res, sir, as every good epic should.'

'This is an official report,' snapped Hornblower. 'It continues the last report I made to Admiral Leighton.'

His tiny cabin only allowed him to walk three paces each way, and crouching nearly double at that – some unfortunate lieutenant had been turned out to make room for him. In a flagship, even in a big three-decker like the *Victory*, the demand for cabins always greatly exceeded the supply, what with the Admiral, and the Captain of the Fleet, and the flag lieutenant, and the secretary, and the chaplain, and the rest of the staff. He sat down on the breech of the twelve-pounder beside the cot.

'Continue, if you please,' he ordered. '"Having regard to these conditions, I therefore proceeded –"'

It was finished in the end – it was the third time that morning that Hornblower had recounted his adven-tures, and they had lost all their savour for him now. He was dreadfully tired – his head drooped forward at his breast as he squatted on the gun, and then he woke with a snort. He was actually falling asleep while he sat.

'You are tired, sir,' said the secretary.

'Yes.'

He forced himself to wake up again. The secretary was looking at him with eyes shining with admiration, positive hero-worship. It made him feel uncomfortable.

'If you will just sign this, sir, I will attend to the seal and the superscription.'

The secretary slipped out of the chair and Hornblower took the pen and dashed off his signature to the document on whose evidence he was soon to be tried for his life.

'Thank you, sir,' said the secretary, gathering the papers together.

Hornblower had no more attention to spare for him. He threw himself face downward on to the cot, careless of appearances. He went rushing giddily down a tremendous slope into blackness – he was snoring before the secretary had reached the door, and he never felt the touch of the blanket with which the secretary returned, five minutes later, tiptoeing up to the cot to spread it over him.

17

Something enormously painful was recalling Hornblower to life. He did not want to return. It was agony to wake up, it was torture to feel unconsciousness slipping away from him. He clung to it, tried to recapture it, unavailingly. Remorselessly it eluded him. Somebody was gently shaking his shoulder, and he came back to complete consciousness with a start, and wriggled over to see the Admiral's secretary bending over him.

'The Admiral will dine within the hour, sir,' he said. 'Captain Calendar thought you might prefer to have a little time in which to prepare.'

'Yes,' grunted Hornblower. He fingered instinctively the long stubble on his unshaven chin. 'Yes.'

The secretary was standing very stiff and still, and Hornblower looked up at him curiously. There was an odd, set expression on the secretary's face, and he held a newspaper imperfectly concealed behind his back.

'What's the matter?' demanded Hornblower.

'It is bad news for you, sir,' said the secretary.

'What news?'

Hornblower's spirits fell down into the depths of despair. Perhaps Gambier had changed his mind. Perhaps he was going to be kept under strict arrest, tried, condemned, and shot. Perhaps –

'I remembered having seen this paragraph in the *Morning Chronicle* of three months ago, sir,' said the secretary. 'I showed it to his Lordship, and to Captain Calendar. They decided it ought to be shown to you as early as possible. His Lordship says –'

'What is the paragraph?' demanded Hornblower, holding out his hand for the paper.

'It is bad news, sir,' repeated the secretary, hesitatingly.

'Let me see it, damn you.'

The secretary handed over the newspaper, one finger indicating the paragraph.

'The Lord giveth, the Lord taketh away,' he said. 'Blessed be the name of the Lord.'

It was a very short paragraph.

We regret to announce the death in childbed, on the seventh of this month of Mrs Maria Hornblower, widow of the late Captain Horatio Hornblower, Bonaparte's martyred victim. The tragedy occurred in Mrs Hornblower's lodgings at Soutbsea, and we are given to understand that the child, a fine boy, is healthy.

Hornblower read it twice, and he began on it a third time. Maria was dead, Maria the tender, the loving.

'You can find consolation in prayer, sir –' said the secretary, but Hornblower paid no attention to what the secretary said.

He had lost Maria. She had died in childbed, and having regard to the circumstances in which the child had been engendered, he had as good as killed her. Maria was dead. There would be no one, no one at all, to welcome him now on his return to England. Maria would have stood by him during the court martial, and whatever the verdict, she would never have believed him to be at fault. Hornblower remembered the tears wetting her coarse red cheeks when she had last put her arms round him to say goodbye. He had been a little bored by the formality of an affectionate goodbye, then. He was free now – the realization came creeping over him like cold water in a warm bath. But it was not fair to Maria. He would not have bought his freedom at such a price. She had earned by her own devotion his attention, his kindness, and he would have given them to her uncomplainingly for the rest of his life. He was desperately sorry that she was dead.

'His Lordship instructed me, sir,' said the secretary, 'to inform you of his sympathy in your bereavement. He told me to say that he would not take it amiss if you decided not to join him and his guests at dinner but sought instead the consolation of religion in your cabin.'

'Yes,' said Hornblower.

'Any help which I can give, sir –'

'None,' said Hornblower.

He continued to sit on the edge of the cot, his head bowed, and the secretary shuffled his feet.

'Get out of here,' said Hornblower, without looking up.

He sat there for some time, but there was no order in his thoughts; his mind was muddled. There was a continuous undercurrent of sadness, a hurt feeling indistinguishable from physical pain, but fatigue and excitement and lack of sleep deprived him of any ability to think clearly. Finally, with a desperate effort he pulled himself together. He felt as if he was stifling in the stuffy cabin; he hated his stubbly beard and the feelings of dried sweat.

'Pass the word for my servant,' he ordered the sentry at his door.

It was good to shave off the filthy beard, to wash his body in cold water, to put on clean linen. He went up on deck, the clean sea air rushing into his lungs as he breathed. It was good, too, to have a deck to pace, up and down, up and down, between the slides of the quarterdeck carronades and the line of ringbolts in the deck, with all the familiar sounds of shipboard life as a kind of lullaby to his tired mind. Up and down he walked, up and down, as he had walked so many hours before, in the *Indefatigable*, and the *Lydia*, and the *Sutherland*. They left him alone; the officers of the watch collected on the other side of the ship and only stared at him unobtrusively, politely concealing their curiosity about this man who had just heard of the death of his wife, who had escaped from a French prison, who was waiting his trial for surrendering his ship – the first captain to strike his colours in a British ship of the line since Captain Ferris in the *Hannibal* at Algeciras. Up and down he walked, the goodly fatigue closing in upon him again until his mind was stupefied with it, until he found that he could hardly drag one foot past the other. Then he went below to the certainty of sleep and oblivion. But even in his sleep tumultuous dreams came to harass him – dreams of Maria, against which he struggled, sweating, knowing that Maria's body was now only a liquid mass of corruption; nightmares of death and imprisonment; and, ever-recurring, dreams of Barbara smiling to him on the farther side of the horrors that encompassed him.

From one point of view the death of his wife was of benefit to Hornblower during those days of waiting. It provided him with a good excuse for being silent and unapproachable. Without being thought impolite he could find a strip of deck and walk by himself in the sunshine. Gambier could walk with the captain of the fleet or the flag captain, little groups of lieutenants and warrant officers could walk together, chatting lightly, but they all kept out of his way; and it was not taken amiss that he should sit silent at the Admiral's dinner table and hold himself aloof at the Admiral's prayer meetings.

Had it not been so he would have been forced to mingle in the busy social life of the flagship, talking to officers who would studiously avoid all reference to the fact that shortly they would be sitting as judges on him at his court martial. He did not have to join in the eternal technical discussions which went on round him, stoically pretending that the responsibility of having surrendered a British ship of the line sat lightly on his shoulders. Despite all the kindness with which he was treated, he felt a pariah. Calendar could voice open admiration for him, Gambier could treat him with distinction, the young lieutenants could regard him with wide-eyed hero-worship, but they had never hauled down their colours. More than once during his long wait Hornblower found himself wishing that a cannon ball had killed him on the quarterdeck of the *Sutherland*. There was no one in the world who cared for him now – the little son in England, in the arms of some unknown foster-mother, might grow up ashamed of the name he bore.

Suspecting, morbidly, that the others would treat him like an outcast if they could, he anticipated them and made an outcast of himself, bitterly proud. He went through all that period of black reaction by himself, without companionship, during those last days of Gambier's tenure of command, until Hood came out in the *Britannia* to take over the command, and, amid the thunder of salutes, the *Victory* sailed for Portsmouth. There were headwinds to delay her passage; she had to beat up the Channel for seven long days before at last she glided into Spithead and the cable roared out through the hawse-hole.

Hornblower sat in his cabin – he felt no interest in the green hills of the Isle of Wight nor in the busy prospect of Portsmouth. The tap which came at his cabin door heralded, he supposed, the arrival of the orders regarding his court martial.

'Come in!' he said, but it was Bush who entered, stumping along on his wooden leg, his face wreathed in smiles, his arms burdened with packages and parcels.

At the sight of that homely face Hornblower's depression evaporated like mist. He found himself grinning as delightedly as Bush, he wrung his hand over and over again, sat him down in the only chair, offered to send for drinks for him, all trace of self-consciousness and reserve disappearing in the violence of his reaction.

'Oh, I'm well enough, sir, thank you,' said Bush, in reply to Hornblower's questions. 'And this is the first chance I've had of thanking you for my promotion.'

'Don't thank me,' said Hornblower, a trace of bitterness creeping back into his voice. 'You must thank his Lordship.'

'I know who I owe it to, all the same,' said Bush, sturdily. 'They're going to post me as captain this week. They won't give me a ship – not with this leg of mine

228

– but there's the dockyard job at Sheerness waiting for me. I should never be captain if it weren't for you, sir.'

'Rubbish,' said Hornblower. The pathetic gratitude in Bush's voice and expression made him feel uncomfortable.

'And how is it with you, sir?' asked Bush, regarding him with anxious blue eyes.

Hornblower shrugged his shoulders.

'Fit and well,' he said.

'I was sorry to hear about Mrs Hornblower, sir,' said Bush.

That was all he needed to say on that subject. They knew each other too well to have to enlarge on it.

'I took the liberty, sir,' said Bush, hastily, 'of bringing you out your letters – there was a good deal waiting for you.'

'Yes?' said Hornblower.

'This big package is a sword, I'm sure, sir,' said Bush. He was cunning enough to think of ways of capturing Hornblower's interest.

'Let's open it, then,' said Hornblower, indulgently.

A sword it was, sure enough, with a gold-mounted scabbard and a gold hilt, and when Hornblower drew it the blue steel blade bore an inscription in gold inlay. It was the sword 'of one hundred guineas' value' which had been presented to him by the Patriotic Fund for his defeat of the *Natividad* in the *Lydia*, and which he had left in pawn with Duddingstone the ship's chandler at Plymouth, as a pledge for payment for captain's stores when he was commissioning the *Sutherland*.

'A sight too much writing on this for me,' Duddingstone had complained at the time.

'Let's see what Duddingstone has to say,' said Hornblower, tearing open the note enclosed in the package.

Sir,

   It was with great emotion that I read today of your escape from the Corsican's clutches and I cannot find words to express my relief that the reports of your untimely death were unfounded, nor my admiration of your exploits during your last commission. I cannot reconcile it with my conscience to retain the sword of an officer so distinguished, and have therefore taken the liberty of forwarding the enclosed to you, hoping that in consequence you will wear it when next you enforce Britannia's dominion of the seas.
   Your obedient and humble servant to command.

J. DUDDINGSTONE

'God bless my soul!' said Hornblower.

He let Bush read the note; Bush was a captain and his equal now, as well as his friend, and there was no disciplinary objection to allowing him to know to what shifts he had been put when commissioning the Sutherland. Hornblower laughed a little self-consciously when Bush looked up at him after reading the note.

'Our friend Duddingstone,' said Hornblower, 'must have been very moved to allow a pledge for forty guineas to slip out of his fingers.' He spoke cynically to keep the pride out of his voice, but he was genuinely moved. His eyes would have grown moist if he had allowed them.

'I'm not surprised, sir,' said Bush, fumbling among

the newspapers beside him. 'Look at this, sir, and at this. Here's the *Morning Chronicle*, and *The Times*. I saved them to show you, hoping you'd be interested.'

Hornblower glanced at the columns indicated; somehow the gist of them seemed to leap out at him without his having to read them. The British press had let itself go thoroughly. As even Bush had foreseen, the fancy of the British public had been caught by the news that a captain whom they had imagined to be foully done to death by the Corsican tyrant had succeeded in escaping, and not merely in escaping, but in carrying off a British ship of war which had been for months a prize to the Corsican. There were columns in praise of Hornblower's daring and ability. A passage in *The Times* caught Hornblower's attention and he read it more carefully. 'Captain Hornblower still has to stand his trial for the loss of the *Sutherland*, but, as we pointed out in our examination of the news of the battle of Rosas Bay, his conduct was so well advised and his behaviour so exemplary on that occasion, whether he was acting under the orders of the late Admiral Leighton or not, that although the case is still *sub judice*, we have no hesitation in predicting his speedy reappointment.'

'Here's what the *Anti-Gallican* has to say, sir,' said Bush.

What the *Anti-Gallican* had to say was very like what the other newspapers had said; it was beginning to dawn upon Hornblower that he was famous. He laughed uncomfortably again. All this was a most curious experience and he was not at all sure that he liked it. Cold-bloodedly he could see the reason for it. Lately there had been no naval officer prominent in the affections of the public – Cochrane had wrecked himself by his intemperate wrath after the Basque Roads, while six years had passed since Hardy had kissed the dying Nelson; Collingwood was dead and Leighton too, for that matter – and the public always demanded an idol. Like the Israelites in the desert, they were not satisfied with an invisible object for their devotion. Chance had made him the public's idol, and presumably Government were not sorry, seeing how much it would strengthen their position to have one of their own men suddenly popular. But somehow he did not like it; he was not used to fame, he distrusted it, and his ever-present personal modesty made him feel it was all a sham.

'I hope you're pleased, sir,' said Bush, looking wonderingly at the struggle on Hornblower's face.

'Yes. I suppose I am,' said Hornblower.

'The Navy bought the *Witch of Endor* yesterday at the Prize Court!' said Bush, searching wildly for news which might delight this odd captain of his. 'Four thousand pounds was the price, sir. And the division of the prize money where the prize has been taken by an incomplete crew is governed by an old regulation – I didn't know about it, sir, until they told me. It was made after that boat's crew from *Squirrel*, after she foundered, captured the Spanish plate ship in '97. Two thirds to you, sir – that's two thousand six hundred pounds. And a thousand to me and four hundred for Brown.'

'H'm,' said Hornblower.

Two thousand six hundred pounds was a substantial bit of money – a far more concrete reward than the acclamation of a capricious public.

'And there's all these letters and packets, sir,' went on Bush, anxious to exploit the propitious moment.

The first dozen letters were all from people unknown to him, writing to congratulate him on his success and escape. Two at least were from madmen, apparently – but on the other hand two were from peers; even Hornblower was a little impressed by the signatures and the coroneted notepaper. Bush was more impressed still when they were passed over to him to read.

'That's very good indeed, sir, isn't it?' he said. There are some more here.'

Hornblower's hand shot out and picked one letter out of the mass offered him the moment he saw the handwriting, and then when he had taken it he stood for a second holding it in his hand, hesitating before opening. The anxious Bush saw the hardening of his mouth and the waning of the colour in his cheeks; watched him while he read, but Hornblower had regained his self-control and his expression altered no farther.

London,

129 Bond Street.

3rd June 1811

Dear Captain Hornblower

It is hard for me to write this letter, so overwhelmed am I with pleasure and surprise at hearing at this moment from the Admiralty that you are free and well. I hasten to let you know that I have your son here in my care. When he was left orphaned after the lamented death of your wife I ventured to take charge of him and make myself responsible for his upbringing, while my brothers

Lords Wellesley and Wellington consented to act as his
godfathers at his baptism, whereat he was consequently
given the names Richard Arthur Horatio. Richard is a fine
healthy boy with a wonderful resemblance to his father and
he has already endeared himself greatly to me, to such an
extent that I shall be conscious of a great loss when the
time comes for you to take him away from me. Let me
assure you that I shall look upon it as a pleasure to
continue to have charge of Richard until that time, as I
can easily guess that you will be much occupied with
affairs on your arrival in England. You will be very
welcome should you care to call here to see your son, who
grows in intelligence every day. It will give pleasure not
only to Richard, but to

> *Your firm friend,*
> *Barbara Leighton*

Hornblower nervously cleared his throat and reread
the letter. There was too much crowded in it for him
to have any emotion left. Richard Arthur Horatio
Hornblower, with two Wellesleys as godfathers, and
growing in intelligence every day. There would be a
great future ahead of him, perhaps. Up to that moment
Hornblower had hardly thought about the child – his
paternal instincts had hardly been touched by any
consideration of a child he had never seen; and they
further were warped by memories of the little Horatio
who had died of smallpox in his arms so many years
ago. But now he felt a great wave of affection for the
unknown little brat in London who had managed to
endear himself to Barbara.

And Barbara had taken him in charge; possibly

because, widowed and childless, she had sought for a convenient orphan to adopt – and yet it might be because she still cherished memories of Captain Hornblower, whom at the time she had believed to be dead at Bonaparte's hands.

He could not bear to think about it any more. He thrust the letter into his pocket – all the others he had dropped on the deck – and with immobile face he met Bush's gaze again.

'There are all these other letters, sir,' said Bush, with masterly tact.

They were letters from great men and from madmen – one contained an ounce of snuff as a token of some eccentric squire's esteem and regard – but there was only one which caught Hornblower's attention. It was from some Chancery Lane lawyer – the name was unfamiliar – who wrote, it appeared, on hearing from Lady Barbara Leighton that the presumption of Captain Hornblower's death was unfounded. Previously he had been acting under the instructions of the Lords Commissioners of the Admiralty to settle Captain Hornblower's estate, and working in conjunction with the Prize Agent at Port Mahon. With the consent of the Lord Chancellor, upon the death intestate of Mrs Maria Hornblower, he had been acting as trustee to the heir, Richard Arthur Horatio Hornblower, and had invested for the latter in the Funds the proceeds of the sale of Captain Hornblower's prizes after the deduction of expenses. As Captain Hornblower would see from the enclosed account, there was the sum of three thousand two hundred and ninety-one pounds six and fourpence invested in the Consolidated Fund, which would naturally revert to him. The lawyer awaited his esteemed instructions.

The enclosed accounts, which Hornblower was about to thrust aside, had among the innumerable six and eightpences and three and fourpences one set of items which caught his eye – they dealt with the funeral expenses of the late Mrs Hornblower, and a grave in the cemetery of the church of St Thomas à Beckett, and a headstone, and fees for grave-watchers; it was a ghoulish list which made Hornblower's blood run a little colder. It was hateful. More than anything else it accentuated his loss of Maria – he would only have to go on deck to see the tower of the church where she lay.

He fought down the depression which threatened to overmaster him once more. It was at least a distraction to think about the news in that lawyer's letter, to contemplate the fact that he owned three thousand odd pounds in the Funds. He had forgotten all about those prizes he had made in the Mediterranean before he came under Leighton's command. Altogether that made his total fortune nearly six thousand pounds – not nearly as large as some captains had contrived to acquire, but handsome enough. Even on half-pay he would be able to live in comfort now, and educate Richard Arthur Horatio properly, and take his place in a modest way in society.

'The captain's list has changed a lot since we saw it last, sir,' said Bush, and he was echoing Hornblower's train of thought rather than breaking into it.

'Have you been studying it?' grinned Hornblower.

'Of course, sir.'

Upon the position of their names in that list depended

the date of their promotion to flag rank – year by year they would climb it as death or promotion eliminated their seniors, until one day, if they lived long enough, they would find themselves admirals, with admirals' pay and privileges.

'It's the top half of the list which has changed most, sir,' said Bush. 'Leighton was killed, and Ball died at Malta, and Troubridge was lost at sea – in Indian waters, sir – and there's seven or eight others who've gone. You're more than half-way up now.'

Hornblower had held his present rank eleven years, but with each coming year he would mount more slowly, in proportion to the decrease in number of his seniors, and it would be 1825 or so before he could fly his flag. Hornblower remembered the Count de Graçay's prediction that the war would end in 1814 – promotion would be slower in peace time. And Bush was ten years older than he, and only just beginning the climb. Probably he would never live to be an admiral, but then Bush was perfectly content with being a captain. Clearly his ambition had never soared higher than that; he was fortunate.

'We're both of us very lucky men, Bush,' said Hornblower.

'Yes, sir,' agreed Bush, and hesitated before going on. 'I'm giving evidence at the court martial, sir, but of course you know what my evidence'll be. They asked me about it at Whitehall, and they told me that what I was going to say agreed with everything they knew. You've nothing to fear from the court martial, sir.'

18

Hornblower told himself often during the next twenty-four hours that he had nothing to fear from the court martial, and yet it was nervous work waiting for it – to hear the repeated twitter of pipes and stamping of marines' boots overhead as the compliments were given to the captains and admirals who came on board to try him, to hear silence close down on the ship as the court assembled, and to hear the sullen boom of the court martial gun as the court opened, and the click of the cabin door latch as Calendar came to escort him before his judges.

Hornblower remembered little enough afterwards of the details of the trial – only a few impressions stood out clearly in his memory. He could always recall the flash and glitter of the gold lace on the coats of the semicircle of officers sitting round the table in the great cabin of the *Victory*, and the expression on Bush's anxious, honest face as he declared that no captain could have handled a ship with more skill and determination than Hornblower had handled *Sutherland* at Rosas Bay. It was a neat point which Hornblower's 'friend' – the officer the Admiralty had sent to conduct his defence – made when his question brought out the fact that just before the surrender Bush had been completely incapacitated by the loss of his foot, so that he bore no responsibility whatever for the surrender and had no interest in presenting as good a case as possible. There was an officer who read, seemingly for an eternity, long extracts from depositions and official reports, in a spiritless mumble – the greatness of the occasion apparently made him nervous and affected his articulation, much to the annoyance of the President of the Court. At one point the President actually took the paper from him, and himself read, in his nasal tenor, Admiral Martin's pronouncement that the *Sutherland*'s engagement had certainly made the eventual destruction of the French squadron more easy, and in his opinion was all that had made it possible. There was an awkward moment when a discrepancy was detected between the signal logs of the *Pluto* and *Caligula*, but it passed away in smiles when someone reminded the Court that signal midshipmen sometimes made mistakes.

During the adjournment there was an elegant civilian in buff and blue, with a neat silk cravat, who came into Hornblower with a good many questions. Frere, his name was, Hookham Frere – Hornblower had a vague acquaintance with the name. He was one of the wits who wrote in the *Anti-Gallican*, a friend of Canning's, who for a time had acted as ambassador to the patriot government of Spain. Hornblower was a little intrigued by the presence of someone deep in cabinet secrets, but he was too preoccupied, waiting for the trial to re-open, to pay much attention to him or to answer his questions in detail.

And it was worse when all the evidence had been given, and he was waiting with Calendar while the Court considered its decision. Hornblower knew real fear, then. It was hard to sit apparently unmoved, while the minutes dragged by, waiting for the summons to the great cabin, to hear what his fate would be. His heart was beating hard as he went in, and he knew himself to be pale. He jerked his head erect to meet his judges' eyes, but the judges in their panoply of blue and gold were veiled in a mist which obscured the whole cabin, so that nothing was visible to Hornblower's eyes save for one little space in the centre – the cleared area in the middle of the table before the President's seat, where lay his sword, the hundred-guinea sword presented by the Patriotic Fund. That was all Hornblower could see – the sword seemed to hang there in space, unsupported. And the hilt was towards him; he was not guilty.

'Captain Hornblower,' said the President of the Court – that nasal tenor of his had a pleasant tone – 'This Court is of the unanimous opinion that your gallant and unprecedented defence of His Majesty's ship *Sutherland*, against a force so superior, is deserving of every praise the country and this Court can give. Your conduct, together with that of the officers and men under your command, reflects not only the highest honour on you, but on the country at large. You are therefore most honourably acquitted.'

There was a little confirmatory buzz from the other members of the Court, and a general bustle in the cabin. Somebody was buckling the hundred-guinea sword to his waist; someone else was patting his shoulder. Hookham Frere was there, too, speaking insistently.

'Congratulations, sir. And now, are you ready to accompany me to London? I have had a post chaise horsed and waiting this last six hours.'

The mists were only clearing slowly; everything was still vague about him as he allowed himself to be led away, to be escorted on deck, to be handed down into the barge alongside. Somebody was cheering. Hundreds of voices were cheering. The Victory's crew had manned the yards and were yelling themselves hoarse. All the other ships at anchor there were cheering him. This was fame. This was success. Precious few other captains had ever been cheered by all the ships in a fleet like this.

'I would suggest that you take off your hat, sir,' said Frere's voice in his ear, 'and show how much you appreciate the compliment.'

He took off his hat and sat there in the afternoon sun, awkwardly in the sternsheets of the barge. He tried to smile, but he knew his smile to be wooden – he was nearer tears than smiles. The mists were closing round him again, and the deep-chested bellowing was like the shrill piping of children in his ears.

The boat rasped against the wall. There was more cheering here, as they handed him up. People were thumping him on the shoulder, wringing his hand, while a blaspheming party of marines forced a passage for him to the post chaise with its horses restless amid the din. Then a clatter of hoofs and a grinding of wheels, and they were flying out of the yard, the postillion cracking his whip.

'A highly satisfactory demonstration of sentiment, on the part of the public and of the armed forces of the Crown,' said Frere, mopping his face.

Hornblower suddenly remembered something, which made him sit up, tense.

'Stop at the church!' he yelled to the postillion.

'Indeed, sir, and might I ask why you gave that order? I have the express commands of His Royal Highness to escort you to London without losing a moment.'

'My wife is buried there,' snapped Hornblower.

But the visit to the grave was unsatisfactory – was bound to be with Frere fidgeting and fuming at his elbow, and looking at his watch. Hornblower pulled off his hat and bowed his head by the grave with its carved headstone, but he was too much in a whirl to think clearly. He tried to murmur a prayer – Maria would have liked that, for she was always pained by his free thinking. Frere clucked with impatience.

'Come along then,' said Hornblower, turning on his heel and leading the way back to the post chaise.

The sun shone gloriously over the countryside as they left the town behind them, lighting up the lovely green of the trees and the majestic rolling Downs. Hornblower found himself swallowing hard. This was the England for which he had fought for eighteen long years, and as he breathed its air and gazed round him he felt that England was worth it.

'Damned lucky for the Ministry,' said Frere, 'this escape of yours. Something like that was needed. Even though Wellington's just captured Almeida the mob was growing restive. We had a ministry of all the talents once – now it's a ministry of no talent. I can't imagine why Castlereagh and Canning fought that duel. It nearly wrecked us. So did Gambier's affair at the Basque Roads. Cochrane's been making a thorough nuisance of himself in the House ever since. Has it ever occurred to you that you might enter parliament? Well, it will be time enough to discuss that when you've been to Downing Street. It's sufficient at present that you've given the mob something to cheer about.'

Mr Frere seemed to take much for granted – for

instance, that Hornblower was wholeheartedly on the government side, and that Hornblower had fought at Rosas Bay and had escaped from France solely to maintain a dozen politicians in office. It rather damped Hornblower's spirits. He sat silent, listening to the rattle of the wheels.

'HRH is none too helpful,' said Frere. 'He didn't turn us out when he assumed the Regency, but he bears us no love – the Regency Bill didn't please him. Remember that, when you see him tomorrow. He likes a bit of flattery, too. If you can make him believe that you owe your success to the inspiring examples both of HRH *and* of Mr Spencer Perceval you will be taking the right line. What's this? Horndean?'

The postillion drew the horses to a halt outside the inn, and ostlers came running with a fresh pair.

'Sixty miles from London,' commented Mr Frere. 'We've just time.'

The inn servants had been eagerly questioning the postillion, and a knot of loungers – smocked agricultural workers and a travelling tinker – joined them, looking eagerly at Hornblower in his blue and gold. Someone else came hastening out of the inn; his red face and silk cravat and leather leggings seemed to indicate him as the local squire.

'Acquitted, sir?' he asked.

'Naturally, sir,' replied Frere at once. 'Most honourably acquitted.'

'Hooray for Hornblower!' yelled the tinker, throwing his hat into the air. The squire waved his arms and stamped with joy, and the farm hands echoed the cheer.

'Down with Boney!' said Frere. 'Drive on.'

'It is surprising how much interest has been aroused in your case,' said Frere a minute later. 'Although naturally one would expect it to be greatest along the Portsmouth Road.'

'Yes,' said Hornblower.

'I can remember,' said Frere, 'when the mob were howling for Wellington to be hanged, drawn, and quartered – that was after the news of Cintra. I thought we were gone then. It was his court of inquiry which saved us as it happened, just as yours is going to do now. Do you remember Cintra?'

'I was commanding a frigate in the Pacific at the time,' said Hornblower, curtly.

He was vaguely irritated – and he was surprised at himself at finding that he neither liked being cheered by tinkers nor flattered by politicians.

'All the same,' said Frere, 'it's just as well that Leighton was hit at Rosas. Not that I wished him harm, but it drew the teeth of that gang. It would have been them or us otherwise, I fancy. His friends counted twenty votes on a division. You know his widow, I've heard?'

'I have that honour.'

'A charming woman for those who are partial to that type. And most influential as a link between the Wellesley party and her late husband's.'

'Yes,' said Hornblower.

All the pleasure was evaporating from his success. The radiant afternoon sunshine seemed to have lost its brightness.

'Petersfield is just over the hill,' said Frere. 'I expect there'll be a crowd there.'

Frere was right. There were twenty or thirty people

waiting at the Red Lion, and more came hurrying up, all agog to hear the result of the court martial. There was wild cheering at the news, and Mr Frere took the opportunity to slip in a good word for the government.

'It's the newspapers,' grumbled Frere, as they drove on with fresh horses. 'I wish we could take a lead out of Boney's book and only allow 'em to publish what we think they ought to know. Emancipation – Reform – naval policy – the mob wants a finger in every pie nowadays.'

Even the marvellous beauty of the Devil's Punch Bowl was lost on Hornblower as they drove past it. All the savour was gone from life. He was wishing he was still an unnoticed naval captain battling with Atlantic storms. Every stride the horses were taking was carrying him nearer to Barbara, and yet he was conscious of a sick, vague desire that he was returning to Maria, dull and uninteresting and undisturbing. The crowd that cheered him at Guildford – market day was just over – stank of sweat and beer. He was glad that with the approach of evening Frere ceased talking and left him to his thoughts, depressing though they were.

It was growing dark when they changed horses again at Esher.

'It is satisfactory to think that no footpad or highwayman will rob us,' laughed Frere. 'We have only to mention the name of the hero of the hour to escape scot free.'

No footpad or highwayman interfered with them at all, as it happened. Unmolested they crossed the river at Putney and drove on past the more frequent houses and along the dark streets.

'Number Ten Downing Street, postie,' said Frere.

What Hornblower remembered most vividly of the interview that followed was Frere's first sotto voce whisper to Perceval – 'He's safe' – which he overheard. The interview lasted no more than ten minutes, formal on the one side, reserved on the other. The Prime Minister was not in talkative mood apparently – his main wish seemed to be to inspect this man who might perhaps do him an ill turn with the Prince Regent or with the public. Hornblower formed no very favourable impression either of his ability or of his personal charm.

'Pall Mall and the War Office next,' said Frere. 'God, how we have to work!'

London smelt of horses – it always did, Hornblower remembered, to men fresh from the sea. The lights of Whitehall seemed astonishingly bright. At the War Office there was a young Lord to see him, someone whom Hornblower liked at first sight. Palmerston was his name, the Under Secretary of State. He asked a great many intelligent questions regarding the state of opinion in France, the success of the last harvest, the manner of Hornblower's escape. He nodded approvingly when Hornblower hesitated to answer when asked the name of the man who had given him shelter.

'Quite right,' he said. 'You're afraid some damned fool'll blab it out and get him shot. Some damned fool probably would. I'll ask you for it if ever we need it badly, and you will be able to rely on us then. And what happened to these galley slaves?'

'The first lieutenant in the *Triumph* pressed them for the service, my lord.'

'So they've been hands in a King's ship for the last three weeks? I'd rather be a galley slave myself.'

Hornblower was of the same opinion. He was glad to find someone in high position with no illusions regarding the hardships of the service.

'I'll have them traced and brought home if I can persuade your superiors at the Admiralty to give 'em up. I can find a better use for 'em.'

A footman brought in a note which Palmerston opened.

'His Royal Highness commands your presence,' he announced 'Thank you, Captain. I hope I shall again have the pleasure of meeting you shortly. This discussion of ours has been most profitable. And the Luddites have been smashing machinery in the north, and Sam Whitbread has been raising Cain in the House, so that your arrival is most opportune. Good evening, Captain.'

It was those last words which spoilt the whole effect. Lord Palmerston planning a new campaign against Bonaparte won Hornblower's respect, but Lord Palmerston echoing Frere's estimate of the political results of Hornblower's return lost it again.

'What does His Royal Highness want of me?' he asked of Frere, as they went down the stairs together.

'That's to be a surprise for you,' replied Frere archly. 'You may even have to wait until tomorrow's levee to find out. It isn't often Prinny's sober enough for business at this time in the evening. Probably he's not. You may find tact necessary in your interview with him.'

It was only this morning, thought Hornblower, his head whirling, that he had been sitting listening to the evidence at his court martial. So much had already happened today. He was surfeited with new experiences. He was sick and depressed. And Lady Barbara and his little son were in Bond Street, not a quarter of a mile away.

'What time is it?' he asked.

'Ten o'clock. Young Pam keeps late hours at the War Office. He's a glutton for a work.'

'Oh,' said Hornblower.

God only knew at what hour he would escape from the palace. He would certainly have to wait until tomorrow before he called at Bond Street. At the door a coach was waiting, coachmen and footmen in the royal red liveries.

'Sent by the Lord Chamberlain,' explained Frere. 'Kind of him.'

He handed Hornblower in through the door and climbed after him.

'Ever met His Royal Highness?' he went on.

'No.'

'But you've been to Court?'

'I have attended two levees. I was presented to King George in '98.'

'Ah! Prinny's not like his father. And you know Clarence, I suppose?'

'Yes.'

The carriage had stopped at a doorway brightly lit with lanterns; the door was opened, and a little group of footmen were awaiting to hand them out. There was a glittering entrance hall, where somebody in uniform and powder and with a white staff ran his eyes keenly over Hornblower.

'Hat under your arm,' he whispered. 'This way, please.'

'Captain Hornblower. Mr Hookham Frere,' somebody announced.

It was an immense room, dazzling with the light of

its candles; a wide expanse of polished floor, and at the far end a group of people bright with gold lace and jewels. Somebody came over to them, dressed in naval uniform – it was the Duke of Clarence, pop-eyed and pineapple-headed.

'Ah, Hornblower,' he said, hand held out, 'welcome home.'

Hornblower bowed over the hand.

'Come and be presented. This is Captain Hornblower, sir.'

'Evenin', Captain.'

Corpulent, handsome, and dissipated, weak and sly, was the sequence of impressions Hornblower received as he made his bow. The thinning curls were obviously dyed; the moist eyes and the ruddy pendulous cheeks seemed to hint that His Royal Highness had dined well, which was more than Hornblower had.

'Everyone's been talkin' about you, Captain, ever since your cutter – what's its name, now? – came in to Portsmouth.'

'Indeed, sir?' Hornblower was standing stiffly at attention.

'Yes. And, damme, so they ought to. So they ought to, damme, Captain. Best piece of work I ever heard of – good as I could have done myself. Here, Conyngham, make the presentations.'

Hornblower bowed to Lady This and Lady That, to Lord Somebody and to Sir John Somebody-else. Bold eyes and bare arms, exquisite clothes and blue Garter-ribbons, were all the impressions Hornblower received. He was conscious that the uniform made for him by the *Victory*'s tailor was a bad fit.

'Now let's get the business done with,' said the Prince. 'Call those fellows in.'

Someone was spreading a carpet on the floor, someone else was bearing in a cushion on which something winked and sparkled. There was a little procession of three solemn men in red cloaks. Someone dropped on one knee to present the Prince with a sword.

'Kneel, sir,' said Lord Conyngham to Hornblower.

He felt the accolade and heard the formal words which dubbed him knight. But when he rose, a little dazed, the ceremony was by no means over. There was a ribbon to be hung over his shoulder, a star to be pinned on his breast, a red cloak to be draped about him, a vow to be repeated and signatures written. He was being invested as a Knight of the Most Honourable Order of the Bath, as someone loudly proclaimed. He was Sir Horatio Hornblower, with a ribbon and star to wear for the rest of his life. At last they took the cloak from his shoulders again and the officials of the order withdrew.

'Let me be the first to congratulate you, Sir Horatio,' said the Duke of Clarence, coming forward, his kindly imbecile face wreathed in smiles.

'Thank you, sir,' said Hornblower. The broad star thumped his chest as he bowed again.

'My best wishes, Colonel,' said the Prince Regent.

Hornblower was conscious of all the eyes turned on him at that speech; it was that which warned him that the Prince was not making a slip regarding his rank.

'Sir?' he said, inquiringly, as seemed to be expected of him.

'His Royal Highness,' explained the Duke, 'has been pleased to appoint you one of his Colonels of Marines.'

A Colonel of Marines received pay to the amount of twelve hundred pounds a year, and did no duty for it. It was an appointment given as a reward to successful captains, to be held until they reach flag rank. Six thousand pounds he had already, Hornblower remembered. Now he had twelve hundred a year in addition to his captain's half pay at least. He had attained financial security at last, for the first time in his life. He had a title, a ribbon and star. He had everything he had ever dreamed of having, in fact.

'The poor man's dazed,' laughed the Regent loudly, delighted.

'I am overwhelmed, sir,' said Hornblower, trying to concentrate again on the business in hand. 'I hardly know how to thank your Royal Highness.'

'Thank me by joining us at hazard. Your arrival interrupted a damned interesting game. Ring that bell, Sir John and let's have some wine. Sit here beside Lady Jane, Captain. Surely you want to play? Yes, I know about you, Hookham. You want to slip away and tell John Walter that I've done my duty. You might suggest at the same time that he writes one of his damned leaders and has my Civil List raised – I work hard enough for it, God knows. But I don't see why you should take the Captain away. Oh, very well then, damn it. You can go if you want to.'

'I didn't imagine,' said Frere, when they were safely in the coach again, 'that you'd care to play hazard. I wouldn't, not with Prinny, if he were using his own dice. Well, how does it feel to be Sir Horatio?'

'Very well,' said Hornblower.

He was digesting the Regent's allusion to John Walter.

This was the editor of *The Times*, he knew. It was beginning to dawn upon him that his investiture as Knight of the Bath and appointment as Colonel of Marines were useful pieces of news. Presumably their announcement would have some influence politically, too – that was the reason for haste. They would convince doubting people that the government's naval officers were achieving great things – it was almost as much a political move to make him a knight as was Bonaparte's scheme to shoot him for violating the laws of war. The thought took a great deal of the pleasure out of it.

'I took the liberty,' said Frere, 'of engaging a room for you at the Golden Cross. You'll find them expecting you; I had your baggage sent round. Shall I stop the coach there? Or do you want to visit Fladong's first?'

Hornblower wanted to be alone; the idea of visiting the naval coffee house tonight – for the first time in five years – had no appeal for him, especially as he felt suddenly self-conscious in his ribbon and star. Even at the hotel it was bad enough, with host and boots and chambermaid all unctuously deferential with their 'Yes, Sir Horatio' and 'No, Sir Horatio', making a procession out of lighting him up to his room, and fluttering round him to see that he had all he wanted, when all he wanted now was to be left in peace.

There was little enough peace for him, all the same, when he climbed into bed. Resolutely as he put out of his mind all recollection of the wild doings of the day, he could not stop himself thinking about the fact that tomorrow he would be seeing his son and Lady Barbara. He spent a restless night.

'Sir Horatio Hornblower,' announced the butler, holding open the door for him.

Lady Barbara was there; it was a surprise to see her in black – Hornblower had been visualizing her as dressed in the blue gown she had worn when last he had seen her, the grey-blue which matched her eyes. She was in mourning now, of course, for Leighton had been dead less than a year still. But the black dress suited her well – her skin was creamy white against it. Hornblower remembered with a strange pang the golden tang of her cheeks in those old days on board the *Lydia*.

'Welcome,' she said, her hands outstretched to him. They were smooth and cool and delicious – he remembered their touch of old. 'The nurse will bring Richard directly. Meanwhile, my heartiest congratulations on your success.'

'Thank you,' said Hornblower. 'I was extremely lucky, ma'am.'

'The lucky man,' said Lady Barbara, 'is usually the man who knows how much to leave to chance.'

While he digested this statement he stood awkwardly looking at her. Until this moment he had forgotten how Olympian she was, what self-assurance – kindly self-assurance – she had, which raised her to inaccessible heights and made him feel like a loutish schoolboy. His knighthood must appear ridiculously unimportant to her, the daughter of an earl, the sister of a marquis and of a viscount who was well on his way towards a dukedom. He was suddenly acutely conscious of his elbows and hands.

His awkwardness only ended with the opening of the door and the entrance of the nurse, plump and rosy in her ribboned cap, the baby held to her shoulder. She dropped a curtsey.

'Hullo, son,' said Hornblower, gently.

He did not seem to have much hair yet, under his little cap, but there were two startling brown eyes looking out at his father; nose and chin and forehead might be as indeterminate as one would expect in a baby, but there was no ignoring those eyes.

'Hullo, baby,' said Hornblower, gently, again.

He was unconscious of the caress in his voice. He was speaking to Richard as years before he had spoken to little Horatio and little Maria. He held up his hands to the child.

'Come to your father,' he said.

Richard made no objections. It was a little shock to Hornblower to feel how tiny and light he was – Hornblower, years ago, had grown used to older children – but the feeling passed immediately.

'There, baby, there,' said Hornblower.

Richard wriggled in his arms, stretching out his hands to the shining gold fringe of his epaulette.

'Pretty?' asked Hornblower.

'Da!' said Richard, touching the threads of bullion.

'That's a man!' said Hornblower.

His old skill with babies had not deserted him.

Richard gurgled happily in his arms, smiled seraphically as he played with him, kicked his chest with tiny kicks through his dress. That good old trick of bowing the head and pretending to butt Richard in the stomach had its never-failing success. Richard gurgled and waved his arms in ecstasy.

'What a joke!' said Hornblower. 'Oh, what a joke!'

Suddenly remembering, he looked round at Lady Barbara. She had eyes only for the baby, her serenity strangely exalted, her smile tender. He thought then that she was moved by her love for the child. Richard noticed her too.

'Goo!' he said, with a jab of an arm in her direction.

She came nearer, and Richard reached over his father's shoulder to touch her face.

'He's a fine baby,' said Hornblower.

'O' course he's a fine babby,' said the wet-nurse, reaching for him. She took it for granted that godlike fathers in glittering uniforms would only condescend to notice their children for ten seconds consecutively, and would need to be instantly relieved of them at the end of that time.

'He's a saucy one,' said the wet-nurse, the baby back in her arms. He wriggled there, those big brown eyes of his looking from Hornblower to Barbara.

'Say "bye bye",' said the nurse. She held up his wrist and waved his fat fist at them. 'Bye bye.'

'Do you think he's like you?' asked Barbara, as the door closed behind the nurse and baby.

'Well –' said Hornblower, with a doubtful grin.

He had been happy during those few seconds with the baby, happier than he had been for a long long time.

The morning up to now had been one of black despondency for him. He had told himself that he had everything heart could desire, and some inner man within him had replied that he wanted none of it. In the morning light his ribbon and star had appeared gaudy gew-gaws. He never could contrive to feel proud of himself; there was something vaguely ridiculous about the name 'Sir Horatio Hornblower', just as he always felt there was something vaguely ridiculous about himself.

He had tried to comfort himself with the thought of all the money he had. There was a life of ease and security before him; he would never again have to pawn his gold-hilted sword, nor feel self-conscious in good society about the pinchbeck buckles on his shoes. And yet the prospect was frightening now that it was certain. There was something of confinement about it, something reminiscent of these weary weeks in the Château de Graçay – how well he remembered how he fretted there. Unease and insecurity, which had appeared such vast evils when he suffered under them, had something attractive about them now, hard though that was to believe.

He had envied brother captains who had columns about themselves in the newspapers. Surfeit in that way was attained instantaneously, he had discovered. Bush and Brown would love him neither more nor less on account of what *The Times* had to say about him; he would scorn the love of those who loved him more – and he had good reason to fear that there would be rivals who would love him less. He had received the adulation of crowds yesterday; that did not heighten his good opinion of crowds, and he was filled with a bitter contempt for the upper circle that rules those crowds. Within him the fighting man and the humanitarian both seethed with discontent.

Happiness was a Dead Sea fruit that turned to ashes in the mouth, decided Hornblower, generalizing recklessly from his own particular experience. Prospect, and not possession, was what gave pleasure, and his cross-grainedness would deprive him, now that he had made that discovery, even of the pleasure in prospect. He misdoubted everything so much. Freedom that could only be bought by Maria's death was not a freedom worth having; honours granted by those that had the granting of them were no honours at all; and no security was really worth the loss of insecurity. What life gave with one hand she took back with the other. The political career of which he had once dreamed was open to him now, especially with the alliance of the Wellesley faction, but he could see with morbid clarity how often he would hate it; and he had been happy for thirty seconds with his son, and now, more morbidly still, he asked himself cynically if that happiness could endure for thirty years.

His eyes met Barbara's again, and he knew she was his for the asking. To those who did not know and understand, who thought there was romance in his life when really it was the most prosaic of lives, that would be a romantic climax. She was smiling at him, and then he saw her lips tremble as she smiled. He remembered how Marie had said he was a man whom women loved easily, and he felt uncomfortable at being reminded of her.

C. S. FORESTER

THE COMMODORE

1812 and the fate of Europe lies in the hands of newly appointed Commodore Hornblower ...

Dispatched to northern waters to protect Britain's Baltic interests, Horatio Hornblower must halt the advance of Napoleon's empire into Sweden and Russia. But first he must battle the terrible Baltic weather: fog, snow and icebound waterways; overcome Russian political and commercial intrigues; avoid the seductive charms of royalty as well as the deadly reach of assassins in the imperial palace; and contend with hostile armies and French privateers. With the fate of Europe balanced on a knife edge, the responsibility lies heavy on a Commodore's shoulders ...

This is the eighth of eleven books chronicling the adventures of C. S. Forester's inimitable nautical hero, Horatio Hornblower.

'Hornblower is Hamlet in command of a battleship' *New York Times*

'I find Hornblower admirable, vastly entertaining' Sir Winston Churchill

C. S. FORESTER

LORD HORNBLOWER

1813, and Horatio Hornblower is propelled toward the heart of the French Empire and his old enemy, Napoleon . . .

Sir Horatio Hornblower has received strict and highly confidential orders from the highest rank: he must embark upon a grave and perilous mission to recapture the *Flame* in the Bay of Seine, where the brutal and foul-tempered Lieutenant Augustine Chadwick is being held prisoner by a mutinous crew. Rescuing the Lieutenant demands all of Horatio's spirit and seafaring prowess – for at the same time, he must contend with capturing two French cargo vessels and take part in negotiations to topple the faltering Napoleon once and for all . . .

This is the ninth of eleven books chronicling the adventures of C.S. Forester's inimitable nautical hero, Horatio Hornblower.

'I find Hornblower admirable, vastly entertaining' Sir Winston Churchill

C. S. FORESTER

HORNBLOWER IN THE WEST INDIES

1815, the Napoleonic Wars are over. Yet peace continues to elude Horatio Hornblower overseas . . .

As an admiral struggling to impose order in the chaotic aftermath of the French wars, Horatio Hornblower, Commander-in-chief of His Majesty's ships and vessels in the West Indies, must still face savage pirates, reckless revolutionaries and a violent hurricane.

And while his retirement at half-pay might well be in sight, Hornblower will need every ounce of his rapier wit and quick thinking – not to mention his courage and leadership – to ensure that the lasting peace in Europe reaches the turbulent seas of the West Indies.

This is the tenth of eleven books chronicling the adventures of C. S. Forester's inimitable nautical hero, Horatio Hornblower.

'I find Hornblower admirable, vastly entertaining' Sir Winston Churchill

C. S. FORESTER

HORNBLOWER AND THE CRISIS

The final Horatio Hornblower story tells of Napoleon's plans to invade England.

Set in 1805, *Hornblower and the Crisis* finds Horatio Hornblower in possession of confidential dispatches from Bonaparte after a vicious hand-to-hand encounter with a French brig. The admiralty rewards Hornblower by sending him on a dangerous espionage mission that will light the powder trail leading to the battle of Trafalgar . . .

Hornblower and the Crisis was unfinished at the time of Forester's death, but the author left notes – included here – telling us how the tale would end. Also included are two further stories – *Hornblower and the Widow McCool* and *The Last Encounter* – that tell of Hornblower as a very young and very old man, respectively.

This is the final book chronicling the adventures of C. S. Forester's inimitable nautical hero, Horatio Hornblower.

'I find Hornblower admirable, vastly entertaining' Sir Winston Churchill

C. S. FORESTER

MR MIDSHIPMAN HORNBLOWER

1793, the eve of the Napoleonic Wars, and Midshipman Horatio Hornblower receives his first command . . .

As a seventeen-year-old with a touch of sea sickness, young Horatio Hornblower hardly cuts a dash in His Majesty's navy. Yet from the moment he is ordered to board a French merchant ship in the Bay of Biscay and take command of crew and cargo, he proves his seafaring mettle on the waves. With a character-forming duel, several chases and some strange tavern encounters, the young Hornblower is soon forged into a formidable man of the sea.

This is the first of eleven books chronicling the nautical adventures of C. S. Forester's inimitable hero, Horatio Hornblower.

'Absolutely compelling. One of the great masters of narrative' *San Francisco Chronicle*

'I recommend Forester to every literate I know' Ernest Hemingway

C. S. FORESTER

LIEUTENANT HORNBLOWER

The nineteenth century dawns and the Napoleonic Wars rage as Horatio Hornblower faces the fury of the French and Spanish fleets combined.

Amidst the hissing of wet wads, the stifling heat of white-hot cannonshot and the clamour of a mutinous crew, new Lieutenant Hornblower will need all of his seafaring cunning to overcome his first challenge in independent command on the high seas. And while blood and violence flow thick and fast aboard a beleaguered *HMS Renown*, the aftermath of war promises intrigue of an entirely different order: Maria, a young señorita, who might just soften the steely resolve of a young lieutenant.

This is the second of eleven books chronicling the adventures of C. S. Forester's inimitable nautical hero, Horatio Hornblower.

'One of the best…Everyone interested in war, or in human nature, should read this fascinating tale' *The Times Literary Supplement*

'I recommend Forester to every literate I know' Ernest Hemingway

He just wanted a decent book to read ...

Not too much to ask, is it? It was in 1935 when Allen Lane, Managing Director of Bodley Head Publishers, stood on a platform at Exeter railway station looking for something good to read on his journey back to London. His choice was limited to popular magazines and poor-quality paperbacks – the same choice faced every day by the vast majority of readers, few of whom could afford hardbacks. Lane's disappointment and subsequent anger at the range of books generally available led him to found a company – and change the world.

'We believed in the existence in this country of a vast reading public for intelligent books at a low price, and staked everything on it'
Sir Allen Lane, 1902–1970, founder of Penguin Books

The quality paperback had arrived – and not just in bookshops. Lane was adamant that his Penguins should appear in chain stores and tobacconists, and should cost no more than a packet of cigarettes.

Reading habits (and cigarette prices) have changed since 1935, but Penguin still believes in publishing the best books for everybody to enjoy. We still believe that good design costs no more than bad design, and we still believe that quality books published passionately and responsibly make the world a better place.

So wherever you see the little bird – whether it's on a piece of prize-winning literary fiction or a celebrity autobiography, political tour de force or historical masterpiece, a serial-killer thriller, reference book, world classic or a piece of pure escapism – you can bet that it represents the very best that the genre has to offer.

Whatever you like to read – trust Penguin.

A SELECTED LIST OF FINE TITLES
AVAILABLE FROM CORGI BOOKS

☐	12504 0	The Smoke	Tom Barling	£2.95
☐	12639 X	One Police Plaza	William J. Caunitz	£2.50
☐	13081 8	Crow's Parliament	Jack Curtis	£2.95
☐	13061 3	Lost	Gary Devon	£2.95
☐	13139 3	The China Card	John Ehrlichman	£3.95
☐	12550 4	Lie Down With Lions	Ken Follett	£2.95
☐	12610 1	On Wings of Eagles	Ken Follett	£3.50
☐	12180 0	The Man from St. Petersburg	Ken Follett	£2.95
☐	11810 9	The Key to Rebecca	Ken Follett	£2.95
☐	09121 9	The Day of the Jackal	Frederick Forsyth	£2.95
☐	11500 2	The Devil's Alternative	Frederick Forsyth	£2.95
☐	10050 1	The Dogs of War	Frederick Forsyth	£3.50
☐	12569 5	The Fourth Protocol	Frederick Forsyth	£3.95
☐	12140 1	No Comebacks	Frederick Forsyth	£2.95
☐	09436 6	The Odessa File	Frederick Forsyth	£2.50
☐	10244 X	The Shepherd	Frederick Forsyth	£1.95
☐	13259 4	The Last Man Out of Saigon	Chris Mullin	£2.50
☐	12417 6	The Salamandra Glass	A. W. Mykel	£2.50
☐	11850 8	The Windchime Legacy	A. W. Mykel	£1.75
☐	12541 5	Dai-Sho	Marc Olden	£2.95
☐	12662 4	Gaijin	Marc Olden	£2.95
☐	12357 9	Giri	Marc Olden	£2.95
☐	12800 7	Oni	Marc Olden	£2.95
☐	12855 4	Fair At Sokolniki	Fridrikh Neznansky	£2.95
☐	12307 2	Red Square	Fridrikh Neznansky & Edward Topol	£2.50
☐	13270 5	Ropespinner Conspiracy	Michael M. Thomas	£2.95

A VERY BRITISH COUP

'Chris Mullin's book is the first for some time that I have stayed awake to finish'
Ken Livingstone, *Labour Herald*

'Entertaining to anyone interested in contemporary politics'
Glasgow Herald

'Compulsive reading'
City Limits

'A curious Molotov Cocktail'
Financial Times

'A very effective political thriller, which has you on the edge of your seat from start to finish'
Oxford Mail

'Entertaining propaganda'
Literary Review

Also by Chris Mullin

THE LAST MAN OUT OF SAIGON

and published by Corgi Books

A VERY BRITISH COUP

Chris Mullin

CORGI BOOKS

A VERY BRITISH COUP

A CORGI BOOK   0 552   13322 1

Originally published in Great Britain by Hodder and
Stoughton Ltd.

PRINTING HISTORY

Hodder and Stoughton edition published 1982
Coronet edition published 1983
Corgi edition published 1988

Corgi Books are published by Transworld Publishers Ltd., 61-63
Uxbridge Road, Ealing, London W5 5SA, in Australia by
Transworld Publishers (Australia) Pty. Ltd., 15-23 Helles Avenue,
Moorebank, NSW 2170, and in New Zealand by Transworld
Publishers (N.Z.) Ltd., Cnr. Moselle and Waipareira Avenues,
Henderson, Auckland.

Printed and bound in Great Britain by
Cox & Wyman Ltd., Reading, Berks.

To Joan,
who will never lose faith

'I could easily imagine myself being tempted into a treasonable disposition under a labour Government dominated by the Marxist Left ... Suppose, in these circumstances, one were approached by an official of the C.I.A. who sought to enlist one's help in a project designed to 'destabilise' this far left government. Would it necessarily be right to refuse co-operation? ... Coming from the representative of any other foreign power such a request would not be entertained by me for a moment. But the United States is not just any other foreign power. I am and always have been passionately pro-American, in all sense of believing that the United States has long been the protector of all the values which I hold most dear. To that extent my attitude to the United States has long been that of a potential fellow traveller.'

When Treason Can Be Right by Peregrine Worsthorne,
Sunday Telegraph, November 4, 1979

1

The news that Harry Perkins was to become Prime Minister went down very badly in the Athenaeum.

"Man's a Communist," exploded Sir Arthur Furnival, a retired banker.

"Might as well all emigrate," said George Fison, who owned a chain of newspapers.

"My God," ventured the Bishop of Bath and Wells, raising his eyes heavenward.

As the Press Association tape machine in the lobby began to punch out the first results of the March 1989 general election it became clear that something had gone horribly wrong with the almost unanimous prediction of the pundits that the Tory-Social Democrat Government of National Unity would be re-elected.

Kingston-on-Thames was the first to declare. The sharp young merchant banker who had represented the seat saw his majority evaporate.

"A mistake," said Furnival when he had recovered his composure.

"Bloody better be," grunted Fison. No one could remember the last time a seat in the Surrey stockbroker belt had returned a Labour Member of Parliament.

The machine was now giving details of a computer forecast to the effect that if the Kingston swing was reproduced across the country Labour would have a majority of around 200 seats.

"To hell with computers," muttered Furnival. Fison took a sip of whisky. The Bishop dabbed his forehead with a purple handkerchief.

There were those who had argued that computers had rendered elections obsolete. That very morning a professor from Imperial College had been on the radio describing how he had fed the entire electoral register into a computer which

had then selected a perfect cross-section of the population. He had polled the sample and confidently predicted that his results would be accurate to within one quarter of one per cent. Harry Perkins was about to put the learned professor and his computer out of business.

"Freak result. Means nothing." The party around the tape machine had been joined by a man in a double-breasted Savile Row suit. Sir Peregrine Craddock's *Who's Who* entry said simply that he was 'attached to the Ministry of Defence', but those who know about these things said he was the Director General of DI5.

For the next few minutes Sir Peregrine's optimism seemed justified. The National Unity candidate held Oxford with a majority only slightly reduced. Braintree stayed Tory. So did Colchester and Finchley. Then at about quarter to midnight came the first results from the North. Salford, Grimsby, York and Leeds East were all held by Labour with doubled, even trebled, majorities. It was at this point that Arthur Furnival disappeared to ring his stockbroker.

At a few minutes to midnight Worcester went Labour, bringing down the first of six Cabinet ministers who would lose their seats that evening. Sir Peregrine took a sip of his orange juice. George Fison rushed back to Fleet Street to dictate an editorial for the late edition of his newspaper. He was last heard shouting that the British people had taken leave of their senses.

By 12.30 it was clear that the National Unity bubble had burst. South of the Wash the Social Democrats were being annihilated. Richmond, Putney, Hemel Hempstead and Cambridge all fell to Labour in quick succession. North of the Wash only the seaside resorts and the hunting country remained in Tory hands.

Like so much else associated with the twentieth century, television sets were banished from the Athenaeum. But in view of the impending national disaster a delegation from the crowd of elderly gentlemen now gathered around the tape machine had been despatched in search of the club secretary, Captain Giles Fairfax. The captain said he would see what he

8

could do and within ten minutes reappeared carrying a small portable set borrowed from the caretaker's flat. It was now installed beside the tape machine on a table taken from the morning room. "All very irregular," said the captain with an apologetic glance at the portrait of Charles Darwin which overlooked the scene. Nevertheless, he stayed to watch.

There was a groan as the television screen immediately focused upon the beaming face of Harry Perkins who was awaiting the declaration of his own result in Sheffield town hall. Perkins, a former steel worker, was a stocky, robust man with a twinkle in his eye and dark, bushy brows. His greying hair was long at the sides and combed over his head to hide his balding crown. His face was deeply lined and rugged, burnished by the great heat of a Sheffield steel mill in the days when Britain had been a steel-producing nation. He was smartly dressed, but nothing flashy. A tweed sports jacket, a silk tie, and on this occasion a red carnation in his buttonhole. Harry Perkins was going to be quite different from any Prime Minister Britain had ever seen. The programme on which he was in the process of being swept to power was quite different from any ever presented to the British electorate.

On the television screen a commentator was now reciting the highlights. Withdrawal from the Common Market. Import controls. Public control of finance, including the pension and insurance funds. Abolition of the House of Lords, the honours list and the public schools.

The manifesto also called for 'consideration to be given' to withdrawal from NATO as a first step towards Britain becoming a neutral country. An end to Britain's 'so-called nuclear deterrent' and the withdrawal of all foreign bases from British soil. There was even a paragraph about 'dismantling the newspaper monopolies'.

For weeks all opinion polls and all responsible commentators had been predicting that there was no hope of the Labour Party being elected on a programme like this. Ever since Harry Perkins had been chosen to lead Labour at a tumultuous party conference two years earlier, the popular press had been saying that this proved what they had always

argued – namely that the Labour Party was in the grip of a Marxist conspiracy. Privately the rulers of the great corporations had been gleeful, for they had convinced themselves that the British people were basically moderate and that, however rough the going got, they would never elect a Labour government headed by the likes of Harry Perkins.

Picture, therefore, the dismay that swept the lobby of the Athenaeum as the television showed Perkins coming to the rostrum in Sheffield town hall to acknowledge not only his own re-election with a record majority, but to claim victory on behalf of his party.

"Comrades," intoned brother Perkins.

"*Comrades*, my foot." Sir Arthur Furnival was apoplectic. "Told you the man's a Communist."

"Comrades," repeated Perkins, as though he could hear the heckling coming from the Athenaeum. He then delivered himself of a dignified little speech thanking the returning officer, those who counted the ballot papers, party workers and all the other people it is customary for a victorious candidate to thank. Then he got down to business.

"Comrades, it is now clear that by tomorrow morning we shall form the government of this country."

He paused to let the cheering subside. "We should not be under any illusion about the task ahead of us. We inherit an industrial desert. We inherit a country which for ten years has been systematically pillaged and looted by every species of pirate, spiv and con man known to civilisation."

"Scandalous," muttered Furnival.

"Disgraceful carry-on," said the Bishop of Bath and Wells.

"All we have won tonight is political power," continued Perkins. "By itself that is not enough. Real power in this country resides not in Parliament, but in the boardrooms of the City of London; in the darkest recesses of the Whitehall bureaucracy and in the editorial offices of our national newspapers. To win real power we have first to break the stranglehold exerted by the ruling class on all the important institutions of our country."

10

"Treason," whispered Furnival, "that's what I call it, downright treason."

Perkins paused and then, speaking slowly and looking directly into a television camera, straight into the eyes of Sir Arthur Furnival, he said, "Our ruling class have never been up for re-election before, but I hereby serve notice on behalf of the people of Great Britain that their time has come."

Such language had never been heard from a British Prime Minister before. Although received with rapture in Sheffield town hall, Harry Perkins' words burst upon the Athenaeum as though the end of the world was at hand. Which, in a manner of speaking, it was.

"South of France for me, old boy," said Furnival.

"Certainly looks like the game's up, Arthur," murmured the Bishop, whose faith in divine providence had temporarily deserted him.

From nearby Trafalgar Square came a burst of firecrackers as crowds of young people celebrated the election result.

By 1.15 the scale of the disaster was apparent to everyone. The television commentators were now citing a computer prediction that Perkins would have an overall majority of around ninety seats. Gradually the cluster of eminent gentlemen around the television dwindled. Some donned overcoats and slipped miserably out into the night. One ancient member dozed on a Chesterfield in the lobby, his head resting on the marble wall, pince-nez dangling from a cord around his neck.

Not everyone went home. Some drifted upstairs to the huge drawing room and sat in urgent little groups discussing what life in Harry Perkins' Britain held in store for them.

"Early days yet." The speaker was Sir Lucas Lawrence, former permanent secretary at the Department of Industry. He was standing at the end of the drawing room overlooking Carlton House Terrace. On the mantelpiece behind him were white marble busts of Alexander Pope and Edmund Burke. Below in the grate a pinewood fire crackled.

"These Labour chappies are all the same," Sir Lucas went on. "Always shooting their mouths off in opposition, but once

11

they've got their backsides in the limousines they're as meek as lambs." After retiring from the Department of Industry Sir Lucas had joined the board of an arms company. There had been one or two raised eyebrows at the time. The odd parliamentary question drawing attention to his dealings with the same company in his capacity as a public servant, but it had all blown over and now Sir Lucas was chairman of the board, his civil service pension intact.

"Pretty damn serious if you ask me," boomed Lord Kildare, a portly landowner with a castle and 30,000 acres in Scotland and a town house in Chelsea. He was standing facing the huge mirror above the fireplace. His considerable bulk rested on the back of one of the green leather armchairs. The mirror afforded a panoramic view of the vast room behind him. In the distance he could see stewards in red jackets and black bow ties silently commuting between the bar and the little groups of elderly gentlemen scattered around the room. He shook his head sadly. A way of life was coming to an end. "Pretty damn serious," repeated Kildare gazing absently into the fire.

Sir Lucas was not convinced. He drew deeply on his Havana and exhaled vigorously. "Mark my words," he said firmly, "once the boys in the private office get to work, these Labour chappies won't know what's hit them."

Kildare side-stepped to avoid being engulfed by an oncoming cloud of cigar smoke. "All very well," he said miserably, "but I've never heard any Prime Minister talk like that fellow Perkins tonight."

Sir Lucas was unruffled. "You forget," he said. "I've seen all this at close quarters. Mind you, I am not saying it was plain sailing. One or two Labour ministers always prove difficult, but in the end we sorted them out."

"How?" asked Kildare, who already had visions of a life in exile. He pictured himself in a white suit and a straw hat sitting alone on the verandah of the Bermuda Cricket Club, a daiquiri in one hand and an out of date airmail edition of the *Daily Telegraph* spread on the table before him. No, thought Kildare, give me the grouse moors any day.

12

Sir Lucas adopted a confidential tone, "I'll tell you how." He lowered his voice and touched Kildare reassuringly on the forearm. "We turned the whole damn machine loose on them. More than any man can stand. Whenever my minister insisted on giving money away to co-operatives or any of his other harebrained schemes, I would give old Handley in the Cabinet Office a ring and put him in the picture. He'd get his people to produce a brief opposing ours which would be distributed to all other departments. If necessary he'd follow up with telephone calls to sympathetic ministers and when the matter came up at Cabinet my minister would find himself totally outgunned. After a while he got the message and resigned. Just as well, otherwise we'd have had him reshuffled."

"All very well, Lucas, when you've only got one or two extremists in the government, but what if you've got a whole Cabinet full of them?" Kildare ran a finger round the rim of his whisky glass.

Sir Lucas smiled wanly. "In that case something bigger's called for." He glanced over his shoulder as though afraid of eavesdroppers. "One or two runs on sterling. A whopping balance of payments crisis. Only takes a few telephone calls to lay this sort of thing on. If you'd seen, as I have, the Prime Minister's face at 2.30 in the morning when sterling's going down the drain at a million pounds a minute, you'd soon realise how right I am."

"If you ask me, we've got a job of work on our hands preserving civilised values." The newcomer to the conversation was Sir Peregrine Craddock, who had been quietly sipping his orange juice on the fringe of the gathering. Speaking as though he was dictating a top secret memorandum, Sir Peregrine continued, "Very serious situation. Whole country crawling with extremists. Everything we stand for threatened. Fight back essential."

With that he placed his glass, still half full of orange juice, on the mantelpiece, turned on his heel and strode out of the drawing room. The lobby was empty now except for the member with the pince-nez who was still dozing. It was silent

13

too, apart from the sporadic patter of the tape machine. Sir Peregrine put on his hat and coat, paused to peer at the latest offerings from the Press Association and walked out into the night. It was exactly 2 am on Harry Perkins' first day as Prime Minister.

Broadcasting House, the headquarters of the BBC, lies just north of Oxford Circus and about a mile from the Athenaeum. On general election nights it is the custom for the Director General to give a small drinks party for the governors, their spouses and a handful of senior executives. The party takes place in a sterile suite adjacent to the Director General's office on the third floor of Broadcasting House, down the corridor from the special radio election unit.

BBC governors are a small body of impartial men and women, whose job is to uphold the commitment to fairness and balance enshrined in the Corporation's charter. Although BBC governors are supposed to reflect a wide cross-section of society, it is fair to say that the political views of Harry Perkins were not within the spectrum of opinion which they embraced. As the alcohol flowed and the scale of Perkins' election victory was becoming clear, the wafer-thin veneer of impartiality which normally shrouds BBC pronouncements began to give way to something less dignified.

"CAT-AST-ROPHIC." The Belfast brogue of Sir Harry Boyd, who twenty years earlier had been the last Unionist Prime Minister of Northern Ireland, broke the gloomy silence around a television set which was delivering a computer prediction of a Labour majority of at least 100 seats. "Catastrophic," repeated Sir Harry quietly, collapsing into an armchair.

"We could be in for civil war," said Jonathan Alford, a rather correct man in his late thirties and a senior television news executive. Civil war was something Alford knew a bit about since he was also a major in the territorial Special Air Services. He was one of a number of senior BBC personnel whose spare time was spent scrambling over assault courses in

14

Herefordshire and attending lectures in army staff colleges on strike-breaking and riot control. The outgoing government had trebled the territorial army budget and left recruits in no doubt that they would have a rôle to play in the event of large scale civil disturbance.

Major Alford was just beginning to enlarge, rather glee-fully, some felt, on the prospects of civil war when he was interrupted by a shrill cry of, "Oh Christ, there goes Roddy," from over by the television set.

The scream, for that is what it was, emanated from the considerable frame of Dame Margaret Carrington, Justice of the Peace and chairperson of the Historic Homes Association. Roddy was Lieutenant-General Sir Rodney Appleton, until now Member of Parliament for Taunton, of whom it was once said, "If there was a canal in Taunton he'd send a gunboat up it." Sir Rodney was a neighbour of Dame Margaret's in Surrey.

Over by the door the Director General, Sir Roland Chance, was administering a stern warning to Jack Lansman, link-man on the breakfast-time radio news programme. It would be Lansman's job to break the news of Perkins' election victory to those members of the British public who hadn't sat glued to their television sets into the small hours. "I do hope we've got this straight, Jack," drawled the Director General. "You can't go on describing these people as 'extremists'. After all, they are now the government."

Lansman was unrepentant. "I've been calling them extremists for years, and nobody's ever complained."

The DG was sympathetic. "You really mustn't take this personally, old chap. I don't like them any more than you do. It's just that they've *won* and we shall have to take them seriously."

"If you say so," sighed Lansman, "but what about the moderates? Surely I can identify a moderate or two? Damn it all, the public have a right to know what they are in for."

"They'll find out soon enough. The public don't need any guidance from you. Just give it to them straight. No more labels. Do you understand?" Lansman nodded sulkily. The

15

DG sidled off to commiserate with Dame Margaret, leaving Lansman muttering, "I'll give it to them straight all right."

On leaving the Athenaeum, Sir Peregrine Craddock crossed Pall Mall and headed up a side street into St James's Square. He cut the corner by the London Library and turning left walked crisply up Duke of York Street, then through Church Place and into Piccadilly, emerging by the Church of St James. Although the buses had long since stopped, taxi cabs were doing brisk business and private cars still cruised towards Piccadilly Circus.

Turning left, Sir Peregrine walked quickly past Hatchards and Fortnum and Mason where he had recently purchased a pound of caviar to celebrate his daughter's birthday. Past the Royal Academy on the other side of Piccadilly, its huge metal gates locked shut, and past the Ritz Hotel. All symbols of everything he found best in the British way of life.

Sir Peregrine was a troubled man. For years he had laboured to keep British public life free from extremism. Every civil servant, every army officer, every MP, every BBC executive whose background betrayed the merest possibility of disloyalty had been quietly blocked from promotion. Now, overnight, all these years of hard work were threatened. Within days the establishment would be crawling with extremists. In Downing Street, the Cabinet Office, the Home Office, the Ministry of Defence, people who until now, thanks to DI5's good work, would not have qualified as doorkeepers in a government department would now be Cabinet ministers. And all because the British public was composed of ignorant clodheads who didn't know what was good for them. Sir Peregrine had never had much time for democracy, but this was the final straw.

By Green Park tube station Sir Peregrine crossed the road and turned right into Bolton Street. Those who did not know better might have assumed that this well-dressed, solitary gentleman was on his way to Shepherd Market where expensive ladies have long been known to provide a wide range of

16

unmentionable services for the upper classes at all times of the day and night. In fact Sir Peregrine was on his way to the DI5 Registry: a seven-storey, fortress-like building of Second World War vintage in Curzon Street, called simply Curzon Street House. Apart from the heavy lace curtains which are features of most secret service décor, there is nothing to indicate what goes on behind the solid walls of Curzon Street House. Those who get as far as the reception will notice only that the internal telephone directory is stamped 'Secret'. In the street directory the building is listed simply as 'central government offices'.

Sir Peregrine entered by the glass doors at the front of the building. Behind these was a steel portcullis with a small door and beyond a reception desk manned by a security officer. Briskly acknowledging the man's attempt at pleasantry, Sir Peregrine went straight to the lift. He emerged on the second floor, turned right and walked a few paces down a carpeted corridor to an unmarked door. Taking his wallet from an inside pocket, he withdrew what appeared to be a plastic banker's card and fed it into a slot in the wall. There was a muffled click as the machine checked the pass code and then, from the door, came the sound of a lock automatically disengaging. Sir Peregrine returned the pass to his wallet, turned the doorhandle and entered.

His office was a large and comfortable room. Wine-red velvet curtains were matched by thick Tibetan rugs. The walls were hung with Vietnamese watercolours and on a table by a lampshade stood a Burmese Buddha: reminders that Sir Peregrine had seen service in the East in his Foreign Office days.

The desk was a large Queen Anne affair, empty save for a tea mug full of felt-tip pens, a teak letter-opener and a framed picture of his wife and daughter. To one side, within easy reach of his swivel chair, stood a visual display unit, still encased in the blue plastic cover in which it had arrived five years ago. Sir Peregrine had only to tap the requisite code into the keyboard of the VDU in order to summon instantly to the screen the most intimate secrets of any one of the two million

17

or so people said to be on the Curzon Street computer. He had only to tap another button and a print-out would slide silently from the belly of the machine.

Gone were the days when clerks and secretaries commuted between the principal floor and the basement of Curzon Street House. Gone were the days of filling in requisition forms, frantic telephone calls to the Registry demanding reasons for delay. Today, on the application of a few simple codes, the secrets of the Curzon Street computer were instantly available.

Not that Sir Peregrine had much time for technology. He was one of the old school, trained in the days of triplicate memoranda and beige files. He had never made any serious attempt to master the VDU and so it stood unused, spurned, beside his desk, an incongruity among the Vietnamese water-colours and the Burmese Buddhas.

Sir Peregrine pressed a buzzer and immediately a side door opened to admit a sharp-featured young man wearing a dark suit and a blue and white striped shirt. This was Fiennes, personal assistant to the Director General. Fiennes was a high-flyer plucked straight from St Antony's College, Oxford, on the recommendation of his tutor.

"Things not going too well, are they, Fiennes?"

"No, sir."

"What have you got for me, then?"

"Actually, sir, there is not very much." He handed Sir Peregrine a beige file labelled 'Perkins, Harold A., Member of Parliament (Labour)'. The file contained about 200 sheets of computer print-out, including records of telephone conversations, photocopies of letters and details of Perkins' voting record on the Labour Party National Executive. There were also some photographs taken at demonstrations. On the top was a short summary of the contents, typed by Fiennes. Sir Peregrine read this and then looked up. "Is this the best you can do?"

"Seems to be all we have, sir."

"What about his sex life?"

"Not married, sir."

"Precisely. The man must have buggered or screwed somebody at some time or other."

"Not to our knowledge, sir. Lived with his mother in Sheffield until she died about ten years ago. Then he moved to London and bought a flat near the Kennington Oval. Leads a fairly humdrum sort of life." Fiennes flicked a lock of his blond hair away from his forehead.

"What about East European embassies? Surely he's in and out of those all the time. Most cf these lefties usually are."

"Perkins never seems to have been much of a one for freebies, sir."

"Well, we are going to have to do better than this." Sir Peregrine closed the file and handed it back to Fiennes. "When the new Cabinet is announced I want you to go through their files with a fine-toothed comb. And not just the Cabinet. Every minister of state, every under-secretary and, above all, any political advisers they bring in with them."

"Yes, sir," Fiennes was heading for the door. "And there is one other thing, sir."

"What's that?"

"Ebury Bridge Road have been on. They want to know if they're to keep the phone taps on Perkins and the other Labour people."

Sir Peregrine smiled. "Why not? Since the Prime Minister or the Home Secretary are theoretically our authority for tapping phones, Perkins and his men will be in the unusual situation of authorising taps on their own phones. I think that's rather amusing, don't you?"

Around the corner from Curzon Street, almost within sight of DI5 headquarters, the nightshift were reporting for duty at Annabel's. Annabel's was not the sort of place where Harry Perkins had a big following.

"Why doesn't someone turn that rubbish off?" A slick young man in a red velvet dinner jacket gestured to the colour

television set on the bar which was displaying the beaming features of Prime Minister-Elect Perkins.

"Sarah couldn't come tonight," said a girl in a light blue jumpsuit. "Her father said if she didn't go down to Sussex and vote Conservative he'd stop her allowance."

"Oh, the beast. Poor Sarah."

"Brilliant idea of Charlie's to come on here. We'd have been cutting our throats with depression at the Cavalry Club. Who's for a drink before we start noshing?" The young man in the velvet dinner jacket reached for his wallet.

At the bar a woman strung with pearls the size of gob-stoppers was saying she was too depressed even to *think* about food.

Someone hung a gravy-stained napkin over the television screen, obscuring the view of Perkins.

"Simply frightening that a man like that could become Prime Minister," said a slightly balding young man parked next to a bottle of champagne. "Shows how low the country's sunk." He was addressing nobody in particular.

"That's Roddy Bluff. He's microchips. Frightfully rich," whispered a slim blonde girl in a Fiorucci skirt. Lady Elizabeth Fain was the daughter of a Somerset landowner. Although she had left a fashionable girls' boarding school in Sussex at sixteen, and her higher education consisted of a finishing school in Switzerland, she knew more about the world than most girls of her background. For a start she read newspapers, a habit that made her unusual among the female clientele of Annabel's. She had also travelled, with a girl-friend, around India and Thailand, staying in cheap hotels and using only public transport. She even had friends who were left-wingers.

One in particular, Fred Thompson, was a journalist working for an impoverished publication called the *Independent Socialist*. Fred often joked that she was his one contact in what he called the master race. "I'm relying on you to use your influence to get me out when the coup comes," he used to say.

They had last met about three weeks ago, just as the

20

election campaign was getting under way. Fred had been in a serious mood. "They'll never let a Labour government headed by Harry Perkins take power," he told her.

"Who're 'they'?" she had asked innocently.

"Your friends in the City, the newspaper owners, the civil servants, all them sort of people."

Elizabeth had laughed at him. "You socialists are all the same – paranoid. Always thinking somebody's tapping your phone or blaming all your troubles on the capitalist press. Of course Perkins will take power, if he wins the election."

"I don't mean he'll be chucked in jail or anything crude like that," Fred had countered. "They'll do what they did at first in Chile. Slowly strangle us by cutting back trade and investment and delivering us into the hands of the IMF and the World Bank. I wouldn't be surprised if our ruling class don't team up with the Americans to help de-stabilise us. They may even organise a few riots, just to stir things up a bit. It's the Allende question all over again."

"The what?"

"Allende was the President of Chile twenty years ago. The Americans organised a coup and kicked him out." Fred's voice had assumed the patronising tone he always reserved for subjects of which he assumed Elizabeth knew nothing.

"I know about *that*," she had responded impatiently. "But what's Allende got to do with us?"

"Very simple," said Fred. "Would an elected socialist government that tried to implement the programme on which it was elected, be allowed to remain in office? Or would it be de-stabilised like Allende was?"

"This is Britain, not Chile," Elizabeth had responded firmly, "and Britain is a democracy. That sort of thing will never happen here."

Sitting in Annabel's with the television pundit now predicting a Labour majority of 100 seats, she reflected on her argument with Fred. She had not taken him seriously at the time because, quite apart from the fact that she had been brought up to believe that parliamentary democracy was the greatest thing since sliced bread, it never really occurred to

21

her that Harry Perkins would win. After all, he was an extremist, and she had also been brought up to believe that the British people would never vote for an extremist.

On the night of the Labour landslide in the 1945 general election a woman at the Savoy Hotel is reputed to have said: "My God, they've elected a Labour government. The country will never stand for it." And now at Annabel's on this fateful night history was repeating itself. "The trouble with the socialists," intoned the lady with the pearls, "is that they don't give a damn for the ordinary people of this country. Like us. They dish out wages to the unions all right, but what about the ordinary people of this country?"

Nearby a straight-faced waiter was presenting a folded bill to a young man sprawling shoeless on a pile of floor cushions. His girl-friend was glued to the television and eating chocolate peppermints. "Con Hold? Julian, where's Con Hold?"

Outside there was a slight drizzle and the young man in the red velvet dinner jacket was puking in Berkeley Square.

Harry Perkins first entered the in-tray of the American President at about 8.30 pm Washington time. The President was giving a dinner party for the executive members of the John Birch Society and their wives when an aide came to whisper the news.

"Jeeeesus Christ," hissed the President, his cigar quivering in sympathy and causing ash to spill on to his lapel. Those mother-fuckers in the CIA had screwed it up again. For months they had been telling him not to worry. This Perkins fellow did not stand a cat in hell's chance, they said. Trust our boys in London, they said. Never been wrong yet. Until tonight.

The President stayed just long enough to make a short speech to the John Birchers, who had made some generous contributions to his campaign funds. Then without going into details he referred to a threat to the Free World which required his urgent attention and headed for the elevator with a posse of secret service agents in tow.

By the time the President reached the Oval Office the head of the Central Intelligence Agency, the chairman of the Joint Chiefs of Staff, the Secretary of State and the President's National Security Adviser were already waiting.

"Okay, George," the President addressed the CIA chief, George McLennon, "how do you explain this one? Only two days ago your people were assuring me that Perkins was a busted flush. Now it seems he's going to be around for some time."

"Sorry, Mr President," stumbled McLennon who was already dreaming of the arses he was going to kick when he got back to Langley. "All I can tell you is what the British boys have been telling us and they've been saying everything was under control."

"That'll teach you guys to take any notice of what that pack of amateurs in London have to say," said the President with venom. Then he nodded towards a man with white cropped hair and cold blue eyes. "Anton, what's your assessment?"

Anton Zablonski, National Security Adviser, an old school world conspiracy man, big on bombing and direct action. Zablonski looked the President straight in the eye, "Mr President, this could be bigger than El Salvador. Perkins' boys have been talking about making Britain a neutral country. That means withdrawing from NATO, kicking out our Third Air Force and doing away with their nuclear submarines. We also lose a base for our cruise missiles. In budget terms Britain is the biggest contributor to NATO, but the main effect would be political, not military. Without Britain the whole alliance could disintegrate."

Despite forty years in the United States Zablonski had not lost his thick Polish accent. The more doomladen his pronouncements, the thicker it became. "Italy's always been wobbly," he went on. "France opted out years ago and the Dutch have never taken the Soviet menace as seriously as we have. Until now Britain has always been our strongest ally, almost a sort of satellite state. We only had to say jump and they jumped."

"Vernon?"

The President had turned to Admiral Vernon Z. Glugstein, chairman of the Joint Chiefs of Staff, the man who had once described 'peace' as the most dangerous word in the English language. Glugstein gave a deep sigh before speaking. "I agree with Anton, Mr President. For all practical purposes Britain's gone over to the other side. Neutrality and Communism are the same thing in my book."

"Easy, Vernon," McLennon interrupted, "it's early days yet. The British Labour Party's notorious for saying one thing in opposition and doing the opposite in government. Let's wait and see what happens."

"Nobody's suggesting we should rush into anything," said the President, "but we'd better make darn sure we're prepared. I don't want any more fuck-ups. The future of Western security is at stake. George, what have we got on the files for de-stabilising Britain?"

"Nothing much, I'm afraid, Mr President. Last thing I can find is dated July 1945. Apparently the Defense Department threw together a plan for a full-scale invasion if the Attlee government went too far. All looks a bit crazy to me."

"Perhaps I can help," interrupted Marcus J. Morgan, the Secretary of State, a corporation lawyer, very fat and very rich. "I had the backroom boys at the National Security Council throw together some options."

"Go ahead, Marcus."

"The key is the British economy. It's in pretty bad shape and not in a position to stand up to much pressure. The first point is, we own about ten per cent of it. Bought it up cheap, after the war. We could easily persuade one or two of the bigger corporations to pull out. Some of them want to anyway."

He was interrupted by the rustle of silver paper. The President was unwrapping a spearmint chewing gum. The President was big on spearmint chewing gum. "Go on Marcus, go on."

"Secondly, there's trade. We account for about twelve per cent of Britain's exports and, if necessary, we could go elsewhere. Thirdly, there's the IMF. Britain is running a very

big balance of payments deficit and before long they are going to have to look for a loan. Since we are the biggest contributors to the IMF, we're in a strong position."

The President palmed the silver paper into a neat ball and, with expert aim, lobbed it into a wastepaper bin by the door. Morgan turned the page of his NSC brief and continued. "Fourthly, there's sterling: the United States and the oil-producing countries hold large deposits in London banks. We could start selling and persuade the Arabs to do likewise. We'd have them by the balls, if we did that. Finally, there's covert action: our embassy in London has a few small programmes running. We could expand these. Buy up a few trade union leaders, some Labour MPs, that sort of thing . . . ."

"We gotta be careful, Mr President," cautioned McLennon, a veteran of too many failed State Department spectaculars to want to be rushed into a new one. It was always the same. A Secretary of State whose knowledge of the geography was largely gleaned from a *Time-Life* Atlas and the currency markets. A President who wanted to be seen acting tough. And when the whole thing blew up in their faces, nobody would want to know. The CIA would be left to take the rap.

"Britain's not some third-rate banana republic," said McLennon. "If we move too fast, we could create a backlash and turn the other European allies against us."

"Sure, George," said the President irritably. Deep down he knew the CIA Director was right. But just now George McLennon was not his favourite person. "What I want to know," said the President, "is can we expect any help from the inside?"

"I reckon we can, sir." McLennon had perked up a bit. "Fact is there are going to be a lot of very unhappy people in Britain after tonight. A lot of very important persons are about to get their toes trodden on and they aren't going to like it. We can expect to find friends in the top levels of the armed forces, the business community and the civil service, not to mention our cousins at DI5. As far as propaganda goes, we can start the fightback right now, since most of the British

25

press is in friendly hands – although Perkins has said he's going to do something about that."

There was a brief silence, broken only by the sound of the President chewing, then he summed up: "Right, gentlemen. Agreed we wait and see how things turn out. Meantime, George, get your people in London to take some soundings and find out who our friends are going to be. Marcus, you get the NSC boys to put some flesh on that de-stabilisation blueprint. And, very discreetly, sound out the rest of the Alliance to see who we could take with us if the worst comes to the worst."

The President paused, took a deep breath, and looked in turn at each man. "Let's be clear. The election of Harry Perkins could be the biggest threat to the stability of the Free World since Joe Stalin. We have to do everything possible to keep him in his place. Everything short of landing the Marines at Dover."

2

Harry Perkins did not intend to become a Labour MP. Having left school at fifteen he followed his father into Firth Brown, the Sheffield special steels plant. From the start he was active in the union, first as assistant branch secretary and later as treasurer.

After five years at Firth's the union paid for him to go on a scholarship to Ruskin College, where he gained a first class honours degree in politics and economics before returning to Sheffield. Before long he was elected convener for the whole plant, which made him chief negotiator for the union side in all dealings with the Firth management. His relations with management were cordial, but not matey. The managing director once remarked, "If I stepped under a bus tomorrow the mills would still be rolling the next day, but if Harry went under a bus the whole place would grind to a halt."

"So long as you realise," Perkins had responded cheerfully.

One evening after he had been back from Ruskin for four years, there came a knock on the front door. It was the secretary of a constituency Labour party on the other side of Sheffield, where a by-election was pending. "We want some-one local, someone who knows about steel and who's on the left. So far all we've got applying are bleeding London barristers and sociology lecturers. Some of the lads thought you might be interested."

Perkins was not keen. His father had been dead twelve years and his mother was getting on in life. Who was going to look after her if he was running up and down to London all the time? But Mrs Perkins, when consulted, said she rather fancied the idea of her Harry being an MP.

Then there was the union, what about the union? They hadn't wasted all that precious money sending him to Ruskin just so he could be a Labour MP. But a phone call to the

27

district secretary confirmed that this was exactly what they had in mind.

Perkins said he'd think about it. He thought for two days before agreeing to let his name go forward. The selection was a walkover; as for the election itself, in Sheffield they weigh the Labour votes. His majority was massive. Next morning his workmates from Firth's turned out in force at the station to see him off to London.

Like many working men who find themselves catapulted into Parliament, Harry Perkins let the place go to his head a little. Although he stayed out of the bars and ate mainly in the Strangers' cafeteria the House of Commons brought out a streak of vanity which had hitherto lain dormant. As time passed he lost the ability to concentrate on what other people were saying. His appreciation of events began to revolve around the part he had played in them. His eyes would start to wander during conversation or he would butt in before the other person had finished speaking.

By parliamentary standards it was nothing serious. Indeed, the trait was almost invisible to anyone who did not know Perkins well, but in Sheffield some of his old friends did remark quietly that Parliament seemed to be going to Harry's head. Even so, no one questioned that Perkins was doing a splendid job of shaking up the parliamentary establishment. For a while he became the scourge of the Tory front bench at question time and on occasion did not hesitate to tear a strip off the Labour front bench as well.

Like many before him, however, Perkins soon realised that wherever power lies in Great Britain it is not in the chamber of the House of Commons. Thus he began to concentrate on leading the fight outside Parliament. For three years there was hardly an invitation to speak which he turned down. The more meetings he addressed, the more the invitations multiplied. Gradually, the rise of Harry Perkins had begun.

When Labour was returned to government Perkins was asked to be Secretary of State for the Public Sector, a new post designed to make the nationalised industries accountable to Parliament. It was a meteoric rise for someone who had

never been so much as a junior minister. With no love lost between Perkins and the Labour leadership, he was under no illusions as to why he had been offered the job. "They're just trawling for a left-winger to make the régime look respectable," he told his friends. All the same, he accepted.

Perkins' spell in government was dominated by what was in later years to become known as the Windermere reactor affair. As Secretary of State for the Public Sector he was responsible for the Central Electricity Generating Board. The Board was in the process of choosing the type of nuclear reactor for a series of new power stations which would generate enough electricity to meet demand until well into the next century. By the time Perkins took office the decision involved a straight choice between a water-cooled reactor made by the Durand Corporation, an American multinational with a reputation for hard sell, and a gas-cooled reactor to be made by British Insulated Industries, a corporation with its head office in Manchester. To the winner the contract was worth a billion pounds.

Every day delegations of hard-nosed businessmen and learned scientists filed through the Secretary of State's second floor office at Millbank. Behind them they left abstruse memoranda setting out their case. The Americans said their version was cheaper. The men from British Insulated claimed they could get back their costs by selling reactors to the Shah of Iran (whose demise at that time was but a twinkle in the eye of the Ayatollah). The Americans said their version was already in use and had proved as safe as houses. British Insulated brought in experts who alleged that it was not.

And so it went on day after day, week after week. Each night when Perkins boarded a number 3 bus he took back to his flat in Kennington red despatch boxes brimming with memoranda arguing the comparative merits of water-cooled and gas-cooled reactors. There were times, as he sat up late into the night poring over papers he could scarcely comprehend, when he wished he was back at Firth Brown's. Alone in the living room of his three-room flat in the small hours of the

morning, the absolute self-confidence he carried through life deserted him. This was no job for a Sheffield steel worker. More than once he reflected on the irony that he, a product of Parkside Secondary School who had barely scraped an 'O' level in Physics, was in a position to over-rule the finest minds in the scientific establishment.

In the end that is exactly what he did. Against the advice of his own civil servants, the Atomic Energy Authority and the CEGB itself, Perkins ruled in favour of British Insulated. The first reactor would be built on the shore of Lake Windermere. The recommendation went to the Cabinet and he talked it through in the face of bitter hostility from his own civil servants. So committed had they been to the American reactor that they refused point blank to provide him with the necessary briefing papers for the Cabinet. Instead he had to commission a report setting out the case for the British reactor from outside academics.

For Perkins the deciding factor was jobs. It was no secret that British Insulated was on the edge of ruin. If they lost the contract a string of factories from Portsmouth to Port Greenock would close. The union men had been to see him. Delegations of shop stewards from every British Insulated factory in the country. In Greenock alone thirty per cent of the town's labour force were employed at British Insulated. Perkins had no desire to be remembered as the man who closed down Greenock. Having satisfied himself that there was nothing to choose between the two reactors on safety grounds, he opted to buy British.

"If you don't mind my saying so, Minister," said Sir Richard Fry, the Permanent Secretary, "I think you have made a big mistake."

"Time will tell," Perkins had replied.

Time did tell. Several years later at Three Mile Island in Pennsylvania an overheated uranium core in a water-cooled reactor led to a radiation leak and the evacuation of a large number of people from their homes. Shortly after the incident Perkins, who had long since returned to the backbenches, received a hand-written note in an envelope bearing the seal

of the Public Sector Department. The note, in elegant italic script, said simply: "You were right. We were wrong." It was signed Richard Fry.

Perkins had the letter framed and hung it on the wall of his room in the House of Commons.

It was during the reactor negotiations that Perkins first met Molly Spence. The managing director of British Insulated had come to see Perkins at the Department. He had brought with him his head of research and development, two scientists to advise on safety aspects and a striking blonde girl who took notes. She was aged twenty-seven, her nose was lightly freckled and her expensive accent had a trace of Yorkshire.

Mid-morning they broke for coffee. Someone from the private office produced a packet of digestive biscuits and the girl took hers and walked over to the window. Perkins followed.

"I like your view," she said, indicating the River Thames. She was standing sideways on to the window, half looking at Perkins, half at the river. The light on her face made her eyes gleam.

"I don't get much chance to look at it," said Perkins, drawing alongside. A convoy of red buses passed over Lambeth Bridge and below, on the river, a barge passed on its way to Hammersmith.

"What's that?"

"What?"

"That sort of castle on the other side of the bridge."

"Lambeth Palace, where the Archbishop of Canterbury lives."

"He's done all right for himself." She smiled lightly.

"Aye," said Perkins, "the Church of England's worth a bob or two."

They were interrupted by a private secretary who came with letters to be signed. Perkins took a fountain pen from his inside pocket and signed, scarcely glancing at the letters. The girl waited in silence, staring out at the river. It was Perkins who broke the silence. "Sounds like you're a Yorkshire lass."

"Sheffield," she said.

"That's where I'm from."

"I know," she said.

Before he could speak again the private secretary was back. "Minister, I think we ought to make a start. You have the Select Committee at noon." There was a clinking of crockery as a lady with a trolley collected the cups. They turned and walked back to the conference table and she said, almost in a whisper, "I think you knew my dad."

"Did I?"

"Jack Spence, works manager at Firth Brown."

"Good heavens," said Perkins, "is he your father?"

She nodded. They did not get a chance to talk again, but when British Insulated came back to the Department two weeks later, Perkins slipped her an envelope. He tried to do it discreetly so that the private office would not gossip, but he had been seen. David Booth, a young high-flyer on second-ment from the Treasury to the nuclear division of the Public Sector Department saw the girl put the envelope in her handbag. At the time he thought nothing of it. The girl was beautiful and the Secretary of State was unmarried. He might have done the same himself had Perkins not beaten him to it.

Molly was dying to open the envelope. On the way out she excused herself and disappeared into the ladies. She cut along the top of the envelope with a nail file. Inside was a single sheet of notepaper which at the top bore the legend "From the Secretary of State". The message inside written in red ink simply said: "Lunch Sunday? Ring me at midnight." And then a telephone number.

There was nothing else. The envelope did not even bear her name. Afterwards it occurred to Molly that this was because Perkins did not know her name. Trembling slightly she stuffed the letter into her handbag and went to catch up with her boss who was waiting in the main reception. That evening, at midnight precisely, she telephoned to say "Yes."

Where women were concerned, Harry Perkins was a late developer. He passed through Parkside Secondary School without ever giving the girls in his class a second glance. It was not that he didn't have friends. There was Nobby Jones whose father was a signalman on the railway. Bill Spriggs, who lived in Jubilee Street, which backed on to the same alley as the Perkins house. And Danny Parker, whose father also worked at Firth Brown. They were all in the same class and went around together. At weekends and during school holidays Nobby's father would sometimes smuggle them into his signal box, where they would sit for hours, with notepads and pencils, jotting down engine numbers. Sometimes when it rained they would go back to Perkins' house and play cards, gin rummy usually. They used to sit round the dining-room table, each with a heap of used threepenny stamps as the stake. Harry never had much luck with cards and very often his supply of used stamps was cleaned out by the end of an afternoon. "Never mind, Harry," Mrs Perkins used to say, "unlucky in cards, lucky in love."

As it turned out Perkins didn't have much luck with love either. By the time they reached the fourth form the other lads had lost interest in train-spotting and gin rummy. Instead they took up girls and pop music.

It was in a rather downmarket coffee bar called Brady's that romance first blossomed. Bill Spriggs and Nobby Jones both did paper rounds and so they could afford to spend the after-school hours sitting round Brady's formica-topped tables tapping their toes to music from the juke box and making a single cup of Brady's awful coffee stretch out over two hours. Occasionally Perkins went with them, but his shilling-a-week pocket money did not run to many cups of coffee, let alone allow for feeding the juke box. Besides, he was not much interested. By the time he was fourteen he preferred to spend an hour browsing through the newspapers in the reading room of the city library. It was the time of the Korean war. Day by day in the *Daily Worker* young Perkins would follow the progress of MacArthur's army as it inched its way up the Korean peninsula towards the border with China.

One evening in Brady's he tried to interest Danny Parker in Korea, but all Danny could talk about was a third-form girl called Lucy Marston whom he had just taken up with. "Last night she let me feel her tits," exulted Danny.

Perkins was disgusted. "Here we are with the world about to blow up and all you're interested in is Lucy Marston's tits." That was the last time he went to Brady's. Most weekends he stayed at home reading. Now and then he would go with his schoolmates to see United play; sometimes a crowd of them would go to the cinema. Danny and Nobby would bring their girl-friends along, but Perkins always played gooseberry. Once they passed themselves off as sixteen year olds and got into an X film called *Flood of Tears*. It was set in America, about a dam that burst and in the floods that followed prisoners escaped from the local jail. Two of the convicts, a murderer and a rapist, end up trapped by the rising waters and seeking refuge in a house with a beautiful girl. What followed was Perkins' introduction to sex. It was pretty tame stuff by today's standards, but for the next few years it was all he had to go on.

Gradually he saw less and less of his schoolfriends. After classes they would go their own ways. Perkins to the library, the others to Brady's. Sometimes on Saturday afternoons, they would meet up at a football match, but that was all they had in common.

Four weeks after Perkins' fifteenth birthday his father was killed in an accident at work. Two steel ingots being loaded by crane on to a lorry fell on him when a cable snapped. But for the accident he would have stayed on at school. His teachers tipped him as Parkside's first candidate for university. Instead he left to take his father's place at Firth Brown.

Perkins' first real girl-friend was Anne Scully. A small, neat girl who was receptionist at the district office of the engineering union. He had been four years at Firth's and met her when he went to pay in the subscriptions from his branch. Anne was quite unlike Perkins. She liked dancing and Buddy Holly and had never read a book – at least not through to the end. That summer they went for long walks in the Pennines and Perkins

34

tried explaining about imperialism (it was the year of Suez) and the goings-on in his union branch. Anne tried hard to understand, but was happier gossiping about who was marrying whom and who was having babies. "You're so bloody serious, Harry Perkins," she scolded him, "always got your head stuck in a newspaper. Why can't you just relax and enjoy life for a change?"

Those days with Anne were the nearest he ever came to relaxing. The high spot of their relationship was a camping holiday in the Lake District. That was in the summer of 1956. For ten days the sun shone brightly. The days they would spend ambling hand in hand along the shore of Lake Windermere, the evenings singing songs with the locals in a pub called The Water's Edge, and the nights snuggled up in the warmth of a single sleeping bag, borrowed from Anne's brother-in-law who ran a camping shop.

They went steady for the best part of three years, until Perkins went to Ruskin. "That'll be the end of us," said Anne sadly. "You'll meet all kinds of fancy people in Oxford and forget about me."

"Don't be daft," he tried to reassure her, but he knew she was right. It was not so much the fancy people, as the distance. At first he hitch-hiked home nearly every weekend. Once Anne came to stay in his digs at Oxford, but the landlady soon put a stop to that. After a while the visits got fewer. The gaps between letters grew longer. In the end they just drifted apart.

By the time he left Ruskin, Anne was married. Perkins got no sympathy from his mother. "That girl was the best thing that ever happened to you," she told him. "If you had any sense, you would have married her while you had the chance." As he passed the years alone he began to think that his mother had been right. Until he met Molly Spence.

"My Dad used to think you were a bit of a bastard," said Molly as she helped herself to salad dressing.

"Between you and I," said Perkins, winking at her, "I was a bit of a bastard."

Molly had never been to lunch with a Cabinet minister before. For the occasion she wore a cotton skirt patterned with red tulips which descended to mid-calf and swirled when she turned suddenly, and a white blouse which did justice to her breasts. Perkins had opened the door to her in his shirt sleeves and a pair of worn brown corduroys.

She was surprised at where he lived. It was a street of late Victorian houses five minutes from the Oval tube station. Perkins' flat was on the third floor. The living room was tastefully, but not extravagantly furnished. Shelves lined with books of Labour Party history and political memoirs. The fireplace had been bricked off, but the mantelpiece remained. Upon it stood a framed photograph of Perkins surrounded by a cluster of small oriental gentlemen.

"Taken in Hanoi," said Perkins when he saw Molly examining the photograph, "two years ago with a delegation."

"And this?" Molly fingered the white bust which sat on the mantelpiece beside the photograph.

"That," said Perkins in a slightly patronising tone, "is J. Keir Hardie."

"Oh," said Molly, none the wiser.

"I don't suppose they taught you anything about him at school."

"Not that I remember."

"Keir Hardie was the first Labour MP," he said, pulling the cork from a bottle of Côte du Rhône.

He poured two glasses and passed one to Molly. "Your health," he said, raising his glass.

"Yours," said Molly, her blue eyes looking straight at him.

They sat at the oak dining table eating the steak that Perkins had just grilled. A Handel organ concerto played on the stereo. They talked about Sheffield. About Firth Brown. About Molly's Dad and Mum who lived in Hallam, on Sheffield's posh side. Perkins told her about the life of a Cabinet minister. Up at six. In the office by eight. Home at midnight. About the red despatch boxes full of letters to sign, memoranda to digest and reports to read. About the time he sat next to the Queen at a lunch for some Arab potentate.

After the steak they had Marks and Spencer's cheesecake and then Perkins suggested a stroll in Kennington Park.

That was how the affair began.

Before she went to bed with Harry Perkins, Molly first looked him up in *Who's Who* to see if he was married. Not that she would have been especially upset if there had been a Mrs Perkins. She just thought she ought to know. Molly was one of those girls who only seem to attract married men. She did not go out of her way to find them. It was just that in the circles in which she moved she had lost the habit of talking to people of her own age.

Affairs with married men had schooled Molly in the art of discretion. At the time the newspapers were engaged in one of their periodic anti-extremist campaigns and Perkins was a prime target. Had Molly been seen with him she would certainly have found her picture on the front page of the popular dailies. The idea appealed to her, but she knew it wouldn't appeal to Perkins.

Molly came once a week, usually on a Sunday. Perkins spent Friday nights and most Saturdays in Sheffield and when he returned he brought with him a pile of constituency mail to be dealt with. More than once Molly arrived expecting to make love and instead found herself sitting up into the small hours typing out what Perkins insisted were urgent letters urging the Home Office not to deport one of his constituents.

From the start Perkins knew there was no future in it. He sensed that she knew too. He was a lonely man, but he had long since reconciled himself to loneliness. Marriage required concessions which he was not prepared to make. He would have had to sacrifice time to small talk and to take an interest in things that bored him stiff. Marriage meant children. Children meant disruption of a life that was already spoken for. There was a time when he might have married. Maybe when he was at Firth Brown. Even perhaps in the early years in Parliament, but not now. Although Perkins would have argued that his life was dedicated to the service of others, it was also a selfish existence in which there was no room for

full-time residents, only the occasional guest. That was where Molly came in.

She made no demands on him. Usually she arrived after dark to avoid the prying eyes. In the lighter summer evenings she would ring first from the Oval tube station and he would go downstairs and open the front door to minimise the risk of alerting the neighbours. The routine rarely varied. There would be a record, usually Brahms or Handel, on the stereo. The table would be set for two. The Sunday newspapers, half read, would be scattered near a floor cushion by the window. Red despatch boxes were stacked in the hallway awaiting collection by a Ministry chauffeur. Another stood open on the writing desk in the corner with half its contents still awaiting attention in a neat pile.

If Perkins was cooking, the meal would be simple. Pâté, a Marks and Spencer pie, vegetables, and a bottle of not very expensive wine. If, as was more often the case, Molly was cooking, the meal might run to a joint of lamb. Since Perkins didn't have time to shop, she would bring the food with her in a wicker basket. He would always insist on repaying her, usually by cheque since he never seemed to have the time to go to a bank.

Conversation centred around what Perkins had been up to in the previous week. Sometimes they gossiped. Molly liked discussing the private lives of public figures. Inside information, however trite, gave her a small thrill. Occasionally Perkins would regale her with an account of a little coup he had scored at a Cabinet sub-committee. Now and then they would discuss politics. Usually it was fairly basic stuff. He would talk of kicking out the American nuclear bases and she would say, "What about the Russians?" They would argue for perhaps five minutes before Perkins gave up, feigning disgust. "You sound like the bloody *Daily Mail*," he would say half seriously. She would kiss him and they would go to bed, leaving the washing up in the sink.

It wasn't much of a love affair and by Molly's standards the Secretary of State was not much of a lover. Her other lovers wooed her with flowers, dinners in West End restaurants and

expensive presents. The only present she ever received from Perkins was a copy of *The Ragged Trousered Philanthropists*. In the front he had written with a red felt pen, "To a slightly Tory lady in the hope that she will see the light." It was signed, "Love, Harry" and followed by three kisses. She struggled through the first fifty pages and then gave up. Molly had never had much time for books.

After about a year Molly stopped coming. Her disappearance was announced in a note which was only a little longer than the one with which Perkins had first brought her into his life. It read: "Dear Harry, on Saturday I'm getting married so we'll have to call it a day. Please understand. Good luck. Molly." For about an hour Perkins was devastated. He made himself a cup of tea and paced his modest living room composing a reply which in the end he did not send. He toyed with the idea of telephoning, but rejected it on the grounds that the telephone might be answered by Molly's prospective husband. Instead he placed the note in his in-tray along with a pile of other unanswered correspondence. A few days later he filed it away in a green folder together with a postcard she had once sent him while on a skiing holiday in Austria and several notes, none more than half a page long, which mainly concerned arrangements for their Sunday night rendezvous and who should get the shopping. He labelled the folder 'Molly' and placed it between similar files labelled 'Micro-chips' and 'Multinationals' in a steel filing cabinet in the spare bedroom. His only other souvenirs were a yellow plastic bathing cap and a Wisdom toothbrush which she left behind in the bathroom.

Perkins had been in the Cabinet for three years when the government started to close down steel mills. He resigned at once to take part in the resistance. The following year he was swept on to the Labour Party National Executive. Three years later he was topping the poll. Looking back, his election as leader of the Labour Party seemed inevitable, but at the time it took everyone by surprise.

3

By the time Harry Perkins became leader of Her Majesty's Opposition, Labour had been out of power for a decade. Although the National Unity government had brought inflation under control, it had only done so at the cost of massive unemployment and great social violence.

The inner city riots which began in the summer of 1981 grew steadily worse as the decade wore on. Shopkeepers began to evacuate. The buses stopped operating after dark when the police said they could no longer guarantee the safety of the bus crews. Brixton High Street became a corridor of estate agents' fading signs and chipboarded shop fronts smeared with graffiti. "Avenge the Railton Five," said one in a reference to five West Indian youths killed in Railton Road when police opened fire on a crowd of petrol bombers. Another said simply: "Burn Brixton," but it had already been overtaken by events.

Gradually, the inner cities were abandoned to roaming bands of unemployed youths and more and more police were required to stop them breaking out into the suburbs where owner-occupiers with jobs lived. In ten years the police budget had doubled. In Brixton, Toxteth, Handsworth, Moss Side and the Gorbals police in armoured cars and bullet-proof jackets patrolled the streets. Around the city centres special units of riot police on permanent stand-by sat fidgeting with their new, lethal nightsticks, imported from America.

In February 1988 Trotskyism had been banned by legislation rushed through Parliament in three days. This had followed the discovery of an arms cache in a derelict house in Islington, said to be used by the International Marxist Group. Some said the guns had been supplied by the IRA, others said they had been planted by the police. No matter, Trotskyism was now illegal. Army camps on Salisbury Plain were filled not only with rioters, but suspected Trotskyists, too. Under

the new law only a single witness, usually an anonymous member of the Special Branch, was needed to secure a conviction for Trotskyism.

The mid-1980s were also the time in which the long struggle between industrial and financial capital was finally resolved in favour of the financiers. For decades successive British governments had pursued policies of high interest rates and manipulation of demand, designed to favour those engaged in speculation rather than production. In these circumstances the only worthwhile investments were short-term ones promising high returns. Even industrial companies already profitable were advised by their accountants to 'go liquid' and hold their assets in cash, gold or oil paintings rather than in new plant and equipment.

As if this were not serious enough, exchange controls (removed by an earlier Tory government) had never been restored thereby making possible what one industrialist, in the privacy of his boardroom, called a 'scorched earth policy'. As the crisis grew worse, the outflow of capital increased.

On the Clyde and the Tyne shipbuilding all but disappeared. A few rusting hulks remained in the yards, half completed at the time British Shipbuilders was allowed to go under. Asset strippers, sharp young men who came from London in Rolls-Royces, wandered among the ruins buying up at bargain prices the cranes and any other movables which they sold at large profits to yards in Spain and France. The hulks that remained were decaying monuments to an industry which had consumed generations of engineers, boiler-makers, welders and fitters. Those who were young enough moved south in search of work. Some went to work in Arabia. Those who were too old or too set in their ways to move stayed put and went down with their ships.

The fishing industry had long since disappeared. In Aberdeen, Fleetwood, Grimsby, Hull and Lowestoft a few rotting trawlers bobbed idly at anchor. They were all that remained of the proud fleets that once roamed the North Sea from the

41

English Channel to the Arctic Circle. One or two more enterprising skippers had converted their trawlers into pleasure boats taking day trippers for rides along the coast during the summer, but it was no way to make a living. The trawlermen blamed the Common Market for their ruin.

In Yorkshire and Lancashire the textile industry finally succumbed to cheap and inferior imports from Taiwan and South Korea. Calls for import controls, delegations to ministries and mass lobbies of Parliament fell upon deaf ears. Men from ministries on index-linked pensions came and looked at the books. It was, they said, a tough old world. If textile workers in Bolton could not compete with those in Taipei and Seoul they would have to go down the plughole.

There was some brave resistance. Scattered work-ins, here and there attempts to set up a co-operative, but there was never really any hope. In the end the textile industry followed shipbuilding and fishing into history.

This did little to damage the political base of the National Unity government. Textiles, ships and fish were the products of Labour strongholds. Elsewhere the belief was widespread that only the inefficient, the idle and the greedy were unemployed, a belief fostered by the popular newspapers. For a time one of Sir George Fison's newspapers even ran a 'Scrounger of the Week' competition, urging people to spy upon unemployed neighbours and offering cash prizes to those who could uncover the most outrageous fiddles.

The collapse of British Leyland was the beginning of the end. Leyland had been the country's biggest export earner and largest employer. One November morning the chairman of Leyland had appeared at the Department of Industry to tell the Secretary of State that his company could no longer service its debts, never mind finance further investment. He needed an extra £500 million immediately and probably the same again next year.

There were emergency Cabinet meetings, a frantic round of negotiations with a Japanese corporation, but in the end the cupboard was bare and most of British Leyland was

42

allowed to go to the wall. The bus and truck company was sold to the Japanese. The Rover plant went to Volkswagen of Germany who promptly turned it into an assembly plant for one of its own models. The collapse of Leyland also triggered off a wave of bankruptcies which swept through components firms in the Midlands. At last the crisis began to lap at the edge of the Unity government's political base.

The third element in the disaster which overtook Britain in the late 1980s was that North Sea oil began to dry up. For most of the previous decade Britain had been self-sufficient in oil. This meant that, besides not having to spend precious foreign exchange importing oil, the government also received huge revenue from the taxes on the profits of the oil companies. In a sane world this temporary good fortune might have been used to provide industry with the investment funds so badly needed. However, most of the oil revenue was squandered on tax cuts designed to buy favour with the electorate.

As domestic oil supplies dwindled Britain was obliged to go back on to the world markets to purchase oil again. It is true that by this time scientists had succeeded in converting sugar cane and other vegetable matter into a substitute for oil, but it was not yet being produced in anything like commercial quantities. Britain's import bill began to increase dramatically. A balance of payments crisis meant that the foreign holders of sterling would start selling. So too would domestic holders, since they were no longer bound by exchange controls.

For those engaged in certain forms of non-productive activity life had never been so good. As money poured out of manufacturing industry, more became available for speculation in commodities, property and works of art. Because the supply of these was relatively limited and the amount of cash chasing them was for all practical purposes unlimited, what went up was not supply, but prices. The value of gold soared; coffee, rubber, tin and a host of other commodities fluctuated wildly as fortunes were won and lost by those who could afford to gamble in futures.

Property boomed, fuelled by the pension funds – the accumulated savings of millions of citizens. The London docks were filled in and replaced by skyscrapers bearing names such as Hay's Wharf Towers and West India House. The names offered the only clues to what had gone before, in the days when Britain had been a trading nation. The 1980s property boom, the craziest of all time, was still in progress when Harry Perkins came to power.

For most of the decade that preceded the election of Perkins and his government the orgy of speculation which lay at the heart of the British disease was, in the minds of many people, camouflaged by the view that political extremists and greedy workers were to blame. By the end of the 1980s, however, certain weaknesses had become apparent in that line of thinking. Real wages had fallen, public spending had been cut back drastically, the trade unions had been neutered; yet still the slide into ruin continued. By the end of the decade the huge campaign to pin the blame for Britain's ills on extremists had finally run out of steam.

The newspapers received the elevation of Perkins with unprecedented hysteria. "Go Back to Moscow," screamed the *Sun*, unable to come to terms with the fact that 'Red Harry' (as the papers insisted on calling him) had never actually set foot in Moscow. "LABOUR VOTES FOR SUICIDE," raged the *Express*, and *The Times* ran a long leading article which argued that the election of Perkins spelled the end of the two-party system since the British people would never be foolish enough to vote into office a government headed by such a man. Even the *Daily Mirror*, traditionally loyal to Labour, thought the choice of Perkins was the end.

Despite their firm belief that a Labour Party led by Perkins stood no chance of winning an election, the press barons took no chances. No one had done more to alert the British people to the perils of extremism than Sir George Fison (indeed, he had been awarded a knighthood for his services in this

44

regard). But the general election of March 1989 was his finest hour.

Day after day in the run-up to polling Sir George's newspapers published lists of 'Communist-backed' Labour candidates. By way of evidence they offered an article in the *Morning Star* or a platform shared by a Labour MP and a member of the Communist Party. A week before election day Sir George's newshounds 'discovered' documents purporting to show that four senior Labour leaders were paid-up members of a Trotskyist cell.

Not to be outdone, the *Express* took to publishing a picture of Perkins daubed with a Hitler moustache, and words such as 'mugging' and 'terrorism' began to creep into discussion of what life in Harry Perkins' Britain held in store. One leading article was headed "Perkins, the demon mugger unmasked." *The Times*, now owned by an American computer company, provided its readers with a slightly upmarket version of the same: claiming at one stage to have discovered a plot by Trotskyites to blow up the Cenotaph in the event of a Labour election defeat. Another paper splashed on its front page an internal Labour Party document outlining plans to abolish tax relief on mortgages and confiscate all personal wealth over £50,000. Enquiry revealed that the document was a forgery, but the retraction was tucked away at the bottom of an inside page.

Only the *Guardian* and the *Financial Times* conceded that there were any issues to be debated and even they concluded that the election of Perkins would be a catastrophe. One commentator went so far as to speculate that this could be the last free election which the British people would enjoy for many years. Events were to prove him correct, though for reasons rather different from those inferred at the time.

But Harry Perkins had no inkling of what was to come as he set out by train for London on his first glorious morning as Prime Minister of Great Britain.

4

Perkins arrived at St Pancras a little after 10 am. He was bearing exactly the luggage with which he had departed for Sheffield on the final morning of the election campaign two days earlier: a British Airways bag containing two shirts and a change of underwear and a rather battered briefcase embossed with his initials – a present from his constituency party on the tenth anniversary of his election.

He had hoped to occupy the journey down sketching out details of his Cabinet and the host of other appointments he would have to make, but from the moment the sleek Advanced Passenger Train glided out of Sheffield he had been harassed by newspaper men who had chosen to ride down with him. For a while bedlam prevailed as reporters, photographers, camera crews, autograph hunters and assorted well-wishers fought to get near. It was not until the train passed Leicester that the ticket inspector, with the aid of a steward from the dining car, was able to restore some sort of order. Perkins began to realise why Prime Ministers did not travel second class.

In the end, all he managed was a glance at the newspapers purchased on the platform at Sheffield. They were mainly early editions and although by the time they had gone to press Labour appeared to be winning, the scale of the victory was unclear. Considering the onslaught to which Perkins and his party had been subjected before the election, newspaper treatment of the impending Labour victory seemed almost generous. "IT'S HARRY," proclaimed the *Daily Mirror* over a large picture of Perkins casting his vote at Parkside Junior School. "PERKINS BY WHISKER," said the *Express* over a report by the paper's political correspondent predicting a 'wafer-thin' Labour majority which, the correspondent added, "should prevent Perkins and his gang from getting up to any of the mischief outlined in Labour's loony

manifesto." Perkins could not resist a chuckle as he pictured the scene on the *Express* editorial floor now that the full result was known. *The Times* tried to set the minds of its readers at rest by recalling the fate which had overtaken previous radical Labour programmes "once the Party's leaders had to face up to the realities of office".

On inside pages the popular press regaled readers with a hurried cuttings job on Perkins' career from his days as a schoolboy at Parkside Secondary School. The picture libraries had been trawled for a class photograph, taken when he was a weedy, freckled youth of fourteen. There was even a picture of young Perkins, aged five years, taken with his mother and father in the back yard of their terraced house in Brightside just before they were bombed out in the second world war. Where the devil did they rake that up from, he wondered.

At St Pancras there were more reporters, photographers and television men with lightweight cameras. Everybody was talking at once. How was he feeling? Who was going to be Foreign Secretary? What did he have for breakfast? And so it went on as Perkins pushed through the throng towards the distant ticket barrier, taking care as he went not to tread on prostrate sound recordists.

After he had fought his way no more than twenty yards, the scrimmage halted. There was a pause and then, as with the crossing of the Red Sea by the Israelites, the ranks of the assembled pressmen suddenly parted to make way for a man in pin-striped trousers and a dark jacket, his cuffs protruding a full three inches from the sleeves and joined by jade links. A silence fell over the assembled multitude, then the man spoke: "Mr Perkins," he said in a voice that rang with self-assurance, "Mr Perkins, my name is Frederick Porter. I have come to take you to the Palace."

Sir Frederick Porter was the King's private secretary. Perkins had been told to expect him at St Pancras. The previous day Downing Street had been on the line to him in Sheffield and explained the procedure for the transfer of power. At the time the votes had still to be counted, the

pundits had still been predicting a Tory victory and yet the man from Downing Street had spoken as though a Labour victory was already a fact. Telepathy? Perkins had wondered. Or just the establishment hedging its bets? In the event Downing Street's caution had proved justified and now the well-oiled machinery for ensuring a smooth transfer of power was in motion. First there was an audience with the King, morning dress optional. He would ask Perkins to form a government. From that moment on he was Prime Minister and he would be taken from the Palace in a Downing Street car. The outgoing Prime Minister would leave Downing Street by a rear entrance. They would not meet, but it was normal practice for the incoming Prime Minister to make Chequers available to his predecessor.

Perkins put down his briefcase and advanced towards Sir Frederick, hand outstretched. Eton, Balliol and the Guards had taught Sir Frederick to display a stiff upper lip in the face of adversity and as he took Perkins' hand his face betrayed no trace of his inner anguish.

"I have a car, sir," said Sir Frederick, indicating with a sweep of his hand the general direction of the Euston Road.

"Car?" said Perkins. "What's wrong with a bus? Number 77 runs down Whitehall from here." Perkins made a fetish of travelling by public transport. Many were the anxious moments chairmen, presiding over mass rallies, had spent looking at their watches because their Party leader's bus was running late. Perkins had resolved that even when he was Prime Minister he would stick to public transport.

For one-hundredth of a second Sir Frederick's face registered dismay, but when he spoke his voice contained precisely the right blend of firmness and humility. "Sir, His Majesty is waiting."

Perkins might have replied that it would do His Majesty no harm to be kept waiting for once. He might even have said that His Majesty could get stuffed. History records, however, that he simply shrugged, handed his bag to the chauffeur and climbed meekly into the back of the car drawn up in the forecourt of St Pancras station.

They drove to Buckingham Palace in silence. As they passed down Kingsway Perkins reflected wryly that he had suffered his first defeat at the hands of the establishment – and he was not yet Prime Minister.

The King and Queen breakfasted together in the private apartments in the north wing of Buckingham Palace. The crockery was Doulton. The cutlery, Louis XIV. The marmalade, Rose's Lime. The Regency windows looked out over verdant lawns. In the distance a gardener crouched planting polyanthus.

The young Queen gazed first across the gardens and then turned to her husband. "I do hope," she said firmly, "that you are not going to go about repeating the sort of things you were saying last night."

The King looked surprised. "I meant every word. This Perkins fellow will be the ruin of us."

"Do be careful, my love. You know the trouble your father used to get into every time he sounded off about politics."

The King sighed. It was not the first time they had had this conversation. "You do exaggerate, darling. Perkins would never dare close us down. He'd have an uprising on his hands."

"He'll be here in two hours. You must bring yourself to be nice to him." With that the Queen buttered a finger of toast and resumed her gaze across the lawns.

Without another word the sovereign placed his napkin on the table, rose and left. A footman glided noiselessly among the tea cups. He had heard nothing.

After seeing the King, Perkins was driven to Downing Street. The car sent by Number Ten to collect him from the Palace was waiting in the inner courtyard. Sir Frederick Porter stiffly ushered Perkins from the private apartments and handed him into the custody of a man in the full uniform of the middle rank civil service. A blue striped shirt, pin-striped trousers

and a dark jacket. The bowler hat and umbrella were visible on a shelf through the rear window of the car.

"Prime Minister," said the man, proffering a manicured hand, "my name is Horace Tweed. I am your principal private secretary."

And with that he opened the rear door of the car, a blue Mercedes driven by a woman in a green uniform (since the Leyland collapse Mercedes had replaced Rovers in the government car pool). Perkins scrambled inside. Tweed closed the door after him, walked round the back of the car and climbed in through the door on the other side. The car slid out of the courtyard. As they passed, the sentries in their lofty bearskins presented arms.

"When I was a kid," said Perkins, "I wanted to be a soldier with one of those hats."

Tweed looked at him blankly. When he was a kid he probably never wanted to be anything but private secretary to the Prime Minister, thought Perkins.

Leaving the Palace they ran a gauntlet of photographers, some of them running out into the road alongside the car. A police car materialised, as if from nowhere, and preceded them down the Mall, its headlights on full beam, despite the daylight.

Tweed was saying something about sterling and the Governor of the Bank of England wanted an appointment, but Perkins was reflecting on his audience with the King. It had gone well. With apparent sincerity the King had congratulated him on his party's victory and charged him with forming a government. After formalities they had indulged in a few minutes of small talk, mainly about football and gardens. Perkins said he had never lived in a house with a garden. The King said he would show him his and Perkins had departed saying he would take up his offer some day.

By the time they reached Downing Street, Tweed was saying something about a phone call from the President of the United States. But Perkins could see only the crowds which spilled out into Whitehall and along the pavement outside the Cabinet Office. As the car turned into Downing Street he

glimpsed a young woman in a white raincoat pressed against the barrier. Her long blonde hair was tucked into the collar of the raincoat; her cheeks were lightly freckled and as he passed she smiled a small, discreet smile. Perkins had scarcely time to think that she reminded him of Molly Spence before the thought was lost amid the cheering of the crowd.

A stone's throw from Downing Street, by a quiet terrace of Queen Anne houses overlooking the south-west corner of St James's Park, a Rolls-Royce was disgorging the portly frame of Sir George Fison. Waiting at an open doorway to greet him was a languid figure swathed in a red corduroy smoking jacket – Sir Peregrine Craddock.

"So good of you to come, George."

"Least I could do in the circumstances, old boy."

In the oak-panelled dining room a maid was clearing away the remains of Sir Peregrine's late breakfast. A pile of newspapers had been cast unread into an armchair; the morning sun streamed in through a bay window overlooking the park; through the plane trees the Treasury edifice was just visible.

Sir Peregrine poured two black coffees from a silver pot, waited until the maid had gone and then spoke quietly. "No doubt you've guessed why I asked you in. At a time like this it's important that those of us who care about civilised values stick together."

"Couldn't agree more," nodded Fison, who had flopped into an armchair by the window. The daylight from behind illuminated his bald crown, creating a kind of halo effect. Sir Peregrine, who was seated facing into the light, was obliged to squint to catch the expression on Fison's face.

The clock on the mantelpiece registered a quarter past the hour in unison with Big Ben, the distant chimes of which were just audible. Sir Peregrine took a sip of coffee and then resumed in the discreet tones he reserved for distasteful subjects: "In order to help people see sense we may have to cut a few corners, if you get my meaning. Float the odd rumour, organise the occasional punch-up." The expression

'punch-up' tripped uneasily off Sir Peregrine's refined tongue and he winced as he pronounced it.

"Absolutely," said Fison, slapping his knee with the flat of his podgy hand. Fison came from a tougher school than Sir Peregrine. He knew exactly what was required. He had started life as an East End barrow boy and a follower of Oswald Mosley. He even had a couple of convictions for incitement under the 1936 Public Order Act. That was a long time ago, of course, but when it came to a bit of bother George Fison could mix it with the best of them. Not that this stopped his newspapers taking a hard line on law and order.

Fison's obvious relish made Sir Peregrine unhappy. "Obviously one doesn't like to think in these terms," he said quickly. "We are supposed to be a democracy and all that, but it's important that people realise what's at stake. Not just the national interest, but the future of the Western alliance." Sir Peregrine's voice rose. He was happier talking global strategy.

Fison slapped his knee again. "Entirely agree, dear boy." The 'dear boy' was an affectation. People didn't speak like that where he came from, but it had been forty years since he moved from Stepney to Chelsea and Fison had been working ever since to adopt what he believed to be the mannerisms of a gentleman.

Sir Peregrine paused to light a pipe. His first of the day. When the blue smoke cleared he continued. "To start the ball rolling, what I had in mind was, I hesitate to use the word," he resumed the *sotto voce* reserved for distasteful subjects, "a smear campaign." He drew on his pipe and then breathed out again, emitting more blue smoke. "Nothing too heavy at first. Just enough to sow the seeds of doubt in the public mind about Perkins and his gang. For the time being we will lay off Perkins himself. His popularity is running high and anything we try to stick on him could blow up in our faces." He looked across at Fison who was nodding intently. "To start with we must concentrate on ministers and advisers. That way we can discredit Perkins without attacking him directly."

With graceful movements of his left hand Sir Peregrine brushed tobacco ash from the lapels of his smoking jacket. He wasn't keen on Fison. The man lacked breeding. He was crude and unsubtle. It stood out a mile. Still, one couldn't choose one's friends in a situation like this. He went on, "I've got a team of chaps standing by and the moment we get details of ministerial appointments they'll be going through the files looking for anything that may be useful. Shady business deals, illicit love affairs, trips to Moscow, articles in the *Morning Star*. Naturally we'll pass everything over and you and the other Fleet Street boys can take it from there."

Sir Peregrine stretched his legs, sank back into the armchair and puffed his pipe. The smoke mingled with the incoming rays of sunlight and caused a cloud to form between himself and Fison. When it cleared he went on, "Normally we'd just shove this sort of stuff in plain brown envelopes and stick it in the post to a few reliable old hands, but this time we want something bigger. That's where you come in." He looked across at Fison, through the haze. Fison was already composing the lecture he was going to give to his senior editors. The nation, he would tell them, was facing catastrophe. In the battle that was to come there were only two sides. Anyone with doubts about which side they were on could collect his cards now. Fison smiled inwardly. He was sure that his services would not go unrewarded. At the very least he was expecting a peerage to provide the final seal of respectability he craved.

The pipe was now clamped between Sir Peregrine's teeth, causing him to speak through the side of his mouth. As he did so the end of the pipe wobbled. "I want you to get together a few proprietors, editors and senior journalists whom we can absolutely count on. You should meet regularly to co-ordinate coverage. As things get hotter, and believe me they will, we're going to need people we can rely on. Can you manage?"

"No problem," said Fison, "no problem at all."

"What about the journalists? Bound to have some trouble with them if we lay it on too thick."

Fison wiped his lips with the back of his hand. "I promise you," he said slowly, "there won't be a peep out of anyone."

"Very embarrassing to have journalists whining on about ethics and press freedom just as we get a decent campaign going."

"My dear boy," Fison leaned towards Sir Peregrine, "take it from me, most Fleet Street journalists wouldn't recognise a real live ethic at five paces. Why do you think we pay them so well?"

"Good, that's settled, then," said Sir Peregrine, rising. He placed the pipe, by now extinct, in an ashtray on the mantelpiece. "One other thing. Very important you don't breathe a word of this conversation to anybody. Nothing we send you must be traceable to us. If Perkins gets a whiff of what's going on, we'll all be in the excreta up to our necks."

Gripping both arms of the chair, Fison heaved himself to his feet, panting slightly with the exertion. He drew himself rigidly to attention, a fitting posture for a man about to serve his King and country, "Don't worry, Peregrine, you can count on me."

Perkins crossed the threshold of Number Ten Downing Street to find the entire staff, private secretaries, clerks, telephonists, footmen and garden girls from the downstairs typing pool lining the corridor that leads to the Cabinet Room. As he entered they applauded. Not entirely spontaneously since many of them confidently expected to be sacked. Only an hour had elapsed since they had gathered on the same spot to applaud the outgoing Prime Minister who had departed by a back entrance.

Guided by the omnipresent Tweed, Perkins crossed the black and white marble tiled floor of the entrance lobby and passed down the corridor to the Cabinet Room, nodding to the right and left in acknowledgment of the applause. He paused respectfully at the entrance to the Cabinet Room as a Catholic might pause in the entrance of a church to cross himself with holy water. Even for a Sheffield steel worker, born and bred with a healthy disrespect for tradition and the

54

trappings of power, the Cabinet Room had something of a presence. Within these walls the British government had first heard of the loss of the American colonies, plotted the downfall of Napoleon, the Kaiser and Hitler and granted independence to India. Now these same walls were to bear witness to the rise, and perhaps the fall, of Harry Perkins.

He entered diffidently and stood at the top of the long table, down either side of which were arranged chairs covered in red leather. Each place at the table was marked with a leather-bound blotter and crystal decanters of water. Perkins made one slow circuit of the table, peering cautiously out of each window overlooking the garden. When he had completed his lap of the room Tweed gestured that he should sit. Perkins sat.

"One or two things we must attend to immediately, Prime Minister."

"Don't I even get to wash my hands?"

"This won't take a moment," said Tweed.

Three private secretaries had now filed into the room and they stood in a crocodile behind Tweed, waiting to be introduced. The first bore a letter from Perkins to his defeated predecessor, placing the Prime Minister's country residence, Chequers, at the disposal of the outgoing Prime Minister until he had made arrangements to go elsewhere. "Just a formality," said Tweed: "Sign here, Prime Minister." Perkins signed.

The second private secretary presented figures showing that three cents had been wiped off the value of sterling in the two hours since the London market opened. Heavy selling was also reported from Hong Kong and Tokyo. "The Governor of the Bank wants an appointment as soon as possible." One was agreed for the afternoon at five o'clock. The Cabinet secretary also wanted an appointment. He was told to come at six.

The third secretary said that the White House had telephoned. The President wanted to congratulate Perkins personally and it had been agreed that the Prime Minister should receive the call in his study in three hours' time.

Formalities complete, Perkins was shown to a small lift in the rear of the building which conveyed him up two floors to the attic flat built into the roof of Number Ten. "This will be your private quarters," said Tweed, as he unlocked the door. "You are planning to live here, of course?"

"Not likely," said Perkins.

"But, Prime Minister, we've already brought your wardrobe here." Tweed ran a manicured hand through his thinning hair.

"You what?"

"We got the key to your flat from your secretary and I sent someone round this morning."

"Then you can just send them back again."

Although it was scarcely an hour since the flat had been vacated there was no trace of the previous occupant. No hint of cigar smoke from the night before. No sign of the whisky bottles that had littered the hearth as the outgoing Prime Minister, surrounded by his closest aides, watched his majority crumble. Before departing for the Palace, Tweed had given instructions that not a trace of the old régime was to remain. The thick carpet had been scrupulously vacuumed. Windows had been flung open. The bed linen and the curtains changed. Even the David Hockney that hung above the fireplace had been replaced by a Lowry print of a Lancashire fairground which Tweed had brought up from the basement. The private office thought of everything.

In a wardrobe in the main bedroom Perkins found his suits, all neatly pressed, in accordance with Tweed's instructions.

"My goodness, you lads work fast," said Perkins.

While he was changing there came a knock on the bedroom door. "Inspector Page and Sergeant Block of the Special Branch," intoned Tweed, who was still loitering in the living room. "These gentlemen will be responsible for your safety from now on."

"That's right, sir," said Page. A thickset, balding man with a Zapata moustache and a face like a closed book. "Sergeant Block and I will take it in turns to accompany you at all times of the day and night outside of Downing Street and the House

of Commons. Naturally we will try to be as unobtrusive as possible.''

Perkins nodded as he selected his brightest tie from a rail along the inside of a wardrobe door.

"One other thing, sir. I understand that you're in the habit of travelling around on buses."

"That's right, Inspector."

"Is that strictly necessary, sir? Makes life very difficult for Sergeant Block and me."

"I am afraid it is necessary, Inspector. You see, my party wants to phase out the private motor car in cities and encourage people to use public transport instead. If we want to be taken seriously, then I've got to set an example.'

"I see, sir," said Page, who clearly didn't see. Not one of my voters, thought Perkins as the Inspector and the Sergeant withdrew. As they left, a private secretary entered to say that the Governor of the Bank had been on again. "He says sterling's going down fast. Can't wait till five o'clock. Must see you immediately."

Lady Elizabeth Fain slept until nearly noon in her mews cottage near Sloane Square, a twenty-first birthday present from her father. Still clad in her nightdress she tripped downstairs to the kitchen, raised the blind to let in daylight and opened the back door to let her dog, a cocker spaniel called Walpole, out into the tiny garden.

She was pouring a glass of grapefruit juice when the phone rang. It was Fred Thompson. "Hi, Lizzie, just called to see how my friends in the Master Race are coping with the revolution."

'Actually, I've just slept through the first ten hours of revolution."

"Don't worry, the tumbrils will soon be rolling through Sloane Square, but I'll see you're okay," said Fred with a chuckle.

"You should have heard them at Annabel's last night. Anyone would have thought Harry Perkins was going to send us all to Siberia the way some people were carrying on."

57

"There are some people I wish he would send to Siberia."

"Such as?"

"Such as that man Fison, for a start. He was on the radio half an hour ago prattling on about the threat to press freedom. Thinks Perkins is going to nationalise his news-papers."

"Isn't he?"

"Course not. All we promised to do was look at alternatives to leaving the newspapers in the hands of fat slugs like Fison. Trusts, co-operatives, that sort of thing. That's not state ownership, is it?"

"If you say so, Fred." At this point Walpole the spaniel passed through the kitchen on his way to the hall and returned with the mail between his teeth.

Telephone in hand, Elizabeth stooped to extract the letters and continued, "I must say that for someone who only last week was predicting a coup if Perkins became Prime Minister, you're sounding remarkably cheerful this morning."

"I never said anything about a coup," protested Fred. "Only that we are going to get a lot of shit from the Americans and your friends in the establishment . . . Anyway, that's not what I rang about. I wondered if you want to come to a party on Sunday. We're celebrating the election result."

"Frightfully sorry, Fred, I'm going to the country this weekend."

"Too bad. You'd have enjoyed it. Lots of left-wing extrem-ists coming."

"No left-wing extremists where I'm going," said Elizabeth. "Chap who's invited me is an army officer, his brother is a Tory MP and his father was something big in the City. They've got a huge house in Oxfordshire."

"Sounds fascinating," said Fred.

"Don't worry, I'll tell you all about it when I get back – providing you manage to keep the tumbrils out of Sloane Square."

At noon precisely Fiennes of DI5 strolled into the coffee shop of the Churchill Hotel in Portman Square. Under his arm he

was carrying a folded copy of the *Financial Times*. He glanced to right and left until his eyes came to rest upon a clean-cut man in his late thirties, in a white, open raincoat.

"Ah, there you are, Jim." Fiennes approached and sat down opposite the man in the raincoat. They shook hands over the table. "Guess you know what I've come about," said Fiennes.

"Sure do." The man's accent was East Coast American.

"Thought we ought to meet on neutral territory. Not wise for me to be seen at the embassy."

The American lit a cigarette without offering one to Fiennes, who went on, "The Old Man thought we'd better liaise directly with your people instead of going through DI6. In any case they'd only balls it up."

"Okay by me." The American took a drag of his cigarette and placed it on the edge of an ashtray. A waiter approached and they ordered two black coffees. "Now what are you guys planning to do about Perkins?"

"The Old Man thinks we ought to take it easy at first. Just feed out a little dirt to the newspapers. Let the civil service and the City do the rest, for the time being."

"What dirt you got on him?"

"That's the problem. There's nothing on our files. We were hoping you might have something."

"Nope. He's clean at our end too. I had the boys at Langley run him through the computer last night. Clean as a whistle."

"Should have more to go on when he starts naming ministers and camp followers," said Fiennes.

"We'll run 'em all through the computer and anything we get we'll pass over to you."

"Better be discreet. No point in going through the usual channels or we'll have DI6 whining to be let in on the act."

"Anything we get I'll hand over personally to you."

The waiter came with the coffees and the bill. They drank in silence. Fiennes paid the bill with a pound note and some coins and got to his feet. "Keep in touch, Jim."

"Sure will."

*

Perkins took the call from the President on the scrambled line in the Prime Minister's study.

"Harry."

"Mr President."

"Harry, I just wanted to congratulate you personally on your magnificent victory."

"Very generous of you, Mr President," said Perkins, reflecting that a flair for hypocrisy was going to be one of the specifications of his new job.

"Harry, we ought to get together just as soon as possible to iron out any little points of difference that may arise between your government and mine."

"Early days yet, Mr President. I've only been in this job three hours so far and as yet I don't have a government."

"Of course, of course, Harry. What I had in mind was to send my Secretary of State, Marcus Morgan, over for a chat as soon as possible. Some time next week, perhaps?"

"Okay by me."

"Fine, Harry, fine. I know how much you share my desire for world peace and I reckon we're going to work together real well. Like you, I have spent my life fighting oppression and exploitation, so you see we got a lot in common."

Perkins listened patiently as the President elaborated on his lifelong crusade for freedom. The conversation, or rather monologue, was finally brought to a close with the President saying that he had to go because he was keeping 'some general from Paraguay' waiting outside the Oval Office.

Scarcely had Perkins replaced the receiver when he was interrupted by a call from the private office to say that the Governor of the Bank of England was at hand.

This was Perkins' second conversation with the Governor that day. The first had taken place in the small hours of the morning – minutes after the outgoing government conceded defeat. Perkins had been in Sheffield town hall when he heard the news and immediately went in search of a telephone. Since the Mayor's parlour was locked up and the Mayor nowhere to be found, Perkins had had to telephone the Bank

of England from a coinbox next to the porter's lodge. Having obtained the Governor's home telephone number from an astonished night duty officer Perkins had proceeded to rouse the Governor from his bed and order him to reimpose exchange control instantly. By moving so swiftly he had hoped to mitigate the impact of his election on the delicate constitution of the foreign exchanges, but it was not to be.

The Governor did not waste time on pleasantries. "Prime Minister, I have bad news."

"Surprise me, Governor." Perkins was given to mild bouts of irony.

"The pound has fallen four cents in as many hours. If it carries on like this, we'll have a slide of catastrophic proportions on our hands."

"Who's selling?"

"Everybody's selling. The Arabs, the Americans, the oil companies. Everybody."

"So what are you proposing?"

"Prime Minister, it is my duty to tell you that the markets need reassuring. Frankly, they are worried that they are going to get a government of . . ." The Governor hesitated.

". . . extremists?" suggested Perkins.

"Something like that."

"In other words," Perkins was looking straight at the Governor, "you are asking me to let a crowd of speculators dictate who I should appoint to my Cabinet."

"Not exactly, no."

"What, then?"

"Only that you take account of feeling in the City."

"And if I don't?"

"Prime Minister, I could not be responsible for the consequences."

"Now let's get one thing straight." Perkins spoke quietly, but firmly. "As long as you are Governor of the Bank of England you *will* be responsible for the consequences. You and your friends in the City may not have noticed, but there has been an election. *My* side has won and *your* side has lost. What's the point in having general elections if, regardless of

the outcome, a handful of speculators in the City of London and their friends abroad continue to call the shots?"

The Governor was taken aback. Accustomed as he was to being the bearer of bad news to a succession of Prime Ministers, he was unused to plain speaking.

Perkins, who had been seated next to the Governor in the semi-circle of armchairs at the end of the study, rose and went over to the windows. They overlooked St James's Park and were half covered by green bullet-proof glass. With his back to the Governor, Perkins continued, "Perhaps you could tell me how much the Bank has spent defending sterling today?"

"Nothing yet," the Governor said, almost under his breath.

"Nothing," said Perkins.

"Nothing," repeated the Governor.

"Why not?"

"Prime Minister, I was advised . . ."

"Don't give me that crap." Still Perkins did not raise his voice. "I'll tell you why you haven't intervened. Because you thought you'd give me a bit of a scare, didn't you? 'New Prime Minister with all sorts of crazy Socialist ideas. We'll soon teach him a lesson.' That's what you thought, isn't it? Let sterling slide for a few hours and then rush round to Downing Street with a list of demands in return for calling a halt."

Perkins turned to face the Governor. "Those days are over. If you know what's good for you, you'll get back in your Rolls-Royce, return immediately to your office and start buying. Fast. If the pound hasn't gained two cents by close of business, I want your resignation."

With that Perkins strode over to the double doors and pulled them open, indicating the exit with a gesture of his left hand. The Governor, his face drained of colour, swept past and on to the landing. He went down the main staircase almost at a trot. Past the portraits of former Prime Ministers, through the entrance lobby with its bust of Disraeli and into the back of his green Rolls-Royce.

By close of business sterling had recovered 2.16 cents against the dollar.

5

Fiennes was pouring himself a coffee from the office percolator when the telex machine in the far corner came to life. Coffee cup in hand he went and stood over the telex. It was the Downing Street press office with the details of Perkins' Cabinet.

As the machine tapped out the first name Fiennes gave a low whistle. The Lord President of the Council and Leader of the House was to be Jock Steeples. Steeples was a former East End docker and veteran left-winger. Despite his undoubted ability he had never been given office of any kind during his thirty years in Parliament, largely because DI5 had fingered him as a possible Communist agent. Steeples would be in charge of pushing the new government's programme through Parliament.

Next out of the machine was the new Chancellor of the Exchequer, Lawrence Wainwright. Wainwright was Oxford educated and had once been a merchant banker. Not an obvious choice for a left-wing government. Fiennes was pleasantly surprised. Maybe Perkins was going to play safe after all.

Any illusions about Perkins being overcome by a sudden fit of moderation were, however, quickly dispelled by his choice of Home Secretary, Mrs Joan Cook. Mrs Cook was one of only a handful of women MPs, an honorary vice president of the National Council for Civil Liberties. She had campaigned for greater public control of the police and the intelligence services. DI5 also suspected she was a crypto Communist. Fiennes groaned.

The Foreign Secretary, Tom Newsome, had been a Yorkshire schoolmaster. DI5 had a file an inch thick on him. In 1968 he had led the huge march to the American embassy in Grosvenor Square. He had been Chairman of the Chile Solidarity Campaign and led numerous deputations to the

Foreign Office to protest against just about every military régime with which Britain traded.

Fiennes placed his coffee cup on the windowsill and with unnecessary vigour ripped the first page of the telex from the machine.

The Defence Secretary headed the second page. This was to be Jim Evans, a Welshman with a fine line in fiery rhetoric. Evans had been a ban-the-bomber since the early days of CND. By now Fiennes was beside himself. This was it. The revolution was unfolding before his very eyes.

So it went on. Four pages of new appointments. Extremists almost to a man. The Northern Ireland Secretary was known to favour British withdrawal. The Minister of Agriculture was a former farm labourer.

"This will send the pound through the floor," said Fiennes half out loud as he tore the final sheet from the telex. He had to restrain himself from running as he went to tell Sir Peregrine the awful news.

Sir Peregrine was composing a memorandum when Fiennes entered. He always composed in long hand, using a blue felt-tipped pen, and he did not like being interrupted. "Yes, Fiennes, what is it?" The irritation in his voice was barely concealed.

"The new Cabinet, sir."

"Oh, yes; bad as we thought?"

"Worse," said Fiennes, handing over the sheaf of telex pages.

There was a full minute's silence as Sir Peregrine ran his eyes slowly down the list. When he looked up there was no hint of dismay in his voice. "Well, Fiennes, we've had a stroke of luck."

"Luck, sir?"

"Wainwright, the new Chancellor. He's on our payroll. We signed him up soon after he got into Parliament. He's been reporting to us ever since."

With a flourish Sir Peregrine returned the telex pages to Fiennes and added, "Perkins has made his first mistake."

*

Fred Thompson was already in bed at his flat in Camden Town when the phone rang. Putting on his dressing gown he stumbled into the living room.

"Sorry to ring at this hour," said a cheerful Yorkshire voice at the other end of the line.

Suddenly Thompson was wide awake. "Harry, or should I say *Prime Minister*?"

"Never mind about that, lad. Listen, I've got a job for you." Perkins paused and then went on, "How would you like to work in my Private Office? I need someone to keep an eye on all these damn civil servants."

For a moment Thompson was stunned into silence. "Will you or won't you?" said Perkins impatiently.

"Of course, Harry, I'd be delighted. What do you want me to do?"

"Just answer a few letters and generally keep your eyes open. I'll tell you more when you start on Monday."

"Monday? But what about the *Independent*? I've got to give notice."

"I've already had a word with your editor. He says he's been trying to get rid of you for years," said Perkins drily.

"What time on Monday?"

"If you come to Downing Street at 8.30 in the morning we can have a cup of tea and I'll show you what's what."

"Okay, Harry," said Thompson, who could think of nothing else to say, so overwhelmed was he by the dramatic change in his circumstances.

"Right, lad, see you Monday." And with that Perkins was gone, leaving Thompson still holding the receiver.

Fred Thompson was one of those journalists who hover on the fringe of the big time, but never quite make it. He had started out on one of George Fison's provincial papers and drifted in the general direction of Fleet Street via a publication called *Municipal News* which operated out of two rooms in Chancery Lane and which folded six months after he joined the staff. After a spot of freelancing, a euphemism for the dole, Thompson landed a poorly paid job with the *Independent Socialist*. It was the sort of journal that everyone had

65

heard of, but nobody seemed to read. If long-serving members of its staff were to be believed, there was a time when the *Independent* had been required reading for every serious left-winger, but those days were long passed. By the time Thompson arrived it was tired and clapped out, snapping harmlessly at the ankles of the parliamentary establishment.

His first encounter with Harry Perkins had been inauspicious. Perkins had telephoned to lambast the editor for transposing a paragraph in an article he had contributed the previous week on the steel industry. In the absence of the editor he lambasted Thompson instead. Next thing he knew Perkins had invited him for a drink at the House.

It was a hot summer evening six months after Labour's second successive election defeat and they sat on the terrace supping half pints of Guinness. Perkins did most of the talking. He was seething with anger at the way the election had been handled. "Serves us bloody right." His brow glistened in the last rays of the sun. "We offer the electorate a choice between two Tory parties and they choose the real one. Now we find ourselves back in the wilderness for five years and the country's going down the plughole." For a moment they sat in silence looking out over the river. A police launch sped past throwing a cloud of spray in its wake. Perkins rested a hand lightly on Thompson's arm in the manner of someone about to impart a great secret. "You mark my words, lad, come the conference heads will roll."

Six days later Perkins announced his intention to challenge the leader. The media had a minor bout of hysteria. Most of his colleagues were mildly amused. For some reason Perkins had never been taken seriously by the clever young lawyers and polytechnic lecturers who seemed to account for about half the Parliamentary Labour Party. In any case, it was whispered that the trade union leaders had met the Shadow Cabinet and agreed to back the status quo.

But if there had been a stitch-up, it came unstitched. Looking back it was amazing that no one saw it coming. Not until the Transport and General Workers' Union delegation met on the morning of the election and threw out the recom-

66

mendation of their executive, was it clear something was up. In the hours that followed, at delegation meetings in clubs and hotel suites all over Blackpool, the block votes began to shift. By evening Perkins was home and dry. In the elections for the National Executive Committee which followed, the left cleaned up. Heads had rolled, just as Perkins had predicted. From that day on he was taken very seriously indeed.

Fred Thompson was the only journalist to tip a victory for Perkins. Week after week the *Independent Socialist* had carried articles documenting the rising tide of anger in the constituencies and at the lower levels of the trade unions. Since no one took the *Independent* seriously, it was not really surprising that Thompson's articles had gone unnoticed. Unnoticed, that is, by all save Perkins.

For some time before he became Labour leader, Perkins had been employing Thompson for occasional bits of research. It was not uncommon for Thompson to spend a morning burrowing in the House of Commons library for figures on West German coal subsidies or imports of special steels from Scandinavia. More and more they would be seen talking earnestly over a cup of coffee in one of the Commons cafeterias or poring together over notes in one of the dark recesses of the Committee Room corridor. After he became leader Perkins gradually came to look more and more to Thompson as his eyes and ears in the party. It was not uncommon, after a ten o'clock division, to see Thompson making his way across the Star Chamber court to the leader of the opposition's rooms for a late-night whisky and a chat about the way the world turned round. So frequent a visitor had Thompson become that the policemen on duty in the lobbies no longer bothered to ask for his pass.

The arrangement was never formalised but by and by it came to be taken for granted that if you wanted access to Harry Perkins, Fred Thompson was the man to speak to. This being so, it should have come as no surprise to Thompson to be awakened from his bed in the early hours by a telephone call from the Prime Minister with an offer of a job in Downing Street. Nonetheless Thompson was surprised and trembled

slightly as he replaced the receiver and went back to bed. It was nearly dawn by the time he fell asleep.

The sun shone brightly over Chelsea as Lady Elizabeth Fain left for her weekend in the country. On the back seat of her new Volkswagen (assembled by robots at the old Rover plant in Solihull) was a small blue suitcase containing two changes of clothes and an evening dress. Beside the case a wicker shopping basket covered by a teacloth contained an apple pie she had baked herself and a bottle of Beaujolais. Walpole the spaniel was upright on the front passenger seat.

Kensington High Street was jammed with Saturday shoppers, but the traffic flowed smoothly. Within twenty minutes Elizabeth was through Hammersmith and on to the M4 motorway. As grey suburbs turned into green countryside she found herself thinking of Fred. On paper at least he was not her type. Had a bit of a chip on his shoulder; always going on about his being working class and how he came from another planet from the one on which she lived. She had a very easy life. Like most of her friends she had a private income and only worked when she felt like doing so. Now she came to think about it, she hadn't a single friend, apart from Fred, who would answer to the description of 'working class'.

Fred was always going on about how corrupt and violent the police were. She had protested that all the policemen she had ever met were kind and courteous. He had replied that the police existed to protect people like her from people like him. At the time she had laughed at him, but as the riots crept closer to Sloane Square she began to think that there might be a grain of truth in what Fred had said.

Walpole curled up on the front seat and fell asleep. Elizabeth exerted pressure on the accelerator. The motorway cut a swathe through lush Oxfordshire pastureland sloping away to a river valley and, beyond, a clump of forest which parted to reveal a country house not unlike the one in which her parents lived. What a contrast with life in one of the great grey skyscrapers in Battersea, where she had once worked for six months in a private nursery school. Somehow people in

68

Battersea even looked different from those she mixed with. The women were pale, pasty, often with unwashed straggly hair and tired eyes. Girls her own age were weighed down with children and shopping baskets and push chairs. Was that what being working class meant? Would she have been like that if she had been born on a council estate in Battersea instead of a country house in Somerset?

About ten miles from Oxford Elizabeth left the motorway at an exit signposted to Watlington. Before reaching the village she turned into an avenue marked 'private'. The avenue was lined on either side by beech trees which united overhead to form a long tunnel. After a thousand yards it swerved sharply right and, suddenly, there was the house.

Watlington Priory was the seat of the Nortons, an ancient Catholic family which traced its ancestry back to the time of King John. The house was a Tudor mansion with two main wings branching off from a centrepiece to which clung several centuries' growth of ivy. The Volkswagen crunched across the gravel forecourt and came to a halt by a walled vegetable garden. As it did so two golden labradors came bounding from the house and rushed in excited circles round the car. From the passenger seat Walpole eyed them cautiously.

The labradors were followed by a young man in faded levis and a tweed jacket with patches on the elbows. "Elizabeth," he called, "how lovely to see you."

Elizabeth had by this time emerged from the car and was being mobbed by the labradors. "Roger," she beamed.

"Jackson, Johnson, get down," the young man bellowed as though giving orders on a parade ground. Instantly the dogs obeyed.

By now Roger stood face to face with Elizabeth. He placed a hand on each shoulder and kissed her on both cheeks. Then, turning, she reached into the car and pulled out first the suitcase and then the wicker basket.

"You shouldn't have bothered," said Roger when she showed him the apple pie and the wine. Taking her case, he ushered her towards the main door of the house. Walpole and the labradors had in the meantime disappeared.

Roger Norton was a major in the Coldstream Guards, his father's old regiment. Home on leave after a spell in Oman. His elder brother, William, the brains in the family, was Conservative Member of Parliament for Banbury. "William's coming for dinner this evening," said Roger as he showed Elizabeth up the creaking staircase to her room in the west wing, "so's Uncle Philip; I think you'll find him interesting."

They dined on roast duck, taken from a deep freeze stocked by Roger in the shooting season. Apart from the presence of Elizabeth it was a family affair. Mrs Norton did the cooking; Mr Norton, a retired banker, carved. Uncle Philip poured the wine. They ate around a large trestle table in the sixteenth-century banqueting hall lit only by candles which cast long shadows.

At first the conversation was dominated by Roger, who regaled them with tales of his exploits in Oman 'bopping the wogs', as he put it.

"Bloody lucky we're there, if you ask me," said Roger, helping himself to more sprouts. "Somebody's got to stick up for democracy, even in that fly-blown dump."

"I thought it had more to do with oil than democracy," said Elizabeth, trying to sound as though she was making an enquiry rather than an assertion.

Roger was taken aback. He didn't have much experience of being contradicted, let alone by a woman. "What do *you* know about Oman?"

"Only what I read in the papers." Elizabeth sipped her wine. She wasn't looking for an argument. Roger was a friend, not a lover. He had been a classmate of her brother's at Eton and they had kept in touch ever since. There was a time when Elizabeth had been attracted by him, but nowadays the more she saw the less keen she was.

It was Roger's brother, William, who first brought the conversation round to the home front. William was in his late thirties, young for such a safe seat as Banbury. Like his father he had started in merchant banking. Folding his napkin and placing it on the table he leaned back and said firmly, "Won't

70

be long before we need someone to stick up for democracy here."

"Ah," said Mrs Norton with relish, "I was wondering how long it would be before we got round to Harry Perkins."

William warmed to his theme. He spoke with the sort of loud self-confidence learned at public school debating societies and rugby club dinners. "Harry Perkins will be the ruin of this country. Nobody in his right mind would invest a penny piece here while he and his shower are in charge. Pound's already going down the chute. Americans are being told to clear out and leave us to the mercy of the Russians. There's even talk of muzzling the press."

"The question is," said Mrs Norton, "what are we going to *do* about it?"

"No good looking to us chaps in the House of Commons," sighed William. "Morale on our side's pretty low. I've never known it so bad."

"Come now, William, dear boy." It was Uncle Philip who until now had hardly spoken. "Picture's nothing near as bleak as you make out."

Uncle Philip paused to cut the end from the cigar he had taken from his top pocket, but no one interrupted. "It's not as though Perkins has got a free hand. Any day now he's going to have to go to the International Monetary Fund for a socking great loan and they aren't going to part with that money without attaching a few strings."

He leaned forward to take them into his confidence. "Between you and me, the chaps in the Treasury are already having a quiet word with their opposite numbers in the finance ministries of the other IMF countries. Do you know what the Treasury chaps are saying? 'Don't bale the bastards out,' that's what they're saying. Let Perkins and his crew stew in their own juice for a while."

Uncle Philip paused again to light his cigar. He went on, "As regards the Americans. If you think they'll just pack their bags and go just because Brother Perkins tells them to, you're quite mistaken. Of course, if the worst comes to the worst they may make a show of leaving, taking a few aeroplanes and

71

soldiers home, but they've got billions of pounds worth of equipment invested in British bases and they aren't going to abandon it. They'll do a deal with the British military to keep it on ice for a while until we get a government with some sense. Then they'll come back and take over where they left off."

Uncle Philip had everyone's attention. The candlelight made the shadows flicker. He took a puff on his cigar and still no one else spoke. "If you ask me," he went on, "Perkins isn't going to make it to the next election. I'd give him a year, maybe two."

"Surely you aren't suggesting someone's going to bump him off?" asked William.

"Not literally, no, but there's other forms of assassination." He tapped the ash from the end of his cigar into a saucer. "Character assassination, for example. You never know what the boys in the media will dig up."

Elizabeth thought she saw a twinkle in his eye, but it may only have been the candlelight.

"Your Uncle Philip seems very sure of himself," she said later as Roger showed her to her room.

"So he should be. Don't you know who he is?"

"Should I?"

"Uncle Philip is the Co-ordinator of Intelligence in the Cabinet Office. The link man between the Prime Minister and the spooks."

On Monday morning Fred Thompson arrived at Number Ten Downing Street at 8.30 sharp. The policeman on the door was expecting him and he was taken immediately up the main staircase to the Prime Minister's study.

"Ah, there you are, lad," said Perkins, stretching out his hand.

"Nice place you've got here, Harry."

"Comes with the job." Perkins gestured Fred towards an easy chair at the near end of the room. "Tea or coffee?"

"Coffee," said Thompson, expecting the Prime Minister to pick up a telephone and order coffee for two. Instead Perkins

72

walked to the far corner of the study and plugged in a kettle which stood on a formica-topped surface behind the writing desk. As the kettle boiled he scooped spoonfuls of Nescafé into two coffee mugs. One of the mugs bore the slogan "Harry for Prime Minister."

"A present from one of the lads at Firth's," said Perkins when he noticed Thompson straining to read the inscription.

The kettle had boiled and Perkins was pouring the steaming water into the mugs. "About this job." As he spoke he stirred in milk from a half empty bottle that stood beside the kettle. "Officially, you'll be in charge of replying to correspondence from party members and trade unions."

Perkins did not ask about sugar. He just plopped two lumps into each cup and carried them back to where Thompson was sitting. He was still wearing a red carnation in his buttonhole. When he was seated in the armchair opposite Thompson he took a sip of his coffee and then resumed in a low voice.

"Unofficially, I want you to keep an eye on the civil servants." He lowered his voice. "To be honest, Fred, I don't trust the bastards an inch. When things hot up, we can expect ferocious opposition to our policies from the Treasury, the Foreign Office and the MoD. I want you to keep your ear to the ground for any underhand tactics. Leaks to the press, withholding information, that sort of thing."

Perkins drained his mug and placed it on the low table by his chair. "I've told the Cabinet Secretary in words of one syllable that we don't want any of the nonsense we had to put up with last time Labour was in government. And I told him to pass the word around."

The Prime Minister stood up and walked to the door. Thompson followed. "Where will I be working?" he asked.

"Follow me and I'll show you."

They turned right outside the study and walked until they came to the staircase at the front of the house. Perkins took the stairs two at a time. On the second floor he opened a door leading from the landing. Inside there was a small room with a low ceiling. The walls were bare except for a Tory Central Office calendar left over from the previous régime and a copy

of the fire regulations. The front wall sloped inwards in line with the angle of the roof. "Used to be the servants' quarters," said Perkins.

Thompson walked to one of the two box windows that protruded from the roof and peered out. The view below was of Downing Street and opposite, the huge metal gates barring the first of a series of archways through the Foreign Office and beyond the Treasury.

"Doesn't catch the sun much, I'm afraid," said Perkins, who had half seated himself on the grey metal desk that stood by the left-hand wall. The wall bore traces of a bricked-up fireplace.

The surface of the desk was clear apart from a Philips word processor and a wire rack containing Downing Street writing paper and envelopes. On the floor by the desk was a table lamp with a long flexible arm, but minus a light bulb.

"Functional, that's the word," said Perkins, who was by now seated on the desk with his feet no longer touching the floor. "Still, I expect you'll brighten the place up a bit. Stick up a few CND posters. That'll give them heart attacks downstairs." He gave a little chuckle. Thompson smiled too.

Outside on the landing Perkins indicated another door to which was glued a hand-painted wooden sign which read: Church of England Crown Appointments Commission. "Your neighbours for the time being," said Perkins, raising his eyebrows. "You should have heard the fuss when I said I was asking the Archbishop of Canterbury to find them a place at Lambeth Palace. Anyone would have thought I'd ordered them to demolish Westminster Abbey."

Thompson moved closer to the door so that he could read the sign. "What on earth are they doing here?"

"In theory the Prime Minister appoints the bishops and all sorts of other worthies." Perkins was now leaning against the wall with one hand in a trouser pocket. "In practice the Archbishop just sends over his nomination and I sign on the dotted line. Ludicrous, isn't it? I haven't set foot in a church since we buried my Mum."

They went downstairs again. This time to the ground floor.

In the entrance hall Perkins introduced Thompson to Inspector Page, who was taking tea with the duty policemen. "This is the gent who keeps me safe from all those vicious Tory ladies." Inspector Page managed only the briefest of smiles as he reached for Thompson's hand.

From the entrance lobby they passed down the long gold-carpeted corridor to the Cabinet Room. Perkins opened the door and they stepped inside. At the far end the early morning sunlight streamed in through the long windows. "This is where it all happens," said Perkins, propping himself against one of the two white pillars which extend from ceiling to floor just inside the door. "The table," explained Perkins, "is shaped like a boat. I sit in the middle" – he pointed to the chair in front of the mantelpiece – "so everyone can see the expression on my face." For a moment they stood in silence and then they turned and left, Perkins closing the door behind them.

The private office adjoins the Cabinet Room. Horace Tweed had just arrived when Perkins' head came round the door. His bowler hat was on a peg by the filing cabinets. He stood as Perkins entered. "Good morning, Prime Minister."

"Mr Tweed, I want you to meet Fred Thompson who is joining my political staff."

"Delighted," said Tweed in a tone of voice that suggested he was far from delighted by the prospect of working with some young Labour Party upstart.

When they were out of earshot Perkins whispered, "Don't forget, Fred, you report to me and only to me. Don't let Tweed or anyone else tell you otherwise." Thompson nodded.

They went back upstairs again to the office that was to be Thompson's. By this time a sack of mail had arrived and was sitting on the floor by the desk. "I assume you'll type most of your own letters," said Perkins, "but if you want any help, the typing pool is in the basement. Garden girls they call them. All twinsets and pearls. That's something we'll have to sort out. Get some of our lasses in." Perkins looked at his watch. He still had some reading to do before the Cabinet meeting.

"Right, Fred, I'll leave you to it. If you want anything, ask Tweed." As he moved towards the door Perkins turned. "There is one thing I should have mentioned." He smiled broadly, causing the lines in his rugged face to sharpen. "You'll have to be vetted by security. To make sure you aren't a threat to democracy."

The Cabinet met at ten o'clock. Ministers arrived at Downing Street on foot as Perkins had given instructions that cars from the government pool were only to be used for emergencies.

In the Cabinet Room Perkins sat with his back to the fireplace in the seat traditionally occupied by Prime Ministers. Above him hung a melancholy portrait of Sir Robert Walpole. Wainwright, the Chancellor, sat on his left. Only a handful of members of the new government had ever held Cabinet rank before and some had never held any government office.

Perkins opened the proceedings with a little homily. "We are about to embark on one of the most exciting programmes any British government has ever dared contemplate. Although we have a clear popular mandate, we can expect to come under the most severe pressure from those vested interests who would rather our programme were not fulfilled. If we are to resist such pressure it is important we should never lose sight of the ideals of the Party that sent us here."

He looked around the table. He had the attention of everyone present. "At the moment we have the advantage of surprise. This will not last long, but while we have it we must use it. As my old Dad used to say, 'Hit 'em hard and when they're down, hit 'em again.' " This elicited smiles from everyone except the Cabinet secretary who sat stone faced.

Item one on the agenda was a paper on the economic situation prepared by the Treasury. Wainwright reviewed the main points and stated his opinion. "They want us to go for higher interest rates and a large IMF loan."

"They don't waste any time at the Treasury, do they?" interrupted Jock Steeples, the Leader of the House. "Before

76

we know where we are they'll be asking for spending cuts and an incomes policy." From around the table there was a sympathetic murmur.

Wainwright ignored the interruption. "As far as the IMF's concerned we don't have much choice. If the pound continues to fall at the present rate our entire reserves will be gone by the end of the month."

Perkins went round the table seeking the opinion of each minister. After each had spoken briefly he summed up, "So we steer clear of the IMF for the moment and talk to the Germans, the French and the Dutch about the possibility of a stand-by credit. If that fails, we'll think again. Meantime interest rates will stay as they are."

The main item was the draft of the King's Speech, which had been cobbled together by civil servants in the Cabinet Office. The law providing for the detention of suspected Trotskyists was to be repealed. A special department, headed by a minister, was to be set up to supervise the reconstruction of the riot-torn inner cities.

All the main manifesto pledges were covered, although one or two had been watered down a little. On the American bases, the draft said simply that "negotiations would be opened with the United States government regarding the future of US military bases in Britain." After some discussion, in which the only strong dissent came from Wainwright, 'withdrawal' was substituted for 'future'.

On British nuclear warheads the draft said simply that they would be phased out. 'Dismantled' was the word the Cabinet preferred.

"Christ Almighty," said Steeples as they filed out into Downing Street two hours later, "the King will have a heart attack when he reads that little lot."

When the details of the King's Speech began to leak sterling went into a nosedive. By the time the markets in New York closed, the pound was a staggering six cents down against the dollar.

6

It was starting to rain when Marcus J. Morgan's bullet-proof Cadillac swept into Downing Street. The Cadillac was preceded by two police motorcycle outriders and a carload of American secret service agents. Behind came a second Cadillac with aides and advisers. Officers of the Metropolitan Police Diplomatic Protection Unit brought up the rear in an unmarked car.

The waiting cameramen scarcely glimpsed the Secretary of State's portly frame as he was propelled through the door of Number Ten surrounded by the secret service men. After him came the American ambassador and a man from the US Treasury.

There was a minor scene in the lobby when Inspector Page told the secret service men that they would not be allowed to accompany their charge to the door of the Prime Minister's study. "If this were America . . ." one of them was heard to say before the inspector cut him short by stating sharply, "This is not America, this is Great Britain and I'd thank you to remember that."

Morgan, happily unaware of the contretemps, was taken to see Perkins. His bodyguards were left pacing up and down in the hallway, chewing gum and muttering curses.

Perkins was waiting on the landing when Morgan, slightly out of breath, reached the top of the stairs.

"Mr Prime Minister," said Morgan without smiling as he extended his hand.

"Mr Secretary of State."

Perkins was nervous. A nerve in the left side of his face twitched uncontrollably and he wondered whether Morgan had noticed. He knew this was going to be an important meeting and he also wondered whether he would manage to conceal his dislike for fat American lawyers. Morgan had a

reputation for crudeness and dealing with him might require more tact than Perkins could muster.

Inside the study, Morgan introduced the ambassador and the man from the US Treasury. Perkins in turn introduced his team, Newsome the Foreign Secretary, and Wainwright, the Chancellor.

Morgan seated himself in one of the two armchairs. Perkins took the other. Newsome, Wainwright and the rest arranged themselves in a semi-circle of hard chairs between the Prime Minister and the Secretary of State. An aide of Morgan's placed a small voice-activating tape recorder between the two men. Tweed, the private secretary, did likewise. He then busied himself serving drinks from a cocktail cabinet at the far end of the study. Morgan had a neat whisky, Perkins an orange juice.

Morgan did not stand on ceremony. "Mr Prime Minister, I'm here because the President is very concerned that your government's programme constitutes a threat to the security of the West."

A pained expression appeared on the face of the American ambassador. In the car on the way to Downing Street he had spent ten minutes advising Morgan to warm up slowly.

"According to your programme," the Secretary of State continued, "you are intending to remove all foreign bases from British soil, scrap nuclear weapons and go neutral." Morgan spat out 'neutral' as though he were referring to a contagious disease which, in a manner of speaking, he was.

He was heard in silence interrupted only by the clink of glasses as Tweed served drinks. "Mr Prime Minister," growled Morgan, "I am authorised to warn you that any attempt to detach Britain from the Western alliance would be regarded by my government as a hostile act and one which would have grave consequences for the United Kingdom."

Morgan was not a man of many words and when he had made his point he stopped. Perkins' face remained expressionless. When it was his turn to speak he did so quietly and slowly. "First, I would like to thank the Secretary of State for

stating his government's position so frankly. I will now try to state our position with equal clarity."

Perkins' opening remarks were heard in silence. "For a long time the British Labour Party has been of the view that the presence of American nuclear weapons on our soil, far from offering us protection, actually makes Britain into a target for Russian missiles. The pledge to remove nuclear weapons was a prominent part of our election manifesto and it was on the basis of that manifesto that we recently won an overwhelming popular mandate."

At this Morgan's lips moved almost imperceptibly. What he said was only audible to those closest to him, but one of the stenographers said afterwards that it sounded suspiciously like "Popular mandate, my ass." The ambassador's face was white.

If Perkins had seen Morgan's lips move, he gave no clue. He went on speaking quietly, "I therefore take the opportunity to inform you that we will shortly be making a formal request to your government to begin the withdrawal of troops and weapons from British soil." He paused to sip his orange juice. "Obviously the details are a matter for negotiation, but we are thinking in terms of a phased withdrawal over two or three years."

Morgan's cheeks flushed. His eyes dilated. "Prime Minister," his voice had acquired a harder edge, "this is grossly irresponsible." He paused to think of something to add. "It's like telling the Soviets, 'We're coming out with our hands up.'"

Perkins could not suppress a smile. "Nonsense," he said firmly, "we are just telling the Russians and anyone else who cares to listen that we don't wish to be annihilated, and inviting them to follow our example."

"And the West Germans," said Morgan, "what about the West Germans? Are you going to abandon them to the Soviets?"

Perkins was feeling confident now. The nerve in his left cheek had stopped twitching. "The West Germans," he said quietly, "have no more interest in being annihilated than we

do. If they want to defend themselves against a possible Russian invasion, they would be wise to develop local militia capable of fighting guerrilla warfare. That is what the Swiss and the Yugoslavs have done and that is how British defence policy will develop in future."

Tweed appeared with the whisky bottle and refilled Morgan's glass. Perkins took another sip of orange juice. Since Morgan had not responded, Perkins added unkindly, "Look at Vietnam. All the nuclear bombs in the world didn't help you there."

At the mention of Vietnam, Morgan's chins began to quiver. He had not come here to have salt rubbed in America's wounds by the leader of some third-rate, clapped-out colonial power. "Prime Minister," he sneered, "I don't think we understand each other very well. Let me spell out our position in words of one syllable."

Tweed lingered in the background, whisky bottle in hand, his ears flapping. The ambassador wished that the ground would open up.

"Let me tell you plain," snarled Morgan. There was a meanness in his voice which had not been apparent until now. "If you kick out our bases, you can kiss goodbye to any help from the United States in putting this ramshackle economy of yours back together again."

Perkins said nothing. Wainwright and Newsome looked blankly at each other. The US Treasury man looked at the floor. The ambassador fidgeted. No one seemed to know what should happen next. Morgan solved the problem. Heaving himself to his feet, he towered over Perkins for a few seconds, then he turned and lumbered towards the door. The man from the US Treasury followed. The aide with the cassette recorder paused only long enough to scoop up his machine. The ambassador, without speaking, stayed to shake hands with Perkins and then scurried after the Secretary of State.

Surrounded by secret service men Marcus J. Morgan climbed back into his bullet-proof Cadillac and was swept away to the ambassador's mansion in Regent's Park. In place

of a press conference, scheduled for noon at the American embassy, a statement was put out saying simply that the Secretary of State and the Prime Minister had a frank exchange of views.

When they heard the King's Speech the executive of the Confederation of British Industry went into special session at its tenth floor offices in Centre Point. Two hours later a statement was issued saying that government plans to force the pension and insurance funds to invest in manufacturing industry would lead to a final collapse of confidence in the currency. They begged the government to think again.

The newspapers next day were rather more forthright. "Recipe for Ruin", screamed the front page headline on the *Daily Mail*. "Downright looney," said the *Sun*. The *Guardian* agonised for ten column inches before concluding that, although Labour's plans made sense, "Now was not the time." Perkins' honeymoon with the press was over. It had lasted just six days.

The weekly meeting of permanent secretaries takes place in the boardroom of the Cabinet Office overlooking Horseguards' Parade. As the senior civil servants in charge of each of the main Whitehall departments, they meet, in theory, to co-ordinate government policy. In practice they also sometimes co-ordinate resistance to government policy.

The Cabinet secretary, Sir Richard Hildrew, was a Balliol man. He had a first in classics and had spent most of his career at the Treasury before taking charge of the Cabinet Office three years previously. "Obviously," Sir Richard was saying, "they can't carry on like this. It's only a matter of time before we get a U-turn. Our job, meanwhile, is to minimise the damage."

"Peter," he turned to a man in a double-breasted, chalkstripe suit seated on his right. "Peter, any news of the stand-by credit yet."

"Nothing final." This was Sir Peter Kennedy, permanent secretary at the Treasury responsible for overseas financial

relations. "My chaps have been on to Bonn and Paris and they seem most unlikely to stump up the funds. The Americans have been putting the screws on and urging them not to co-operate."

"Hardly surprising after yesterday's débâcle." The newcomer to the discussion was Sir Michael Spencer, who was in charge of Defence. Although none of the permanent secretaries had been present at the meeting between Perkins and the American Secretary of State, every one of them knew exactly what had taken place. News travels fast on the Whitehall network.

Spencer paused from doodling logarithms on his blotter: "As I see it we have at least six months before we have to start giving the American bases the heave-ho. By that time the government will have had a taste of the real world and may be in a mood to think again."

"The IMF loan is going to be the key." It was Kennedy of the Treasury again. "With any luck the terms will be so stiff that the foreign bankers will do our job for us."

Outside, the rain had stopped for the first time in two days. Shafts of sun streamed through the Regency windows to form puddles of light on the floor in front of each window.

Sir Richard gathered his papers into a neat pile. "So we're agreed, then, gentlemen." He glanced around the table. "No one does anything precipitate until we see which way the wind blows. Delay is our strategy."

In the distance the chimes of Big Ben could be heard striking eleven o'clock. From nearby came the clip-clop of horses' hooves at the Changing of the Guard.

"Three Communists, one Trotskyite and a queer." Fiennes was almost licking his lips as he placed the last beige file on the desk in front of Sir Peregrine. The other files, about twenty in all, were arranged in three piles. "Not to mention that His Majesty's Foreign Secretary seems to be screwing some ripe little twenty-one year old from Hampstead Labour party."

Sir Peregrine leaned back in his chair. "Not the sort of stuff that brings down governments," he sighed.

"Surely, sir, three Communists?"

"But that was thirty years ago, Fiennes. People do all sorts of silly things at university." He picked up one of the files and flicked through the pages of computer print-out. "In any case we can't make too much of the Communist angle. One of them was Wainwright and he's ours now."

"How about the Trot?" Fiennes passed another file.

Sir Peregrine opened it and read aloud: " 'Ted Curran, aged sixty-two, Minister for Overseas Development, until 1962 a member of the Socialist Review Group, a forerunner of the Socialist Workers' Party.' " He looked up at Fiennes. There was the merest hint of a smile on his lips. "Nineteen sixty-two; that's leaving it a bit late to go respectable. What have we got in the way of pictures?"

A pile of full plate black and white pictures lay on the desk beside the files. Fiennes picked them up and quickly leafed through them. "This one's not bad. Taken at a CND demonstration in the late Fifties." He passed the picture to Sir Peregrine. "Curran's in the donkey jacket on the left, the fellow next to Jim Thomas. Today he's National Secretary of the SWP."

Sir Peregrine held the picture close to his face while he studied it carefully. "Hmm, promising. Even shows the SWP banner in the background." He laid the photo on the desk. "Any evidence that Curran is still in touch with Thomas?"

"Not as far as we know."

"Pity. Still, we can't have everything."

Fiennes stood up and gathered an armful of files. "Shall I pass this on to Fison?"

Sir Peregrine thought for a moment. "No, I wouldn't do that. A cheap rag like his is a bit too obvious for this sort of thing. How about *The Times*? We've got a man on *The Times*, haven't we?"

"Yes, sir."

"And while you're about it," Fiennes was almost at the door when Sir Peregrine spoke again, "why don't you check out that girl Newsome's sleeping with?" He smiled thinly.

"Quite a turn-up for the books, if we found the Foreign Secretary sleeping with a Trot."

By the end of his first week in Downing Street, Fred Thompson was only halfway through the backlog of mail. It was mostly letters of congratulation. Requests for interviews he passed on to the press secretary who had an office off the main hallway. Invitations to speak at Labour Party or trade union functions were passed to Perkins' personal secretary, Mrs Kendall, a plump, greying lady in her late fifties who had worked for Perkins since he entered Parliament. She took the invitations through to the Prime Minister and he would simply write 'Yes' or 'No' in the top right-hand corner. Mrs Kendall would return them to Thompson and he would reply accordingly. Abusive letters he filed without replying. Threatening letters were passed to the Special Branch.

If a letter was received from a trade union general secretary, a Labour Member of Parliament or a personal friend of Perkins, Thompson would draft a reply and take it to the Prime Minister for signature. Usually Thompson would take the letters for signing to the Prime Minister's study in the early evening, after Perkins had returned from the House of Commons. Before setting out Thompson would buzz Mrs Kendall and she would tell him if the Prime Minister was free. Sometimes Perkins would make them both a cup of Nescafé, using the kettle behind his desk, and then they would sit and gossip for ten minutes.

During the day Thompson saw little of Perkins. Once, after he had been in Downing Street three days, Perkins had put his head round the door and enquired how he was getting on. The Prime Minister's flat was on the same floor, but since he was still living in Kennington he only used it as a changing room.

The attitude of Tweed and the other private secretaries towards Thompson can best be described as 'correct'. They were never rude, but never went out of their way to be helpful. The men from the Church of England in the office next door gave Thompson little more than the time of day. He assumed they were sulking over their impending eviction and

after the first day he gave up trying to make friends with them.

To Thompson's surprise the garden girls were on the whole friendly. Since they had worked for the previous régime they knew their way about and Thompson went to them when he needed help.

Mrs Kendall was a dear. She was always neatly turned out and with long grey hair tied in a bun at the back of her head. She had strong political views of her own and was, if anything, to the left of Perkins. She did not hesitate to tick him off if she thought he was pulling his punches. Thompson got on well with her and since she was on better terms with the private office he channelled requests for such things as filing cabinets through Mrs Kendall.

On his first morning Thompson was given a long form to complete and return to a box number in the Ministry of Defence. He was asked to list every address he had lived at over the last ten years, the names of any Communists, Trotskyites or Fascists with whom he had ever had dealings, and to give two referees.

Two days later a Special Branch man with a rolled umbrella and a navy blue Marks and Spencer mackintosh came to see him. An ex-CID sergeant in his fifties who had been pushed sideways, he was bitter at never being made inspector. "My job is to make sure there are no subversives in Whitehall," he said without a trace of humour.

"According to the newspapers the place is crawling with subversives," replied Thompson mischievously. "Only problem is they're all elected."

The Special Branch man did not attempt a smile. He refused an offer of coffee and sat down without so much as unbuttoning his raincoat. "You in debt to anyone?"

"No."

"Have you a girl-friend?"

"Several."

Solemnly the man recorded each answer in his standard

issue notebook. "Which system do you support?"

"I beg your pardon?"

"Our system or theirs?" There was irritation in his voice. Thompson was not treating him seriously.

"What do you mean, *ours*?"

"The King, Parliament . . . "

"And *theirs*?"

"The Russians."

Thompson struggled to keep a straight face. The man sat waiting, biro poised, for an answer. "I am a member of the Labour Party. There's all sorts in the Labour Party."

"Which sort are you?"

"Is that really relevant?"

The man's voice hardened. "I'll decide what's relevant and the longer you piss about the longer this will take."

It took two hours and as he left the man did not attempt to conceal his annoyance. Civil servants treated the Special Branch vetting with respect because their careers depended on security clearance, but political appointments were made by ministers who usually did not give a toss what the Special Branch dredged up. Thompson could afford to be cocky.

"You'll be hearing from us again," said the Special Branch man as he departed, but he knew he was wasting his time.

When Thompson left Downing Street, it was already getting dark. He walked up to Whitehall and took a number 24 bus back to his flat in Camden. Indoors he switched on the kettle for a cup of tea and just caught the headlines at the end of the radio news. Sterling was still sliding. That day it had dipped under two dollars for the first time since the early 1980s.

Before the kettle had boiled the phone rang. It was Elizabeth Fain. "Fred, at last. I've been trying to get you all week."

Thompson told her about his new job and then asked about her weekend in the country. She sounded agitated. "That's what I want to talk to you about. It's important."

"Fire away."

"No, Fred, not on the phone."

"Now who's paranoid?"

They met that evening in a Holborn wine bar. At eight o'clock next morning Thompson saw Perkins alone in his study.

7

Every morning at ten a blue Mercedes deposited the Chancellor of the Exchequer, Lawrence Wainwright, at the main entrance to the Treasury. Despite the Prime Minister's memorandum ordering ministers to limit their use of government cars, Wainwright insisted on being driven the 300 yards from Number Eleven Downing Street. Not that Wainwright was lazy or incapable of walking. On the contrary, he was a man of iron constitution. He insisted on being driven to the Treasury each morning only because Perkins had asked him not to. It was as simple as that. Had Perkins insisted ministers go by car, Wainwright would probably have walked.

Wainwright was a bitter man. By rights he and not Harry Perkins should have been in Number Ten. At least, that was what he told himself. That was also what the newspapers said. And so did a surprising number of Labour MPs in the privacy of the tea rooms. Wainwright knew that had history taken its natural course he would have been leader of the Labour Party. It was no secret that a comfortable majority of Labour MPs would prefer him to Perkins any day of the week. But just as Wainwright had been poised to enter upon what he regarded as his rightful inheritance, the rules had been changed. Instead of leaving the choice of leader up to the MPs, the party had set up this damn fool electoral college. The result was Harry Perkins.

Wainwright had toyed with the idea of leaving politics, of taking a job with the World Bank or NATO and coming back to haunt Perkins in a new incarnation. There had been no shortage of offers, but in the end he had decided to stay. For one thing it was only a question of time before Perkins and his friends ran into deep trouble. When that happened there might well be a role for Wainwright. He might be just the man to step in and fill the breach when Perkins ran aground. This was what Wainwright's friends were saying. Stick around,

Lawrence, they said. We may need you soon. So Wainwright had stuck around. The result was an offer of a senior Cabinet post.

At first Wainwright had been surprised when Perkins offered him the Chancellor's job, but the more he thought about it, the more he realised he was doing Perkins a favour by accepting. Firstly, because he probably represented more of a threat outside the government than inside. Second, because his contacts in the City were impeccable. In opposition Wainwright had accepted directorships on the board of a leading merchant bank and a multinational chemical company. He had of course to resign the directorships when he went back into government, but the contacts were still there. Wainwright moved very easily in the world of high finance. Being the only moderate in the Cabinet he was virtually a prisoner. The more he thought about it, he was an obvious choice for Chancellor.

The Treasury was a gloomy place. The building was designed originally for the British Raj in New Delhi and intended to exclude the Indian sunlight. For some reason it ended up being built in Whitehall rather than Delhi and excluding British rather than Indian sunlight. The corridors are built around a circular courtyard and account for more than a quarter of the entire surface area. They are wide enough to accommodate six people walking abreast and all day long messengers pushing little wicker baskets ply back and forth.

The Chancellor's office is on the second floor overlooking King Charles Street. Sir Peter Kennedy, the senior permanent secretary, was waiting when Wainwright arrived.

"Bad news, sir." Kennedy's eyes betrayed a tiny gleam of satisfaction as he spoke. "No go with the stand-by credit. The Americans didn't want to know. The Germans said only if the Americans co-operate and the French said 'Get stuffed'. Only the Dutch seem prepared to lend a hand."

Wainwright placed his red despatch box on the oak desk, walked to the other side and sat down. "Do the markets know?" he asked Kennedy.

"Not yet, sir, but it's only a matter of time," said Kennedy, affecting regret.

"When they do, I suppose they'll wipe another billion off sterling." Wainwright was toying with a paper knife.

Kennedy did not reply, but remained hovering like an obsequious butler. "I told the Cabinet," said Wainwright self-righteously, "I told them we were wasting our time even asking, but they would insist." He placed the paper knife by the base of a large lampshade on the right hand corner of the desk. "That only leaves us one option, the IMF."

That was Kennedy's cue. "I've already been on to Washington," he said quickly. "They say they could have a team here by Wednesday."

"Wednesday?" Wainwright raised an eyebrow. "They don't waste any time, do they?"

"Actually, sir," said Kennedy with a smile, "we did warn them we might be calling." And then he added hastily, "Unofficially of course."

"Of course," said Wainwright, who knew very well that behind his back the Treasury mandarins were in daily contact with the IMF. For all he knew they may even have agreed the conditions. Probably all that remained was to get the Chancellor's signature on a letter of application.

He looked up at Kennedy. The man never put a foot wrong. Yet everyone in the Treasury knew that it was he and not Wainwright who was boss. Long after Wainwright had gone from the Chancellorship, Kennedy would still be steering the British economy.

"We'll need a summary of our financial position to show the IMF."

"There's a draft in your tray, sir."

"And a position paper for the Cabinet."

"The first draft is being typed now," said Kennedy, clasping his hands and tilting his head to one side. Will that be all? he seemed to say.

"I'd better tell Perkins." Wainwright pressed a button on the intercom connecting him to his private office. "Get me the PM," he said.

Marcus J. Morgan was back in his Washington office when he heard that the British were sending for the IMF. He thumped the desk in triumph. "Now we'll screw the bastards."

Morgan was a mean man and he was proud of being mean. "I didn't get where I am today by helping old ladies across the street," he was fond of telling subordinates.

That night top secret cables went out from the State Department to American ambassadors in Nigeria, Saudi Arabia, Kuwait and other countries holding reserves in sterling. The cables instructed the ambassadors to apply *all legitimate pressure* to persuade the governments to which they were accredited to start converting their reserves into any currency but sterling. Legitimate pressure included offers of increased military aid.

The British were on the run. Morgan planned to make them run even faster.

Sir Philip Norton, the Co-ordinator of Intelligence in the Cabinet Office, had just returned from lunching at the Reform Club when he was summoned by the Prime Minister. "PM's in a bit of a flap," said Tweed as he ushered Sir Philip into the presence.

"Ah, there you are, Norton," said Perkins, indicating the seat in front of his desk. "I've got a little job for your fellows."

Perkins paused to take off his reading spectacles. It was the first time Sir Philip had seen Perkins wearing glasses. They made him look more of an intellectual than his public image suggested. "I've had reports," Perkins went on, "that civil servants in the Treasury have been privately advising foreign finance ministries not to provide the stand-by credit we have been trying to negotiate. Do you know anything about that?"

Inwardly Sir Philip was aghast, but his face betrayed not a flicker of emotion. "New one on me, Prime Minister."

Perkins placed both hands palm downwards on the desk. "As far as I am concerned there is one word to describe a situation where a servant of His Majesty's government conspires with officials of a foreign government against the British national interest: *treason*." Sir Philip winced at the

word. Really, this was laying it on a bit thick. "Tell DI5 I want the names of those involved. Tap the phones at the Treasury if necessary." Perkins paused and then added with a smile, "About time DI5 had something useful to do. A change from photographing CND demonstrators and spying on trade union officials."

Sir Philip did not share Perkins' amusement.

"May I enquire what your source is for this information, Prime Minister?"

"The source is my affair, but you can take it from me it's reliable."

Too damn reliable, thought Sir Philip.

"While you're here," said Perkins, "perhaps you can tell me, do DI5 keep files on members of my government?"

"These days, Prime Minister, it's all on computer. Curzon Street will have something on every Member of Parliament. Mostly just name, age, school, assets. Standard procedure."

"How do I get at them?" Perkins took a Kleenex tissue from a box on his desk and started to clean his glasses.

"I beg your pardon, Prime Minister." Sir Philip was sitting bolt upright.

"The files, tapes or whatever you call them. How do I get them? It's the ones on Cabinet ministers I'm interested in." He breathed on the lenses of his spectacles, causing them to mist over.

"Prime Minister, I must advise you that it would be most irregular for any member of the government to see those files."

Perkins cocked an eyebrow. "But I thought the Prime Minister is supposed to be the head of the security services. Surely I can see what I like?"

In eight years as Co-ordinator of Intelligence and before that as head of DI5 Sir Philip had served three Prime Ministers and four Home Secretaries. Never had any of them asked to see files except on the recommendation of the security chiefs. Sir Philip was embarrassed, but firm. "Prime Minister, there is a convention that ministers do not concern themselves with particular cases. It was set out in a directive by the former

Home Secretary, Sir David Maxwell Fyfe, in 1952. I can provide you with a copy."

Perkins was incredulous. "You are not seriously suggesting I should be bound by a memorandum from some Tory Home Secretary nearly forty years ago?"

Sir Philip wrung his hands. That was precisely what he was suggesting.

"Because if so," Perkins replaced his glasses and leaned across the desk, "you are quite mistaken. I want copies of everything that damn computer has on members of my Cabinet. And I want it today."

Four hours later Tweed wheeled in twenty-four small bundles of computer print-out. One for each Cabinet minister. Perkins sent each minister his own and asked for comments. What he did not know is that before parting with print-outs, DI5 had carefully weeded out juicier snippets such as the Foreign Secretary's affair with the girl in the Hampstead Labour party. The reference to the photograph of the Overseas Development Minister marching alongside the National Secretary of the Socialist Workers' Party was also missing. It turned up a few weeks later on the front page of *The Times*. The photo was published under the headline "A Trot in the Cabinet" and the story underneath went on to imply that he was just one of many. *The Times* had even managed to dredge up a couple of Curran's old SWP colleagues who reminisced at length about the minister's days as a revolutionary Marxist.

The story caused a mild flurry in the popular newspapers and the *Daily Telegraph*, and Tory backbenchers had some fun at question time in the House. By and large, however, the only people who were shocked were those who wanted to be, since Curran had never made any secret of his political past.

"That'll do for starters," said Sir Peregrine when Fiennes placed the press cuttings in his in-tray. Then he added, with the nearest he ever came to a smile, "Next we'll give the Foreign Secretary's love life an airing."

*

The first thing Sir Philip Norton did when he got back to the Cabinet Office was to ring his brother. The phone rang for a full minute before a refined voice said, "Watlington Priory."

"Andrew." As Sir Philip spoke his secretary placed a cup of tea on the desk in front of him. "Andrew, I wanted to thank you for that awfully nice dinner the other evening."

From the other end of the telephone came a couple of minutes of "Jolly decent of you to come, old boy . . ." Sir Philip clasped the telephone receiver with one hand, stirred his tea with a spoon in the other, and, occasionally, uttered a "Yes" or "No". When the babble at the other end subsided, he replaced the teaspoon in the saucer and came to the point. "Who was that girl with Roger?"

"What girl? Oh, you mean Elizabeth? Fain's girl. Charming . . ."

Sir Philip had taken from an inside jacket pocket a gold-topped fountain pen. *Fain* he wrote on a sheet of Cabinet Office notepaper. "Any idea what she does for a living?"

"Not a clue. Father was an equerry to the King." There was a silence at the other end of the phone and then, "I say, old boy, nothing wrong?"

"Of course not. Just curious, that's all." Sir Philip laid the pen on the desk and reached for his tea. "Sorry Andrew, must rush. Thanks again for dinner."

He replaced the receiver and put the top back on his fountain pen which he returned to his inside pocket. On the Cabinet Office notepaper Sir Philip had written under *Fain* the words *Equerry* and *King*.

His next call was to Sir Peregrine Craddock to whom he related the details of his conversation with Perkins. When that was done he flipped a switch on his desk intercom. "Get me some background on Lady Elizabeth F-A-I-N," he said into the machine. "And when you've found out where she lives tell Ebury Bridge Road to put a tap on her phone."

The men from the IMF arrived two days later. They checked into Brown's Hotel in Mayfair under assumed names. Their anonymity did not last long. A story in the *Financial Times* the

95

next day blew their cover. News of their arrival caused the pound to rally by half a cent, but the recovery did not last long.

There were five of them: an American, a Dutchman, a Japanese, a German and an Englishman, Bill Whittaker, a former deputy chief cashier at the Bank of England. Whittaker was a hard, humourless man, who had not come to look up old friends. He was here to look at the books and offer a diagnosis. He was not concerned with the political consequences of this diagnosis, only with the facts. The facts in this case were that Britain was asking for the biggest loan in the IMF's history. Inevitably the price would be high.

Everywhere the IMF team went they were trailed by pressmen. Photographers were waiting outside the Treasury, the Bank of England and Downing Street. As if to underline the gravity of the mission, rain started soon after the IMF team arrived in London and continued almost without respite until they left. Every day the newspapers published pictures of five unsmiling men in mackintoshes, getting in and out of chauffeur-driven cars, king-sized umbrellas held aloft. And with every day that passed the pound continued to fall until the reserves were nearly exhausted.

Only a three per cent increase in Minimum Lending Rate staved sterling's complete collapse.

One rain-sodden night after the IMF team had been two weeks in Britain a Royal Air Force DC10 took off from Northolt in Middlesex. On board were three men whose identity was known only to the captain and the steward who were sworn to secrecy. The three passengers boarded the plane after darkness from a car which was driven to the aircraft steps. The DC10 left Northolt at 2100 GMT and flew west over the Atlantic until it was well clear of European airspace. Then it veered south, skirting Spain and Portugal. Just before the Canary Islands the DC10 turned east towards Morocco. It crossed Morocco behind the Atlas Mountains and then turned north east. At 0130 GMT the DC10 landed at Dar El Beidah airport, Algiers.

The plane taxied to a dark corner of the airport and stopped. Two black Mercedes, one containing a high official of the Algerian government, were waiting. Even before the engines were switched off, a gangway was in place. The doors opened and the three passengers emerged, each carrying a briefcase and a small suitcase.

While a chauffeur put their luggage in the boot of the first Mercedes the three men each shook hands with the Algerian official. Then they climbed into the car and were driven away to a secluded villa on the Mediterranean coast. The crew of the plane followed in the second Mercedes.

The three Englishmen were the Foreign Secretary, Tom Newsome; his parliamentary private secretary, Len Fuller; and a political adviser, Ray Morse.

In London the IMF team were commuting between the Bank of England and the Treasury. At the Bank they talked about interest rates and devaluation. At the Treasury they discussed the Public Sector Borrowing Requirement and income policies.

Between officials at the Bank, the Treasury and the men from the IMF there was little disagreement about what was necessary. They had all been brought up to believe that borrowing was basically immoral and should be heavily penalised. They believed that government spending was far too high and that free trade was sacred. The only problem was how to convince the government. As Sir Peter Kennedy said, "The government has just won a huge election victory based on exactly the opposite analysis of the situation."

When, after two weeks of deliberation, the IMF men unveiled their terms for a loan, even Wainwright was taken aback. They wanted £10,000 million off public spending in two years. Even on Treasury estimates that would add another million to the dole queues. It would also require a rigid incomes policy, something the government was pledged not to introduce. On top of this the IMF also wanted guarantees that the government would not introduce import controls

or any other restrictions on free trade. "I'll never get that through the Cabinet," Wainwright told them.

"Your problem, not ours," said the American member of the IMF team, and it was he who did most of the talking. He went on, "We're bankers, not politicians. We don't make any distinction whether we are dealing with British social democrats or Turkish Generals."

"All very well," replied Wainwright, "but Turkish Generals have ways of dealing with public opinion that aren't open to British social democrats."

At 0800 GMT (ten o'clock local time) Tom Newsome had an audience with the Algerian President at the Casr Es Shaab Palace. Later he spent an hour with the Prime Minister and the Finance Minister after which he was driven to the airport. At noon local time Newsome was airborne again, this time bound for Tripoli.

In London Annette Newsome phoned the private office and said that her husband was unwell and would work from home. She added that since he had lost his voice he could not be contacted by telephone. Arrangements were made for the red despatch boxes to be delivered by car to his home in Camberwell.

The Foreign Office press department issued a short statement saying that the Foreign Secretary was indisposed and had cancelled all engagements until further notice.

When the IMF terms were put to the Cabinet there was uproar. "What do they think we are, some banana republic?" raged Jock Steeples.

"Tell them where they can stuff their bloody money," said Jim Evans, the Defence Secretary.

The Home Secretary, Mrs Joan Cook, was more rational. "Even if we wanted to, we couldn't get a package like that through the Parliamentary Labour Party, let alone the National Executive Committee," she said quietly.

In the end it was agreed to defer any decision until Wainwright and the Prime Minister had had another talk with the

IMF. If necessary the managing director of the Fund was to be invited over from Washington.

Evans was asked to prepare a paper outlining drastic cuts in Britain's NATO budget, including the complete withdrawal of the British Army on the Rhine. News of this decision was to be leaked to the lobby correspondents when Perkins had them in for an off-the-record briefing later that day. As Perkins told Fred Thompson over a whisky in the Prime Minister's study that evening, "When our friends in NATO realise that defence will be the first casualty of any cuts, they may take more interest in getting the IMF off our backs."

In Libya Newsome lunched with the young colonel who had succeeded Gaddafi in a bloody coup two years before. Then he was driven back to the airport by the colonel's personal chauffeur. There was an awkward moment when it was discovered that the British ambassador was there seeing his wife off to London on a shopping trip. Fortunately the ambassador did not notice the DC10 with British markings parked a discreet distance from the terminal buildings. Heaven knows what he would have said had he known his Foreign Secretary was hiding from him in the Men's lavatory of the VIP lounge.

By 1500 GMT Newsome was en route to Baghdad.

8

Fourteen direct telephone lines connect the office of the Chancellor of the Exchequer with the outside world. They lead to Number Ten Downing Street and to each of the main government departments. Two lines connect with the official residence of the Chancellor at Number Eleven Downing Street (one to the sitting room and the other to the study). But the most important line connects the Chancellor's office with the Bank of England, which is obliged to clear with the Treasury every £10 million of reserves spent defending the value of sterling.

All the telephone lines pass through a concentrator in the Chancellor's private office. Incoming calls are indicated by a light flashing above the appropriate line on the concentrator. During a sterling crisis the light above the Bank of England line flashes with increasing frequency. Every time that light flashes everyone in the private office knows that the Bank has kissed goodbye to another £10 million.

When word reached the foreign exchanges that negotiations with the IMF had broken down the light above the Bank of England line to the Chancellor's private office began to flash every fifteen minutes. Tiny beads of sweat formed on the brow of the normally imperturbable Sir Peter Kennedy.

"Reserves down to £500 million, sir," said the junior private secretary who took the last call from the Bank. He handed Sir Peter a scribbled note with the latest details. The Bank was spending £30 million an hour from the reserves. At that rate they would be bankrupt in two days.

Kennedy crossed the red lino corridor which separated his office from the Chancellor's. He entered without knocking. Although Wainwright's desk was by the window most of the light was excluded by the Foreign Office building opposite. On the wall behind Wainwright hung an oil of the Relief of

Lucknow. Sepia was the predominant colour and it only added to the gloom.

"The Saudis and the Nigerians are selling," said Kennedy, his voice doomladen. "We're down to $1.47 and the cupboard's almost bare."

Wainwright was already preparing his alibi. "I told them," he said, "but they wouldn't listen."

"Couldn't you try the PM again?" Kennedy pleaded. "Something's got to give soon."

"I had Perkins on ten minutes ago. All he could say was we should keep our nerve." Wainwright did not attempt to conceal the contempt in his voice. "Seemed to think something would turn up by the special Cabinet tomorrow morning."

Kennedy withdrew shaking his head and mumbling to himself. He now seemed certain to go down in history as the permanent secretary who had presided over the collapse of the currency.

In the private office the intervals between the calls from the Bank of England grew shorter. And every time the light flashed on the concentrator apprehension shivered through the inner sanctum of the Treasury.

The DC10 bringing Newsome and his two colleagues from Baghdad touched down at Northolt at 0932 GMT. The Cabinet was due to meet at ten o'clock and the London foreign exchange market opened at the same time.

An official Mercedes was waiting to take them to Downing Street. Newsome sat in the front passenger seat; Len Fuller and Ray Morse in the back. Although tired the three men were exhilarated.

As they were passing through Willesden, Newsome dialled Downing Street on the radio telephone. "He's just gone into the Cabinet." It was Tweed's voice on the other end.

"Then get him out," said Newsome.

There was a delay of about forty-five seconds, most of which was spent waiting for traffic lights in Willesden High Street, before a voice said, "Perkins here."

"Harry, we've got it," Newsome was hardly able to contain his excitement.

"Everything?"

"Everything."

"Well done, lads," said Perkins. "How quickly can you get here?"

Newsome consulted the driver. The traffic was bad, but he said he knew a short cut through St John's Wood.

"About twenty minutes."

"I'll put the kettle on," said Perkins.

Newsome replaced the receiver on its rest between himself and the driver. Then, reaching in his briefcase, he took out a small battery operated shaver and began to shave.

Ministers were glum as they arrived for the Cabinet. Everybody knew this was the crunch. Batteries of television cameras waited outside.

"It's so unfair," said Mrs Cook to Jock Steeples, as they went in. "We never even had a chance."

Sir Peter Kennedy had been busy overnight preparing a brief outlining in the direst terms the consequences of a crash. By eight o'clock that morning every permanent secretary in Whitehall had a copy of the document in their hands. By 9.30 every Cabinet minister had been briefed on the alternatives facing them: the IMF or bankruptcy.

Jock Steeples came prepared to resign rather than accept the IMF terms, but he was in a minority. In the face of three days' intense pressure the majority against the IMF at the last Cabinet had melted. They had only been in office six weeks and already the hope that had attended their election was about to evaporate. The bankers had outwitted them in record time. They felt ashamed.

Only Perkins had a spring in his step when he returned to the Cabinet room after taking the telephone message in the private secretary's office. "What's he so cheerful about?" whispered Jim Evans, the Defence Secretary, to his neighbour as the Prime Minister sat down. He didn't have to wait long to find out.

"Comrades." The Cabinet Secretary winced at the use of the word. Such language simply was not used in Downing Street. "Comrades," repeated Perkins, "I have an important announcement."

They listened, not expecting to hear anything that would make the day more bearable. "Half an hour ago the Foreign Secretary arrived back in this country after a visit to Algeria, Libya and Iraq." Jim Evans' eyes widened. It was only half an hour since he had phoned Tom Newsome to find out if he would be well enough to make the Cabinet. Newsome's wife had said he was propped up in bed inhaling Friar's Balsam.

Perkins went on, "The Foreign Secretary has concluded an arrangement with these countries to make available to us a standby credit of up to £10,000 million on very generous terms."

From around the baize-covered table there was an audible gasp. First of disbelief, then relief. A miracle had happened. "The cunning old bugger," said Steeples. It was not clear whether he was referring to the Prime Minister or the Foreign Secretary.

Perkins allowed a few seconds for the good news to sink in and then tapped his pen on the table to call order. "The Foreign Secretary will be here in fifteen minutes and he will then be able to fill in the details."

When Newsome came through the door the Cabinet stood and applauded. Like the use of the word 'comrade' to address Ministers of the Crown, standing ovations are not a common feature of Cabinet meetings. Only the Cabinet Secretary remained in his seat.

Newsome outlined the details briefly. The new credit facilities would be available for an initial period of two years, renewable for a further two should the need arise. Interest payable at ten per cent annually on any money drawn.

Questions about the terms went on for twenty minutes. "What did you give away on Israel?" asked Wainwright, his voice betraying a note of sourness. He, after all, should have been told what was going on.

"Only what's in our programme." Newsome smiled benignly. "A homeland for the Palestinians."

"And what did you tell them about our relationship with the Americans?" persisted Wainwright.

"Told them we were going to kick out the bases," said Newsome looking round at his colleagues. "We are, aren't we?"

"You bet your life," growled Steeples.

From around the table there was a murmur of assent.

After the Cabinet, Newsome was driven home to Camberwell where he kissed his wife on the forehead, bathed, changed his clothes and left again. By three o'clock he was on his feet in the House of Commons.

The Chancellor's statement drew prolonged cheers from the Labour benches. The only note of dissent came from the Zionist lobby who feared that Israel had been sold out, but their doubts were swept aside in the general euphoria.

Scenting blood, the Conservatives had turned out in droves for the Chancellor's statement. They were stunned by the announcement. Questions to the Prime Minister followed. Perkins rubbed in the news. "You can tell your friends in the City," he roared at the subdued Tories, "that their attempt to subvert the democratically elected government of Great Britain has failed."

News of the Arab loan came too late in the day to have much effect on the London exchange, but by the time it closed at 4 pm the slide had eased. When the New York market closed five hours later the pound was one cent up on its value at the start of business.

As the Far East markets opened buying was feverish. The Arabs and the big corporations appeared to be leading the spree. The value of sterling began to climb fast. By the end of the week it had passed $1.60 and was still rising. Disaster had been averted.

*

The mandarins were less than overjoyed to see the government get off the hook so easily. At their weekly meetings in the Cabinet Office the permanent secretaries indulged in a fit of collective pique.

"You should have heard them crowing," said Sir Richard Hildrew, the Cabinet Secretary. "Actually stood up and applauded him there and then. Have you ever known government ministers who behave as though they are at a football match?" He shook his head wearily. What was the country coming to?

Sir Peter Kennedy had made a complete recovery from the prospect of going down in history as the permanent secretary who presided over the collapse of the currency. Now the threat had receded, his mind was turning to another vexing question. "Why wasn't the Treasury told? That's what I want to know." He stabbed the air with the forefinger of his right hand. "Not even Wainwright knew. No one even told the Chancellor."

Sir Cedric Snow, Foreign Office, was even more indignant. "I was told that Newsome was ill in bed at home when all the time he was gallivanting around the Middle East. Lied to by my own minister." He stressed the word *lied* as though it was the first time in the history of diplomacy that a lie had ever been told.

"Anyone would think," Sir Cedric went on, "that this government doesn't trust its own civil service."

A full thirty seconds elapsed before anyone else spoke.

When Marcus J. Morgan heard the news his chins began to quiver. He had barely finished reading the cable from the London embassy when the scrambled telephone on his desk began to bleep. It was the President, wanting to know "How the hell can a British Foreign Secretary travel 6,000 miles to three Arab countries and meet three heads of state without the CIA or the State Department picking up even a whisper?"

Morgan didn't know, but he was sure going to find out. "Meantime, Mr President, it's back to the drawing board."

*

Sir Peregrine Craddock was putting golf balls into a horizontal Nescafé jar as Fiennes entered with news of the Arab loan. He was in mid putt when Fiennes began describing the Foreign Secretary's secret visit to Algeria.

"Algeria?" He looked up just as the putter made contact with the ball. Fiennes was forced to side-step to avoid obstructing the ball as it rolled towards him, missing the Nescafé jar by more than three feet. Sir Peregrine now stood erect, brandishing the putter as though it were a sword. "Fiennes, do you mean to tell me that the Foreign Secretary has spent the last thirty-six hours in Algeria and that those nitwits in DI6 didn't even get a sniff?"

The ball had come to a halt just short of the doorway that led to the outer office. Fiennes shifted uneasily. "And Libya and Iraq," he said quickly.

Sir Peregrine leaned the putter against his desk. In silence he walked around the desk and settled himself in his swivel writing chair. It was a full minute before he spoke again. Fiennes wondered whether his presence was still required. At length Sir Peregrine looked up; his hands were joined beneath his chin as if he were in prayer. "Fiennes," he said slowly, "the time has come to sort out the Foreign Secretary's love life."

9

Maureen Jackson preferred older men. She was the youngest of the three daughters of a Politics professor at the London School of Economics. When she was still a third former at Camden School for Girls she was going to parties with her sisters, borrowing their clothes and reading their books. She was fifteen when she read *Fanny Hill*.

Maureen had little to do with boys of her own age. Her first lover was a third year student of her father's who came to their Hampstead house for tutorials. She was sixteen at the time.

By the time she was twenty, Maureen was working as a reporter on the *Hampstead and Highgate Express* and going out with men ten years older. She had wide eyes, perfect teeth and a complexion that rendered make-up superfluous. Although abnormally intelligent she did not get good enough 'A' levels to go to university. Her poor results were put down to her active social life and the amount of time she spent working for the local Labour Party. At least that is what she said she had been doing. Her mother had doubts.

Her parents took a tolerant view of their daughter's sex life. Both Maureen's elder sisters had been allowed to bring steady boyfriends home for the night. Even when her mother came home unexpectedly one weekday afternoon and found Maureen in bed with a man the fallout need not have been too disastrous.

Except that the man was His Majesty's Foreign Secretary.

Tom Newsome first met Maureen Jackson when she came to interview him for her newspaper. At the time Labour were in opposition and he was a junior foreign affairs spokesman. If he had known that in a year's time he would be the Foreign Secretary, he might have resisted getting involved. But New-

some had always had an eye for the ladies. As a schoolmaster in Yorkshire he had flirted with the young female teachers, but it was not until becoming a Member of Parliament that he realised the possibilities.

Power, as Dr Kissinger once said, is a great aphrodisiac. Not that backbench MPs have any power, but as Newsome quickly discovered, dinner in the Members' Dining Room of the House of Commons, followed by a drink on the terrace (weather permitting) did go down well with the ladies.

For his first five years in Parliament his wife, Annette, remained in Leeds looking after their two sons. When the sons left home Annette moved south and they bought a house in Camberwell. For a while Newsome behaved himself. He and Annette were a good team. Their politics were the same and she helped him with his constituency work.

Not until that spring morning when Maureen Jackson walked through his front door was Newsome again tempted to stray from the straight and narrow.

They chatted for two hours. Much of the time he spent interviewing her. By the time she left he knew where she lived, that she didn't have a steady boyfriend and what she thought of nuclear weapons.

That evening he rang Maureen from the House. He knew he should not, but he could not resist. Did she fancy a spot of dinner? When? Central Lobby at eight o'clock. After that it was back in the old routine. A meal in the Members' Dining Room, a drink on the terrace, even a stroll after dark round the lake in St James's Park.

The next day in the lobbies they were ribbing him. "Who was that young floosie I saw you with last night, Tom?" asked a Member from South Wales with a wink.

"Just some journalist in for an interview," said Newsome, trying to sound casual.

After that he was more discreet. Maureen never came to the House again. Usually they met in one of the parks. When they started sleeping together it was in a cheap hotel in Pimlico, booked under the name of Mr and Mrs Murray. But anyone could see at a glance that she was young enough to be

108

his daughter. In fact one of his sons was older than Maureen. There was a knowing look in the hotel receptionist's eye.

All very sordid, but what else could he do? They couldn't go to his home because Annette was there. They couldn't go to her place because she still lived with her parents.

Then came the election. Labour won. Newsome to his astonishment became Foreign Secretary. Overnight his life was transformed. Cabinet meetings, state receptions, overseas tours, private secretaries to organise every detail of his life and everywhere he went he was followed by the red despatch boxes.

There was scarcely any time for Annette, never mind Maureen. The affair should have ended there and then. More than once he was on the point of ringing her and ending it, but he could not bring himself to. Newsome was in too deep.

Then came that awful September morning. He had given the private secretaries and the red despatch boxes the slip. "Come back to my place," she had said, "Mum's out all day."

He must have been mad, but he went. It was the first time he had ever been home with her. They were in bed within half an hour. Their love-making was just reaching fever-pitch when Maureen suddenly went rigid. He looked up and found himself looking Mrs Jackson straight in the eye at five paces.

She never said a word. Just stood there staring straight at him. For nigh on a minute the only sound was the ticking of the clock on the dressing table. Then she turned and was gone. They heard the front door slam behind her.

Foreign Secretaries are not supposed to panic, but this one did. His hands were shaking as he pulled on his trousers. "Oh, Christ, Maureen, maybe she's gone for the police."

"Don't be silly, Mum would never do anything like that. It's not as if I'm under age." Young Maureen remained as cool as a cucumber.

Newsome was out of the house within minutes. He glanced to right and left but there was no sign of Mrs Jackson. Then he practically ran all the way to Hampstead Underground station.

For days afterwards he held his breath and waited for the storm to burst. But life went on. Maybe Mrs Jackson hadn't

recognised him? A moment's thought told him this was inconceivable; his photograph had been everywhere since the Arab loan triumph. Yet there was not a whisper in the newspapers. Nothing from DI5 or the Special Branch. His secret seemed safe.

Maureen didn't contact him for two weeks. For all she knew his phones might be bugged (they were, as it turned out). They met in a café at Euston at eight in the morning and after a quick conference decided to carry on. But one problem remained. After a row with her parents Maureen had decided it was time to leave home. The simplest solution would have been for Newsome to rent her a small flat but Maureen rejected the idea, saying that she was not going to be a kept woman. Instead she moved into a girl-friend's flat near Chalk Farm. Maureen failed, however, to tell Newsome that her friend was a member of the Workers' Revolutionary Party.

Sir Peregrine's face lit up when he saw the file. "How about that?" he kept repeating as Fiennes showed him the photographs of the Foreign Secretary walking hand in hand with the lovely Maureen.

"Shot with a 300 mm lens in Kew Gardens," said Fiennes.

"And these?" Sir Peregrine's eyes lingered over a 10″ × 12″ of Newsome planting a kiss on Maureen's right cheek.

"Euston at eight-fifteen in the morning. Our chaps had to get up early for that one," smirked Fiennes.

Sir Peregrine placed the prints on the desk and looked up. Fiennes had never seen the old man looking so happy. "Quite a turn-up for the books, that she should be sharing a flat with a Trot," said Sir Peregrine. "An unexpected bonus."

He thought for a moment. "There are two ways we can play this. We can either throw it to the press and let public opinion do the rest. Foreign Secretary in blackmail situation. Threat to security and all that. Or . . ." He tapped the desk with the flat of his hand. ". . . or we can go to Perkins and demand the resignation of Newsome on security grounds. Then we can leak it to the press anyway."

Sir Peregrine revolved his desk chair towards the window.

"I think we'll take the second option. That way we get the best of both worlds."

He spun back towards Fiennes again. "Does his wife know?"

"Not a dicky bird."

"In that case," said Sir Peregrine, "she's in for an unpleasant surprise."

Not every visitor to the Prime Minister enters Number Ten Downing Street through the front door. Certain very important persons, whose existence is not officially acknowledged, enter by way of the double doors leading from the Cabinet Office. Sir Peregrine Craddock and Sir Philip Norton were two such persons.

Walking one behind the other and led by a private secretary bearing the key, the two men walked in silence. They passed through the Cabinet Office to the sturdy door leading into Downing Street. The private secretary unlocked the door and they passed through, still without speaking. Tweed was waiting on the other side. Behind they heard the key turn in the lock.

"The PM is in the study," said Tweed as he led them up the main staircase. Still they walked in single file, still without speaking. A solemn little procession, in keeping with the distasteful task they had to perform.

Perkins was waiting for them in one of the armchairs just inside the door. "Sit down, gentlemen." He gestured to a settee in the centre of the room. "What can I do for you?"

Sir Philip looked over his shoulder to check that Tweed had withdrawn. Then he told the Prime Minister about Tom Newsome and Maureen Jackson and the flat she shared with a girl from the Workers' Revolutionary Party. Sir Peregrine sat in silence, his face shrouded in a funereal expression.

Perkins listened with his chin resting in his right hand and his elbow on the arm of the chair. As he listened he sank deeper into the armchair. Having outlined the facts Sir Philip went on to review the implications. "First, there is the blackmail potential. His wife doesn't know."

It was late October. St James's Park lay under a thick covering of leaves. The sky was cold and clear. The last rays of sunlight filtered weakly through the bullet-proof glass on the windows. "Second," said Sir Philip, "there is the fact that she shares a flat with a Trotskyite."

When he had finished Perkins thought for a moment in silence. A deep melancholy settled over his normally cheerful countenance. At length he raised his chin from his hand and asked, "So what are you advising?"

"Prime Minister," said Sir Philip gravely, "you have no choice. You have to ask the Foreign Secretary for his resignation."

But Perkins did not share his intelligence chief's perception of the threat to the nation posed by one twenty-two-year-old female Trotskyite living in Chalk Farm. "Is there any evidence that security has been breached?" he asked, looking first at Sir Philip and then at Sir Peregrine.

Sir Philip took a deep breath. "With great respect, Prime Minister, that is not the point."

"Very much the point as far as I'm concerned," said Perkins.

"In any case, Prime Minister," Sir Peregrine Craddock was speaking for the first time, "there is still the blackmail question."

"That can be disposed of quite simply," said Perkins. "All Newsome has to do is tell his wife and the threat of blackmail disappears."

Sir Philip tried to conceal his dismay. "Prime Minister, our advice is very strongly that the Foreign Secretary must be asked to resign."

Perkins stood up. The interview was at an end. "Thank you, gentlemen. I shall bear your advice in mind, but my inclination is to call in Newsome and suggest he tell his wife immediately. As far as the girl is concerned, he can either stop seeing her or she can move to a flat without a resident Trotskyite."

Tweed appeared, as if from nowhere. The two security chiefs turned to leave. Perkins walked to the door with them.

"One other thing, gentlemen." The Prime Minister looked first at Sir Peregrine and then at Sir Philip. "I'm not expecting to read anything about this in the newspapers tomorrow morning."

"Too late," said Sir Peregrine gravely, "the affair is already common knowledge in Fleet Street." In fact no one in Fleet Street knew Tom Newsome's secret, but they soon would. DI5 would see to that.

Perkins saw Newsome that evening in the Prime Minister's room at the House of Commons. Newsome reacted calmly to the news that Maureen had been discovered. For months he had lived in fear of being found out and now the time had come he was almost relieved. He asked for twenty-four hours to consider his position. Perkins agreed. "Think carefully, Tom," he said, "you're one of the most valuable members of my team and I can't afford to lose you."

The *Daily Express* got the story first. When the tip-off came the editor sent one of his best photographers, Bill Ham, to sit outside Maureen Jackson's flat with a telephoto lens trained on the front door.

Ham had had to spend an uncomfortable night before his big break came. He could hardly believe his luck when just after breakfast a green Volkswagen drew up and out stepped the Foreign Secretary. Ham was seated in his own car on the opposite side of the street. He wound down the front window. Before Newsome had reached the doorstep Ham was halfway through his first roll of Tri-X.

Newsome was inside the flat for half an hour. Ham was just about to light a cigarette when the front door opened again and there she was, Maureen Jackson in the arms of the Foreign Secretary. They embraced for a full three minutes before finally parting. If Ham had been closer, he would have noticed that Maureen was crying. And if he had been closer still, he would have noticed that Newsome was also crying.

*

113

After seeing Perkins, Newsome had made up his mind quickly. He would tell Maureen it was all over and then he would drive home and come clean with Annette. The next morning he was out of the house well before eight. He told Annette he was borrowing the car and drove, as fast as the early rush hour traffic would allow, to Chalk Farm. Normally he would have looked around before getting out, but that morning there was too much on his mind. He did not see Bill Ham's Nikon lens pointing directly at him as he locked up the Volkswagen.

The scene with Maureen was heart-breaking. She did not try to talk him into changing his mind. They both knew it had to end. For half an hour they held hands in the living room. An uneaten Ryvita and a cold cup of coffee, Maureen's interrupted breakfast, lay on the table. On the mantelpiece was the gold charm bracelet he had given her on her twenty-first birthday. She had never dared wear it in public in case anybody asked.

He said not to mind about seeing him out, but she followed him downstairs all the same. He was already on the doorstep when she flung herself into his arms. If he had thought for a moment, he would have known it was madness, but then the whole affair had been madness from start to finish.

When at last she let go he kissed her lightly on the forehead and walked away down the garden path. He did not look back, but he knew she was watching because he did not hear the door close.

In the car, driving back to Camberwell, Newsome tried to compose himself. Now he had to face Annette. Truly, he thought as he crossed the river at Waterloo, this must be the worst day of my life. But he was wrong. The worst day of his life was still to come.

The *Express* went to town on the story. Most of the front page was taken up with Bill Ham's exclusive shot of Newsome saying goodbye to Maureen. FAREWELL, MY LOVELY said the headline. The story inside was dominated by a picture of Newsome walking away from the house with Maureen watching forlornly from the doorstep.

To make matters worse she was still in her dressing gown. As well as a close-up of Maureen and a picture of Newsome and Annette taken at an embassy reception a few weeks earlier, there was even a photograph of the girl who shared Maureen's flat. The accompanying story said that "Security chiefs were last night urging the Prime Minister to sack Newsome." It went on to point out that Maureen's flatmate was a member of the Workers' Revolutionary Party. The story had DI5's fingerprints all over it, but no one would ever prove anything.

The first edition of the *Express* arrived at Downing Street within an hour of coming off the presses. Perkins saw it when he returned from the vote at the House. Twenty minutes later the Downing Street switchboard was jammed by calls from other newspapers demanding a statement.

Poor Newsome buried his head in his hands when Perkins showed him the *Express*. "Fancy letting yourself be photographed kissing this lass on the bloody doorstep," said Perkins, but he did not rub it in. Newsome looked as if he were cracking up. He offered to resign there and then, but Perkins refused to discuss the subject. "Go home and see Annette before the rats from the gutter press get to her."

By the late editions the story was leading every front page. The phone started ringing at 10.15 that evening and did not stop until Annette took it off the hook. Newsome arrived home to find a horde of newspapermen camped in the front garden. Annette was in the kitchen with a mug of tea and a cigarette. It was a year since she last smoked. She was wearing the silk dressing gown he had bought her at a recent foreign ministers' meeting in Tokyo. Her eyes were red, but she was not crying.

She made him tea and they sat and talked. He tried to apologise, but in the circumstances it did not seem very adequate. Annette wanted to know about Maureen. When had they first met? How often? Where? She received the information calmly. Sitting on the opposite side of the table, puffing her cigarette and sipping her tea. Never quite looking him in the eyes. Taking care that her feet under the table did not touch his.

115

He told the story quietly, dispassionately. Giving more detail than was strictly necessary. As the words tumbled out, Newsome was conscious for the first time of the extent of his treachery.

They went to bed around two o'clock. Annette said she preferred to sleep in the spare room and Newsome did not argue. Neither of them slept well. Quite apart from everything else, the doorbell kept ringing.

Newsome got up around seven. Peeping through the curtains he could see that the crowd of pressmen had grown. There were television cameras too. He turned on the radio and the story was leading every bulletin.

At seven-thirty he rang John, his eldest boy who was in his second year at Magdalen. He rented a flat in Oxford with two other students and news of the furore had not yet reached him. Newsome advised him to keep a low profile. He offered to come home at once and fend off the press, but Newsome said that would not be necessary. It would all blow over.

The younger boy, James, was working as a waiter in the South of France. Improving his French before going up to Cambridge next year. Newsome searched in vain for a telephone number. Eventually he gave up. The call could wait a couple of hours. It would be a while before the hacks managed to trace him.

At nine Newsome rang the Foreign Office to say he would not be in. The private secretary did not sound surprised.

All day long the chorus of demands for a statement grew louder. By Prime Minister's questions that afternoon, these had turned into calls for Newsome's resignation.

That evening Newsome saw Perkins alone in the study at Number Ten to hand in his resignation letter. This time Perkins did not demur. They both knew resignation was inevitable. The two men shook hands and then Newsome drove for the last time to the Foreign Office. He planned to clear up his papers and then take Annette away somewhere quiet for a few days to give the uproar a chance to die down.

*

When he got back to Camberwell it had gone eleven. The house was in darkness. He turned the key in the front door and switched on the hall light. Annette's coat was hanging on a peg by the door, so she had not gone out. She must be in bed. Not wanting to wake her he trod lightly on the stairs.

The bedroom door was open. In the light from the landing he could see Annette lying on the bed, fully clothed, one leg trailing over the edge.

"Annette," he whispered, but there came no answer.

He listened for the sound of her breathing, but he could hear nothing.

"Annette," he screamed, jamming on the light.

She lay on the bed. Very pale and perfectly still. On the table by the bedside was a glass half full of water and beside her on the bed an empty bottle. The label on the bottle said, "Maximum dosage: three tablets."

10

The weather in November 1989 was bitter. The lake in St James's Park froze and the keepers had to break a hole in the ice for the ducks. Even the Astrakhan pelicans sought refuge from the cold in the shrubbery on an island in the lake and disappeared from public view.

The weathermen forecast a white Christmas and as the evenings drew in the clear sky turned grey. "What we need now," said Sir Peter Kennedy to Sir Richard Hildrew, as they took a lunchtime stroll across the park, "is a nice long miners' strike."

The trade union leaders filed into the Great Parlour at Chequers and took their seats around the polished mahogany table. Before he sat down Bill Knight of the Engineers' Union caressed the oak wall panelling. "This is what I call *class*," he said and as he spoke his hand drifted to the blue and white porcelain on the mantelpiece. Despite impeccable proletarian origins most union leaders quickly adapted to the comforts of high office.

Chequers, the country residence of the Prime Minister, is a huge Tudor mansion in Buckinghamshire donated to the nation by a patriotic magnate who would no doubt have revolved in his grave if he could have seen Harry Perkins sitting at his dining table.

Or maybe he would not. For Chequers with its galleries and terraces and Old Masters had transformed generations of Labour Prime Ministers into country squires. When he first took office Perkins vowed he would have nothing to do with Chequers, but he was there before the year was out.

"Gentlemen," said Perkins, turning the cover page of the Cabinet Office brief on the table before him. The document was entitled "The first five years," and across the top a private secretary had written in longhand "first draft". The trade

union leaders all had copies before them and they turned the cover page in unison with the Prime Minister. "Gentlemen," Perkins repeated, "we are here to reach an understanding between the government and the trade unions on the management of the economy for the remainder of our term of office." As he spoke tea was served by girls in the blue uniforms of the WRNS, seconded to Chequers for such occasions.

Perkins chose his words with care. Every such 'understanding' between a Labour government and the unions had started by embracing prices, pensions, public ownership and a range of other issues dear to the hearts of trade unionists and ended up as a disguised incomes policy. This was a sore point with union leaders and Perkins was keen to reassure them. "Let me be clear," he was saying, "we will deliver our share of the bargain." The government would take control of the pension and insurance funds. Industrial capital would be made available at low rates of interest. There would be quotas on the import of manufactured goods, particularly cars and textiles. He was heard in silence and his pauses were punctuated only by the ticking of the fine grandfather clock in the corner.

Not everyone was listening. Bill Knight of the Engineers' Union was gazing out of the window at the frost-tinted north lawn. Reg Smith, general secretary of the United Power-workers was wondering if the portrait of Oliver Cromwell on the opposite wall would suit the living room of his house in Virginia Water. There are not a lot of power workers living in Virginia Water, but then Smith had come a long way since his days as a stoker in Battersea Power Station.

Perkins stopped and asked for comments. Cups were re-filled and the Wrens wheeled away their trolleys. Knight spoke first. "What about wages. You ain't said nothing about wages."

"That's right," said Smith, "my lads will be asking for fifty per cent." This news was greeted by a low whistle from Jim Forrester, the railwaymen's leader. His lads would be lucky with ten per cent.

Perkins concealed his anger, but his cheeks were flushed. Here were two men who had devoted years to fixing Labour

party conferences into voting down just about every progressive demand on the agenda. Now here they were with their hands out at the first opportunity.

"Wages," said Perkins calmly, "will have to be part of the whole package. If we are going to put money into social services and industrial investment, then we have to go easy on wage claims for the moment."

"My members will accept that," said Bob Sanders of the local government workers. Even as he spoke he was nervous. He had seen four Labour governments in his working life. Each one started by promising the moon and ended up turning on the unions. But he would give it a try. He was now a year off retirement and his lifelong dream seemed to have come true. Britain had a real Socialist government at last. He did not want to see it become bogged down by wage militancy. "Providing," added Sanders, "and only providing that the government keeps faith on its share of the deal."

"My members only earn half as much as yours." Sanders was speaking directly to Reg Smith. "Of course they'd like a fifty per cent increase too but they recognise it's a question of priorities. They attach higher priority to reducing unemployment than to higher wages."

"We're here to represent the employed, not the unemployed," snapped Smith. Then he stopped abruptly because he knew he'd gone too far.

"Speak for yourself," said someone at the end of the table.

After that the meeting went more Perkins' way. It was agreed that there would be no limit on public sector wage claims. Trade union negotiators would however be asked to bear in mind that there were other ways of improving living standards beside higher wages. Not everyone went along with this. Smith declared that his power workers would be going all out for as much as they could get. And he was heard to say that, if Perkins did not watch out, he would have a strike on his hands.

*

Sir Philip Norton was casting an eye over the Cabinet minutes when the phone rang. It was Fiennes of DI5. "You wanted some background on Lady Elizabeth Fain."

"At last," said Sir Philip.

Fiennes read from his notes, "Daughter of the fourth Earl. A former equerry to the King, a thousand acres in Somerset, former colonel in the Coldstream Guards. Retired from the army seven years ago."

"Never mind the father," said Norton impatiently, "what about the girl?"

"Aged twenty-five. Private income of £11,500 a year. A mews house near Sloane Square. All fairly predictable really," said Fiennes wearily.

"And the phone tap?" Sir Philip drummed his fingers on the desk top.

"Nothing much. Her life mainly seems to consist of organising dinner parties or being invited to them."

A blind alley, thought Sir Philip. Still, it had been worth a try. He was just about to thank Fiennes for his trouble when Fiennes said, "One curious thing, sir. She has made a couple of calls to a number in Camden. Chap by the name of Fred Thompson lives there. Seems to be that young leftie who works in the Prime Minister's office. Strange, someone with her background mixing with a chap like Thompson."

"Yes," said Sir Philip, "very strange." Thanking Fiennes for his help he replaced the phone. So that was how Perkins knew about the conversation at Watlington. In future he would be more careful. You couldn't trust anyone these days.

The phone rang. It was Fiennes again. "One other snippet that might interest you, sir."

"Go ahead, Fiennes."

"This Fain girl has just started a job as a research assistant in the Shadow Cabinet office at the House of Commons."

"Has she by jove?" said Sir Philip. "We'll see about that."

Fred Thompson was in his Camden flat preparing to set out for the launderette when the phone rang. It was Elizabeth Fain. She sounded upset. "Fred, I've been fired."

Thompson dropped the bundle of dirty shirts he had been stuffing into a pillowcase and sat on the floor by the telephone. "Why on earth . . . ?"

"They said my work wasn't up to scratch, but I've only been there a week and nobody complained until yesterday." Poor Elizabeth. She was almost in tears. Normally she was so composed. "I asked why they hadn't complained before and they came over very funny. Said they had really been looking for someone who knew about economics but they never said a word about economics when I was interviewed." Her voice trailed off.

Thompson was about to commiserate, but before he could say a word Elizabeth spoke again. "Fred, you don't think it has anything to do with what I told you about my weekend in Oxfordshire with the Nortons?"

"How could it? I told no one except . . ." He had been going to say, "except the Prime Minister," but stopped himself just in time. Yes, of course that was it. He knew exactly what had happened.

"Except who?"

"Elizabeth, let me buy you lunch. I'll be over in twenty minutes." Thompson put down the phone and scooped the pile of fifty pence pieces he had been saving for the launderette into the pocket of his raincoat.

Out on the street he hailed a taxi to Sloane Square. They lunched at a bistro on the King's Road and afterwards drove in Elizabeth's Volkswagen to Hyde Park. Walpole the spaniel came too. That afternoon they held hands for the first time.

"Coming on to snow," said Sir Peter Kennedy as he brushed the flakes from his Aquascutum raincoat. The sky was greyer than ever and the lake in the park remained frozen. An old lady was feeding breadcrumbs to the ducks although the sign said she shouldn't.

"No sign of that miners' strike you were hoping for," said Sir Richard Hildrew, as they hurried across the park towards Whitehall.

"No," said Sir Peter, "but looks like the next best thing.

The power workers are threatening a go-slow after Christmas." By the time they reached the steps leading into Downing Street the snow was falling fast.

11

One reason why the British ruling class have endured so long is that every so often it opens ranks and absorbs a handful of its worst enemies. Reg Smith was a case in point.

He was six feet six in his bare feet. His greying hair was closely crew-cut and this, combined with a broken nose and half closed eyes, gave him a somewhat menacing appearance. Out of earshot, he was known to most of his colleagues as Odd Job. Within earshot he was referred to with deference. Reg Smith had presence.

He started life in a crumbling terrace of back-to-back houses in Chester-le-Street, County Durham. But for the second world war he would have followed his father down the pit, but instead he was conscripted into the army at the tail end of the war. A sergeant by the time he was demobbed, he signed on as a stoker at Battersea Power Station.

Chairman of his union branch within no time, after two years he was sent as a delegate to the national conference of the United Power Workers' Union. At about this time he joined the Labour Party and before long he was attending the annual conference as a union delegate. Those with memories long enough recall the day when Reg Smith was at the sharp end of the class struggle. There was even a time when he would not have taken offence at being described as a Marxist.

But times changed. At the end of the 1950s a ferocious battle was taking place to wrest control of the United Power Workers' Union from Communists. Smith saw the way the wind was blowing and weighed in on the side of the moderates. Not long after, a vacancy as a district organiser was advertised in the union journal. Smith applied, got the job and never looked back.

He first came into contact with the Americans at a conference organised by the Ditchley Foundation in the summer of 1981. The Ditchley Foundation is not exactly secret, but nor is

124

it exactly public either. Its purpose, according to the prospectus, is "to provide opportunities for people concerned with the formation of opinion from the United States and Britain . . . to meet in quiet surroundings."

The 'people concerned with the formation of opinion' tend to be mainly bankers, businessmen, politicians and diplomats. Occasionally a right-wing trade unionist is invited to discuss how to keep his members under control. That was where Reg Smith came in.

The 'quiet surroundings' are a magnificent eighteenth-century mansion secluded among oak and beech trees in the rolling countryside of Oxfordshire.

After his first Ditchley conference Smith found that he was plugged into an international network of very powerful people. Like all powerful people they were obsessed with the notion that someone somewhere was plotting to take away the power and status they had amassed.

The American embassy arranged for Smith and his wife to go on an expenses paid tour of the United States to learn about American labour relations. In Washington they even arranged for him to spend five minutes with the President and a photograph of the event occupied pride of place on the mantelpiece of his Virginia Water house.

The powers-that-be knew that one day Reg Smith would come in handy. And with the election of Harry Perkins, Smith's hour had come.

Negotiations between the Electricity Council and the United Power Workers' Union broke down in mid-January. The employers, prompted by the government, wanted to take the dispute to arbitration, but Smith would have none of it. Instead he summoned a special meeting of his executive for the following Wednesday. Item one on the agenda would be a proposal for a work to rule to start forthwith. No one doubted it would be carried. The snow began to settle for the first time that winter.

*

The executive of the United Power Workers' Union met in the seventeenth floor boardroom of the union's smart new premises on the Euston Road. The offices had been an investment by the power workers' pension fund and built on an old British Rail goods yard. The union occupied the top five floors with the other twelve rented out at considerable profit. When they first became public the plans for the lavish new offices had provoked criticism from some members. Several letters were sent to the union journal pointing out that the power workers were supposed to be against property speculation. The letters were not published. Smith saw to that. "Nothing's too good for the working class," he told the critics.

To the south the boardroom overlooked Bloomsbury and beyond that the Thames. The river meandered in a grey ribbon from Tower Hamlets to Wandsworth. St Paul's Cathedral, Nelson's Column and the tower of the House of Lords stood out clearly, and in the far distance, the television mast at Crystal Palace and beyond that the beginnings of the Kent countryside. On a clear day you could even tell the time by Big Ben. Reg Smith enjoyed nothing better than showing visitors the view from his boardroom, particularly after dark when the whole panorama was a mass of twinkling lights. "One word from me," he was fond of telling his guests, "and that lot would be in darkness."

Smith took his seat at one end of the solid oak table in the centre of the room. He brought the meeting to order by slapping the polished surface with the flat of his hand. There was immediate silence. "Brothers," said Smith in an accent that owed more to Virginia Water than the Durham mining town of his birth, "it's very simple. We're asking for fifty per cent and an extra week's holiday. The Board are offering us ten per cent and no extra holiday."

He cast an eye around the table in search of dissenters. There being none he continued, "We have made our position clear from the start. If there is no more money on the table, then we will be forced to take industrial action."

Again Smith scanned the faces. Despite the indignant tone

in which he addressed them, his remarks provoked no nods of agreement. Left to themselves most members of the executive would have settled at ten per cent. They were moderates almost to a man. Indeed most of them owed their seats to the fact that they had featured on a slate of moderate candidates published in certain popular newspapers at the time of the election. Now they were being asked to agree to industrial action in support of a wage demand that most of them privately considered was outrageous. It was a strange old world.

"This afternoon your president," Smith indicated a balding hollow-cheeked man immediately on his left, "and myself went to see the minister at the Department of Employment. All he could offer us was arbitration. We . . ." Smith looked again at the president, ". . . we told the minister that arbitration was completely unacceptable and that in view of the government's intransigence we would be forced to take industrial action. To which the minister asked us to spare a thought for the economic situation of the country and the efforts the government was making in other areas. I . . ." Smith paused, ". . . we told him that this had no bearing whatever on the merits of our case."

Not everyone could bring themselves to look at the general secretary while he addressed them. When it came to the vote he could count on most of them but their hearts were not in it. Smith came to the point. "I therefore propose that we instruct our members to commence working-to-rule as from midnight tonight." He paused to draw breath. "Any comments?"

Midway down the table a large, debauched looking man raised the forefinger of his right hand. His shirt collar was concealed beneath an overhang of chin.

"Brother Walker."

Tommy Walker represented the north-east division. His support was a certainty. "I agree with the general secretary." He paused to muster synthetic indignation. "I think it is a scandal the way we've been treated. All these years we've been sliding down the pay league and now the time has come to put the power workers back where they belong. At the

top." He underlined the last phrase by bringing his hand down with a slap on the surface of the table.

"Thank you, Tommy," said Smith. A man at the end of the table was indicating he wished to speak, but Smith ignored him and scanned the other executive members. No one else indicated and so he returned to the man at the end of the table. "Brother Clwyd."

Barry Clwyd was a younger man than the rest, in his mid-thirties. He represented South Wales. There was no love lost between him and Reg Smith. Smith had been through the rule book in search of reasons to declare Clwyd's election invalid. "What I don't understand," said Clwyd, "is why we can't go to arbitration. Why is the general secretary so keen on industrial action all of a sudden?"

"You're the one that's supposed to be a revolutionary," sneered Smith.

"If you'd let me finish, Brother Smith," Clwyd's lilting Welsh voice contrasted with the harsh tones of the general secretary. "Everyone here knows that if there were a ballot tomorrow our members would vote overwhelmingly against this work-to-rule."

"You're out of order." It was Smith again. "Under the rules a ballot is only required before strike action. A work-to-rule is the responsibility of the executive."

This time Clwyd did not attempt to respond. He knew from experience that it was useless to argue. Few executive members could be swayed by argument. The rest took their cue from the general secretary. Three other members contributed to the discussion. Two for, one against. Then Smith took the vote. There were only three dissenters. "Right then, brothers, that's it." Smith stood up. "We take action from midnight."

Picking up his file he walked to the window. Far below, the lights were coming on all over London. The Euston Road was gummed with traffic. A train sounded its two-tone horn as it pulled into St Pancras. "Pity Downing Street has its own generator," said Smith quietly, "otherwise I'd pull the plug myself."

*

After the executive meeting broke up Smith spent an hour dictating a memorandum on the conduct of the work-to-rule for circulation to all district officers of the union. He also issued a terse statement to the Press Association blaming the dispute on the intransigence of the government which, he said, was refusing to allow the Electricity Board to negotiate freely.

He was then driven to Victoria Station. The pavements were thick with snow pounded to slush by the footfalls of rush-hour crowds. Along the Strand an automatic salt-spreader was stuck in a traffic jam. The last of the day's commuters, bent double against a cruel wind, trickled into Charing Cross. Newspaper vendors sought refuge from the cold in shop doorways. At Victoria, Smith dismissed the chauffeur, waited until the car was out of sight then walked briskly away from the station and into Buckingham Palace Road. He crossed the road and continued in the direction of St James's Park, perusing the shop fronts as he went. After about two hundred yards he came to a halt outside a restaurant called Bumbles. Reaching in the pocket of his overcoat he drew out a piece of paper and checked the name against a scribbled address. Then, looking to the right and left, he pushed open the door and entered.

The American, who was already seated at a table towards the rear of the restaurant with an evening newspaper spread before him looked up when Smith entered. He was wearing a white raincoat, open at the front, the one he had worn when he had last met Fiennes of DI5 in the coffee shop of the Churchill Hotel.

"Jim." Smith bore down upon the American, his right hand extended.

"Reg." The American was on his feet now. A waiter took Smith's overcoat and scarf. His heavy briefcase he placed on the floor by the table. "I see you boys are in the headlines." The American indicated the front page of the paper he had been perusing. The headline story was about the impending power dispute. Smith turned the paper towards him and glanced at the story which included a rather unflattering

129

picture of himself taken at a press conference two weeks earlier.

The waiter fussed around them. Did they want apéritifs? The American already had a Scotch and Smith ordered the same. He specified Chivas Regal; nothing was too good for the working classes.

"To victory," said the American raising his glass.

"Victory," said Smith, his heavy jowls emitting a modest smile. Victory over whom or what, they did not say.

The American was Jim Chambers, first secretary, political section, at the embassy. The British Labour movement was his brief. He had a caseload of middle-rank Labour MPs and trade union leaders. His job was to pinpoint rising stars and get in close. It was all above board, so far at least. In the three years he had served in Britain, Chambers had become a familiar face in the bars at Labour party conferences and TUC congresses. Every snippet of information or gossip he had carefully noted and filed away. As a result he had identified the drift to the left in the Labour Party long before it had become apparent to his masters in Washington. At least three members of the new régime were regular guests at the dinner parties Chambers held at his home in Connaught Square. He had entered into the spirit of his job. Many was the drunken evening he had spent with his arm around a Labour politician singing the Red Flag or a chorus of Avanti Popolo.

Chambers was an old hand. His earlier assignments had included spells in El Salvador and Portugal. President Ford had claimed that saving Portugal from Communism was one of the achievements of his presidency. Jim Chambers had played his part.

Now Chambers was in London. He had thought he was in for a quiet life. At least there won't be a revolution in England, they had joked with him in the State Department, when he was posted. Little did they know. But Chambers was ready. He had been one of the few to tip a victory for Perkins. Now he was one of the few to predict that Perkins would not last the course.

Chambers had assembled his British caseload with pre-

cision. It offered him contacts in every significant faction of the Labour movement. He even had a contact on the central committee of the British Communist Party. It was he who had set up Reg Smith's visit to the United States three years earlier. He had persuaded Smith to attend the conferences at Ditchley. The beauty of it was that no money had changed hands and no one had done anything they would have to lie about. His only outlay had been the occasional bottle of Scotch, the odd expenses-paid tour of the States and a little harmless entertaining.

They started with oysters washed down with white wine. Duck in orange sauce followed. "What exactly is a 'work-to-rule'?" asked Chambers. "We don't have them on my side of the Atlantic."

"A work-to-rule," said Smith in between mouthfuls of duck and spinach, "means that my members will do exactly what is in their contracts and no more. There will be no overtime worked, all productivity agreements will be cancelled and, if someone is off sick, no one else will do his job."

"How long before it bites?"

Smith wiped a trickle of orange sauce from his jaw with a napkin. "The lights will start to go out within two or three days. By the end of the first week there will be lay-offs in the factories. Within a fortnight the government will have disaster on its hands."

Chambers had finished eating and pushed his plate to the middle of the table. "How long will it last?"

"Until we win."

"Is your executive behind you?" Chambers sat with his forearms resting on the table.

"More or less." Smith served himself another helping of spinach from a tureen in the middle of the table. "A couple of them cut up rough. Wanted to know why I was pushing a strike now when I advised against when the Tories were in."

"What did you say?"

"I gave them the usual." The waiter removed Chambers' finished plate and the vegetable dish. "Five years of restraint

131

under the Tories. Power workers now are well down the wages' league. Time we caught up."

This was not by any means the whole story. The truth was that Reg Smith hated Harry Perkins. For years he and other right-wing trade union leaders had worked to keep the Labour Party in the hands of the moderates. Labour leaders had looked to Smith to deliver a majority of the trade union block vote on crucial issues at the party conference. And for years Smith and his friends had delivered.

The reward for loyal service had been an unending flow of quangos and honours doled out by a grateful Labour Party establishment. For tame trade union leaders there were seats on the boards of nationalised industries and places on the vast array of public authorities, committees, commissions and enquiries that were in the gift of a reigning Prime Minister. The ultimate accolade, and one upon which Smith had set his sights, was retirement to the House of Lords.

The election of Perkins had put an end to all that. Under Perkins the Labour Party was pledged to abolish the honours system and whatever public appointments were going, Smith could not expect to benefit.

Reg Smith was a bitter man and the focus of his bitterness was Harry Perkins. He wanted to see Perkins humiliated, and closing down the power stations seemed the best way of going about it.

"The advantage of a work-to-rule," he said as the coffee arrived, "is that we don't have to cough up any strike pay because our members will still be drawing their wages. If we had an all-out strike, our funds would dry up in two weeks. With a work-to-rule we can hold out indefinitely and inflict maximum damage."

12

Reg Smith proved spot-on in his estimate that the work-to-rule would start to bite within three days. The coal-fired power stations were the first to go out of service. They consumed up to twenty thousand tons of coal a day and required constant maintenance. Each boiler and generator was serviced by a team consisting of a leader, an assistant and several attendants. Under the terms of the work-to-rule, if one man did not turn up, the rest of the team stopped work and gradually the huge boilers became clogged with clinker.

The Littlebrook station on the south side of the Thames estuary was the first to be hit. By noon on the third day the manager reported that his number five boiler had accumulated a thousand tonnes of slag. He would have to close it down. Once the boiler cooled and the slag solidified it would take a team of men with pneumatic drills ten days to clear. Every boiler that closed down meant a 500 megawatt generator out of service and the supply of electricity to the national grid reduced accordingly. Within twenty-four hours of the Littlebrook shutdown, coal-fired stations at Pembroke, Didcot, West Burton and Battersea had each closed down a boiler. By the end of the first week the national grid had lost twenty per cent of its capacity. All that week the temperature hardly rose above freezing. It was the coldest January on record. Demand for electricity had never been higher. Smith could hardly have picked a better time.

As the boilers were closed down, the blackouts began. At the Grid Switching Centre in Streatham sweat was glistening on the brow of control engineer Wally Bates as he snapped out orders to men in white overalls who sat in a circle around the edge of the room before a bank of dials and switches. "Give it back to Lambeth, take out Putney and Southwark." As he spoke he scribbled calculations on a notepad.

133

One of the four telephones rang. He reached for it without looking up. "Yup," he barked. It was the West London Hospital. They were in the middle of a major operation and having trouble with the emergency generator. Could he spare them for another hour? He promised to do his best and before he replaced the receiver another phone was ringing. It was the Control Centre at East Grinstead. Could he save another fifty megawatts? They were running low. He groaned. Why didn't they ask St Albans? He already had two boroughs in darkness.

He slammed down the phone, tapped a series of numbers into his calculator and entered the answer on a sheet attached to a clipboard in front of him. Then he shouted, "Tell Horseferry Road to stand by for shutdown in one hour." He permitted himself the merest trace of a grin. The Horseferry Road sub-station took in the House of Commons and most government ministries.

The phone rang. It was East Grinstead again. No, St Albans were already taking more than their share. He would have to take out another London borough. More tapping on the calculator. More scribbling on his clipboard. "Tell Wandsworth to stand by in one hour," he barked. Then, drawing a handkerchief from his trouser pocket, he wiped his forehead. "Jesus," he said to himself, "this is only the first week."

The Cabinet went into emergency session the morning after the work-to-rule began. Everyone was agreed that the demands of the power workers could not be met. "We'll have every bleeding union in the country at our throats if we give in to this one," growled Jock Steeples.

The Energy Secretary, Albert Sampson, reported on the likely effects if the dispute dragged on. Sampson was a Yorkshire miner. He owed his place in the Cabinet more to a feeling that the miners ought to be represented than to his ability. Even before the dispute there were those who had questioned whether Sampson was up to the job. "According to my Department," Sampson read ponderously from the

134

brief in front of him, "normal demand at this season of the year is around 50,000 megawatts. So far we have lost about 9,000 megawatts generating capacity. Some of that can be absorbed by surplus capacity but next week we can expect to lose double that."

As Sampson droned on Perkins' attention wandered. He had always regarded Reg Smith as a malicious bastard, but this took the biscuit. In ten years of Tory government Smith had never even threatened industrial action, yet within weeks of a Labour victory he was suddenly posing as a super-militant. Sampson was now listing the emergency measures recommended by his department to conserve electricity. A five-inch limit on bathwater, powers to limit illuminated advertising, shop-window lighting and floodlights at football matches. And if the dispute went into a third week, they would have to put industry on a three-day week.

Outside, the sky was grey. A chill wind whipped up snow-flakes which whirled against the windows of the Cabinet Room. Wainwright was calling for a state of emergency. If necessary troops would have to be used to run the power stations.

"Hang on a minute," said Perkins, "if you think I'm flying up to Balmoral to get the King's signature on a bit of paper allowing a Labour government to use troops against the power workers, you can think again. We'd be a bloody laughing stock if we fell for that one." There was a general murmur of agreement around the table and Wainwright, seeing that he was outnumbered, did not press the point.

It was agreed that Perkins should ask the TUC General Secretary to try and bring the power workers' union to the negotiating table. The army would be asked to make available generators for hospitals. The Cabinet Office would be asked to draft emergency legislation giving the government tem-porary powers to restrict the use of electricity for con-sideration by the next Cabinet meeting. In the meantime the Civil Contingencies Committee would be asked to advise on further measures.

*

Jonathan Alford was the first to arrive at Sir George Fison's home in Cheyne Walk. A Philippine maid in a black dress answered the door. Alford hovered in the hallway while the maid disappeared with his coat and scarf. "Sir's in the drawing room," she said on her return. Alford followed her up the stairs to the first floor. The wall was lined with prints of eighteenth-century London. There was one of Park Lane in the days when it was a lane and the only traffic were carriages bearing ladies with parasols. Another showed Westminster Abbey viewed from a field in Millbank at about the spot which is now the headquarters of Imperial Chemical Industries.

The maid pushed open the ornate double doors that led from the first-floor landing and then stood aside to let Alford pass. The drawing room, which extended from front to back of the house, was illuminated by table lamps, one on the marble mantelpiece and two on low coffee tables in the left-hand corner. Fison, brandy glass in hand, was standing alone by the front window, apparently gazing at the traffic on the Embankment. He turned as Alford entered and lumbered towards him, hand outstretched.

"You'd be the chap from the BBC," said Fison in his poor imitation of an upper-class accent. Alford nodded. The maid lingered. "Get Mr Alford a drink," snapped Fison in the harsher tone he reserved for addressing servants.

"A whisky and ginger, please," said Alford relinquishing Fison's weak handshake.

"Glad you could come. Peregrine Craddock told me you could be relied upon. Just as well. Reliable chaps are thin on the ground at the Beeb, these days." Alford's chest swelled. He was flattered to think that he should be known to the chief of DI5. The little Philippine maid presented his whisky and withdrew in silence. As they drifted towards the window, Fison rumbled on about left-wing extremists who seemed to be running the BBC these days. Alford contributed only the occasional nod.

Downstairs the doorbell rang again. Fison was still denouncing extremists in the BBC when the maid reappeared to announce the editor of *The Times*. In the ten minutes that

followed Alford found himself being introduced to the owners or editors of just about every newspaper in Fleet Street. There was also the chairman of the Independent Broadcasting Authority and the editor of Independent Television News. My goodness, thought Alford, this is for real.

Like his father before him Alford's view of the world was fashioned by Winchester, Oxford and in the Guards. It was at Oxford that he had first become aware of the extremist menace. He saw how Communists and Trotskyites wormed their way into the Oxford Union. How they used the union debating society as a platform for promoting their extremist views and how easily ordinary students were misled by smooth-talking agitators. It was at Oxford that he first resolved to do whatever he could to resist the rising tide of extremism. Alford's opportunity came when his tutor offered to put him in touch with "someone in the right line of business".

The result was an interview with a man from London who gave his name as Mr Spencer and who left a telephone number where he could be contacted at any time. The number connected with the switchboard at the Department of Trade, but led in fact to an office in the West End. Alford used to ring the number about once a month with snippets on who was organising meetings on Ireland and demonstrations against the military régime in Chile. He also reported on Iranian students organising opposition to the Shah.

Alford had never lost touch with the secret world. Soon after obtaining his commission in the Guards he was seconded to Military Intelligence. He did a spell in Ireland, mainly desk work evaluating reports from agents in the field. The Ireland tour ended abruptly when two of his agents were assassinated by the IRA.

There followed a year in Hereford teaching political theory to SAS recruits until one May morning in the early Eighties he was summoned to Curzon Street and asked how he felt about leaving the army for a career in Civvy Street. "As what?" he had asked. "Television," they said. "Job coming up at the Beeb. Nothing very taxing. Just want you to keep the air-

137

waves clean for us." There followed a crash course in journalism at a polytechnic in Harlow and six months in the Ministry of Defence Information Department until the BBC advertised for a Defence Correspondent. Alford was told to apply and was boarded for an interview. "A formality," said Curzon Street. Sure enough, Alford was appointed. Now, still only in his late thirties, he was Editor News and Current Affairs, and responsible for every syllable the BBC addressed to its subjects on the state of the nation and much else besides.

"Gentlemen, if I could have your attention?" Fison was tapping a wine glass with the blunt side of his fish knife. They were seated around a polished oblong table which fitted together in three sections. Including Fison, there were a dozen of them. The maid had withdrawn, leaving them alone with the port and the cheeseboard. "You all know why I invited you here," said Fison. "We've got to decide what we're going to do about this damn government."

The cheeseboard reached Fison and he lopped off a generous portion of Stilton. "In the coming months," he continued, "things are going to get pretty rough. Perkins has already made it clear that he intends to evict the American bases, and that will destroy the Atlantic alliance and play straight into the hands of the Russians."

There was a "Hear, hear," from Lord Lipton swathed in cigar smoke halfway down the table. The Lipton Corporation's holding included over one hundred provincial newspapers, a merchant bank, a chain of wine merchants and four oil tankers.

"Withdrawal from the Common Market," Fison went on, "will be the end of Britain as a trading nation." He paused for a sip of port. "There is even talk of a plan to dispossess the owners of our national newspapers which would be the end of the free press we all cherish." Fison was playing on home ground here. There was a sustained outbreak of "Hear, hears".

He cut himself a sliver of Stilton and munched as he spoke, "What we are engaged upon is a battle for survival. No holds barred. We have to recognise that in the task that lies ahead of

138

us old-fashioned concepts like free speech and democracy might have to be suspended." The editor of *The Times* shuffled his feet. What Fison was saying might be a necessary expedient, but did it have to be stated quite so boldly? Fison's voice rose as he reached his climax. "This government has to be brought down. Those of us who control public opinion have a special part to play in bringing the nation back to its senses."

Amid the cheese, the cigars and the port there followed a discussion of what was to be done. Lord Lipton took the hardest line. He said the armed forces must resist withdrawal from NATO but did not specify what form the resistance should take. The editor of *The Times* advised caution. He was sure that once Perkins had taken stock of what he called "the hard realities", he would do a U-turn. Everyone agreed that Newsome's downfall had been an unexpected bonus and Fison was indiscreet enough to hint that DI5 might have had a hand in the affair. It was at this point that Alford came in. "What we have to do," said Alford, "is to drive a wedge between the government and its support in the country. In that sense this dispute with the power workers is a god-send. We have to back the power workers and lay the blame for this dispute squarely on the government."

This was too much for Lord Lipton. "Since when have we ever backed strikers?" he interrupted.

"Poland," interjected someone at the end of the table.

"Quite different," snapped Lipton.

"On the contrary," said Alford. "The analogy with Poland is very helpful to us. We backed the Polish strikers because they were striking against a Communist government. It didn't matter that some of their demands were ridiculous. The point was they were attacking Communism." He stressed this point with a wave of his finger. "Since Perkins and his government are Communists for all practical purposes, it follows that we should be backing the power workers and anyone else who cares to strike against the government."

It was generally agreed that Alford had a point. Stories about old ladies dying of hypothermia and denunciations of

the strikers for greed and heartlessness would have to be played down. Instead every effort would be made to present the power workers' case as a good one. Emphasis would be placed on the importance of the service they provided and how undervalued their services were. If the power workers extracted a decent settlement, that might spark off a rash of extravagant wage claims which would bring the government into conflict with its trade union base. It was quite the opposite of the line newspapers normally took on wage claims but then, as Fison drily remarked, "A little inflation is a small price to pay for bringing down a government of extremists."

It was after midnight when the party broke up. This was only a beginning, Fison said as they departed. The removal of Perkins and his government was in the national interest. Since between them, they controlled access to just about all the information in the country, they would play a vital rôle. In view of what was at stake they could not afford to be too scrupulous. It was, he said, the end that mattered, not the means.

As January turned into February the snow had turned to sleet. The demand for electricity remained constant, but the supply declined. One by one the great power station boilers clogged with clinker and generators went out of service. By now every major city was without electricity for at least two hours a day. Where possible the Electricity Board tried to give notice by publishing a roster of areas to be hit, but with the amount of electricity in the national grid declining hourly notice was not always possible.

The House of Commons debated the crisis in a Chamber lit by paraffin lamps. The opposition wanted to know why Perkins hadn't declared a state of emergency? Why weren't troops being used to run the power stations? Did he have any figures for the number of old people who had died of cold? How much production was being lost? What steps was he taking to settle the dispute? Perkins was less than impressive. He fumbled his lines. He contradicted himself. On the possibility of a settlement he was evasive.

In truth there was absolutely no sign of a settlement. Reg Smith wasn't budging at all. He had refused arbitration and rejected the good offices of the TUC General Secretary. He had not even scheduled a meeting of his union's executive to discuss terms for negotiation.

The newspapers carried stories of residents in high-rise flats marooned by the failure of power to the lifts. In Coventry a thirteen-year-old girl was killed in an accident at traffic lights which were not working during a power-cut. In Glasgow a man on a kidney machine had to be rushed to hospital when the power failed without warning. The Volkswagen plant at Solihull was working mornings only.

By the end of the second week public opinion was turning ugly. Bricks were being thrown through electricity board showroom windows. A farmer who had lost one thousand baby chickens when his incubators were cut off, drove into Whitehall and dumped the corpses at the end of Downing Street. Perkins had to abandon his daily practice of arriving at Downing Street by bus after a passenger tried to assault him and was only prevented by the speedy intervention of Inspector Page.

The Civil Contingencies Committee, CYI as it was known in Whitehall jargon, met in the Cabinet office every morning at ten o'clock. The Secretaries of State for the Home Office, Energy and Defence were present, together with their permanent secretaries and the army Chief of Staff, General Sir Charles Payne. Even Perkins created a precedent by attending.

From day one the permanent secretaries and Sir Charles were pressing for a state of emergency. The permanent secretary at the Home Office, Sir Oliver Creighton, appeared one morning waving a draft Order in Council which he proceeded to try and sell to the committee like a salesman promoting some cure-all wonder drug. "Valid for seven days without the approval of Parliament," enthused Sir Oliver. "His Majesty's signature is all that's necessary."

"Then what?" asked Perkins, his voice betraying a hint of sarcasm.

"Then you simply order the power men to work normally," said Sir Oliver cheerfully.

"And if they refuse?"

"Arrest them." It was Sir Charles' first contribution to the discussion. A small, dapper man with square shoulders and a trim moustache, he had been in the army thirty years and only ever seen action in Northern Ireland. In the absence of a Russian invasion this was his last chance before retirement.

"All twenty-two thousand of them?" said Perkins, raising an eyebrow.

"If necessary, sir," said Sir Charles, who did not appear to realise he was not being taken seriously. "We have the capacity. A string of camps up and down the country for just such an emergency. All in working order. Even some vacancies in the Salisbury Plain camps since the Trots were released."

Sir Oliver Creighton's face had assumed a pained expression, as though a secret had been let out of the bag. "I think Sir Charles is referring to our civil defence preparations which, if you'll forgive my saying so, are not relevant here," he said soothingly. Sir Charles was just about to protest that, on the contrary, he was referring to the plans for dealing with strikers drawn up by the previous government but never implemented, when he was silenced by an icy stare from Sir Oliver. The Prime Minister said nothing, but made a mental note to enquire further when the crisis was over.

"I don't understand," said Perkins to Fred Thompson over a late-night whisky in the Prime Minister's study. Spread out on the desk before them were the first editions of tomorrow's newspapers. "ACTION NOW" demanded the *Sun* in a front-page headline two inches high. The editorial below began, "How many more old-age pensioners have to die of cold before Prime Minister Perkins climbs down off his high horse and starts talking to the power men?"

Perkins read the sentence aloud and then tossed the paper back on to the desk. "I don't understand," he repeated miserably. "Last time the power workers came out the *Sun* was

142

practically demanding they be boiled in oil and Reg Smith was described as public enemy number one. This time they treat him like a bloody hero." He turned to the centre pages of the *Daily Mail* which carried a sympathetic profile of Smith. It was headed "The Reluctant Militant" and showed a picture of the United Power Workers' general secretary with his family. "No one regrets this more than I," Smith was quoted as saying, "but the government just won't listen to reason." Perkins read it aloud.

"Hypocrite," said Thompson who was leafing through *The Times*. "The power men have a case" was the heading over the main leading article. For a full minute there was silence, broken only by the rustling of newspapers. It was nearly midnight and the silence pervaded the whole building. The private office was in darkness. The lady on the switchboard was halfway through a crossword. The policeman on duty in the entrance lobby was lightly dozing.

At length Perkins spoke again, "It can't go on like this, Fred. Sooner or later something's got to give." He was leaning back in his chair his head resting on the high back, the whisky glass cradled in his right hand. Thompson was perched on the edge of the desk. "The civil service are pushing for the use of troops. I'm coming under pressure in Cabinet. Even Jim Evans seems to be weakening. A week ago, I'd never have believed it, but now . . ." his voice trailed off. A police car raced up the Mall, its sirens wailing.

"For Christ's sake, Harry," said Thompson harshly, "if you send troops into the power stations, we'll find ourselves at war with the whole movement. The miners will black the coal. The supervisors will come out in sympathy, and we'll turn Reg Smith into a national hero."

Perkins did not reply. He knew that Thompson was right. He put the half empty glass on the desk and ran his hands over his aching eyes. He was dog tired. Since the dispute began he had averaged less than five hours' sleep a night. He no longer went home to Kennington, but slept in the flat in Downing Street. Another victory for Tweed and the private office. Since the day Perkins arrived in Downing Street Tweed had

143

been taking bets on how long it would be before Perkins stopped catching buses and living at home and started behaving like a Prime Minister. It had taken just nine months.

Thompson took a last swig of whisky and said he must be off. He left behind a pile of letters to be signed. There was no need for the Prime Minister to sign any letters but Perkins had always insisted on the personal touch. As with riding buses and living in Kennington, he was finding it harder than ever to deal with letters personally. Tweed and the private office had been against the idea from the start. Prime Ministers have more important things to do, they argued. Perkins, however, was determined not to allow Tweed to chalk up another small victory. With a sigh he took the bundle of letters, each with an addressed envelope embossed with the Downing Street seal, and signed the top one in blue felt pen. It was to a Labour Party member in Glasgow who was advising him to stand firm against the power workers. The writer had said a number of uncomplimentary things about Reg Smith, even going so far as to suggest he was in the pay of the CIA. Thompson had drafted a tactful reply. Since the man had addressed Perkins as "Dear Harry" (so many Party members seemed to consider themselves on first name terms with the Prime Minister) Perkins signed himself "Harry" in clear blue letters. That would make someone's day in Glasgow.

In the distance Big Ben struck midnight. No other sound reached the Prime Minister in his study. Downstairs in the hall the policeman was still dozing, disturbed only by the occasional patter of an unattended telex machine somewhere on the ground floor. The telephonist had abandoned her crossword and was also dozing. Only one dim light lit the main staircase. The brighter light from inside the study showed clearly the crack between the door and the carpet.

After twenty minutes Perkins put down his pen; pushed away the bundle of letters with both arms outstretched and sunk back in the deep, comfortable chair. On the desk, by a tea mug full of old pens was a small framed portrait of an elderly woman, her face lit by a wide smile not unlike that for which Perkins was famous. She had the same full cheeks, the

same wrinkles around the eyes. It had been ten years now since Perkins' mother had died. How chuffed she would have been to see her Harry in Downing Street. She wouldn't have stood any nonsense from those stuffed shirts on the Civil Contingencies Committee. She would have told them what they could do with their state of emergency.

He put the cap on his pen and returned it to an inside pocket. As he did so his eye caught the front of the *Daily Mirror*. It was dominated by a picture of Number Ten, taken at night with all lights blazing. The caption beneath explained that, unlike most houses, the Prime Minister's residence had a generator of its own and he was not inconvenienced by the electricity cuts. The headline above read, "ALL RIGHT FOR SOME PEOPLE."

As the work-to-rule entered its third week the snow stopped, the slush melted into puddles reflecting a clear blue sky. By now the electricity in the grid was down to half the normal supply. At the Streatham Switching Centre Wally Bates was on the edge of a nervous breakdown. Most factories were working only twenty hours a week. A huge balance of payments deficit was forecast for the end of the month. Television was reduced to a single channel, but that had not stopped the BBC from carrying a sympathetic profile of Reg Smith and a documentary setting out the power workers' case in terms which were broadly favourable. There were some isolated acts of public vengeance. Some power workers in Yorkshire had had the tyres of their cars slashed. A doctor in Manchester refused to treat power workers. By and large, however, the media was remarkably successful in laying responsibility for the dispute at the door of the government. Perkins' opinion poll rating dropped to an all-time low.

But Reg Smith knew he had to settle. As the days passed it became clear that many power workers did not have their hearts in the dispute. Many were saying openly that the claim was too high. The head office on the Euston Road received an increasing number of letters from members urging a settlement. Surprisingly, or so it seemed to many people, the

145

newspapers did not highlight the opinions of the men in the power stations. An opinion poll commissioned by Sir George Fison's main daily newspaper had found that over eighty per cent of power station workers were prepared to settle. It was quietly suppressed on direct orders from the proprietor.

Smith knew he couldn't carry the normally docile members of the executive indefinitely. There had been rumblings at the last meeting. Even Tommy Walker, the ultra-loyalist from the North-East, had said he couldn't keep his members under control much longer. So, the day before the regular executive meeting Smith picked up the phone in his sixteenth-floor office and ordered his secretary to dial Congress House. "Reg here," he said gruffly when the TUC General Secretary came on the line. "We're ready to talk."

The talks took place by candlelight at the Department of Employment in St James's Square. The government had authorised the Electricity Council to go all out for a settlement. Smith took them to the limit, double the original offer. The newspapers hailed the result as a triumph for Smith and humiliation for the government. An opinion poll published on the morning of the settlement showed that an instant general election would result in a Tory victory. Reg Smith was not a Tory, but he could not suppress a secret smile.

13

Half a dozen senior ministers and their permanent secretaries attended the defence conference at Chequers. The Chiefs of Staff were also present together with sundry colonels, group captains and lieutenant commanders. All weekend military men in civilian clothes were to be seen bustling up and down the stairs between the Hawtrey Room and the Great Parlour, bearing huge rolled-up maps depicting the Soviet threat. Outside on the gravel forecourt gleaming black Mercedes were drawn up in a neat semi-circle. Government chauffeurs in green uniform and matching caps stood gossiping and smoking in clusters. Others reclined in the back seats of their cars with noses buried in the sports pages.

The forecourt was screened by a high brick wall and beyond the drive led away through an avenue of young beech trees to a pair of lodge houses which marked the main entrance. Here the press were assembled. Photographers festooned with cameras and long lenses stood, hands in pockets, windcheaters zipped to the chin, stamping their feet in frustration. There were to be no photo calls, no press conferences. All they could do was attempt to snap the participants as their cars slowed down to check with the policemen on the gate. Television crews with the latest lightweight cameras kept on the alert. Interest was not confined to the British press. Correspondents filled in the time by recording face-to-camera pieces describing the conference with phrases like "vital to the future of the Western alliance" and "a turning point in Anglo-American relations".

Security was tight. The policemen carefully scrutinised the passes attached to the windscreen of every car that went in. Away across the green parkland policemen with dogs could be seen patrolling the fields that divide the public footpath from the grounds of the Prime Minister's country residence.

Inside the atmosphere was tense. The Chiefs of Staff made

little secret of the fact that they regarded Perkins and his government as a greater threat than the entire Soviet army. The permanent secretaries sympathised discreetly. The ministers knew, or at least strongly suspected, that their civil servants were in cahoots with the Chiefs of Staff. Even the Wrens who served the tea remarked to each other on the atmosphere as they scuttled in and out of the Great Parlour.

The dozen places at the stout mahogany table were occupied by the ministers and the Chiefs of Staff. The permanent secretaries and the military advisers sat behind them in a wider circle around the table on chairs poached from the White Parlour. The Prime Minister sat with his back to the window. On a sideboard in the bay of the window rested a bowl of yellow chrysanthemums. God knows where you get chrysanthemums from at this time of year, thought Defence Secretary Evans, as he took from a red despatch box the paper he was about to present.

Perkins called the meeting to order without ceremony and invited Evans to speak first. Copies of his paper had been circulated in advance and he summarised it page by page, inviting questions as he went along. "So far as we have been able to establish," began Evans, "the United States has over one hundred bases and other military facilities on the soil of the United Kingdom. These you will find listed in Appendix One." There was a rustle of paper while everyone searched for Appendix One.

"What do you mean 'so far as we have been able to establish'?" interrupted Jock Steeples.

"To be perfectly frank," said Evans with a quick glance at the general on his left, "I have not had the co-operation I would have liked in the preparation of this paper." He went on to explain that it had taken three requests before his private office had been able to come up with what now appeared to be a complete inventory of American weaponry and related installations. Even now there was some dispute about the exact rôle of the communications facilities, some of which appeared to be targeted against the host country rather than against any real or imagined external threat. He would

deal with this in more detail. Meanwhile he would only say that there were some members of the British defence establishment who apparently believed that the Secretary of State could not be trusted with all matters relating to the defence of the realm. At this, there was much foot-shuffling and sideways glancing among the Chiefs of Staff and their advisers, but no one thought it wise to argue.

Evans resumed his summary. "US forces in Britain have the use of twenty-one airbases, nine transport terminals, seventeen weapon dumps, seven nuclear weapon stores, thirty-eight communications facilities and three radar and sonar surveillance sites." He paused, "You will find details of each of these in Appendix Two." There was more rustling of paper and a rattle of tea cups as Wrens with the trolleys arrived.

"The United States," Evans went on, "has about seven thousand warheads and of these about two hundred are stored in Britain. Those for the Poseidon submarines are kept in underground chambers at Glen Douglas near Holy Loch. The other main storage depots are at Caerwent near Newport and Burtonwood near Warrington. There are also nuclear weapons stored on or near American air force bases at Upper Heyford, Mildenhall, Lakenheath, Bentwaters, Brize Norton, Wethersfield, Woodbridge, Greenham Common, Marham, Sculthorpe and Fairford." Evans recited the names slowly, in the manner of a British Rail announcer. A uniformed Wren leaned across his right shoulder and placed a cup of strong tea on the edge of his blotter.

"In the event of war," Evans was no longer reading from the brief in front of him, "especially equipped Boeing 757s would take off immediately from Mildenhall in Suffolk and would become the US European Command."

"Exactly how much control do we have over this little lot?" asked Mrs Cook, the Home Secretary. She was seated almost opposite Evans. Her bright red jacket made her conspicuous among the dark lounge suits and military uniforms.

Evans plopped two lumps of sugar into his tea and stirred gently. "None whatever," he said quickly.

"With respect, sir." It was Air Chief Marshal Sir Richard Gibbon, RAF Chief of Staff. "With respect, we have an *understanding.*"

"Not worth the paper it's written on," said Evans without waiting for the air marshal to finish. He had had the same argument with his officials twice already this week. "I had my officials go back through the archives. No treaty was ever signed. All they could come up with was a note, dated October 1951, prepared by the British ambassador in Washington and initialled by an American under-secretary of state which says that the use of the bases in an emergency is a matter of joint decision 'in the light of the circumstances prevailing at the time.' The full text is in Appendix Three." They turned to Appendix Three.

"I can only say," snorted the air marshal, "that in the ten years I've been dealing with them, I've always found that our American allies work very closely with us." He leaned back in his chair as though that was the final word on the subject, but it was not.

"Fact of the matter is," said Evans quietly, "that over the years the US air force has installed its own communications network, and it can now operate quite independently of the MoD. Isn't that so Air Marshal?"

The air marshal did not reply. There was a brief silence during which Evans glanced triumphantly around the table as though expecting a round of applause.

"What I'd like to know," said Harry Perkins who had until now sat silently with his chin in his hands, "is against whom are we defending ourselves?"

"I'm sorry, Prime Minister, I don't quite follow." Air Marshal Gibbon had assumed, without any particular reason, that the question was directed at him.

"For the last forty years," said Perkins, "all our defence plans have been based on the assumption that the only threat to our security comes from the Soviet Union." He paused. Through the bay windows behind him two policemen could be seen pacing the north lawn, one of them held an alsatian on a lead. "Supposing," continued Perkins, "just supposing, that

the real threat to our security were to come not from the Soviet Union, but from the other side of the Atlantic?

"We'd not be very well prepared, would we?"

Lunch was a buffet in the Long Gallery. Perkins spent most of the lunch hour describing the treasures on display there to anyone who cared to listen. There was Nelson's gold pocket watch, Napoleon's despatch case and a ring reputed to have belonged to Queen Elizabeth the First. Jock Steeples and Mrs Cook stood watching from a distance as Perkins stooped over a glass case trying to decipher a letter from Oliver Cromwell for the benefit of the navy Chief of Staff. "This place brings out the lord of the manor in Harry," said Steeples with a grin.

The Prime Minister's final remarks at the morning session were the main topic of conversation among the military men and the permanent secretaries. Nothing in their training had prepared them for the possibility that Britain might need protecting against the United States. One permanent secretary, having first glanced over his shoulder to make sure he was out of earshot of the politicians, said that so far as he was concerned the Atlantic alliance was all that stood between freedom and tyranny in Britain. And in a discreet corner, a colonel from the MoD Planning Department was heard to say that the way things were going he would not be surprised if Britain soon became a fully paid-up member of the Warsaw Pact.

The afternoon began with a slideshow downstairs in the Hawtrey Room at which a succession of military men sought to impress upon ministers the overwhelming superiority of Soviet conventional forces in relation to those of the West. As Jock Steeples murmured to Mrs Cook, it was a bit late in the day for this sort of argument. The government said clearly that it intended to get the Americans out and only the practicalities remained to be settled. That was why they were here: to work out the practicalities, not to go through the same old arguments all over again.

Steeples was still whispering when the first slide came up on

the screen. It purported to show the balance of NATO and Warsaw Pact forces in central Europe. Mrs Cook had waited until the room was in darkness to put on her glasses. She peered through the haze of smoke from Jim Evans' pipe. "Where's France?" she asked.

"Madam," said the colonel who was giving the commentary, "France is not a member of the NATO Command." He spoke in the slightly patronising tone that experts sometimes use when dealing with the hopelessly ignorant.

Mrs Cook repaid in kind. "I am aware of that, thank you, Colonel." Her voice betrayed the tone of irritation that ministers sometimes use with experts who treat them like fools. "But if the Russians invaded Western Europe, I imagine we could count on the French to lend a hand, couldn't we?"

The colonel said he hoped so.

"In that case," said Mrs Cook flashing him one of her steeliest smiles, just visible in the light from the projector, "perhaps you could show us some figures that include the French?"

A major was despatched to find details of the French armed forces. Meanwhile the colonel pressed a button and a picture of a Soviet T-72 tank appeared on the screen. "One moment, Colonel," said a voice from the gloom, "would you mind taking us back again?" He pressed the reverse switch and the tank was replaced by the chart depicting the East/West balance. "Aren't the American figures a bit on the low side?" It was Ted Curran, Minister for Overseas Development. He was not in the Cabinet, but had asked to be included in the Chequers weekend since defence was his particular hobbyhorse.

The colonel shifted his weight from one foot to the other. His right hand clutched a stick, about the length of a billiard cue, which he used for pointing to the screen. "They include all American troops based in central Europe," he said stiffly.

"But not those based in the United States and earmarked for Europe in the event of emergencies?" asked Curran from the back of the room.

"No, sir."

"And the Russians?" Because he was looking into the light of the projector and the smokescreen thrown up by Jim Evans' pipe, the colonel was denied a view of Ted Curran's face.

"We count all Soviet troops west of the Urals."

"Not a very fair comparison, is it, Colonel?"

"That's how we've always done it in my time, sir." In the front row the Chiefs of Staff were on edge. Air Marshal Gibbon was plucking at the expanding metal strap on his watch. General Payne was brushing his lapel with exaggerated gestures of his right hand. The First Sea Lord affected to be dozing, but was in fact wide awake.

They moved on to tanks and it was the same again. Mrs Cook wanted to know if the figures included obsolete Russian tanks. Ted Curran wondered aloud whether precision guided missiles had not rendered the tank almost useless and, in any case, why had no mention been made of anti-tank weapons? Then they turned to aircraft. Did the figures include planes based in America, but earmarked for Europe? If not, why not? How many of the Soviet planes were interceptors? Why was no distinction made between interceptors and attack aircraft?

And so it went on. The beads of sweat that formed on the colonel's forehead showed clearly in the beam of the projector. By about the third slide the tone of crisp, military self-assurance that he had carried with him since Sandhurst had disappeared. General Payne, in the front row, fixed him with a glassy stare and did not let go for a full minute. The permanent secretaries were silently appalled. Surely the MoD could put up a better show than this? They must have known they were in for a rough ride. "Trouble with the chaps at MoD," whispered Sir Peter Kennedy to his opposite number at the Home Office as they filed out when the show was over, "is that, until now, they've always had ministers who accept whatever nonsense is put in front of them." He blinked rapidly as they came into daylight. "They don't seem to realise those days are over."

*

Perkins was the first to surface on Sunday morning. Or at least he thought he was until he crossed the landing overlooking the Great Hall and saw Mrs Cook ensconced in one of the deep armchairs with the papers. "Morning Joan." She looked up sharply as Perkins appeared at the balustrade.

"Ah, there you are, Harry. I want a word with you."

"Fire away." Perkins was leaning on the banisters which turned the first floor landing into a sort of gallery overlooking the hallway.

Mrs Cook, who was standing by now, shook her head. She placed the papers on the chair in which she had been sitting and indicated silently that he should come down. She was waiting at the foot of the stairs and without speaking, save a mumbled "Good morning" to the policeman on duty in the porch, they went outside. In the forecourt they turned left and through a gate in the brick wall that surrounded the south terrace. There had been a frost in the night and their feet made light imprints on the stone terrace. Mrs Cook did not speak until they were out of earshot of the house and going down the steps into the rose garden.

"Harry," she said, "there's something you ought to know."

"There's a lot of things I ought to know," smiled Perkins.

"I had the Prison Room last night," continued Mrs Cook. The Prison Room, an attic bedroom so called because it had once acted as a place of detention for a lady of the court who had fallen foul of Queen Elizabeth the First, stood apart from the other bedrooms at Chequers and could only be reached by a spiral staircase from either the Hawtrey Room on the ground floor or the Great Parlour immediately above. "After dinner I did some work on my despatch box and set off for bed around midnight. I was just about to cross the parlour on my way to the spiral staircase, when I heard voices."

Mrs Cook described how she had hovered in the doorway and managed to identify the voices as belonging to Lawrence Wainwright, the Chancellor, and Air Marshal Gibbon. The parlour was lit only by a single lampshade on the mantelpiece

154

and peeping round the door she could see that the two men were seated, port glasses in hand, close by the entrance to the staircase. Not wanting to disturb them she retraced her steps down the main staircase and into the Hawtrey Room. From there she had entered the spiral stairway up which she crept until she drew level with the first floor. "The door leading from the staircase into the parlour was ajar and I had not switched on the light on the staircase for fear of alerting Wainwright and Gibbon. I couldn't hear everything, but Wainwright was saying he had planned to resign but Craddock had advised him not to."

"Craddock?" said Perkins. "Would that be the D15 Craddock?"

"Who else?"

They had completed a circuit of the rose garden and were now back by the steps leading to the terrace. Mrs Cook indicated that her story was not yet finished and so they commenced a second circuit. "Wainwright said that Craddock had advised him to stay on at least until the Americans had been consulted."

"The sly bastard," said Perkins almost under his breath.

"Then Gibbon piped up and said that he'd be in Washington next week and would take the opportunity to sound out the Americans then."

"Sound them out about what?"

"They didn't say, but I imagine it's got something to do with the bases. Gibbon did say something about seeing the Secretary of State and maybe even the President."

As they returned to the house they ran into Wainwright on his way out. He greeted Perkins with a hearty "Morning Prime Minister", but Perkins could not help noticing that Wainwright avoided looking him straight in the eye.

When they assembled in the Great Parlour for the morning session there was one new face among them. A small man in his early sixties with thick black eyebrows and a shock of white hair. He was seated on the right of Perkins who introduced him as Sir Montague Kowalsky, chief scientific

155

adviser to the Ministry of Defence. "Sir Monty's going to tell us how we get rid of the bomb," said Perkins.

The small man gave a nervous smile. "Gentlemen," he said and then, with a nod of the head in the direction of Mrs Cook, "and Madam." He fumbled with the documents in front of him. "You should all have a copy of my paper. I shall make a short summary."

He spoke with a central European accent. "A nuclear warhead is a very delicate instrument. To remain functional it requires constant maintenance and the regular replacement of sensitive components. Withdraw the facilities for maintenance and refurbishment and you lose the capacity to retain nuclear weapons." Sir Monty's forearms rested on the table. "Warheads rely for detonation upon such elements as plutonium, tritium and in the old days, polonium."

The mention of these words caused the eyes of the audience to glaze over. Seeing this, Sir Monty added, "I need not trouble you with the details."

He paused and looked around the table. "Suffice it to say that the effective life of a nuclear warhead is between four and ten years. After that time it has to be transported to the Royal Ordnance Factory at Burghfield for renewal. The simplest way to dispose of our nuclear arsenal would be, therefore, to dismantle each warhead as it arrives at Burghfield."

On the landing outside, the rattle of cups foreshadowed the coming of the Wrens with tea. Sir Monty joined the palms of his hands as though in prayer. "However," he said, "I imagine you would wish to complete the run down of our nuclear arsenal in somewhat less than ten years. There is some scope for speeding up the process at Burghfield. Reasonably, I estimate that you could dismantle all the warheads within three to five years."

This news he announced with just a trace of a smile. Sir Monty was a rare phenomenon among the defence establishment: a scientist who was opposed to nuclear weapons. He was a Jew born in Poland, the son of a goldsmith from Poznan. When the Nazis over-ran Poland he was living with an uncle in Golders Green. His parents were despatched to

156

the concentration camp at Treblinka and he never saw them again. By the end of the war he was a student at Imperial College. His PhD was on the effects of radiation. Hiroshima and Nagasaki provided no shortage of case studies. From that time onwards he was convinced of the evil of nuclear weapons.

For years Sir Monty had concealed his aversion to the bomb, at least to his professional colleagues. He had taken care to speak in the measured, balanced tones expected of a scientist. He hoped that he still did so, even though he found it hard to conceal his excitement. He was within two years of retirement and had long despaired of seeing an end to the bomb in his lifetime. Now, suddenly here was Harry Perkins and his government pledged to rid Britain of the bomb. And here was Montague Kowalsky sitting at a table in Chequers, telling them how to go about it. Truly, these were exciting times.

The Wrens served tea and left. Jim Evans puffed at his pipe and Mrs Cook waved away the smoke with her hand. Ted Curran had a question. "How do we make sure," he asked, "that no future government is able to revive a nuclear weapons programme?"

The faces of the Chiefs of Staff simultaneously assumed a pained expression.

"You cannot be sure, but you can make it extremely difficult and very expensive," Sir Monty replied with what he hoped was the appropriate air of scientific detachment. "You must close and disperse the facilities at Aldermaston and the Royal Ordnance Factory near Cardiff. That is where the components for the warheads are made."

He paused to sip tea. "Also, as soon as all existing warheads have been dismantled you must close and disperse the facilities at Burghfield."

"And how many people will be put out of work?" It was Wainwright's first contribution to any of the discussions that weekend.

Funny how the Treasury never worried about putting people out of work if it involved cutting public spending in any

other department, thought Joan Cook. Only when it comes to saving money on bombs that they start worrying about lost jobs. From the look on the face of Harry Perkins, she could see that he was thinking the same.

"There are about 5,000 people employed at Aldermaston," said Sir Montague calmly. "And maybe another 2,000 at Burghfield and Cardiff. You may also lose some jobs in the naval dockyards at Devonport and Rosyth. As regards the Polaris submarines or the Tornados and Jaguar planes which carry warheads, these need not necessarily be scrapped. They can easily be adapted for conventional use."

Wainwright pressed the point. "So you would estimate at least 10,000 lost jobs?"

"If I may make a personal observation?" Sir Montague turned to the Prime Minister. He was not in the habit of offering his opinion, but with the exception of Wainwright, the ministers seemed well disposed.

Perkins waved his hand as if to say, "All right by me."

Sir Monty proceeded to offer his opinion. "With proper planning there is no reason why these people should lose their jobs. Many of them are highly skilled. Certainly the scientists could be redeployed."

"Exactly," said Mrs Cook. Wainwright did not respond.

Jock Steeples spoke next. "You have said nothing about disposal of the American warheads based in Britain."

Sir Monty ran a hand through his white hair. "The Americans," he said, "are another matter. If you ask them to go, they will take their warheads with them, probably to Germany and Spain. They will take with them their submarines, planes and other delivery vehicles." He paused as though deliberating whether to venture another personal opinion. Why not? he thought. "After they have gone, you will want to dismantle all the storage facilities on the bases. Otherwise there would be nothing to prevent their return under another government."

Kowalsky looked innocently around the table. He hoped he had not overstepped his brief. Wainwright and the Chiefs

of Staff, seated in a cluster at the opposite end of the room, looked aghast.

Unabashed, Sir Monty added one last personal observation. "I imagine," he said mischievously, "that the Americans will not be very keen to go."

14

The President was on a fishing holiday in Maryland when the cables from London confirmed that the British were going through with their plan to evict all American bases. And not just the bases. In his broadcast to the nation, recorded in the Great Parlour at Chequers that Sunday evening, Perkins had specified that the Americans would also be asked to withdraw from General Command Headquarters (GCHQ) at Cheltenham, to close Menwith Hill in Yorkshire and the chain of other communications facilities used for monitoring all telephone, telegram and telex traffic to Europe and the United States. The timetable, said Perkins, would be a matter for negotiations, but he envisaged that the American withdrawal would be complete within three to five years.

Within an hour of the broadcast the President was reading the full text in his log cabin by the Potomac river. Two fishing rods and a gaff were propped up against the wall by the door. Laid nearby were two gleaming salmon, the day's catch. The President was slouched in a folding camp chair the bulging canvas of which was hard put to accommodate his considerable frame. He sat there clad in an anorak, gumboots and old tartan trousers splashed with mud. Around him, motionless and with their arms folded, stood aides dressed incongruously in blue blazers and trousers with impeccable creases.

No one spoke while the President ran his eye down the three foot length of teletape. After several minutes of intense concentration he put the tape on the table, unwrapped a spearmint chewing gum; then he shouted so loudly that even the fish in the Potomac must have heard. "Damn, blast and shit," he said.

There followed a hurried conversation with Secretary of State Morgan over a scrambled radio telephone. Morgan was already in his office at the State Department. Their brief conversation over, the President walked out of the cabin and

160

strode to a waiting jeep. Behind him doors slammed as aides and secret service agents climbed into their vehicles. Then the little convoy set off bumping along the rough forest track. After twenty minutes they came to a clearing in which stood a white helicopter, its fuselage emblazoned with a circular coat of arms around which was written in clear black letters, "The President of the United States." Two hours later, the President, still in gumboots and mud-spattered trousers, was back in the Oval Office.

They were seated in a semi-circle of easy chairs around the fireplace, logs freshly lit burning in the grate, and a portrait of George Washington above the mantlepiece. The President sat to the right of the fireplace, to his left Admiral Glugstein still in evening dress, having driven to the White House directly from the Hilton Hotel where he had been hosting a dinner for the head of the Chilean navy. Marcus J. Morgan, the Secretary of State was next. Morgan had brought with him a pile of cables from London, the latest saying that the Chiefs of Staff were threatening to resign. Opposite, on the sofa, was the President's national security adviser, Anton Zablonski, who was leaning forward with hands on his knees like a crouching rugby full-back expecting the ball to come his way at any moment. Beside Zablonski sat the CIA chief, George McLennon. On the way up in the elevator McLennon had been composing small talk to break the ice. He had planned to ask the President about his fishing trip, but changed his mind when he saw the look on the President's face. This was no time for small talk.

With the exception of McLennon, they were all big men with heavy jowls and large bellies. The heaviness of their jowls lent gravity to the occasion.

The President spoke first. "Let's be clear. There is no way we can afford to lose Britain. No way at all." Zablonski was nodding in agreement. The President went on, "We lost China in 1949 and got by. We lost Vietnam in 1975 and got by. But if we lose Britain, we're done for."

161

"Right on, Mr President," whispered Zablonski.

"If we were prepared to invest two-billion dollars a year and forty thousand American lives to try and save a dump like Vietnam, then the sky's the limit when it comes to saving Britain." The President spoke slowly, every phrase punctuated by the sound of his jaws processing chewing gum. "Whatever the cost we've got to stop those bases falling into enemy hands – and by enemy I mean the British government."

For a moment there was no sound save the crackling of the log fire. The President looked at each man in turn. "Gentlemen, this is war. I want to know how we get rid of Harry Perkins and his government." He nodded towards Morgan. "Marcus, you first."

The Secretary of State ran a plump hand across the stubble on his unshaven chin. "To start with, Mr President, we gotta play for time. Emphasise the technical difficulties. Slam in a nice bill for compensation. Demand the return of every piece of equipment that we've ever installed in the British defence system, down to the last paper clip. Meanwhile we get our European allies to pile on the pressure, get the bankers to heat up the economy a little and quietly prepare for the worst."

"Anton?"

Zablonski sat up straight, slicked back his hair and tightened the knot of his tie as though he were rising to address an audience of thousands. "I reckon," he said firmly, "it's about time we stopped babying the British. Tell them straight to get into line or else. We could start by organising a trade boycott and, if it comes to the worst, we could blockade the ports."

"That's plain crazy." McLennon could not restrain himself. "If we do that we'll end up taking on the whole world."

"So what would you do," snapped Zablonski, "put Perkins down for a Nobel Peace Prize?"

McLennon ignored this. In his view Zablonski was a dangerous lunatic who enjoyed far too much access to the President. Lunatics like Zablonski had already driven half the

world to Communism and, if they continued to have their way, it would not be long before the other half followed.

"We have one thing going for us," said McLennon. "British public opinion. Perkins is not as popular now as he was six months ago. That dispute with the power workers was very damaging. On top of which many people in Britain are worried about the Soviets. We must play that one for all it's worth." He paused to look across at the President who was making notes. *Play Soviets*, the President had written on a pad of white paper embossed with his seal.

"And here," McLennon went on, "I must pay tribute to the British intelligence boys. We often laugh at them, but I must say they have got their media sewn up tighter than a gnat's ass-hole. Apart from a Communist rag, which no one takes seriously anyway, every national daily, every Sunday paper, just about every local newspaper from Surrey to the Scottish Highlands is on our side on this one. So is the BBC and most other television networks. All hammering Perkins and his crew every day. All playing the Soviet threat for everything it's worth. In most countries we have to pay for that kind of coverage. In Britain we get it for free." There was envy in his voice. If only the American establishment had a media half as friendly, half as unenquiring. "Sooner or later," he said, "public opinion in Britain is bound to swing our way." He paused and looked at Zablonski. "Unless we screw it all up by declaring war on them."

"George is right Mr President, we gotta play this cool." It was Marcus Morgan. McLennon looked up in surprise. It was not often he had the Secretary of State on his side.

"What we need," Morgan went on, "is a bit of so-phist-ica-tion." The word rolled slowly off his tongue. Sophistication was not something widely associated with corporate lawyers. "If Anton had his way, we'd be training British mercenaries in Camp Hale by now."

"As I see it," said Admiral Glugstein, who until now had sat back in silence, "our key objective must be to maintain the installations." He pinched his trousers at the knee to preserve the crease. "The warheads are no problem. If the worst comes

163

to the worst we can play the Brits along by flying them out to Germany or Spain. The submarines can also be temporarily relocated, if necessary. But the infrastructure, that's another matter."

The admiral's polished shoes gleamed in the light of a lampshade. His cuffs protruded a full two inches from the sleeve of his dinner jacket. "Yes sir," he went on, "we got thirty billion dollars tied up in infrastructure. Communications, storage facilities and the like. If we lose that little lot we're in trouble deep."

"That's where the British military come in." Morgan had taken a cigar from his top pocket and was fumbling for a lighter. "Providing we hand over to the British military, they should be able to babysit for us until the next election."

"And if Perkins wins the next election?" jeered Zablonski.

"That," said the President with a thin smile, "is item two on today's agenda."

The RAF DC10 bringing Air Chief Marshal Sir Richard Gibbon to Washington touched down at Andrews Air Force Base at around 9 am Washington time. Officially he was coming to talk to the American air force about an updated version of the F-18 which the RAF were hoping to buy. The visit had been scheduled months in advance. Unofficially, however, he had come to give the Americans a full briefing on the Chequers weekend and to sound them out on what was to be done. Although he was met at the airbase by a USAF staff car, he was driven not to the Pentagon, but to the State Department. To avoid the possibility of recognition he was dressed in civilian clothes. He entered the State Department by a service entrance at the rear of the building and was taken immediately to the office of the Secretary of State.

If anyone had suggested to the air marshal that what he was engaged upon was treason he would have replied crisply that, on the contrary, he was engaged in an act of patriotism. If pressed, the air marshal would have argued that the citizen's loyalty to the State was conditional upon the State recognising a responsibility to provide protection for the

citizen. By withdrawing from the Atlantic alliance the British government was failing to honour its share of the bargain. Therefore, the air marshal was perfectly entitled to withdraw his loyalty from the State. He was not alone in this line of thinking. In one way or another such arguments were to be heard around the dinner tables and in the drawing rooms of gentlemen's clubs the length and breadth of St James's. They were to be heard in the officers' mess at the Army Staff College at Camberley. And in the boardrooms of some of Britain's grandest corporations. They were even, on occasion, to be heard between the four walls of a permanent secretary's office in Whitehall.

Very often such arguments were embellished by the suggestion that the loyalty of many government ministers was in doubt. If there was any treason going on, it was argued, it was more likely to be found in the Cabinet Room or behind the Georgian façade of Labour party headquarters at Walworth Road. To say nothing of some of the Marxist trade union leaders who made no secret about where their loyalties lay. This reasoning rarely made the newspapers, at least not in so crude a form. But it was what many very important people in Britain were thinking as the winter of 1989 faded into spring of 1990.

Of course no one in their wildest dreams would have envisaged a situation where any British Cabinet minister or even a Marxist trade union leader would actually undertake a trip to Moscow for the specific purpose of briefing the Soviet Foreign Minister on the secret deliberations of the British government. Everyone knew that Soviet sympathisers were a little more subtle than that.

Yet here was an air marshal, who only hours before had been party to the highest level and most secret deliberations of the British government, seated in the office of the American Secretary of State, spilling the beans with gusto. Call it treason or patriotism or what you will.

Marcus J. Morgan was in shirtsleeves, which did justice to his mighty biceps. Cold winds blew outside, but inside an air conditioner hummed gently. Or was it an extractor fan ab-

sorbing the endless screen of cigar smoke which wafted up from behind his paper-strewn desk? On a table by the window was a scale model of the B-1 bomber, the biggest, fastest and most expensive ever built. The air marshal gazed longingly at it and wondered aloud if the Royal Air Force would ever be able to afford a squadron of B-1s. "Don't worry," Morgan assured him, "Britain will get her share just as soon as we've extended the runways at Mildenhall."

"Let's get one thing straight right from the start," said Morgan after the air marshal had told him there was talk of resignations, "we don't want to see any resigning. The battle's only just beginning and we're going to need you boys to stick in there. So stay stuck in." The air marshal nodded. He could see the point, though he had never before heard the Chiefs of Staff of His Majesty's armed forces referred to as "you boys".

"Another thing," said Morgan after the air marshal had told him of the plan to dismantle the British warheads. "Instead of taking the warheads to Burghfield, just fly them to Germany and we'll take care of them for you until the all clear sounds. Then you can have them back again." He flicked the ash from his cigar into an ashtray made from the wing of a Soviet MIG shot down over Afghanistan. "You can put a few through Burghfield to keep Perkins happy. If necessary, soup up the figures a bit." The air marshal nodded again. Yes, he thought that could be done. The real problem would be when the time came for Burghfield and Aldermaston to be dismantled. When that happened there would be no hope of Britain ever again maintaining an independent deterrent.

"That's when you start to take it easy. Throw a spanner or two in the works. Tell the government it's more complicated than you thought. Get the workers to go-slow." Morgan chuckled. "Going-slow is what you British are good at, isn't it?"

The air marshal managed only a weak smile. At home he would have been the first to laugh at any joke about the idleness of the British working man, but he did not like to see a foreigner running down his countrymen. "That might not be as easy as you imagine," he said, "the running down opera-

tion is likely to be in the hands of the chief scientific adviser to the MoD, an old Pole named Kowalsky. We're not sure we can count on him to play ball. At Chequers on Sunday I rather got the impression that he might actually be in favour of doing away with nuclear weapons." The air marshal's voice betrayed incredulity, as though he could not conceive a scientist, let alone one working for the Ministry of Defence, who would be against the bomb.

"A pinko?" asked Morgan, one eyebrow raised.

"I wouldn't go *that* far," said Sir Richard quickly.

They talked for another half hour. Mainly about the chain of communications bases run by the American National Security Agency. This was really not Sir Richard's department. More an intelligence matter. But he knew enough to venture an opinion. He was slightly taken aback when Morgan remarked casually that it was being used to monitor all British government communications, including the Downing Street switchboard. "There's virtually nothing that bastard Perkins says that won't find its way to this desk within six hours," said Morgan patting a file of computer print-outs in his in-tray. At first Sir Richard assumed that American bugging the British government communications had been prompted by recent events, but Morgan soon put him straight. America, he said, had been bugging friendly governments for the last thirty years. Including all British governments, Conservative and Labour. "We started during the Suez crisis," beamed Morgan, "and never kicked the habit."

From the State Department Sir Richard was taken to see the President. They went in Morgan's car. To avoid leaks the meeting took place not in the Oval Office, but in a suite in the Executive Office Building which the President used for off-the-record meetings. The President asked mainly about the political situation in Britain. How long did Gibbon think Perkins would last? Was there anyone else in the Labour Party who could take over if Perkins was ousted? Gibbon had replied that being a military man he was not well up on politics, but it was his impression that Perkins would lead the

167

Labour Party into the next election and that he stood a good chance of winning.

With that Gibbon was driven to a house in Georgetown which the State Department used for VIP guests. Here he bathed, shaved and changed into his air marshal's uniform. From there he was taken to the Pentagon where he lunched with the USAF Chief of Staff. Even here the F-18s were discussed only perfunctorily. Most of the talk was about the bases in Britain. Finally he was driven back to the RAF DC10 which was refuelled and waiting for him at Andrews Air Force Base. By the small hours of Tuesday morning he was back in London.

15

The spring brought out the crocuses and daffodils in St James's Park. On the Thames the pleasure boats made their first trips of the season to Kew Gardens, and in Hyde Park military bands began playing again on Sunday afternoons.

Spring also saw the launch of a huge offensive against the government's plan to do away with nuclear weapons. It started a few days after the Chequers conference with a statement from the US State Department to the effect that while the United States would always respect the sovereignty and territorial integrity of the United Kingdom and any other NATO member, there were wider issues at stake. By effectively withdrawing from the alliance, the statement continued, the government of the United Kingdom places in jeopardy not merely the security of their own people, but that of Western Europe as a whole. The German, the Spanish, Belgian and Italian (though not the Dutch) governments each delivered separate protest notes. Meanwhile the Chiefs of Staff made what was supposed to be an unpublicised visit to Perkins to protest at the decision, but when they arrived at Downing Street batteries of cameras were waiting to record the event.

Press coverage grew steadily more outrageous. Ministers were presented as unwitting agents of the Soviet Union. One cartoon depicted Perkins standing on a map of Europe and opening a door for Russian tanks. Another showed a column of Russian tanks in front of the Houses of Parliament with America, Germany and other NATO allies, standing to one side, saying to Britain "Serves you right". The *Daily Mail* described the decision to ask the Americans to leave as the "biggest betrayal of Europe since the Molotov-Ribbentrop Pact". *The Times* said that Britain would never be able to hold her head high again and the *Guardian* commented that while a case might be made out for severing military ties with the

United States, now was not the time. Attempts to point out that Sweden and Switzerland had prospered as neutral countries were brushed aside, as was all mention of Canada which had unilaterally renounced nuclear weapons three decades before without any discernible ill-effects.

The public was still being given a wholly false picture of the balance of forces in Europe. Despite a personal memorandum from the Secretary of State's office and several reminders from Downing Street, the MoD press office continued to brief journalists using tables which omitted all mention of French forces and which excluded all British and American troops stationed outside central Europe.

Perkins staged a slight recovery in the opinion polls, which recorded a majority of British citizens in favour of the government's stand, but the findings were not widely reported. Only in May when in the face of a continuous propaganda barrage the majority against the bomb started to decline, were the opinion polls headline news again.

Gradually the going got rougher. The West German railways cancelled a ninety million pound order for locomotives and rolling stock to be built in Huddersfield. Spain pulled out of an order for two naval patrol vessels being built at Barrow. Saudi Arabia, which had been on the point of signing a contract with a British company for a huge construction project at a port on the Red Sea, withdrew at the last moment. These were the first in a spate of cancellations. The *Boston Globe* reported that American embassies around the world had instructions to persuade friendly governments to take their business elsewhere than Britain. Only the *Financial Times* took up the story.

Also about this time American-owned multinational corporations began transferring huge sums of money out of Britain. At first there appeared no reason for the transfer since British exchange rates compared favourably with those in Europe and the United States. Later a rumour circulated the money markets that the corporations were acting in response to pressure from the US Treasury which had privately guaranteed them against losses arising from these trans-

actions. When the rumour persisted the American ambassador was summoned to the Foreign Office and asked to confirm or deny. His denial was less than watertight.

At the same time it was reliably reported from Washington that the Secretary of State had told a group of right-wing congressmen in an off-the-record briefing that America had no intention of vacating its bases in Britain. "When the time comes," he was quoted as saying, "we'll just sit tight and see what happens."

At this news the colour drained from Perkins' face. "I'm beginning to think we've bitten off more than we can chew," he said to Fred Thompson during one of their late night chats. Thompson was amazed. It was the first piece of pessimism he had ever heard from Perkins. "You know, Fred," Perkins had continued, "membership of NATO is about as voluntary as membership of the Warsaw Pact." He spoke as though he was kicking himself for not having realised that earlier. "We aren't going to be allowed to leave. If economic pressure doesn't work, they'll try blackmail. If that doesn't work, they'll try and subvert us. And if that fails, they'll send tanks. Just like the Russians did in Hungary."

Trade Unionists for Multilateral Nuclear Disarmament was launched at a crowded press conference at a suite in the Dorchester Hotel. The Dorchester was not an obvious venue but then, as Reg Smith never tired of saying, nothing is too good for the working classes. Smith was the chairman of TUM, as it became known. The secretary was a dapper young man called Clive Short who had lately graduated from Oxford. At Oxford he had formed a breakaway Labour club because the original one had, it was alleged, been taken over by extremists. It was in this capacity that he had come to the attention of Reg Smith.

Two other general secretaries, the leaders of the steel workers and the shop workers, shared the platform with Smith at the Dorchester. They were, however, careful to emphasise that they were present in a personal capacity. Also on the platform were shop stewards from union branches at

Aldermaston, Burghfield and the Devonport dockyard. Their interest was easily identified: their members' jobs were at stake.

In answer to questions, Smith did most of the talking. TUM, he said, was his brainchild. It was designed to act as a rallying point for the millions of moderate, sensible trade unionists who realised that Harry Perkins and his government were surrendering the country to the Russians. He wanted to stand up and show that it was not only Tories who cared about their country and about freedom.

Was TUM in favour of nuclear disarmament? Yes, of course, but not at any price. It was not right to ask the Americans to pull their bases out of Britain, unless the Russians pulled out of Eastern Europe.

Where was TUM's money coming from? From affiliation fees and a large bank overdraft. So far only the United Power Workers' Union had affiliated at national level, but a number of union branches had already signed up and at least one of the major civil service unions, which had a lot of members in the defence industry, was expected to affiliate shortly.

Was TUM a CIA front organisation? This question came from a reporter on the *Independent Socialist* who had managed to slip in to the invitations-only press conference. But Smith was an old hand at his game. He easily parried the question with just the right blend of indignation and humour to be convincing. "And while we're on the subject of front organisations," he added to general laughter, "is there any truth in the rumour that the KGB is funding the *Independent Socialist*?"

Press coverage the next day was lavish. Every paper carried a picture of Smith and ten to twenty column inches of sympathetic reporting. Papers which had only half heartedly supported the power workers' go-slow a few weeks earlier now had a campaign they could get their teeth into. The *Daily Mirror* was particularly effusive. Here at last, said an editorial, was a man prepared to stand up to Perkins on his own ground. A trade unionist who put the security of Britain before party politics.

172

TUM placed a series of advertisements in national news-papers appealing for members and money. Donations poured into its third-floor office in a terrace of early Victorian houses near the Euston Road headquarters of the United Power Workers' Union. So great was the flood of mail that Smith had to second a couple of union secretaries to help. By the end of the first week, Smith was able to announce donations totalling forty thousand pounds. He wisely declined to speculate as to the kind of people who would contribute funds to Trade Unionists for Multilateral Nuclear Disarmament. For one thing, many of the donations were anonymous. For another, as many of the accompanying letters made clear, much of TUM's support was coming from people who believed neither in trade unionism nor disarmament.

Sir Peregrine Craddock knew even before most CND mem-bers that the Campaign for Nuclear Disarmament were plan-ning a major demonstration. Quite apart from the routine telephone taps, he had a man on the CND general council. It was one of DI5's most successful penetrations, yielding a complete set of minutes, not only of executive meetings but also of the secret discussions that took place between leading members of CND and Harry Perkins when he was leader of the opposition.

Sir Peregrine had long regarded CND as the most subver-sive organisation on DI5's books. Its subversive nature lay in the breadth of its appeal. Besides the usual gaggle of Com-munists, Trotskyists and layabouts, CND's membership took in Christians, Social Democrats, Liberals, Buddhists, veg-etarians and even a few Young Conservatives. In the early days DI5 had made a number of hamfisted attempts to discredit CND as a Soviet front. Sir George Fison's news-papers even helped out with stories of CND delegations on expenses-paid trips to Moscow or by quoting from articles in *Pravda* in praise of CND. But none of this had the slightest effect on public opinion and CND's membership continued to grow. Worse still, it was effective. For years DI5 had invested thousands of man hours and weeks of computer time meticu-

lously infiltrating, bugging and logging the details of every little Trotskyist sect that had ever raised a placard outside Brixton tube station on a Saturday morning. Yet none of these had ever caused the slightest hiccup in the orderly conduct of the nation's affairs. CND, meanwhile, had turned the nation's defence policy upside down in the space of a decade. And there appeared to be nothing DI5 or any other organ of the State could do to stop it. Yes, thought Sir Peregrine turning a half circle towards the window in his swivel chair, CND was a very dangerous organisation indeed.

From below in Curzon Street, a screech of car brakes momentarily penetrated the double glazing and lace curtains of Sir Peregrine's inner sanctum. He spun his chair sharply back from the window towards the desk and pressed a button by the telephone which caused a red light to flash in the outer office. The door at the far end of the room opened and Fiennes entered. As usual he was wearing a white shirt with blue stripes, a dark blue suit and the thinnest of thin smiles.

"Fiennes," said Sir Peregrine without looking up, "I think we ought to lay something on for this CND demo next month. Get on to Special Ops and see what they suggest."

"Good idea, sir." Fiennes would have said it was a good idea whether or not he thought so.

"What I have in mind," Sir Peregrine went on, "is a bit of a punch-up. Something that will detract from any favourable press coverage."

"I'll get on to it right away, sir."

Fiennes had turned back towards the door when Sir Peregrine spoke again. "Just a punch-up, you understand, Fiennes. I don't want anybody killed or maimed." As an after-thought he added, "Above all, I don't want any of those psychopaths from Hereford involved."

"No sir," said Fiennes quietly, though he could not bring himself to think of the members of the Special Air Services as psychopaths.

The crowd began to assemble at Speakers' Corner long before midday. All weekend people had poured into London for

what CND had promised would be the biggest demonstration in British political history. It had been billed in CND literature as "The Final Push". The aim, according to the leaflets, was to show that "in spite of the unanimous hostility of the media and the establishment the British people stood behind their government's decision to do away with the Bomb."

The organisers had confidently predicted a quarter of a million people and even by the normally cautious estimates of the Metropolitan Police it seemed they could be right. Special trains and coaches were streaming into London from Scotland and the North of England, from Wales and the West Country. To the dismay of Jim Chambers, who was observing from the American embassy, there were even contingents from the West German Social Democratic Party and from Holland, Italy, Greece, Norway, Belgium and Spain. Nearly every country in NATO was represented. The spectre of a neutral Europe which had haunted Pentagon defence planners for so long was looking more and more probable.

As is customary at such gatherings, the Special Branch was well represented. Though not carrying banners they were readily identifiable. Heavy young men in green anoraks, faded jeans and plimsols. Some posed as press photographers, but gave themselves away by chatting too readily with the uniformed officers. Others were given away by the tell-tale bulge of a police radio under their jackets. They were to be glimpsed operating long-range cameras from rooftops all along the route of the procession, but particularly from vantage points overlooking Trafalgar Square, which would be the climax of the demonstration.

Fred Thompson was pointing all this out to Elizabeth Fain as they walked hand in hand along Park Lane towards Speakers' Corner. "Those cameras are so powerful," he was saying, "that they can identify an individual at a hundred and fifty yards." Thompson waved cheerfully at the men on the roof of the Hilton.

"By now," he teased, "they'll have you on file and before long all your friends in high places will know you have been

seen in the company of a dangerous extremist. It'll be the talk of Annabel's."

"I wouldn't be seen dead in that place these days," said Elizabeth nudging him playfully. It was true, Elizabeth's outlook on life had changed since she first met Thompson. She had started to read between the lines of what she read in newspapers and, at Thompson's prompting, was now halfway through a book on the origins of the Cold War. Unlike many of her friends, Elizabeth had always been prepared to accept that the Americans were not necessarily the champions of freedom that she had been brought up to believe. However, it came as a revelation to discover the existence of a point of view, apparently supported by documentary evidence, which saw America as the centre of a worldwide network of tyranny, terrorism and suppression. It had turned her world upside down. She was not exactly converted. She was confused.

"I can see it's going to take a long time to repair the damage caused by that expensive education of yours," Thompson had said when she questioned him one evening about the coup in Chile. He had added with a grin, "Count yourself lucky that you've been saved while there was still time."

He had put his arm around her and kissed her lightly on the cheek. "Just imagine if you'd married one of those awful Hooray Henrys from the Cavalry Club."

"Do shut up, Fred," she had said half in anger, but she knew he was right. In her mind there suddenly loomed a vision of the awful Roger Norton and his tales of "bopping wogs" in Oman.

"Think about it," Fred had continued, "by now you might have been living in the Shires breeding a new generation of Hooray Henrys to run our country for us."

With that they had both burst out laughing. She had kissed him. "Yes," she admitted, "I had a very narrow escape."

By now they were more or less living together. Elizabeth had taken a job in an oriental bookshop near the British Museum, and during the week she would stay at Thompson's flat in

Camden Town. At weekends Thompson went to her house near Sloane Square.

This was the first demonstration they had ever attended together. "I can't imagine what my father would say, if he could see me now."

"He'd probably disinherit you."

"Probably." She squeezed his hand.

They were nearing Speakers' Corner now. A stream of people, some clutching banners headed in the same direction. In the park itself the crowd was so dense that it stretched as far as the cafeteria on the corner of the Serpentine. A policeman said he had not seen anything like it since the firework display the night before Prince Charles got married.

Stewards were trying to marshal the throng into some sort of order. "North-East region to the front, South Wales in the middle, trade unionists in the third column," a man with a loudspeaker was shouting. By a miracle, Thompson spotted the Holborn Labour party banner and he and Elizabeth fell in behind that.

All around there were people selling magazines and newspapers. Obscure journals with names that Elizabeth had never heard of before: *Tribune*, *Militant*, *Sanity*, *New Socialist*. To pass the time while they waited Thompson bought a copy of a paper called *Socialist Worker*. The front page led with a story about a police plot to sabotage the demonstration with an outbreak of violence. It said secret instructions had been given to units of the Special Patrol Group, but offered no clue as to the source of this information. "That's the trouble with all these Trot journals," said Thompson, "high on hysteria, low on facts."

Far away the head of the demonstration, led by a brass band of Yorkshire miners, was now moving off into Park Lane. Through a gap in the railing they could see wave after wave of banners passing, but still the numbers in the park seemed to grow no smaller.

In the centre of the crowd the speeches had begun. The speakers were crowded on to the back of a lorry with a hydraulic platform normally used to repair street lights, and

177

one by one they were elevated above the crowd. Thompson and Elizabeth were too far away to recognise the speakers by sight, but their voices came over clearly on the carefully placed amplifiers: Labour politicians, a Church of England bishop, and even a well meaning brigadier who was received politely, but without enthusiasm. The biggest cheer of all was reserved for a Methodist peer in his late eighties. And all the while a police helicopter, with huge zoom lens cameras on either side, whirred above the great throng.

Thompson and Elizabeth waited more than two hours before their section of the crowd started to file out of the park. Even then more than half the crowd still remained to follow. "At this rate," said Thompson, looking at his watch, "we are going to miss Harry's contribution." The Prime Minister was scheduled to speak at 3.30 pm, the first time anyone could remember a serving Prime Minister addressing a demonstration in Trafalgar Square. The private office had come out strongly against, sending memos all week advising him not to speak. First they gave security as the reason. Then they tried to persuade him to entertain the Irish Prime Minister to lunch at Chequers instead. Finally, they said it demeaned the dignity of his office. "Nonsense," Perkins had replied, "the only thing that demeans this office is the long list of broken promises by successive Prime Ministers."

The demonstrators moved briskly to Hyde Park Corner shepherded between a thin line of policemen. The demonstration was a good-natured affair, with some singing, some chanting of inane slogans such as "Yanks out," and "Americans go home." It was only as they moved into Piccadilly that the police lines thickened. Behind the railings in Green Park, clearly visible from the road, stood uniformed police in helmets with visors, riot shields and truncheons at the ready.

"Expecting trouble, are we?" said Thompson quietly. Elizabeth held his hand tighter. Above, the police helicopter whirred. The air of goodwill began to evaporate. "Aren't our police wonderful?" shouted someone behind.

They passed the Ritz. St James's was cordoned off. Behind the cordon Thompson caught sight of half a dozen identical

mustard coloured vans with rear windows blacked out parked in a convoy. "The Special Patrol Group," he whispered to Elizabeth.

Twenty yards further on, outside Fortnum and Mason, a group of heavy young men in plimsolls and green anoraks stood smoking nervously. Just before Thompson and Elizabeth reached them, the police cordon parted and four of the men slipped through to mingle with the demonstrators about five yards ahead of Thompson. The other demonstrators gave them a wide berth. Thompson was not the only one who noticed what was happening.

The strangers marched in step with the demonstrators. Thompson saw that two of them were carrying plastic bags that appeared to contain something heavy. They passed Hatchards and the Church of St James's, crossed Piccadilly Circus and moved into the Haymarket. By the time they reached the American Express office beyond the Haymarket Theatre, Thompson had almost forgotten them. It was then that he heard the sound of breaking glass.

He looked round in time to see one of the plate glass windows on the American Express office splinter inwards. Instantly a burglar alarm began to ring. As he watched a half brick arched up from the crowd just ahead of him and smashed through another window. He looked around for the four strangers, and identified them trying to push their way out of the crowd on to the pavement on the opposite side of the road from the American Express office. One man was still clutching a half brick.

"Fred, look out." It was Elizabeth, holding his hand tighter than ever. The crowd around them began to scatter. Everyone was shouting. From distant amplifiers came the sound of the speeches in Trafalgar Square. To judge by the applause it sounded as though Perkins was speaking. The original burglar alarm had now been joined by others. Above the din Thompson could hear clearly the sound of horses' hooves. "Look out," Elizabeth screamed again. The crowd around them parted to reveal police, scores of them on horseback, pouring out of Charles II Street wielding batons to right and left.

The first of the horsemen had already overtaken them. Wailing police sirens now vied with the burglar alarm. So did the screaming. The noise drowned the whir of the police helicopter directly above. No one even looked up.

They were running as fast as they could now. Elizabeth had still managed to keep hold of Thompson's hand. The horsemen were in hot pursuit clubbing to the right and left. Banners were trampled underfoot. They passed one boy with blood pouring down his face from a wound in his forehead. Ahead of them a girl was screaming.

The panic spread in both directions. It passed up the Haymarket in waves and back towards Trafalgar Square which was already jammed with people. For some reason the section of the crowd in the north part of the Haymarket, instead of retreating, continued to press forward forcing those at the front into the path of the horsemen. This may have been because, as Thompson later learned, both ends of the demonstration had come under attack. At almost exactly the moment the bricks went through the window of the American Express building, the police with riot shields had emerged from behind the railings in Green Park and started to lay into the demonstrators. Those in the middle had at first been unaware of what was happening.

Thompson and Elizabeth continued running until they reached the bottom of the steps at Carlton House Terrace where, they reasoned, the horsemen could no longer follow. It was here that they again caught sight of the four strangers jogging along the edge of St James's Park that borders the Horse Guards Parade. Following them was easy. By the time they drew level with the end of Downing Street they were walking. Two of the men paused to light cigarettes. They were laughing and joking as they climbed over the low rail at the edge of the park, crossed the Horse Guards Road and made for the steps leading into Downing Street.

Two uniformed policemen were on duty at the end of Downing Street. The men spoke briefly to them and then disappeared up the steps. When Thompson and Elizabeth arrived one of the policemen held out his arm to bar the way.

"Not today, thank you, sir." He pointed in the general direction of Piccadilly. "A bit of bother up the road, you see."

"I work here," said Thompson flashing his plastic laminated Number Ten pass under the policeman's nose.

The policeman stood aside without another word. The four strangers were almost at the top of Downing Street by the time Thompson and Elizabeth entered and they had to run to catch up. Whitehall was practically deserted, having been sealed off to keep the demonstrators away from the government buildings. The men had turned right. They crossed the road by the Cenotaph and walked another fifty yards before turning left down a narrow street opposite the Treasury.

"Where does that go to?" asked Elizabeth.

"Three guesses," said Thompson.

As he spoke a convoy of mustard coloured vans overtook them and turned into the same street. They reached the turning just in time to see the four strangers enter a forecourt bounded by a high railing. To one side in a sentry box sat a uniformed police officer. The mustard coloured vans followed.

"Cannon Row Police Station," said Thompson.

"Oh," said Elizabeth quietly, "aren't our police wonderful?"

The next day's newspapers were full of it. Perkins had the early editions delivered to his flat in Kennington that evening. He continued to spend weekends there in preference to the flat at Downing Street.

"Anti-Bomb mob on rampage," screamed the *Sun* front page headline over a picture of the American Express building with its two broken windows. The inside pages displayed pictures of an injured policeman and a crowd charging helter-skelter down the Haymarket. The caption said they were running wild, but in fact they were fleeing the police horsemen. "Mob attacks American Express – 400 arrested," said the *Telegraph* headline. All the other papers carried similar reports and pictures. There was scarcely any mention of the

size of the demonstration or its purpose. Perkins' speech was referred to only in passing.

The only comment that was reported with any prominence was a statement from Reg Smith in his capacity as chairman of Trade Unionists for Multilateral Nuclear Disarmament. The riot, he said, proved what he had always argued. Namely, that CND was run by a number of irresponsible hotheads who were motivated more by hatred of the United States than by a desire for nuclear disarmament. He appealed to all decent, sensible people who may have allowed themselves to be misled into supporting CND to reconsider their position.

"Bastard," said Perkins as he flung the papers in a heap on the floor. For weeks he had been looking forward to today as a chance to get the case for removing the bases across to the public in a way that not even Sir George Fison's papers could ignore. He was sure the disruption was organised, but proving it was going to be another matter.

Thompson had telephoned soon after Perkins arrived home and described what he and Elizabeth had seen. Perkins had rung the Metropolitan Commissioner immediately and demanded an explanation. "But I don't suppose I'll get one," he had said to himself as he replaced the receiver. "After all, I'm only the bleeding Prime Minister."

Sure enough, an hour later the Metropolitan Commissioner rang back to say that he had personally checked with Cannon Row police station and no men answering the description given by Thompson had been seen on the premises.

Meanwhile Thompson, on the advice of Perkins, had contacted the BBC and ITN offering them his eyewitness account of what had happened. The BBC Television news desk referred him at once to a senior executive, Jonathan Alford. Mr Alford was courteous, but sceptical. He said he would ring back, but did not. ITN, on the other hand, immediately whisked Thompson to its Wells Street studio. But the recorded interview was not shown. "You know how it is," said an embarrassed news editor when Thompson rang to enquire what had happened, "you were crowded out, not enough time."

But both BBC and ITN did find time to show the demonstration leaving Hyde Park. They used near identical clips in both of which a Communist Party banner stood out clearly.

Perkins switched the television off and poured himself a whisky. He had not felt so depressed at any time since he became Prime Minister. The other side were winning the propaganda war and he was almost powerless to hit back. For a moment he caught himself wishing he ran a dictatorship where he could simply order the newspapers to print what he said.

When he climbed into bed that night he felt lonelier than for a long time. As he drifted to sleep he found himself thinking of Molly Spence. It was getting on for thirteen years since she had passed out of his life. She was the last woman he had slept with. She would be getting on for forty now. He wondered whom she had married. How many children she had. Whether she had voted for him in the election. He did not suppose he would ever find out.

How wrong he was.

16

Molly Spence had married her boss, the managing director of British Insulated Industries. They had two children, a girl aged twelve and a boy aged ten, and lived in a converted mill in the Peak District of Derbyshire. Her husband commuted each day to British Insulated's twelve-storey head office in the centre of Manchester.

The mill, which could not be seen from the road and was approached by a winding drive of grey stone chippings, was on the floor of a valley and overlooked on three sides by sloping bare hills which were green, grey or purple depending on the time of year or the disposition of the sun. The highest of the plateaux, Kinder Scout, was a favourite place in the summer for parties of campers and ramblers.

Despite its isolation the mill was never a silent place, what with the sheep on the hillside and the running water from the nearby stream. Only when the wind howled too loudly or the rain beat too hard upon the windows could the water not be heard. And every hour or so there was the rattle of a one-coach diesel railcar that ran along the floor of the valley. It was one of those lines that British Rail was always threatening to close, but never did.

Molly's husband, Michael Jarvis, was fifteen years older. Even by Molly's standards that was pushing it a bit. She had thought hard before accepting his persistent offers of marriage. He had two children by his first wife and she did not get on with them. He drove a Jensen, though that was neither here nor there. He was powerful and, if Molly was honest with herself, she did have a soft spot for powerful men. In the end she said "Yes" because it seemed less trouble than saying "No". Off and on she had been going with Michael Jarvis for four years. Everyone in British Insulated knew. She did not want to devote the best years of her life to being someone's

mistress and then end up being dumped in favour of a woman younger and prettier.

She had not told Michael about the affair with Harry Perkins. It had only been possible because he had based himself in London to negotiate the reactor deal. Although she had told Perkins that she shared a flat in Kensington with another girl, she in fact lived with Jarvis in an apartment owned by British Insulated. On Thursday nights Jarvis usually returned to Manchester to deal with business at head office. He would stay the weekend in Manchester and always spent Sunday with his children. It was these weekly visits to Manchester that made Molly available for Harry Perkins at weekends.

She had never loved Harry Perkins though she was as fond of him as she had been of anyone. She had liked him for being different. She liked his sense of humour. She liked him because he was famous. She liked him because he was interesting. But she always knew there was no future in the affair. Every Sunday when she caught the tube to the Oval she wondered whether to tell him it was the end. As the tube sped under the river, and through Kennington, she would sit composing her opening lines. But when she arrived, she could not bring herself to do it. There was Harry as warm and witty and optimistic as ever. There was the Handel organ concerto on the stereo. The bottle of Côte du Rhône on the table. She knew that deep down Harry Perkins was a lonely man. She knew that behind his façade of self-assurance, behind his steely willpower and his crammed appointments diary, there was an area of emptiness which she filled. She could tell by the way he clung to her. By the way he closed his eyes so tightly when they made love. By the way he lay with his head on her breasts.

So when the time came she had not the heart to tell him. She had carried on seeing him right up to the end. Right up to the Saturday before the wedding. The nearer the day came, the harder it got to tell him. In the end she had written him a long letter explaining about Michael and going into all sorts of unnecessary detail about her feelings. Then she had torn up

the letter and substituted a simple statement of fact: *On Saturday I'm getting married so we'll have to call it a day. Please understand. Good luck. Molly*. She told herself that this was the sort of memorandum Cabinet ministers liked. Short and to the point.

Even so, she had not forgotten Harry Perkins. How could she? There he was in the newspapers every day. There he was every time she turned on the television. Not the Harry Perkins she knew. This was a much harder man, tough talking and belligerent. All the same, she felt a pang of guilt every time she saw him. She thought how much older he looked and wondered if the daily barrage of vilification was getting him down. She noticed too that the optimistic twinkle had disappeared from his eyes.

Molly kept her souvenirs of Perkins in a blue vanity case amid a pile of old boxes in the attic. They included that first note on official paper. *Lunch Sunday? Ring me at midnight*. And then the telephone number. Not even signed.

There was *The Ragged Trousered Philanthropists* with the message inscribed on the inside cover: *To a slightly Tory lady in the hope that she will see the light. Love, Harry* and then the date. There were several other notes, mainly re-arranging the time of their weekly rendezvous, one on ministry notepaper, a couple on House of Commons paper and the rest on blank scraps. There was also a cheque for £5.20 drawn on the account of Harold A. Perkins at the Co-operative Bank, Leman Street, London, E.1, in payment for shopping. Because he was famous she had decided the cheque was worth more to her uncashed. And that was it. Not a lot to show for a love affair that lasted more than a year. She kept her souvenirs hidden because she did not want Michael to know. He would have seen the dates and worked out for himself that she had two-timed him almost to the day of their marriage.

Perkins would have been pleased to know that she voted Labour in the election. Actually it was no big deal. Michael and most of the top management of British Insulated had probably voted Labour, if the truth were known. After all they owed their jobs to Perkins. Had he not fought so hard for

their reactor, British Insulated would have gone to the wall. Instead it had landed contracts to build four nuclear reactors in Britain with an option on two more. That in turn had led to orders from Saudi Arabia and Brazil. Thanks to Harry Perkins British Insulated had gone from strength to strength. And, who knows, they might one day have led the world, but for the disaster at Windermere.

The Windermere reactor was not simply a triumph of technology. It was also a triumph of politics. The splitting of the atom was as nothing compared with the five-year battle that raged between the Central Electricity Generating Board and the Save Windermere Society. There were public inquiries, High Court injunctions, parliamentary select committees and, when all else failed, sabotage.

The scientists argued that their nuclear power station was clean, safe and aesthetic. The Save Windermere Society said it was dirty, poisonous and ugly. The society argued that the Windermere reactor would drive away tourists, destroy wild life and one day perhaps incinerate Lancashire. The society had mobilised the National Trust, the Countryside Commission, Cumbria County Council and the Lake District National Park Authority, to say nothing of the Kendal Conservative Association and the Newby Bridge Amenity Society. Between them these organisations could count on more colonels, brigadiers and generals than the Duke of Wellington took to Waterloo. Yet in the end they met defeat. Whitehall decreed that the Windermere reactor should be built. Parliament and the judges endorsed it. And up it went.

But slowly. The building of it took four years longer than scheduled. Sugar was poured into the fuel tanks of the bulldozers that came to clear the site. There was an inter-union dispute over the lagging of pipes which led to a six-month shutdown. When the pipes were finally fitted many were found to have faulty welds. Then the boilers leaked. And then there was the little matter of the uranium that came off the rails somewhere between Liverpool docks and Preston.

There were times when British Insulated teetered on the edge of bankruptcy. There were times when the board seriously considered pulling out of reactors. There were times when Michael Jarvis wished he had been a schoolteacher, a postman or anything but the managing director of British Insulated. Yet in the end the Windermere reactor was built.

It occupied a shelf of land blasted out of the hills that run along the west shore of the lake. By no stretch of the imagination was it a thing of beauty except perhaps to nuclear engineers and architects. But neither was it dirty or poisonous. Not to begin with anyway.

The reactor dwelled in a huge windowless temple of sheer white concrete inlaid with aluminium. Inside the temple was crisscrossed by steel pipes and walkways all as spick and span as a hospital operating theatre. Down the centre a towering structure of yellow steel, not unlike a lighthouse, ran back and forth on rails feeding the god on enriched uranium. In all of this the intervention of human beings seemed irrelevant.

The god itself was encased in a concrete holy of holies seventy feet high and twelve feet thick and lined with steel, capable, or so it was said, of enduring heat at temperatures of up to seven hundred degrees centigrade and pressure of six hundred pounds per square inch.

The uranium pellets on which the god was fed were passed to it through the roof of the concrete chamber. The great heat given off by the uranium was blasted by carbon dioxide into water boilers which produced steam, which drove turbines which in turn produced electricity. That at least was the theory. And so it was in practice, until that fateful day in May when the Windermere reactor went out of control and almost took out Liverpool.

Jerry Turnbull was in charge of the control room when the temperature gauges started to rise. "Bloody gauge is playing up again," he muttered, hammering the glass panel with his fist. The needle on the gauge did not move.

Phil Prescott, control assistant, came and stood behind Turnbull. He was yawning. It was the first hour of the night

shift. "No sign of the red light." He gestured towards the panel of lights which came on automatically in the event of an equipment failure. "Must be the gauge."

Turnbull hammered on the gauge again. Still it didn't move. He was not unduly worried. There had been two false alarms in the ten days since Windermere had been operating at full capacity and both had been traced to faulty wiring in the instrument panel. "Marvellous, isn't it?" said Prescott. "We can split the atom, but we can't wire a bloody circuit."

Turnbull picked up a phone and dialled the instrument maintenance engineers. There was no answer. "Another fucking tea break," he said loudly and slammed the phone down. Opening the log book he wrote the following entry: "2130, reactor coolant temperature gauge reading too high. Rang instrument maintenance. No reply." At least my arse is covered, he thought as he closed the log.

Jerry Turnbull had risen about as far as he was going to get in the hierarchy of the power industry. Even now he was working above his grade. The regular nightshift controller had taken sick two days ago and Turnbull was filling in. He was forty-nine years old and bitter. He worked nightshifts because his wife had left him and because nights were quieter. "Mr Turnbull likes a quiet life," his annual report had said. And it was true.

Unfortunately for Mr Turnbull, however, tonight was not going to be quiet.

He was dozing lightly when somehow his eye came to rest on the meter that measured radiation in the reactor hall. It was reading two hundred and fifty millirems per hour. He came to with a jolt. Carbon dioxide was leaking.

Turnbull looked at his watch; it was 0215. The reactor temperature gauge was still creeping up although there was no sign of a red light. He looked around for Prescott, but Prescott had gone for an early breakfast.

Trembling slightly Turnbull switched on the video scanner that monitored the pipes carrying the carbon dioxide into the reactor. The camera ran along the length of the pipes, hovering over the welds. There was no sight of a leak. He looked

189

again at the radiation meter. It had gone up another twenty millirems.

Next, he turned on the scanner that monitored the pipes taking the steam out of the reactor to the generator. He scanned them once, twice. Turnbull was panicking now. He had worked seventeen years in nuclear power stations without once being near the scene of an accident. Now for the first time he found himself in sole charge.

He rang the canteen. Where the hell was Prescott? Gone down to the lakeside for a smoke. He rang instrument maintenance. The bastards still were not answering.

Even at this point, so the manuals assure us, there is no cause for alarm. All the reactor components essential to its safe functioning are duplicated. If the pumps which bring the coolant gas into the reactor fail, there are duplicates waiting to take over. If one of the pipes bringing the coolant into the reactors or taking the steam away should leak, there are others which will take the strain.

If all else fails, so the text book says, the reactor will automatically shut itself down. But none of this happened at Windermere that night.

By the time a nearly hysterical Turnbull got the general manager out of bed the meter reading for radiation in the reactor hall had risen to four hundred millirems an hour, ten times the permitted level.

Engineers in protective clothing were inside the hall searching for the source of the leak. The temperature gauge had reached seven hundred degrees but there was no sight of an automatic shutdown. When the general manager appeared on the scene around 0545 he found Prescott and Turnbull arguing furiously. Prescott wanted the reactor shut down. Turnbull was shouting that he was not going to be the man who shut down the Windermere reactor.

By the time the dayshift came on duty the radiation level in the reactor hall was over six hundred millirems. Medical checks on the engineers who had been inside the hall showed they were seriously contaminated. The general manager im-

mediately ordered a shutdown of the reactor but some of the control rods appeared to have warped, making a complete shutdown impossible. Inside the reactor the uranium was melting. In the reactor hall automatic sprays had been activated, but they were insufficient to cope with the huge quantities of radioactive carbon dioxide now leaking from the reactor.

Tests in the atmosphere outside the reactor building showed no significant radiation leakage, but it was clearly only a question of time. The police were asked to stand by to evacuate everyone within a five mile radius. At 0800 Downing Street came on the line. The Prime Minister wished to be kept informed.

He was not the only one. A twenty-mile-an-hour wind was blowing due south. At that rate a cloud of radioactive carbon dioxide would take just fifteen minutes to engulf the village of Newby Bridge at the end of Windermere. Then, assuming no change in the direction of the wind, the radioactive cloud would continue south over Morecambe Bay and would reach Blackpool within little over an hour. Within three hours it could be over Liverpool.

"Facilities for the orderly evacuation of Liverpool do not exist," said the Chief Constable of Merseyside when informed of the news.

By 0935 the Windermere engineers managed to get the emergency cooling system working which stopped the uranium melting, but the radiation level in the reactor hall was higher than ever. The meter reading was showing nearly one thousand millirems in the area of the reactor and even men wearing protective clothing could only work there for a few minutes at a time.

By midday, with the help of experts from London flown in by army helicopter, the engineers managed to insert the warped control rods and close down the reactor. Tests outside the building showed that radiation was reaching dangerous levels. Disaster had been averted. Just.

*

191

The preliminary investigation showed that the cause of the leakage was a series of hairline cracks in the base of the concrete pressure vessel which contained the reactor. The cracks had developed into fissures when the reactor over-heated due to the failure of the emergency cooling system. Later enquiries revealed that the cracks occurred because the concrete used in the construction of the pressure vessel did not match the specifications laid down by the designers and approved by Nuclear Installations Inspectorate. Neither had the vessel been adequately tested despite documentation that said otherwise. In other words, British Insulated Industries had a few questions to answer. A public enquiry was immediately announced, but it was not only British Insulated who would face questions.

On the Sunday morning after the accident at Windermere, David Booth made himself a pot of tea and sat out in the garden with the papers. It was the first time that year that the weather had been good enough to sit outside. His wife had taken the children to lunch at her mother's, so he would not be disturbed.

The papers were full of the Windermere disaster. The *Sunday Times* Insight team had traced the whole history of the project and their report filled a special four-page pull-out. Most of the papers had been quick to pounce upon Harry Perkins' role in the affair. There were long articles describing how he had forced the deal through in the teeth of bitter opposition from his own civil servants, the Atomic Energy Authority and the Central Electricity Generating Board. Several editorials called on Perkins to make a statement.

David Booth took more than a casual interest. He was a principal in the foreign exchange department at the Treasury, but thirteen years ago – exactly at the time the deal with British Insulated had been negotiated – he had been on a six-month secondment to the nuclear division of the Public Sector Department. Indeed he had actually taken part in some of the negotiations.

At the time, Booth had formed a sneaking regard for Perkins. He had been deeply impressed by the way Perkins had stood his ground over the reactors against virtually the entire establishment. He had also been appalled at the way his civil service superiors had behaved: refusing to circulate briefing documents; withholding from the minister information that did not tally with the case they were putting forward. There had been times when he had seriously wondered whether or not some of his colleagues were actually in the pay of the American reactor company.

But none of this concerned Booth that sunny Sunday morning. He was worrying that he knew what the *Sunday Times* Insight team did not, something that would cause a sensation if it became generally known. David Booth knew that, at the time Harry Perkins had been pushing British Insulated's case through Cabinet he had been having an affair with the secretary to the managing director of British Insulated. Booth had seen the Secretary of State discreetly hand the girl that envelope during the negotiations at the department one morning. He had watched them drinking coffee together by the window overlooking the Thames. And in the weeks that followed he had seen the knowing winks and nods, the occasional pat of the elbow that the Secretary of State and the girl had exchanged.

The question was, what should he do about it? In all probability the affair was entirely innocent. Foolish perhaps for a man in Perkins' position, but nevertheless innocent. He had no wish to do Perkins down. God knows, the man had enough trouble on his hands without all this being raked up. In any case he had worked with Perkins. The man was as straight as a die – even his worst enemies would concede that.

On the other hand, a doubt nagged him. Supposing the girl had influenced the decision over the reactor? Supposing she had led him, however unwittingly, to come down in favour of British Insulated? Almost certainly there was nothing in it, but it was his duty to report what he had seen.

Booth wrestled with the problem all weekend. He did not

finally make up his mind until he arrived at his desk on Monday morning. Then he asked for an immediate appointment with his permanent secretary, Sir Peter Kennedy.

17

When the memorandum from Sir Peter Kennedy arrived on Sir Peregrine Craddock's desk the DI5 chief's eyes lit up. Sir Peregrine was not much given to displays of emotion, but he got up, paced his office and slapped his thigh with the flat of his hand. If this is true, he said to himself, we've got the bastard at last.

Composing himself Sir Peregrine returned to his desk and buzzed Fiennes.

"There's a man called David Booth who works in the Foreign Exchange Department of the Treasury. I want to see him immediately."

"Yes, sir."

"Then I want to get on to our man at the Public Sector Department. Ask him to get me the names and addresses of everyone from British Insulated Industries who took part in the reactor negotiations at the Department thirteen years ago." He looked up at Fiennes who was standing almost to attention. "Everyone. Do you understand? Typists, clerks, stenographers, the lot."

"At once, sir."

"And when you've done that," Sir Peregrine was still looking at Fiennes, "get on to the Special Branch inspector in charge of the Prime Minister's security. Tell him I would like to see him as soon as possible, but that he is not to let anyone know he is coming here. Neither his superiors nor the Prime Minister. Especially not the Prime Minister."

What's all that about? wondered Fiennes, as he closed the door behind him and returned to the outer office. He knew better than to ask questions, however. He would find out soon enough.

David Booth arrived at Curzon Street House within the hour and was shown straight to Sir Peregrine's office. His hands

were shaking slightly as Fiennes showed him in. Even now he was not sure he had done right. Perhaps there was something in it after all. All the same, he never expected to be summoned by the head of DI5.

Sir Peregrine was in an affable mood. When Booth entered, he leaned across his desk and shook hands. "So good of you to come, Mr Booth. I shan't keep you long." He waved Booth to an armchair.

The interview lasted about ten minutes. Booth repeated what he had already told his permanent secretary that morning. Sir Peregrine went over the details carefully. Had he actually *seen* Perkins hand the envelope to the girl? Yes, he had. Did he have any idea what was in it? No, he did not. Could it have been connected with the reactor negotiations? Yes, possibly. Perhaps the Secretary of State had simply handed over some document for safe keeping that she would afterwards pass on to her boss? Possible, but unlikely. And in any case there was all that nodding and winking.

"Quite so," said Sir Peregrine crisply, "but even Secretaries of State are not above occasionally making eyes at a pretty girl. That didn't mean he was sleeping with her."

Not necessarily, agreed Booth. He was beginning to feel that it was all in his imagination. There was nothing in Sir Peregrine's reaction to indicate whether he believed the story or not.

"One final question," Sir Peregrine was saying. "Have you told anyone about this apart from Sir Peter Kennedy?"

"No sir."

"No one at all? Not even at the time."

"No."

"Good." Sir Peregrine smiled benignly. "Then I'd be obliged if you would continue to keep the whole thing under your hat."

The DI5 chief rose and Booth rose with him. They walked towards the door. "I am sure you appreciate," said Sir Peregrine confidentially, "that if any of this got out, there would be the most awful stink."

*

Inspector Page nearly fell over backwards when he received the summons to Curzon Street. Of course in his job he often dealt with DI5, but only with the liaison man in Downing Street or other government departments. Usually these dealings only involved routine checks on people scheduled to meet the Prime Minister. Occasionally he drew the odd threatening letter to DI5's attention. But a meeting with the chief himself, that was another matter.

Page arrived at Curzon Street House in the early evening. Fiennes had stressed that he was not to tell anyone and so he waited until he went off duty before setting out. Fiennes met him in the lobby and took him by lift to the second floor. He offered no clue as to what it was all about. The truth was that Fiennes did not know. When he had handed over the list of names and addresses of the British Insulated Industries people that had arrived that afternoon, Sir Peregrine had received it without comment.

When Fiennes entered with Inspector Page he noticed that the list was lying on Sir Peregrine's desk and that one of the names had been circled in red. He was not close enough to see which one.

Sir Peregrine waited until Fiennes had left the room before he spoke. "Inspector," he said, "does the name Molly Spence mean anything to you?"

The inspector's forehead creased to a frown. After a moment's thought he said, "No, sir."

"Mrs Jarvis, perhaps?"

"No sir."

Sir Peregrine was sitting sideways on to the window, his elbows resting on the arms of his chair and his fingers joined at the tips. To look at the inspector he had to turn his head sharply to the right. "Am I correct in thinking that you have been looking after the Prime Minister since the day he took office?"

"Yes sir."

"And as far as you know, no one of that name has visited him during that time."

"That's right sir."

Sir Peregrine stared straight ahead, his chin touching the tip of his joined fingers. "Is it conceivable that a lady of that name could visit him without your knowing?"

The inspector smiled. The idea of Harry Perkins receiving secret visits from a young lady was one that appealed to his sense of humour. "Possible, but not likely, sir."

"When he visits his constituency in Sheffield perhaps?"

"If he goes to Sheffield either I or the sergeant go with him. Normally he returns to London the same night."

"Or to his flat in Kennington."

"Nowadays he only stays at Kennington one or two nights a week," said the inspector. "In which case there would be a uniformed man on duty in the lobby downstairs, day and night. I would expect to be told of any visitors."

Sir Peregrine turned back towards the inspector. Reaching his arm forward, he pressed the switch on a desk lamp. It illuminated the space between them, giving the inspector his first clear view of the DI5 chief's face.

"Do you have access to the Prime Minister's flat, Inspector?"

"Yes sir, I have a key."

"Good." Sir Peregrine smiled. "I want you to do something for me."

The inspector stiffened a little. "Sir, I normally get my instructions from the Branch."

"I'll clear this with your superiors," said Sir Peregrine brusquely. He went on to explain that he wanted the inspector to search the Prime Minister's flat for any trace of the woman called either Molly Spence or Mrs Jarvis. He was to look for photographs, letters, dedications on the inside of books and to search desks, cupboards, drawers and filing cabinets. He was to leave everything exactly as he found it. He was to take no one with him and, above all, to breathe not a word to anyone.

Sir Peregrine scribbled a number on a scrap of paper which he passed to the inspector. "This is my direct line. You are to report to me personally and to bring with you whatever you find."

*

198

Inspector Page waited until Friday when the Prime Minister left for his weekly visit to Sheffield under the watchful eye of Sergeant Block. Then he drove to Kennington. He felt distinctly uneasy. It was not every day he was ordered to commit burglary, let alone in the home of the Prime Minister. He might have felt happier had he been told the reason for the interest in this woman Spence or Jarvis or whatever her name was. In any case, why couldn't DI5 do its own dirty work? And so what if Perkins was having it off on the quiet? Good luck to him.

Page had been looking after Perkins for over a year now. Politically they were miles apart. Page was a bit of a law and order man himself, but he did not mind admitting that Perkins was a decent enough bloke. Over the last few months Page had often found himself alone with the Prime Minister. Sharing compartments on trains, sitting together in the back of an official car on the way to a speaking engagement, even sharing a seat on the top deck of those damn buses that Perkins still insisted on riding now and again. Perkins had listened patiently to Inspector Page's views on what should be done with strikers, rioters and Northern Ireland and sometimes they had engaged in good-natured argument. Perkins was forever asking about the inspector's family. On one occasion he had even invited Page to bring his wife and two small sons to Downing Street and had shown them round in person. The inspector would not exactly have described himself as a close friend, but he was as close as a bodyguard is ever likely to get to a Prime Minister.

And now he was being asked to sneak into Perkins' flat and sift through his personal effects. Page would do it because he was under orders, but he did not like doing it. Not one little bit.

To avoid prying neighbours he parked his car in the Clapham Road and walked back round the corner about fifty yards to Perkins' flat. He glanced quickly up at the window of neighbouring flats and, when he was sure no one was looking, let himself into the front entrance hall with a Yale key. He glided up the three flights of stairs, taking the steps two at a

time, turned the two Chubb locks on Perkins' front door and let himself in, closing the door quietly behind him.

It was, thought Page, a very modest home for a Prime Minister, being rather smaller than the inspector's own semi in Willesden. There were two bedrooms and a medium-sized living room. The smaller of the two bedrooms was a store-room. There were boxes of papers and magazines, piles of bound volumes of Hansard, and two metal filing cabinets. This is going to take all bloody night, thought Page, as he surveyed the flat.

He started by looking at the photographs. The one on the desk in the living room of an elderly lady with grey hair was, he guessed, Perkins' mother. On the mantelpiece there was a picture of Perkins with some orientals. On the wall in the bedroom a large photograph, taken in the bar of a Sheffield Labour club, showed Perkins surrounded by party members. In the wardrobe Page found an old shoebox full of black and white prints, some of them dating back to Perkins' childhood. There was one girl in her early twenties, but it seemed to have been taken years ago and the name Anne was scribbled on the back.

Next he went through the letters on the desk. They were in wire baskets labelled 'Constituency', 'Personal' and 'Party'. Page flipped through the basket marked 'Personal'. It consisted mainly of unpaid bills, some bank statements and two or three letters from people who appeared to be relatives. There were drawers in the desk and he went through them one by one. Postage stamps, typewriter ribbons, paper clips, a pile of old election addresses and several books of old Co-Op coupons. Jesus, thought Page, it must be ten years since the Co-Op stopped giving stamps.

He had been there about an hour when he started on the small bedroom. He tugged at the top drawer of one of the filing cabinets. It was open. Inside it was crammed with green folders, all neatly labelled. He ran his eye quickly along the labels which were in little plastic mounts clipped on to the metal ridge of the files. Every so often he came to a folder that was not labelled and drew it out for inspection. They mostly

contained newspaper cuttings, many of them about Perkins, some dated years back. There were copies of letters sent on behalf of constituents to various government departments and to the housing department of Sheffield City Council.

Page did not strike lucky until he reached the third drawer. The folders now seemed to consist of old newspaper cuttings arranged under subject headings . . . CIA . . . Indian Ocean . . . Income Tax . . . they did not seem to bear much relation to each other . . . Microchips . . . Molly . . . Multinationals . . . Molly, Molly. That was it. The name of the girl he was looking for. He whisked the folder out and walked with it into the living room. Opening it, he laid the contents out on the desk. There was very little: a postcard from Austria dated March 1977 and half a dozen notes on scraps of blank paper. These were variously signed Molly, Moll and M, but bore no address. Some were dated, some were not. They mainly concerned shopping arrangements. Surely the head of DI5 had more important matters with which to concern himself? Page shrugged. His was not to reason why.

He scooped the notes and the postcard back into the green folder, closed the filing cabinet and glanced around the flat to make sure everything was as he had found it. Then, with the folder under his arm, he let himself out of the front door.

At the end of the street he found a phone box and rang the number Sir Peregrine had given him. It was after seven o'clock on a Friday evening, but the DI5 chief was at his desk. Page drove directly to Curzon Street.

If Sir Peregrine was disappointed at the meagre contents of the Molly folder, he did not show it. Using the photocopier in the outer office he made two copies of each item and then returned the folder to Page. "Put this back where you found it," he ordered. "And remember, not a word to anyone."

Molly Jarvis had just finished loading the dishwasher when she noticed a tall man striding down the gravel drive towards the house. He would have stood out anywhere in Derbyshire, indeed anywhere north of Mayfair. He was dressed in a perfectly cut navy blue suit with a waistcoat. On his lapel she

caught the glint of a watch chain. On his head he wore a hat, a homburg she thought it was called. An umbrella was hooked over his left arm and in his right hand he carried a black leather briefcase of the sort that is standard Civil Service issue.

Drying her hands on a teacloth she went to the front door. She had opened it even before the man reached the house. The man doffed his hat. "Mrs Jarvis?" he said from a distance of about five yards.

"Yes."

"My name is Craddock." He had reached the doorstep now and was standing, hat in hand. Molly guessed he was aged about sixty. A handsome man by any standards. His greying hair still covered the top of his head. His square chin and straight back suggested he might once have been an officer in the Guards. "I'm with the security people in London," he added in a voice which reflected generations of refined breeding.

"Oh," said Molly.

"One or two questions to ask. Hope I'm not disturbing you." He took another step forward.

"Not at all," said Molly standing aside to let him enter. If the man had said he was the Prince of Wales, she would not have argued.

They passed into the living room. The man had to stoop slightly to avoid hitting his head on the oak beams in the ceiling. There was a Handel organ concerto playing softly on the stereo.

"Like Handel, do you?" asked the man.

"Yes," said Molly.

He arranged himself on the sofa and laid down the hat and the briefcase at his side. The umbrella he propped against the arm of the sofa. Molly went to make a cup of tea and while she was out of the room the man got up and inspected the bookshelf. When she returned he was standing by the window leafing through a biography of Harry Perkins. It was not a very good book. Molly had bought it on the spur of the moment at a shop in Sheffield two years ago.

"You once knew Harry Perkins, I believe." Molly nearly dropped the teatray.

"Yes," she said, "in my old job at British Insulated we had to go and negotiate with him once or twice. About reactors."

"No," said the man turning to face her, "that wasn't what I meant."

Molly was seated by now. The tray was on the floor at her feet. The Handel concerto was still playing softly. "How did you know?" she whispered.

"Never mind about that." His voice seemed harder now. He walked to the bookshelf, replaced the volume and returned to the sofa. Molly poured the tea. "Mrs Jarvis," he said eventually, "I want you to tell me everything you know about Harry Perkins, starting from the day you first met him."

She told him of the meetings at the Public Sector Department. About the note Perkins had slipped to her. About that first lunch at his flat in Kennington. About all the other Sundays. About how she used to ring first from the Oval tube station so that he would leave the door open for her.

The man had taken a notepad from his briefcase and a felt-tipped pen from an inside pocket. Occasionally he scribbled on the pad. Sometimes he asked a question.

"And all this time you were living with Michael Jarvis?"

"Yes," said Molly quietly, her eyes downcast.

"And all this time Mr Jarvis was negotiating the sale of his company's reactors with Perkins."

Molly's eyes widened. Suddenly it dawned on her where all this was leading. No, she protested, her affair with Perkins had nothing to do with the reactors. Michael knew nothing about it. Even to this day she had not told him. She had never discussed the reactors with Perkins. No, never. Not once, not ever. It was a love affair, nothing more.

The more she protested, the more the man probed. Had she ever given Perkins a present? A watch, a pair of cufflinks perhaps? Not even at Christmas?

No, she said, it wasn't like that. She was crying now and the man's voice became more gentle. The chimes of the grandfather clock in the hall reminded her that it was almost time to collect the children from school. The man said he would soon be finished.

"Mrs Jarvis," he said, "did Perkins ever give you a present?"

"No," she said quickly. And then she remembered *The Ragged Trousered Philanthropists*. He asked if he could see the book and she led him up the wrought iron spiral staircase to the attic room where she kept her souvenirs of Perkins in the blue vanity case.

She blew the dust from the case. It had been at least two years since she last opened it. The key was in a jamjar on the window sill. She unlocked the case and took out the book. Its paperback cover had faded. The man opened the book and read the dedication on the inside of the cover: *To a slightly Tory lady in the hope that she will see the light. Love, Harry*, and then the date. Molly looked embarrassed.

"And these letters," said the man indicating the half dozen or so envelopes bound together with an elastic band. "From Perkins, were they?"

Molly nodded.

The first was the note Perkins had passed her that day in the Public Sector Department: *Lunch Sunday? Ring me at midnight*. It was undated, but the notepaper was inscribed at the top: 'From the Secretary of State.' The man shook his head in amazement. How indiscreet politicians could be.

Taking each of the other notes from the envelopes, he inspected them and put them back. Molly stood in silence, watching.

Then he came to the cheque for £5.20 drawn on Perkins' personal account. "For shopping," said Molly quickly.

The man raised an eyebrow.

"What the hell do you think it was for?" said Molly sharply.

The man said nothing. He collected the envelopes and the cheque together and bound them again with the elastic band.

They went downstairs in silence. The man was carrying the letters and the book.

"Mrs Jarvis," he said when they were back in the living room, "I am afraid I must borrow these."

What was he going to do with them, she demanded? Michael would be furious if he found out about her affair with Perkins. And as for Perkins . . . Her voice trailed off as the awful panorama of possibilities opened up before her eyes.

The man's voice was reassuring again. "My dear, you have nothing to worry about. All this will remain a secret between you and me." He was putting the book and the letters in his briefcase. "In due course they will be returned to you." He paused and glanced around the room. "It's just that, if any of this got into the wrong hands, the Prime Minister would be gravely embarrassed." He spoke as though embarrassing the Prime Minister was the last thing he wanted to do. "Particularly," he added, "in the light of the accident at Windermere."

The man then collected his hat, umbrella and briefcase and walked to the front door. Molly offered him a lift to the station. He thanked her, but said he would rather walk since he did not get to the country very much these days.

With that he strode away up the gravel drive. Molly stood on the doorstep and watched him go.

Sir Peregrine was back at his home in Queen Anne's Gate by about eight that evening. His maid had prepared a light meal which he ate alone in his study overlooking the park. Before settling down for the evening with a glass of port and a book of John Donne's poems, he made just one telephone call on the scrambled line. It was to Sir George Fison at his home in Cheyne Walk.

"George, dear boy." He toyed with the port glass. "The PM's been looking a bit off colour this evening, don't you think?"

Fison said he thought so too.

"Strain's beginning to tell at last," said Sir Peregrine.

Fison gave a little snort of laughter and said he would not be in the least surprised.

"I was wondering," said Sir Peregrine, "if you could get your chaps to run a little speculation on the PM's health."

Fison said he would see what could be done.

18

Indeed Perkins had not been feeling well for months. The colour had drained from his cheeks. The optimism had gone from his eyes. He smiled less often now and when he did his smile looked artificial. Thompson had been advising him for months to take it easy, but the advice went unheeded. Everyone in Downing Street was talking about how worn he looked. The garden girls, the policemen on the door, the housekeeper, even Tweed and the civil servants in the private office.

There was a time when he had ignored what the newspapers said about him, but nowadays he seemed obsessed by them. Every night when the first editions arrived he would spend an hour poring over them, sometimes by himself, sometimes with Thompson. "Lying bastards," he would shout as he read the editorials, particularly those in the *Express* or the *Mail*.

"Take it easy, Harry," Thompson would say.

But Perkins did not take it easy. As the attacks in the media mounted, he became bitter and short tempered. It showed in his performance on the floor of the House. The Tories could see when he was riled and jibed him mercilessly.

For some weeks now, ever since the Chequers conference, there had been reports of a plot against him in the Parliamentary Party. There was talk in the tea rooms of a substantial revolt over the proposed cuts in the defence budget. Up to one hundred MPs were, it was said, prepared to abstain or vote with the Tories. There was even talk of the Parliamentary Party choosing a leader of its own. A small group of MPs around Wainwright were said to be behind the rebellion. Relations between the Prime Minister and the Chancellor had sunk to an all-time low.

The accident at Windermere had shaken Perkins. Though he maintained a studied silence in public, in private he held himself responsible. "If only I had listened," he said to

Thompson. There was nothing anyone could do to convince him it was not his fault. At one stage he was talking about resigning and it was all that Thompson, Jock Steeples and Mrs Cook could do to talk him out of it. From the wall of his room in the House of Commons he took down the framed letter from Sir Richard Fry: *You were right. We were wrong*, it said. Perkins wondered what Fry was saying now.

On top of everything else, there was the growing crisis in relations with the United States. The US ambassador had been to Downing Street with a list of impossible demands for compensation and assurances before his government would even consider withdrawing the bases. Indeed American leaders were now saying openly that they had no intention of going, but would sit it out until the next election. And the way things were going Perkins was unlikely to survive the next election. The opinion polls were showing a substantial Tory lead and the last two by-elections had seen Labour seats fall to the Tories.

By the time the newspapers began carrying a spate of reports about his health, it no longer seemed like a media conspiracy, just a reflection of what people around the Prime Minister had been saying for weeks.

Whatever the state of Perkins' health, it was not improved by a memorandum from Sir Philip Norton, the Co-ordinator of Intelligence in the Cabinet Office, requesting an appointment for himself and Sir Peregrine Craddock to discuss a security matter of the utmost urgency.

They came one Wednesday evening in July, entering through the secret door that divided Downing Street from the Cabinet Office. Tweed unlocked the door to admit them and locked it again after they had passed.

As usual they formed a solemn little procession as they made their way along the ground floor corridor and up the main staircase to Perkins' study. They walked in silence, one behind the other. Their footsteps fell in unison. They wore long, doleful faces which seemed to say that they had a regrettable but necessary public duty to perform. Pinky and

Perky, Perkins had taken to calling them behind their backs.

"Come in gentlemen," said the Prime Minister as the two intelligence chiefs hesitated at the doorway of his study. And then Perkins could not resist adding, "Which of my ministers have you come to stick the knife into this time?"

Craddock and Norton looked at each other blankly and sat down in the comfortable chairs. Perkins joined them.

Craddock and Norton looked again at each other as though they had not decided who should speak first. Craddock clutched tightly at the thin green folder on his lap. Norton broke the ice.

"Prime Minister," he said quietly, "it concerns the reactor at Windermere."

"Oh," said Perkins sitting bolt upright. He had not been intending to take the intelligence chiefs very seriously, but now they had his full attention.

"I believe," continued Norton, "that you were the minister responsible for commissioning the reactor."

"I was the Secretary of State, but it was a Cabinet decision," corrected Perkins.

"Quite so." Norton avoided catching Perkins' eyes.

"Prime Minister," Craddock was speaking now, "did you know a girl called Molly Spence?"

Perkins gulped. Where the hell had they dug her up from? "So what if I did?" he said quickly.

Craddock ignored his question. "And were you having an *affair* . . ." his tongue lingered over the word, "with her at the same time as you were negotiating with British Insulated over the purchase of their reactor?"

"Now look here," said Perkins struggling to suppress anger, "if you think there was any connection between . . ."

He did not finish. Craddock cut in with another question. "And were you aware that during the whole time of her relationship with you, she was living with Michael Jarvis, the managing director of British Insulated, the man with whom you were negotiating?"

"Impossible," Perkins almost shouted. And then he stopped because he realised it was perfectly possible.

"And were you further aware," Craddock was heading for the winning post now, "that she subsequently married Jarvis and that the wedding took place only three days after she finished with you and only three weeks after British Insulated won the contracts for the reactor?"

Craddock could not have delivered a more devastating blow if he had hit the Prime Minister square on the head with a cricket bat. Perkins fell back into the chair, his hands rested limply on the arms. The silence was broken only by the distant hum of traffic in the Mall and by the laughter of children in the park. Perkins could even hear the ticking of his watch.

When he spoke again, he did so quietly, "Has she been trying to sell her story to the newspapers?"

"No," said Craddock, "but there's always the possibility."

"It was just an affair," said Perkins weakly, "just a small love affair."

"*We* know that Prime Minister," said Craddock, "but it doesn't look very good, does it?" As he spoke he handed Perkins the green folder that until now had rested on his lap.

Perkins opened it. The contents were photocopies of notes he had written her. Craddock had omitted to include the copies of notes that she had written to him. There was no point in letting Perkins know his flat had been raided.

There were no more than ten sheets of photocopy. Perkins examined each in turn. There was the inscription from *The Ragged Trousered Philanthropists*. He remembered how he teased her about her ignorance of working class history. There was the note that had started it all. On Department notepaper. Perkins shook his head. He must have been mad. There was the cheque. He could not even remember writing it.

"She said it was to pay for some shopping she did for you," explained Craddock seeing his bewilderment.

The rest of the notes would have meant nothing to anybody but himself and Molly. Just meeting times and who was going to do the shopping. As he leafed through them it all came back to him. The Sunday lunches. The Côte du Rhône. The Handel organ concertos. The afternoons in bed. For a whole

210

year she had been the bright spot of his life. He shook his head sadly. How could she do this to him?

For a moment he tried to put a brave face on it. He closed the folder and returned it to Craddock. "Nothing very incriminating there," he said, trying to sound cool.

"Except the dates, Prime Minister."

He shook his head. Of course, it was the dates that landed him in it. For a moment he glimpsed the headlines when the newspapers found out: P.M. IN REACTOR LOVE TANGLE or PERKINS IN WINDERMERE SCANDAL – TORIES DEMAND ENQUIRY. He shook his head again. It was going to come down very hard.

Sir Philip Norton had apparently sensed what the Prime Minister was thinking. "There is another way," he said.

"Oh?" said Perkins numbly.

"Ill health, Prime Minister. You have been looking poorly recently. Everyone's been saying so."

"Go into hospital and then resign, you mean?" It was the first time anyone had used the word *resign*. "Who the hell is going to believe I resigned through ill health?"

"Don't see why not," said Norton, "Eden got away with it after Suez."

"Of course there will be a fuss," said Craddock, "but it will soon die down. People have very short memories." And then he added almost hopefully, "We could make the necessary arrangements very quickly."

Perkins took a deep breath. "I'll let you know in half an hour," he said.

After they had gone Perkins remained seated for five minutes exactly as they had left him. Then he got up and walked to the window. His head came just above the bullet-proof shields. He looked out over the empty garden of Number Eleven, over the wall to the park beyond. He saw children playing. He saw lovers walking hand in hand. Why had she done this to him? He shook his head again.

Then he walked slowly to his desk and tried to raise Fred Thompson on the internal phone. There was no answer. He

rang Thompson's home number. Again no answer. Then he rang Jock Steeples' room in the House. Then Mrs Cook's direct line at the Home Office. Then her House of Commons number. No answer. No answer. No answer. What else did he expect at dinner time on a fine summer's evening?

He sat down at the desk and ran his hands over his eyes. All his instincts told him that he should never make a decision like this without seeking advice. But he was tired, very tired. Besides which, who was there to advise him? For the time being Molly Spence was a secret he shared only with DI5. If he delayed another twelve hours, he might find himself sharing Molly with the whole world.

He was still seated at the desk, rubbing his eyes when Norton and Craddock returned. They knocked gently and entered. He looked at them, blinking.

"Shall we go?" said Norton as though the answer was a foregone conclusion.

"I'll go upstairs and pack," he said.

"No need," said Norton, "we'll take care of that."

From the desk Perkins picked up the framed picture of his mother and slid it into the pocket of his jacket. It was only a small picture and so fitted easily. He walked to the double doors where Craddock and Norton awaited him. He turned and looked around the room in the last fading light of the summer's evening. Then the three men stepped on to the landing. A footman outside silently drew the doors closed behind them.

They went down the main staircase in silence. Norton in front, Craddock behind. They walked across the hall into the lobby. The policeman on duty stood up when they passed but Perkins did not acknowledge his greeting. There was no sign of Inspector Page or Sergeant Block or of any of the other Special Branch officers responsible for his security.

Outside there were only a couple of passing tourists. They waved when they recognised him, but he did not respond. They were the only witnesses to the fall of Harry Perkins.

A black Rover was waiting, one of the last off the produc-

tion line before British Leyland had collapsed. A policeman held the door while he climbed into the back seat followed by Sir Philip. Sir Peregrine walked round the back of the car and climbed in through the rear door on the other side. That was how they sat, one on either side of him, as if they were afraid he might try and jump out at the traffic lights.

The Rover moved out of Downing Street and turned left into Whitehall. It was not the Prime Minister's official car and Perkins did not recognise the driver. They drove around three sides of Trafalgar Square, cutting through the lane reserved for buses and taxis. They turned left after the National Gallery and sped away towards Hampstead.

One hour later the following statement was issued from Downing Street:

> At 2130 hours the Prime Minister was admitted to the Royal Free Hospital for medical tests. On the advice of his doctors, he will be receiving no visitors.

The first the Prime Minister's doctors knew of his illness was when they read about it in the newspapers next day.

19

Perkins remained immured on the ninth floor of the Royal Free Hospital for seven days. An entire ward had been evacuated and sealed off, the corridors patrolled by unsmiling young men who talked to each other through walkie-talkie radios and whose jackets featured a prominent bulge under the left shoulder.

Shortly after the Prime Minister was admitted the hospital switchboard became jammed and for some hours callers heard only the engaged tone. When it was possible to get through again the operators had been instructed that no calls were being put through to the ninth floor. After failing to get through by telephone Jock Steeples drove to the hospital. He arrived a little after midnight and found Fred Thompson in the main hall. Thompson had apparently tried to get out of the lift at the ninth floor and been bundled back again by the unsmiling young men who were patrolling the corridors. The production of a Downing Street pass had made no impression.

Steeples and Thompson made one more attempt. This time getting out of the lift at the eighth floor and making their way up the fire escape to the floor above. On arrival they found the doors locked and curtains drawn.

The battery of pressmen who had descended on the hospital had no better luck. Some had put on white coats and posed as hospital orderlies. Others tried bribing genuine orderlies to go up and take a look. But everyone who tried to get out on the ninth floor had the same reception.

Steeples was fuming. He demanded to speak to the hospital's chief administrator. The man was eventually woken up at home and brought to a telephone. All he could say was that the matter was out of his hands. The ninth floor had been taken over by DI5. Next, Steeples rang the Cabinet Office and demanded Sir Philip Norton's home number.

214

The duty officer declined to believe that the caller was Steeples and refused to part with the number. Steeples then drove to the Cabinet Office and virtually beat the number out of the wretched man. All to no avail. Sir Philip's telephone did not answer.

At ten o'clock next morning Downing Street issued a further statement. It read as follows:

The Prime Minister has been advised by his doctors that he is suffering from exhaustion and requires a long period of complete rest. He has, therefore, tendered his resignation to His Majesty the King, effective from noon today.

Copies of a signed statement to this effect were circulated to the press. The signature was quite clearly Perkins'.

When Steeples eventually ran Sir Philip Norton to ground and demanded to see Perkins, all he got was "Terribly sorry old boy. PM was adamant. No visitors."

As deputy leader of the Labour Party it naturally followed that Jock Steeples would now take over as acting Prime Minister until the autumn when the Party would elect a new leader at its annual conference. It only remained for an emergency meeting of the Labour MPs to be convened to confirm Steeples in his rôle.

It soon became apparent, however, that events might not follow the anticipated course. A meeting of Labour MPs was called for the following Monday, but the statement convening the meeting spoke of 'electing' a new leader. This did not go down well with Labour Party members since it was nearly ten years since a party conference had relieved MPs of sole responsibility for choosing the Party leader.

All weekend delegations of Labour MPs were seen going out of the Chancellor's residence at Number Eleven Downing Street. The Sunday papers were full of speculation that Lawrence Wainwright would shortly announce that he was a candidate for the leadership. When the General Secretary of

the Labour Party rang to ask Wainwright to confirm or deny the speculation, she found Wainwright evasive.

Sure enough, when the MPs assembled on Monday evening Wainwright was a candidate. In the election which followed he beat Steeples by a comfortable majority. About fifty left-wingers abstained on the ground that the election was unconstitutional. The following morning an emergency meeting of the Labour Party National Executive unanimously endorsed Jock Steeples as acting leader.

The result was an unprecedented constitutional crisis. The King found himself with a choice of two Prime Ministers, both claiming to represent the Party with a majority of seats in the House of Commons.

The King was at Windsor when the crisis occurred. Three hours before the Parliamentary Labour Party was due to meet, a black Rover containing Sir Peregrine Craddock was admitted to the castle. He was received in a drawing room overlooking the long straight sweep of the Great Park.

There is no record of what was said. It is known only that Sir Peregrine was closeted with the King for about twenty minutes, after which he was driven back to London. Later the same day several prominent members of the judiciary were received and still later four senior members of the Privy Council.

The next day it was announced from Windsor Castle that His Majesty had asked Lawrence Wainwright to form a government.

The news was received with dismay by Labour Party members throughout the country. There were a number of arrests for the daubing of anti-Royalist slogans. In Glasgow serious rioting occurred on successive nights. In London all police leave was cancelled and security was intensified in public buildings.

The Labour National Executive applied to the High Court for an injunction, arguing that Wainwright was not the properly elected leader of the party. This was refused on the

ground that it was established practice for the sovereign to choose as Prime Minister the person who commanded the confidence of a majority of members of the House of Commons. The fact that he did not command the confidence of the Labour Party was neither here nor there. The case was thrown out by the Appeal Court and the House of Lords for the same reason.

Wainwright's Cabinet did not contain a single member of the outgoing government. Steeples was offered a minor post, but declined.

At its first meeting the new Cabinet announced that the request to America to withdraw its bases and other military facilities would be revoked. Britain would remain a full member of NATO and would only renounce nuclear weapons when the Russians did the same.

It was also announced that Chequers, the country residence of the Prime Minister, would be placed at the disposal of Harry Perkins for the purpose of convalescence. Ministers were unanimous in wishing him a speedy recovery.

That night at the Athenaeum rejoicing was unconfined. The head porter said afterwards he could not remember anything like it since VE day. Members who had not been seen in town for years showed up. Sir Arthur Furnival was there, looking fit and tanned after a sojourn in the South of France. The Bishop of Bath and Wells was there too, looking years younger. So was Sir Lucas Lawrence, a retired permanent secretary. Lord Kildare had come down from his castle in Scotland for the first time since that awful night when Perkins had been elected.

There was much backslapping and handshaking. Champagne corks popped late into the night (so much so that Berry Bros. and Rudd had to be especially opened to bring in fresh supplies).

Away from the hubbub, in a quiet corner of the dining room, Sir George Fison was giving a small dinner party. The editor of *The Times* was present. So was Sir Philip Norton from the Cabinet Office and Sir Peter Kennedy from the

Treasury. There was also a younger man called Alford, who was said to be a rising star in the BBC. And there was the mysterious Sir Peregrine Craddock.

Not all their conversation was audible to the waiters or the other guests, but the gist was overheard. "This time last year," Fison was saying, "who would have dreamed we'd be sitting here tonight celebrating the survival of all we hold dear." A waiter poured champagne as Fison went on to enumerate, "The Atlantic alliance, the Common Market, the House of Lords . . ." He had been going to propose a toast, but was interrupted by a telephone call. It was the night editor of his principal daily newspaper with a query on the front page editorial that Fison had dictated that afternoon. It was to be headed "A victory for sanity."

When Fison rejoined his guests, Alford was telling a story about how a fellow called Jack Lansman, the anchorman on the BBC Radio Four breakfast programme, had done a little jig in the corridor outside the studio when he heard that Perkins had resigned. "Been nothing quite like it since the night Allende was overthrown in Chile," Alford was saying.

Sir George proposed a toast to Craddock. "The British public," he said, "would never know how much reason they had to be grateful to Sir Peregrine."

Craddock smiled modestly and raised his glass of orange juice. "Everyone should feel proud," he said. There had been no tanks on the streets. No one had gone to the firing squad. Apart from the odd demonstrator on the receiving end of a police baton, no one had even been injured.

In fact, he said with a wan smile, "It was a very British coup. "

Postscript

Harry Perkins was not seen again in public for nearly a year. For most of that time he remained in seclusion at Chequers. Security was very tight. Once or twice a photographer with a long lens managed, by sneaking round to the back of the house, to get a shot of a lonely figure pottering around the rose garden. Fred Thompson, Jock Steeples and Mrs Cook were allowed the occasional visit. If the sun was shining they would sit with Perkins on the south lawn, drinking tea and reminiscing about what might have been. Neither Steeples nor Mrs Cook ever held office again.

When Perkins did return to the House of Commons he seemed a broken man. He wandered the lobbies and the tea rooms and sat on the occasional committee, but he contributed little. He remained popular with his constituents in Sheffield, however, and the City Council put a little plaque on the council house where he and his mother had lived.

When the New Year's honours were announced, Reg Smith of the United Power Workers became Lord Smith of Virginia Water. Sir George Fison also received a peerage. "For services in the cause of truth and freedom," the citation said. Jonathan Alford was knighted and is widely tipped as a future BBC Director General. There was one surprise buried deep in the honours list: a CBE for David Booth, a young civil servant in the Foreign Exchange Department of the Treasury. No one – least of all Booth himself – seemed to know why he had been honoured.

Sir Peregrine Craddock retired to Somerset where he now grows prize-winning roses and plays the occasional round of golf. Once in a while he comes up to town and has a quiet lunch at the Athenaeum and a browse around the bookshops in Bloomsbury.

After the Windermere disaster Molly Spence's husband, Michael, lost his job with British Insulated. He now works in

Saudi Arabia. Molly and the children live with her parents in Sheffield. When she realised what had happened, she wrote Perkins a long letter explaining that it was all a terrible accident, that she had never meant to harm him, and begging him to forgive her. There is no reason to suppose Perkins ever received the letter. Anyway, he did not reply.

As for Fred Thompson, he married Elizabeth Fain and they moved away to Scotland where he now has a job on the *West Highland Free Press*. Thompson is said to spend his evenings writing a book which will tell what really happened to the government of Harry Perkins. There must, however, be some doubt as to whether it will ever be published.

THE LAST MAN OUT OF SAIGON

BY CHRIS MULLIN

The Fall of Saigon. And every American is pulling out, desperate to leave the doomed city before the victorious North Vietnamese Army sweeps in.

Every American except MacShane.

For MacShane isn't there to run the war: his orders from CIA headquarters at Langley are simple – organize a network of agents after the fall of the city. But that isn't so easy for someone like MacShane, a South American specialist who has never been to Vietnam before. Particularly when he discovers his two contacts are useless and his cover has been blown.

Nothing in MacShane's training has prepared him for what follows. And nothing in his background has cut him out to be THE LAST MAN OUT OF SAIGON.

'An excellent thriller, told convincingly'

Graham Greene

'Excellent, professional, authentic . . . as unputdownable as Graham Greene'

Robert Kee

'Chris Mullin . . . proves himself in this book to be a fine storyteller.'

John Pilger

0 552 13259 4

THE ROPESPINNER CONSPIRACY

BY MICHAEL M. THOMAS

As topical as today's most worrying financial headlines, THE ROPESPINNER CONSPIRACY is the story of a brilliant and insidious Soviet plot to infiltrate the West's banking system and lead it to self-destruction, aided and abetted by one of America's most prominent capitalists. Here is a novel filled with breathtaking suspense and vivid characters, a tale for our times told with Michael Thomas's elegance, wit and profound insight. And it offers something more: a grave warning (for those who will listen) about the ways in which the West's financial structure has been imperilled by the men who lead it.

0 552 13270 5

THE CHINA CARD

BY JOHN EHRLICHMAN

With this startlingly authentic novel John Ehrlichman steps into the front rank of the masters of espionage fiction. At the heart of THE CHINA CARD is the possibility that the Chinese Communists have planted a 'mole' deep within the Nixon administration, within the White House itself. In the hands of an author who *was* one of Richard Nixon's closest advisers, the premise takes on a chilling plausibility that places the President's China 'initiative' in a shocking new perspective.

THE CHINA CARD is a novel of stunning force in which the reader becomes engaged in the dramatic power plays of history itself.

0 552 13139 3